Copyright © 2025 T.D. Bogart

All rights reserved

The characters and events portrayed in this book are fictitious. Any similarity to real persons, living or dead, is coincidental and not intended by the author.

No part of this book may be reproduced, or stored in a retrieval system, or transmitted in any form or by any means, electronic, mechanical, photocopying, recording, or otherwise, without express written permission of the publisher.

Print: ISBN-13: 979-8-9927130-0-8
Ebook: 979-8-9927130-1-5

Cover design by: T. D. Bogart
Library of Congress Control Number: 1-14802439591
Printed in the United States of America

DISSEMBLANCE

T. D. BOGART

CONTENT WARNING

Reader discretion is advised it explores intense and difficult topics, read responsibly as these topics may be distressing to some audiences. **If you are not impacted by triggers, and do not want aspects of this book spoiled, please feel free to skip the next paragraph.**

This novel explores **heavy themes**, including domestic violence, sexual assault, psychological manipulation, self–harm, underage sex (not depicted), and trauma related to infertility and loss.

The portrayal of these topics is raw, unfiltered, and graphic. Please take caution if you've experienced similar traumas, as the content may be triggering. It also delves deeply into adult relationship dynamics, navigating complex and sometimes troubling terrain. Trust yourself in deciding if this is something you can handle.

DEDICATION

Dissemblance is dedicated to readers who have walked a fine line between desperation and hope, and to those who are still waiting for their rainbow.

DISSEMBLANCE: (n) The act of concealing or hiding one's true intentions.

PLAYLIST

Tennessee Whiskey, Chris Stapleton

Mayday, Wild Rivers

I want you here, Plumb

Get Ur Freak On, Missy Elliot

The Kind of Love We Make, Luke Combs

Wet Dreams, Artemas

Skin and Bones, David Kushner

Guilty as Sin, Taylor Swift

Heaven, Kane Brown

My Home, Myles Smith

A Little Bit Happy, Talk

Beautiful Life, Benson Boone

PROLOGUE
FIFTEEN YEARS AGO

Mark lay on his back, staring at the ceiling, the Penn banners above his bed barely visible in the dim light. He wiped the sweat off his forehead, shifting the black hair out of his brown eyes so that he could get a better look at her. The air was thick with the scent of summer, warm and heavy, filtering through the cracked window. Outside, cicadas hummed, the occasional rustle of wind slipping through the trees.

Josie was curled against his side, her bare leg hooked over his, her fingertips tracing absent patterns along the dark quilt covering them. She pulled it higher, pressing closer.

"We should get up," she murmured.

He didn't answer right away. The room smelled like her, like them, and he wasn't ready to let go of it yet. Not when the weight of reality pressed at the edges of the moment, waiting to suffocate them both. "A few more minutes."

His bedroom hadn't changed much since he was a kid. The bookshelves were still packed with textbooks and sports trophies, the same desk sat in the corner where he'd spent years preparing for an Ivy League education, because nothing less would please his father. A lifetime of expectations pressed down from the walls, but Josie had been the only thing that made any of it feel real.

They had known each other since childhood, family get-togethers, backyard parties, the kind of history that made her feel more like a sister, until one day, when he realized the feeling he had for her ran deeper than that.

They hadn't seen each other in months, and when she walked through the sliding glass doors and into the back yard, his entire body responded. She looked different, her breasts had filled out, her body more like a woman than a girl. Mark's stomach fluttered, a familiar pang of desire invading him as he walked toward her, unable to take his eyes off her tall slender figure, her long black hair, the way her lips pursed together before she flashed that brilliant smile.

The air was thick with barbeque smoke as he called to her, winding his fingers through hers as he led her away from the crowd, past the tree lined property, and into the woods. They moved toward a clearing, the sun spilling into the grass filled pasture, capturing her laugh with his mouth as she stood in the grass, grinning up at him. He had hesitated, knowing she was younger, knowing people would talk. But then she had looked at him like that, like he was something more than what everyone else saw, he had kissed her anyway, and she had let him.

Mark glanced down at her now, her body soft against his, but the weight in her eyes pulled him from the memory.

"You alright?" he asked.

She shifted, her eyes searching his, like she was looking for something only he could give her. "Just tired," she replied, but Mark didn't believe her. He knew better than anyone how much she carried inside, but she hid it well, like always. Josie never let herself crack in front of him, not even when the world seemed to push her into a corner.

"I hate it when you lie to me," he murmured, his fingers brushing the black strands that had fallen over her face. "You don't have to pretend with me, Josie."

Josie's lips pressed together, as if the truth was a heavy

weight she couldn't let go of. "I'm not pretending," but the tremor in her voice betrayed her. "It's just… I don't know what's gonna happen."

"Neither do I," Mark replied, "I'm here, okay? We'll figure it out together."

Josie turned her face up to him then, her hazel eyes bright in the dim light, but there was a sadness in them that caught in Mark's throat. It was the look she always wore when she thought of the future, uncertain, fragile, like she was always waiting for it to slip away.

She took a deep breath, her hand brushing his where it rested on her stomach. Mark's heart stuttered, the gesture so small but so heavy it felt like it shifted the entire room. His fingers followed hers, tracing the panes of muscle, his touch hesitant and gentle.

"I've been thinking," Josie paused, "About what this means, about us."

Mark's hand stilled for a moment before resuming its slow path, his fingertips brushing against bare skin. "You won't have to do it alone," he murmured. "You know that, right? Whatever happens… I'm here."

Her heart thrummed faster, and he felt it more than he heard it. "I know. It's just… everything's different now. I don't even feel like myself anymore. And there's school, and you're leaving for Penn."

"You're still you," he uttered firmly. "Maybe things are changing, but that doesn't change who you are. Who we are. I can take a gap year, transfer, hell, join the military."

Josie didn't respond right away, her hand covering his as if anchoring herself to him. He felt her shift against him.

She sighed, and the sound carried a thousand unsaid words. "You're not scared?" she asked after a long pause, her voice quieter than before.

Mark's mouth formed a faint smile. "Terrified," he admitted, "But I've got you, and that's all I need."

She tilted her face up to press her forehead against his jaw. "I don't want to mess this up, I want to do this right."

Mark's hand moved again, this time brushing over her lips. He exhaled. "Marry me, Josie. Even if we can't do it right away, let's get married."

Tears fell as she nodded, her hands framing his face as she took his mouth with hers.

The room fell silent again, but it wasn't the heavy silence of uncertainty. It was something deeper, something that spoke of quiet promises and the unshakable bond between them. Josie's breathing evened out, her body relaxing fully for the first time that day. Mark held her close.

The first crack of the door opening was quiet, until it flew open with a force that rattled the hinges. Mark froze, his heart thundering. Josie's gasp caught in her throat, her trembling fingers clutching at the sheet like it could shield her from the storm that had just entered the room.

"Jesus fucking Christ," his father spat, stepping inside. His shadow stretched long across the floor, suffocating the air in the room. "What the hell is this?"

"Dad, wait–" Mark started, his voice cracking, but he didn't get to finish. His father's hand shot out, grabbing him by the arm and yanking him to his feet.

"You couldn't control yourself for five goddamn minutes?" His breath was sour against Mark's face. His eyes snapped to Josie. "And *you*, get dressed. Now. You do not leave this house, do you understand me?"

Josie didn't move, her tear-streaked face pale and frozen.

"I said *go*." His father's voice dropped, cutting like a blade. She scrambled for her clothes, her hands shaking as she pulled them on. She didn't look back as she fled the room.

The door clicked shut behind her, leaving Mark alone with the man whose shadow had loomed over his life for as long as he could remember.

"What *the fuck* were you thinking?" Every word was laced with disdain.

Mark stood his ground, tugging his jeans on with trembling hands. "I love her."

His father's laugh was sharp. "Love?"

Mark swallowed hard. "She's—"

"Don't." His father held up a hand, cutting him off. "Don't insult me with excuses."

Mark stiffened; his jaw clenched. "She's pregnant."

The words landed like a gunshot.

His father's eyes closed for a moment. Then, in one swift motion, a palm connected with Mark's cheekbone, jerking his head sideways. The room spun as he righted himself, blood dripping onto the floorboards as the metallic taste of blood filled his mouth.

"You arrogant little shit," Doctor Morales hissed, the words sharp enough to flay. "Do you have any idea what you've done? What this means?" His voice rose with every word. "You've thrown away your future. My career. Our name. Everything I've worked for."

Mark sat with his back to the edge of his bed, his chest heaving, his muscles tense.

His father's foot connected with his abdomen before Mark even registered the movement, forcing the air out of his lungs. "You love her?" Doctor Morales spat, standing over him. "You don't even know what love is. Do you know what happens to children who think they're men?"

Mark steadied his breathing as he rose to his knees, glaring up at his father.

XV

"They go to prison," his father was leaning so close, Mark could feel his breath. "You're eighteen. You're a legal adult. And she's fifteen. Do you know what the law calls that, Mark?"

Mark didn't answer, but the slight twitch in his brow betrayed him.

"Rape," he paused for effect. "S*tatutory rape*," his father seethed. "That's a felony. They'll call you a predator. They'll put you on a registry. You'll never get into college. You'll never get a job. You'll be the guy who ruined his life before it even started."

Mark shook his head, his hands curling into fists. "That won't happen. She won't let it"

"She doesn't get a choice!" Doctor Morales snapped. "You don't get to rewrite the law because you think you're in love. This isn't a fairy tale, this is real life, and in real life, people like you lose everything for mistakes like this."

Mark's defiance faltered, the weight of his father's words sinking in like lead.

Doctor Morales straightened, his eyes cold and calculating. "This ends tonight. Or I will end it for you."

Mark wiped the blood from his lip, glaring up at him. "No. She wants this, we want this."

The silence stretched, taut and dangerous. His father leaned toward him. "She will see you for what you are; broken, selfish, and weak. Just like I do." Air escaped his father's clenched teeth.

"No, this ends now. Come." His fathers nails dug into his arm.

ONE

Amy lay still, her muscles tense with anticipation as she watched Mark move over her, His dark eyes were clouded by the black hair that fell into his face. She focused on the clean lines of his jaw, drifting to the jagged scar that snaked down his neck, the faint scent of aftershave enveloping her senses. His minty breath was cool against her shoulder, his movements deliberate but mechanical, a careful choreography of indifference. She gripped the sheets, trying to focus on making a baby rather than the pain it was taking to get there.

The injections from their sixth round of fertility treatments had left her body painfully sensitive. Her ovaries felt heavy, a lingering sting radiating through every nerve ending. Each drive felt like her pelvis was being torn from the inside out. Her body tensed beneath him, a reflex she couldn't control, her muscles screaming for relief. *Don't cry, don't cry.*

Mark's movements became faster, harder as he tried to maintain himself. *Just get through it.* His thought felt hollow, but it was the only thing keeping him moving. He glanced at her face, noting the tension in her features, the way her lips pressed tightly together. She wasn't into this either, but the look on her face. He closed his eyes briefly, willing himself to stay focused, to stay interested. But the pressure of what this was supposed to mean, what it was supposed to accomplish, felt suffocating. It was as if his body had become a traitor, refusing to cooperate in even the simplest of ways.

The familiar, clinical conclusion came without warning or emotion. She tilted her hips automatically, trying to direct his release to where it might matter most. He pulled away abruptly, collapsing onto his side of the bed as he reached for his phone on the nightstand.

Mark glanced at Amy again, his fingers hovering over the phone. She had been so hopeful lately, clutching to the idea of their future with a desperation that made him feel suffocated. She didn't just want a child, she wanted *him*, wrapped up in her plans, her dreams, her carefully constructed version of their life together.

And he had played his part. He always did.

But every day, the cracks grew wider, the lies harder to sustain. There were moments, fleeting but sharp, when he wanted to let it all collapse. To walk away. To let her see the man behind the façade, the man who didn't want what she did, who wasn't capable of giving her what she needed. But then what? What would that make him? A failure? A monster?

Her cold fingertips grazed his arm, snapping him back to her.

He propped himself up against the headboard, his eyes fixed on his phone. "My editor loved the last draft. Best seller material."

Mark's psychology practice and published research made him successful, but his social media posts catapulted him to stardom. The journey had been rapid, almost dizzying. His polished, sharp video clips of provocative relationship advice, delivered with his trademark confidence, had snowballed into a phenomenon. People didn't just watch Mark, they believed him. His insights on modern love, intimacy, and personal fulfillment had struck a chord, resonating with an audience desperate for answers. And Mark? He delivered, packaged perfectly for the algorithm–driven masses.

Amy forced a smile, through the cramps. Her throat felt tight as she shifted closer, placing her head on his ribcage. "That's great. You deserve it, your research is ground breaking." Her lips brushed his bicep as she curled into him, her voice carrying a hint of the anxiety she couldn't quite conceal.

Mark leaned back. "Feels like yesterday I was stuck in clinical trials and writing papers no one would read."

Amy laughed softly, though her shoulders tensed. "It's more than that, though. People connect with you. The way you explain things, relationships, control, sex, vulnerability, all of it–it resonates."

He nodded, his finger absently tracing the scar on his jaw. His thumb flicked across the screen with practiced ease, replying to comments faster than she could read them. "My agent's already setting things up for a July launch. Press conferences, a few TV appearances, maybe even some speaking gigs. Big moves coming."

Amy studied his face, her fingers grazing his chest. "That sounds amazing."

Mark's hand brushed hers briefly, his attention still divided as he skimmed his notifications. "I'll try to keep things manageable. I know this hasn't been easy on you."

The words gave her a flicker of hope, even as she felt his focus slipping further away. Her eyes dropped to her lap. *If she could just give him a baby, something that was a part of them both, he'd come back to her.* She could feel it. She had to believe it.

Mark was engrossed in his screen. "Three million followers."

She pulled herself close, resting her head against him. "Maybe… maybe this will be lucky cycle number seven?"

Mark nodded, giving her shoulder a gentle squeeze. "Yeah, maybe." he murmured, though he lacked conviction. He leaned over, kissed her, and pulled himself out of bed.

As he headed to the shower, muscles flexed and jaw set, she watched him brush his dark, hair from his forehead. A quiet ache settled in her chest. She lay there, staring at the ceiling, wondering how far she could stretch herself to hold onto the life they'd once dreamed of. The sound of water hitting the tile made her move. Swinging her legs over the mattress, she stood and stretched, grabbing and looping her arms through her robe as she made her way to the kitchen to make coffee.

The drip gurgled as she sectioned her shoulder length hair into three sections, weaving her fingers through her black tresses until they formed a braid. The coffee pot beeped and she poured two cups as Mark's presence loomed into her periphery.

"Fast shower, you smell good." She kissed his cheek as she handed him the beverage.

"What do you think about this?" Mark asked, turning the screen toward her. It was a post promoting his latest project, an artsy black–and–white shot with a caption that read: *"Visionaries see the world in shades others can't."* The self–congratulatory tone grated on her, but she could see the appeal.

Amy's head tilted as she contemplated the composition. "It's…nice."

Mark's lips twitched upward, but his expression was critical. "Nice? That's not exactly helpful, Amy. Kaitlyn's been pushing me to be more engaging. Something that pops… you know?"

Kaitlyn. Of course. His agent always had ideas, and they always seemed to involve more of Mark's time, more of his attention, leaving Amy to hold together what was left of their shared life.

"Well," she considered carefully, "if it's about engagement, maybe post something more personal? People like seeing the real you."

Mark smirked. "The real me? Not sure that's marketable." He stood, brushing crumbs off his lap. "I'll think about it. Kaitlyn's got some ideas about the book that she wants to run by at our next meeting."

"That's next week?" Amy asked.

"Yeah. We're finalizing some plans." He looked up briefly, offering her a half–smile. "It'll be good."

Amy nodded. She wanted to be supportive, but the cracks in their marriage felt wider than ever. She thought about her own career shift six months ago, when she had left real estate to become the Program and Marketing Manager at The Riverview, Charlotte and Lincoln's latest business venture. It was a role she was proud of, yet it felt overshadowed by Mark's relentless climb. *His deserved climb.* She felt a pang of guilt for the resentment.

A buzz from her phone pulled her out of her thoughts. It was Charlotte.

"Hey," Amy answered, leaning back in her chair.

"Morning! Just a heads–up, I need to swing by the coffee shop to drop off some schematics before heading to the mill. Want to meet there? Or should I bring you a cup."

Amy smiled. They had been college roommates and stayed close ever since. Now, they were working together at the Riverview as it prepared for its grand opening after months of renovations. Amy laughed, but she knew what Charlotte meant. It wasn't just any old building, it was a piece of Hudson Valley's history, a relic from the region's industrial past. Perched near the river, the mill had once been the lifeblood of the small town, its towering brick walls and massive wooden beams a testament to the craftsmanship of another era.

"I mean, you have to admit, it's got a hell of a story," Amy paused, "I'll see you at work, if you could bring me a green tea, that'd be great, I have some stuff to help Mark with marketing wise."

"Great. See you later."

"Yeah, see you then." After hanging up, Amy cleared the table and laced up her running shoes. She needed more than just a walk; she needed to clear her head.

Amy's phone buzzed on the counter, the screen lighting up with the familiar Instagram notification: *Doctor Mark Rodriguez just posted a new reel.*

She tapped the screen, and the post opened to Mark's face, perfectly framed in the warm, inviting tones of his office. *I mean I did a damn good job with that design.* She thought.

The familiar sight of him on camera made her breath catch, just as it always did. His sharp jawline was softened by the faintest shadow of stubble, a concession to the busy week he'd had. His deep brown eyes, thoughtful and kind, seemed to hold the viewer captive, as though he was speaking directly to them. His shirt, open at the collar, framed the smooth lines of his neck, and even though Amy had seen him in this space countless times before, the way he filled the screen was magnetic. It was the same charm that had captivated her years ago at a college party, disarming her with his wit, and that sexy edge.

Mark began speaking, each word carrying the weight of his professional poise and personal conviction.

"As many of you know, relationships are the cornerstone of what I do and what I'm passionate about. Today, I want to talk about something deeply personal to me; our journey through infertility and how it has affected my marriage."

Amy's stomach tightened. "What the fuck, that's not what I meant."

Mark paused, his hands gesturing lightly as he leaned toward the camera, a practiced move to convey intimacy.

"My wife and I have been navigating this road for years now, and it's one of the hardest things a couple can go through. There's grief, frustration, and moments where it feels like the world is asking more from you than you have to give. It's so easy to lose sight of each other in the process. To let the stress replace the connection that brought you together in the first place."

Amy's throat constricted. He said it all so eloquently, but the words pierced her in a way she hadn't anticipated. She sank onto one of the kitchen stools, the phone resting in her trembling hands.

Mark's expression shifted, his voice softening. "But here's the thing: even in those dark moments, there's an opportunity.

An opportunity to choose kindness, to communicate openly, to prioritize your partnership above everything else. Because that's what marriage is; it's choosing to show up for each other, over and over again."

A faint smile curved his lips, the kind that had made Amy fall in love with him in the first place. "One thing I always tell my clients is this: be honest, even when it's hard. Share your fears, your hopes, your doubts. It's not about fixing each other; it's about walking through the challenges hand in hand. And if you're out there struggling, please know, you're not alone. Seek help, talk to someone, and don't let shame silence you."

The reel ended on a caption that read: *"Infertility and Marriage: Navigating Together | #MentalHealthMatters #InfertilitySupport.*

Amy stared at the screen, a swirl of emotions rising to the surface. His words had been heartfelt and beautifully delivered, crafted to resonate with anyone who stumbled across the post. But what gnawed at her most wasn't what he'd said, it was what he hadn't. The raw, private moments of their marriage, the nights she'd cried herself to sleep while he worked late or the days when his optimism felt like a crushing weight against her own despair.

He had painted a picture, yes, but only in the broadest strokes. As much as it stung, she couldn't deny that he was good at what he did; better than good.

His image was flawless, he was perfect.

TWO

Charlotte adjusted the pillows on the couch, her brown eyes flicking to the baby monitor on the coffee table. Genevieve was napping upstairs, her rhythmic breathing crackling through the speaker. The house smelled like fresh coffee and vanilla, the remnants of Lincoln's morning waffles. Now that she had a moment to breathe, she made her way to their home office to finalize some things for work the next day.

She sat at her desk, surrounded by spreadsheets, architectural renderings, and a coffee that had long gone cold. The Riverview was so close to completion, and the final push was always the hardest. Through the many photos scattered on her desk of her husband Lincoln's architectural designs and blueprints, she could piece together the floor-to-ceiling windows, the Hudson River stretching out under the morning light.

The renovations for the mill had taken over a year; gutting the interior, reinforcing the structure, modernizing the space while keeping its history intact. The exposed brick, the steel-framed windows, the sprawling event space that could shift from weddings to corporate retreats. After years of discussions between Lincoln, Jack, and herself about the abandoned structure's potential, this vision was finally coming to life.

The coffee shop had been Charlotte and Jack's first business venture, small but successful. The Riverview was their next move, a gamble that would either solidify their place in Hudson's business scene or sink them completely. And now, with Lincoln's firm gaining traction, and their opening event celebrating all its success, the stakes had never been higher.

She exhaled, clicking through the latest budget revisions. If the city backed Lincoln's redevelopment project, it wouldn't just boost his firm, it would put The Riverview on the map. That kind of exposure could turn their sleek new venue into a go–to destination, attracting high–end clients from Hudson, and with luck, Albany and the City.

Her buzzing phone cut through the peace. She picked it up without looking.

"Hey," she answered, tucking the phone between her shoulder and ear as she stacked Lincoln's blueprints of the mill back into a neat pile.

"I was just about to call you, I was looking over plans and spreadsheets. Can you send me a pic of the marketing samples? Still stuck on color."

"Hold on a sec, I actually have them laid out on the counter. I personally love the green more than the red." Here. Charlotte heard the snap of the camera. "Sent." Amy cleared her throat before continuing. "I've been working on marketing angles–press releases, targeted campaigns for corporate sponsors. We need a strategy that makes this project feel personal. Hudson isn't just looking for redevelopment, they're looking for legacy. The mill should be positioned as the heart of this transformation. If we get the right people behind us, this isn't just Lincoln's deal, it's ours."

"Yes, I see what you mean. You're the best thing to happen to this team, Amy. Go with green, and send it to the printers, this is perfect."

"Awe, thanks. You've got it. Will send over the files this afternoon."

Amy's voice was tight, like she was holding something in. Charlotte frowned, sinking onto the couch. "Sorry for dominating the conversation, we can talk about this tomorrow. You called me. What's going on?"

A pause. "I'm staring at a pregnancy test and can't bring

myself to take it."

Charlotte exhaled, leaning forward, forearms braced on her knees. This was familiar territory. "Want me to stay on the phone while you do it?"

There was a pause. "I can't keep doing this." Amy's footsteps echoed through the phone, her pacing quick and restless. "Mark's gone, again. Another trip in the books for him, we might as well move to the city, I hate doing this alone." Amy had read all the books, tried all the wives' tales, told herself she'd accept whatever came. Yet, every month, without fail, the desperation pulled her back into its grip, making her beg the universe all over again.

Charlotte sighed as she leaned against the cushions of the couch. She knew that Mark was immersed in his work, but he always made time for Amy, always accompanied her on appointments, always made the effort. "You know he would be there for you if he was in town, just breathe."

Charlotte absentmindedly reached for a nearby pen, twirling it between her fingers. Amy's sharp intake of breath derailed the conversation, catching them both off guard.

"What is it?" Charlotte interjected, leaning forward, she pressed her ear to the phone.

"It looks like it could be a line? Wait. It's just the dye activating. Amy forced a hollow laugh. "God, I swear I do this every time." Charlotte could hear the trepidation, something she had heard so many times before.

"Grab yourself a cup of coffee. By the time you get back, it should be time to look at the test." Charlotte suggested.

"Good idea, though decaf isn't going to do much. One positive of this cycle not working will be the return of caffeine." Amy forced a laugh as she poured a cup.

Then came the dreaded words. "The test is negative," The strain of holding back tears was evident in every syllable.

Charlotte took a breath. "Okay. I love you. We're going for

a run. Clear your head a little. Meet me at the park in ten." She hung up before Amy could refuse, grabbed two cups of coffee, and carefully made her way upstairs.

Charlotte texted her for good measure: I mean it, I'm getting dressed right now.

Charlotte stepped into the master bedroom, finding Lincoln propped against the headboard, a binder of plans for The Riverview open beside him and his phone in hand. At the sound of her footsteps, he glanced up, setting the phone aside.

"I have a phone call scheduled with Summitline Architecture in Manhattan, it looks like they're interested in the merger with our firm."

"How's Amy?"

She sighed, her thoughts drifting into the depth of her coffee cup as she sat beside him. "Could be better, the test was negative."

Lincoln wrapped an arm around her waist, scooching her body closer to his. His brow creased with concern. "Is there anything we can do for them? I could take Mark out for a round of golf or something."

She let herself relax into him, as his hands gripped her shoulders, kneading her tense muscles. "That might help. Anything to remind them they're not alone in this."

He pressed a kiss to her temple, pulling her close. "You're a good friend, Char."

"I haven't told Amy about the pregnancy." she murmured. "It feels too soon. I don't want to hurt her more than she is already."

Lincoln nodded. "When the time is right, you'll know. Don't stress it." he exhaled.

Charlotte leaned into him, "that's amazing news. I know they will come around, it's a great business deal for both of you." She glanced at her watch. "Alright, see you later. Got to get ready."

She rose from the bed, hopping on one foot as she slipped her sock on.

Charlotte tried thinking of what she'd say to Amy this time, but the short drive made that a useless effort.

The tires of her emerald Ford Edge lulled to a stop in the near barren parking lot of Henry Hudson Riverfront Park. The trail was the epitome of scenic beauty, captivating to residents and visitors alike. The early morning light cast fire to the water in blaring contrast against the hulls of boats docked in the water.

Amy was arranging her dark hair into a messy bun as charlotte walked up to her. She let out a breath, her shoulders sagging. "I really thought this time…" She trailed off, her gaze drifting to the water. "I mean, I *knew* it probably wouldn't happen, but there was this little part of me that kept thinking–maybe."

Charlotte swallowed the lump in her throat and reached for Amy's hand, squeezing gently. "It *will* happen. Maybe just not like this. There are other options, new meds, adoption."

Amy tensed. "I don't want to think about that yet."

Charlotte nodded quickly. "Right. I hear that." A beat of silence stretched between them.

"Mark posted about it."

Charlotte frowned. "What do you mean?"

Amy sighed. "A fucking Instagram reel. Some dramatic video about infertility and staying strong, and all the comments are just–'Mark, you're such an amazing husband,' 'You guys are so inspiring.'" She shook her head. "Meanwhile, I was still in the bathroom staring at a negative test."

Charlotte hesitated. "Maybe that's just how he's processing it."

Amy's expression wavered. "I don't know," she admitted. "It just feels… Like he shares more with *them* than with me. Like he needs their support more than mine."

Charlotte tapped her shoulder. "I think he's just trying to help people. He's always been good at that, hasn't he? Making people feel less alone."

Amy let out a slow breath, her fingers knotting together. "Yeah, you're right."

Charlotte nudged her gently. "And he is here for you. He tries so hard, I think men get the brunt of this, they're never really thought of when it comes to the stress of trying to have a baby, you know?"

Amy's lips parted like she wanted to argue, but no words came. Instead, she nodded, her shoulders slumping. "I know, you're right."

"He loves you so much, he wouldn't be posting about it if he didn't." Charlotte tried.

Amy exhaled as she bent down to grab her ankle for a stretch. "Let's just run. First one back buys lunch."

Charlotte nodded, "You got it, girl."

The trails were Amy's sanctuary, a place where she could lose herself in the rhythmic pounding of her feet against the pavement. As she ran, the weight of her unspoken worries pressed down on her. The struggles to conceive, the growing distance with Mark, the loneliness she couldn't shake, it all churned in her mind.

The trail wound along the river, offering fleeting moments of serenity. Amy flinched, a searing pain made her stop to catch her breath, staring out at the water, she couldn't shake the feeling that something had to change.

Finally drawing level with Amy, Charlotte could see the strain etched on her friend's face, her features contorted with agony. "Hey, what's wrong?" she placed a hand on Amy's shoulder.

Amy's hands were pressed to her side. "I think it's another cyst," she managed between shallow breaths. "It's been a pain in the ass for days."

They came to the end of the trail, placing her hands on her

knees as she took a little breather for the way back.

"I'm so sorry, girl, I have some ibuprofen in the car, want me to run ahead and grab some for you?" Amy shook her head, with a dismissive wave of her hand.

"Let's walk it off. Come on."

They started back in silence, their footsteps crunching over the gravel path. The air was thick, weighted with everything unsaid. Amy's gaze drifted past the trees, the soft hum of wind through the branches barely registering. "I thought this time would be it." Her voice was thin, almost distant.

Charlotte pulled her in, wrapping her arms around her. At first, Amy resisted, stiff in her hold. But then something broke, and she leaned into her, her shoulders shaking, hot tears soaking into Charlotte's shirt.

Charlotte felt her own eyes sting. It wasn't fair. None of it. *And the guilt.* While Amy was drowning in disappointment, she was carrying a secret she hadn't found the right moment to say, and it gnawed at her.

Her hands tightened on Amy's back. "I'm here," she whispered. It was all she could give.

Amy exhaled as she pulled back, swiping at her damp cheeks. "I don't even know why I'm crying," she muttered. "It's not like this is new."

Charlotte gave a small, sad smile. "That doesn't make it hurt any less."

Charlotte heard a sharp inhale, as Amy staggered.

Amy's grip slackened, her body pitching forward before Charlotte could react.

"Amy?"

Her name barely left Charlotte's lips before Amy's legs buckled completely. The sudden dead weight wrenched Charlotte down with her, gravel biting into her hands as Amy hit the ground hard. The air cracked with a strangled, gut-wrenching scream.

"Oh my God! Amy?" She scrambled, heart pounding, eyes darting over her friend's face. "What, what the hell?"

Amy didn't answer. She was curled in on herself, hands fisting in the dirt, her breaths coming too fast, too uneven.

Panic clawed its way up Charlotte's throat. "Amy, look at me." She reached out, brushing the damp hair from her friend's face, her hands shaking. "Talk to me. You're scaring me."

Amy's lips parted like she wanted to say something, but no sound came. Just the ragged rise and fall of her chest.

Charlotte barely got Amy's name out before her legs buckled. The weight of her wrenched Charlotte down too, gravel biting into her palms as Amy hit the ground hard.

The sound that tore from Amy's throat didn't even seem human. Raw, strangled, like something breaking open.

"Oh my God. Amy?" Charlotte's hands were on her before she could think, panic surging through her. "What–what the hell?"

Amy didn't answer. She was curled in on herself, fingers digging into the dirt, her breathing too fast, too uneven.

Charlotte's chest tightened. "Amy, look at me." She reached out, brushing the damp hair from her friend's face, her fingers shaking. "Talk to me. Please."

Amy's lips parted like she was trying, but nothing came. Just the ragged rise and fall of her chest.

Charlotte fumbled for her phone, nearly dropping it as she swiped at the screen. "Call…"

Amy's eyes rolled back.

Her body went slack.

Charlotte's stomach lurched. "Shit. Shit." She pressed her fingers to Amy's clammy skin, her own pulse hammering so hard it made her lightheaded.

She barely registered the operator's voice when they

answered. Her words came in a rush, her breath uneven. "I need an ambulance. My friend–she just collapsed."

Her free hand hovered over Amy's shoulder, unsure if touching her would make a difference. She felt utterly useless, stuck in the space between panic and action, between fear and the awful possibility that this was something she couldn't fix.

"Yes, Hudson Park."

"Please hurry," she whispered.

△△△

Mark's phone buzzed against the table, its vibration cutting through the low hum of conversation in the room. He glanced at the screen, his brow furrowing as Charlotte's name lit up. A sigh escaped his lips, a mix of frustration and annoyance.

He let it ring twice before seeing her incoming text of it being an emergency. Swiping to answer, pressing the phone to his ear.

"What's wrong?" he asked. He was steady, controlled, trying to act businesslike.

The words left his mouth, but the rest of him betrayed his composure. A rippled sensation surged through him, starting low in his abdomen and spreading outward.

Stop. His eyes sharpened, but his body refused to obey. *Fuck, he was so hard.* His head tilted back as he felt her nails scrape lightly along his thigh, her lips tightening around him.

No. he mouthed.

The urgency pulled him back. "It's Amy. She collapsed during our run, had to call an ambulance. I'm on my way to the hospital." Charlotte told Mark.

His stomach knotted at her words, but not enough to drown out the heat pooling low in his pelvis. He shifted in his seat, the leather creaking beneath him as he exhaled sharply. She didn't slow down, and his hand gripped the strands of her hair.

"Are you there?" she asked.

"What happened?" He stood abruptly, needing to create distance, but it only made things worse. Her hands followed, sliding up his torso with a maddening slowness. A shudder ran through him, his knees nearly buckling as he braced himself against the wall. The pressure, the relentless rhythm she refused to break, blurred the lines between agony and ecstasy.

His jaw clenched as he felt her teeth gently graze his shaft, a sharp contrast to the softness of her lips as he came. His free hand shot out, gripping her shoulder with enough force to stop her. For a moment, the room fell silent, except the uneven rhythm of his breath.

Charlotte continued, oblivious. "She was complaining of pain earlier, but she thought it was just another cyst. Paramedic thinks it's probably her appendix, maybe a rupture."

She stumbled back, her gaze flicking between desire and amusement as she wiped her mouth with a finger.

"Is she–" He cleared his throat, trying again. "I'm on my way."

"She's in good hands, I'll see you soon."

THREE

The drive to the hospital was quiet, the hum of the tires filling the space between them. Josephine watched buildings blur past, why did he take this route? Her stomach flipped as they passed a row of medical offices, immediately pulling her back to another drive, another night, when the silence between them had been even heavier.

She pressed her palms together, rubbing them absently, grounding herself against the creeping unease. The sterile office. The cold metal of the exam table beneath her legs. Mark's father standing over her. The taste that burned the back of her throat.

> The office was cold and sterile, the kind of place where no good news was ever delivered. Josie hesitated at the door, but Doctor Morales' firm grip on her arm left no room for argument. Mark trailed behind them, his bruised face pale and tense.
>
> Josie sat stiffly on the exam table, the thin paper beneath her crinkling with every tremor as she heard the door lock. She wrapped her arms around herself, her knees pressed tightly together as if she could shrink small enough to disappear. Mark stood against the wall, his hands shaking at his sides, his bruised cheekbone swollen and dark.
>
> Doctor Morales snapped on a pair of gloves, the sound echoing in the small room like a gunshot. "You have two options," he'd said coldly, "You can take the medication, or I'll handle it myself."

Josie's wide, tear-filled eyes locked on Mark. "You can't—"

"I can," Doctor Morales interrupted, his tone hard and final. "And I will. You are fifteen. You don't have the capacity to make this decision. I do."

"Dad, stop," Mark stepped forward. "You can't do this."

"Sit the fuck down," his father barked. "One more fucking word, and I'll call the cops on you myself." His cold stare snapped back to her, and she felt like she was going to puke.

Mark hesitated, his fists tightening, but Josie shook her head at him, silently begging him not to make it worse. He backed away, his chest heaving as he pressed himself against the wall.

Doctor Morales turned to her, his tone softer now, but no less insidious. "Josephine," his tone almost gentle, "I've known your parents for years. I've watched you grow up. You're a smart girl, too smart to throw your life away over a mistake."

Her hands began to sweat. "It's not a mistake." she whispered.

He ignored her, pressing on. "Do you have any idea what this would do to your family? To your mother?" He shook his head, a disappointing sigh escaping him. "Your mother is a devout Catholic. What do you think she'd say if she found out her only daughter got pregnant at fifteen? Out of wedlock? She'd be mortified. Embarrassed. Do you want to put her through that kind of shame? Because that's exactly what this would do."

Tears spilled over Josie's cheeks, her hands twisting in her lap.

"And Mark?" Doctor Morales continued, his gaze

sharp. "Do you know what happens to an eighteen-year-old who impregnates a minor? He goes to prison, Josephine. Prison. They'll call him a predator, a sex offender. His life will be over before it even starts."

She shook her head. "We love each other. We'll figure—"

"No, you won't," he interrupted, "You won't figure out anything because the world won't let you. College? Gone. Careers? Gone. This will follow both of you for the rest of your lives."

Josie's sobs grew louder, her whole body shaking.

Doctor Morales stepped closer. "I'm not saying this to hurt you. I'm saying this because I care about you. About Mark. This isn't about love. It's about doing what's right for both of you. This is your chance to fix this before it's too late."

Stop crying, he internally snapped before exhaling. He pulled a small packet of pills from his pocket and set them on the counter. "This is the only way," his expression firm, "Take these, and it's done. No one has to know. Your parents don't have to know. Mark doesn't go to prison. Your life stays on track."

Josie stared at the pills, her vision blurred by tears.

The room seemed to tilt, the walls closing in around her as her breath came in shallow, panicked gasps. She looked at Mark one last time, desperate for him to say something, to do something.

"Josie," Mark choked out, "You don't have to—"

"She does," his father snapped, turning on him with a glare that silenced him instantly.

Josie's hands shook as he placed them in a cup and handed it to her. Every part of her wanted to scream, to run, but her body refused to move. She brought the pills to her lips and swallowed, the water burning like acid as it slid down her throat.

Mark's voice cracked. "Dad–"

"It's done," his father cut him off with a cold finality. He turned to Josie, his tone suddenly calm, "You'll experience some cramping. It'll feel like a normal period. This will all be over before you know it."

Josie slid off the table, her legs buckling beneath her. She caught the edge with a trembling hand, her breath sharp and uneven. The room swayed. Cold sweat prickled at her skin. She wouldn't look at him. Couldn't.

Something inside her was gone. Not just taken, ripped away. Her relationship, her choices, her dignity.

Her fingers curled against the sterile paper lining the table, crumpling it in her fist. A hollow, cavernous ache spread through her ribs, swallowing everything. She pressed her lips together, tasting salt, swallowing the sob clawing its way up her throat.

Doctor Morales stepped toward her, blocking her path to the door. His expression was carefully composed. "Josephine," he paused for effect, "this was for the best. You're young. Impulsive. This would have destroyed you. You don't see it now, but I saved your life tonight."

She refused to look at him, her gaze fixed firmly on the floor.

"No one will ever know," he continued, his tone almost soothing. "Not a soul. Isn't that what you wanted? For everything to go back to normal?"

Josie's expression was blank. "I want to go home."

Doctor Morales didn't answer, stepping aside to let her pass. Mark rushed to her side, his hands brushing hers as they walked silently to the car. She didn't pull away, but she didn't grip his hand, either.

She swallowed hard, trying to tether herself back to reality as she looked over at Mark, still bewildered that he was here, that they had found one another again after all these years, that this was even possible. She swallowed hard, the pressure in her chest making it difficult to breathe.

Looking at Mark now, older, sharper, more guarded, she couldn't reconcile the boy who had stood helpless in that office with the man gripping the wheel beside her." "I still think about that night," she admitted, breaking the silence.

Mark's grip tightened on the wheel. "I don't."

Josie turned to him, brows knitting. "You don't?"

His jaw flexed. "I try not to."

She hesitated, realizing, too late, what she hadn't considered. He hadn't just lost their baby that night. He'd lost everything. "Mark, I–"

"Don't." His tone was firm. His fingers flexed against the steering wheel, then relaxed as he exhaled slowly. "It's over. It happened, I've made peace with it."

She nodded, not pushing it, but the weight of it settled deep in her ribs.

A long stretch of silence passed before Mark shifted, reaching for her hand. His touch was warm, steady. "Let's get away," he murmured. "Just us."

Josie glanced at him, her fingers lacing with his. "Where?"

"Anywhere you want. A cabin in the mountains, a beach. Just you and me."

She smiled faintly, leaning into the fantasy. "That sounds perfect."

"It will be." He paused, "One day, we'll leave all of this behind, start fresh."

Her chest ached with how much she wanted to believe that. But reality wasn't that simple. "When?" she asked, "When are you going to end things?"

Mark's grip on her hand tightened, just enough for her to notice.

She met his gaze, and something flickered in his eyes, something unreadable, something cold beneath the warmth he'd shown just moments ago.

"There's a lot at stake, you know that."

Josie's muscles tensed. She did know. She knew what he was risking. What they were risking.

His hand squeezed hers again, firmer this time. "Trust me."

The words weren't a request.

She swallowed, nodding slowly. "I do."

A long stretch of silence passed before Mark reached across the console, settling his palm against the back of her hand. His warmth bled into her skin, steadying, grounding. "Good." Mark's gaze shifted between the road and Josie as she flipped the mirror down, braiding her long black hair to the side. Her movements were easy, familiar. The way she drew in her bottom lip when she concentrated, just like Amy always did, brought a fleeting sense of something deeper, something too close. Her eyes, a soft hazel that always seemed to be searching for something beyond the moment, locked with his for just a second longer than he expected. The same steady, unspoken understanding between them that he used to share with Amy.

The hospital came into view, and Josephine exhaled, untangling their fingers as they pulled into the parking lot. "I should go. My shift starts soon." She shifted to kiss him.

Mark nodded, but as she reached for the door handle, his hand closed over her wrist. "I'll pick you up tonight, we'll grab dinner. I love you." He eyed her. "Josie, those scrubs are fit you so well. Remind me to buy some more for you."

She met his gaze, "Okay. Love you too."

She walked away, disappearing through the hospital doors. Mark stayed in the car, gripping the wheel, staring at the dashboard like it held the answer to something he hadn't figured out yet. He checked the notifications as he watched Josie disappear through the main entrance of the hospital, giving her ample time for them to not run into one another.

Then, with a slow breath, he opened the door and stepped out, adjusting his tie, as he readied himself to go inside.

The hospital room was unnervingly quiet besides the soft beep of monitors and the occasional shuffle of a nurse's shoes in the hallway. The shadows of exhaustion darkened Amy's heavy eyes, still deeply sedated from the anesthesia.

Mark sat by her bedside, his posture relaxed, one leg crossed over the other as he scrolled through his phone. A flood of notifications awaited him; tweets, comments, and likes, a surge of emails and texts from Kaitlyn, his publicist, about upcoming press appearances.

He glanced at Amy, noting the soft curl of her fingers against the blanket, the way her lips parted slightly as she slept. His thumb hovered over a message from his agent.

> Kaitlyn: Congrats on three million, we've got the location booked for your keynote and signing, ticket sales will be posted soon.

A grin tugged at his lips. He adjusted his tie, the movement instinctive despite the casual setting. Rising fame suited him, the validation of his work, his mind, his ability to spin a narrative others devoured without question.

His marriage to Amy had become the antithesis of everything he had built for himself. The emails, the constant reminders of his success, of his place in the world, felt like a veil over his real feelings. A veil he hid behind because the truth was, he didn't know who he was without it. Without Amy, without the reputation, without the image. He felt like a man in a cage of his own making.

How much longer could he play the part of the devoted husband when all he felt was trapped? *Trapped in his image*, trapped in a marriage that had long since worn thin.

His fingers trembled slightly as he tapped at the screen, trying to drown out the noise in his head. Trying to escape the sickening pull of conflicting emotions. His need to *leave*, but his obligation to stay. His desire for freedom, and his drive to maintain control. His body was restless, his thoughts scattered. He should care about Amy, should feel something deeper than obligation. When he looked at her, he felt nothing, nothing that he *should* feel.

She wasn't his escape. She was his anchor, and that's what made it worse.

The earlier phone call replayed in his mind. The tension, the urgency of Charlotte's words, the sharp, guttural *pleasure* that had coursed through him in that singular moment.

Mark leaned back in the chair, his fingers grazing his jaw. He had tried to break it off with Josie, the timing was terrible with everything happening with his book, and his career.

Her tenacity, her nails against his skin, the way she worshiped him, her mouth insistent despite his murmured protests. The thrill that raced through him when Charlotte's voice cut through, completely oblivious. He felt his dick twitch.

He hadn't wanted it to happen, but there was something intoxicating about the duality of the moment, the collision of crisis and pleasure. It set him in a cold sweat, goosebumps tracing both arms. The weight of the power it gave him was undeniable.

Mark's fingers tapped against his phone's screen, rhythmically, as though to drown out the intrusive thoughts. He looked at Amy again, still unmoving.

When Charlotte had told him Amy had collapsed, he'd felt a rush, not of concern, but of something darker. *Control.* The situation had demanded him. It had been an opportunity to be seen, to be the husband everyone believed him to be.

And then there was her mouth on him. The way she'd smiled, the way she'd whispered *Let me finish* against his skin.

He shook his head, raking a hand through his hair.

He didn't know how to break free of it. He couldn't escape the script he'd written for himself, no matter how much he ached for a change. The facade was crumbling, and he knew it. *But what would happen if he let it go?*

What was left if he walked away from the life he'd built?

Mark stood, his mind spinning as he moved toward the door.

He was still here. And the truth, ugly as it was, was that he couldn't leave. Not yet. Maybe never.

The phone buzzed again.

Kaitlyn: Event sold out. Keep the momentum going.

He sighed. This was who he was now. This was what he had to be. The nurse walked into the room, and Mark excused himself to answer a call.

∆∆∆

Charlotte made her way down the hall with two cups of coffee. Mark was standing outside Amy's closed door, speaking to someone on the phone. The sight of him brought a fleeting sense of relief as she thought about how he was so good to her, such a grounding presence.

"Hey you, I warn you, this is swill." Charlotte handed him the steaming cup. "Everything okay? Docs come in yet?"

Mark nodded, his facade wavered for a moment, a flicker of vulnerability crossing his features. "The nurse is working on her drains right now. She had a lot of blood in her abdomen, so the drains will help alleviate that pressure. Doctors found out what has been causing her issues with conceiving," his tone was reassuring.

As Mark filled Charlotte in on the news, his unease was palpable, evident in the way he switched uncomfortably from foot to foot, his gaze avoiding hers as he spoke. "The surgery was more complicated than anticipated," Mark began, "They found a lot of endometrial tissue, her organs were coated with it. He said he would come in later to discuss the findings in depth when Amy comes around."

Charlotte drew in a sharp breath. "That's terrible news." She wasn't sure she knew what endometriosis was, exactly, and was looking forward to hearing what the doctor had to say about it. "Were they able to clear it all out?" Charlotte nervously wound a strand of hair around her finger.

"How do you feel about it?" Charlotte shifted her weight, crossing her arms across her chest as she leaned against the wall.

Mark shifted focus, nodding politely as the nurse opened the door.

"She's awake." The nurse swiped her hand under the hand sanitizer dispenser, before moving down the hall. "I'll let the doctor know that she's up."

As Mark and Charlotte entered the room, Charlotte moved closer to Amy, grasping her hand gently as she took a seat adjacent to the bed. Before she could pull away, her attention was drawn back to the door as it creaked open. Doctor Lofner, Amy's surgeon, stepped in.

"Good evening Mrs. Rodriguez, I wanted to provide you with an update on your question about discharge. Because of the complexity of the procedure, we want to keep you here for another twenty four hours."

Amy nodded thoughtfully as she wound the sheet around her finger. "That makes sense. I had one more question, the nurse didn't know." She glanced at Mark, her expression betraying her anxiety, then turned her attention back to Doctor Lofner. "When will it be okay for us to start trying to conceive again?"

Doctor Lofner hesitated for a moment, "I would recommend waiting at least eight weeks. Given the complexity of the surgery and the number of lesions we had to remove, it's important to give your body time to heal."

Mark cleared his throat, "Doctor Lofner, can you explain the diagnosis to her like you did for me? I don't think she understands what is going on." His tone was condescending and somewhat agitated. Charlotte suddenly felt uncomfortable, like she needed to leave the room, but Amy extended a hand for her to join her. Charlotte crept closer to the bed where Amy tightly took hold of her hand.

Doctor Lofner took a piece of paper from her chart and clicked his pen." When the tissue that lines the uterus grows outside the organ itself, it's like an invasive tumor. It attaches itself to other organs and parts of the body and it can cause a lot of issues. It was major abdominal surgery, Mrs. Rodgriguez. We had to open you up instead of doing small incisions. There are four stages of endometriosis. Given your findings, your case was deemed a stage three." He wrote a note on the clipboard before continuing. "I would defer to your reproductive endocrinologist for specific guidance on timing. You may encounter continued difficulty with trying to conceive, and require treatments, though it may very well be that you are able to conceive on your own, should your body heal appropriately."

Amy nodded, expression falling with disappointment.

"Do you have any additional questions?"

"No, thank you for everything Doctor Lofner."

He smiled. "I'll be back to check on you in the morning. If you have any additional questions, feel free to page the nurse, and she will get in contact with my office." He shook hands with Mark. As the physician left the room, Amy studied Mark, sensing a disconnect. He seemed distant, his attention elsewhere.

"Waiting eight weeks seems a bit much, doesn't it?" Amy glanced at Charlotte for support.

Mark's response was measured as he ran his hands through his hair. "The doctor knows best, Amy. We shouldn't rush into anything." Charlotte could tell he was irritated, but keeping his cool because of her presence. Charlotte's phone rang. *Thank God.* She thought as she held up the screen. "I'll be right back." She slipped out of the room, relieved to escape the impending argument.

Amy's face hardened as the door closed. "But what if we wait and nothing changes, or worse, our window closes and this is our only chance?"

Mark flexed his fingers, his knuckles cracking in the silence. "Only chance?" The words came out blunt, almost cold. "This is going to *improve* your chances, not limit them. Trust the process."

Amy shifted her weight to sit up, pressing against the mattress for leverage, but the drain in her abdomen pulled. She yelped, recoiling from the pain, but Mark's expression didn't soften.

He leaned forward, his gaze hard. "Which is precisely why we're waiting." His hand brushed over the cigarettes in his pocket, a brief flicker of distraction as he tapped the box, then lowered his head toward her. "You need to start listening to your doctors. This is not up for discussion." His tone was flat, final.

There was a knock, and Lincoln and Charlotte walked back in with a large basket of flowers and a bottle of wine.

"Hey Amy, the wine is for later." Lincoln, placed the arrangement on the counter, turning his attention to Amy, he took a seat in a nearby chair. "How are you feeling?"

Amy's smile was evident. "A hell of a lot better than I have in years." She gave him a thumbs up.

Lincoln returned the gesture. "Awesome news." turning to Mark, Lincoln gathered his stressed state. "Hey man, want to come with me to get some coffee? Apparently, there's a Starbucks near the gift shop."

"Gah, really? That would have been nice to know." She poured the now cold liquid down the sink. "Can I have a Jasmine tea then? Ask if they can add some lemon and ginger too."

Mark nodded, relief washing over him as they turned for the door. "Need anything?"

She shook her head as Charlotte sat down on the foot of Amy's bed. "No, thanks." She exhaled. "Take your time, girl gossip is always the worst for you two." Amy laughed, wincing at the discomfort of her contracted muscles. Her gaze drifted towards the door, a mixture of emotions flickering across her face. She took a deep breath, gathering her thoughts.

"Sorry you had to see that earlier, we butt heads on this more often than I would like to admit." she sighed, "I think– I think Mark's just been under a lot of stress lately," Amy began, hesitating as she searched for the right way to express the situation. "Between the book, work, and everything else, it's been really hard on him too."

Charlotte listened closely, her expression softening with empathy as she took in Amy's troubled tone.

"Trying for a baby has taken a toll, it's hard for him to show positive emotions with it." Amy continued, "But I know he's trying his best, in his own way."

Charlotte leaned forward, her fingers gently wrapping around Amy's hand. "Mark is trying his best," she said, her voice soft but uncertain, as if fumbling for the right words. "I can't imagine what you both must be going through. But you've got each other. That's something, right?"

Amy took a steadying breath, her gaze unfocused as she let her words sink in. "For the first time, the pain… it's gone. All these years, I didn't know it wasn't normal. I thought that's just how it was supposed to feel." She paused, swallowing the lump in her throat. "It used to be like a constant, dull ache. And then, sometimes, it would hit so hard, like something was tearing inside me. I couldn't even get out of bed. No one believed me."

Charlotte's heart twisted, her fingers squeezing Amy's, though she still couldn't fully comprehend what Amy was describing. "I can't even imagine what that must have been like," Charlotte exhaled. "It must have been awful. I don't get how something like that can just be missed for so long."

Amy nodded, her chest tight. "I just lived with it. It was like I was being punished for something I didn't understand." Her voice broke for a second, but she kept going. "I didn't even know how bad it had gotten until it stopped. And now it's gone. I don't know how to feel about that. I never thought I'd feel this kind of relief, like I can actually move forward."

Charlotte's gaze softened as she saw the raw emotion on Amy's face. "But at least now you know what it is. Now that they've fixed things, you can finally take back control of your body. That's a huge thing."

Amy sniffed, nodding. "Yeah. For the first time, it feels like something might actually be possible. I can finally picture what being a mom could look like, instead of just wondering if it was ever going to happen."

Charlotte's hand tightened on Amy's again, though she couldn't help but feel that familiar disconnect, an emptiness of understanding. "You've been through so much. I just know things are going to work out for you."

Amy smiled weakly, the tears still slipping down her face. "Thanks. I hope you're right."

FOUR

Callum glanced at his phone, the glow of the screen casting soft light against his sharp features. His wavy brown hair, a face that seemed permanently caught between a smirk and focus. He scrolled through the email Amy had sent earlier, a detailed list of houses for sale in the area. While Amy no longer practiced real estate full time, her license was still active, and she'd offered to help. There were links to photos, asking prices, and short descriptions she'd clearly taken the time to annotate with her own thoughts.

Too small for someone your height.

Nice yard for your imaginary dog.

This one has good bones, just not in the basement.

He shook his head and let out a chuckle. *She really didn't miss a thing.*

His apartment downtown had always been temporary, a space to fill while he got his bearings after his divorce. The Riverview was finally finished, and the contract he'd signed six months ago meant he'd be sticking around for the long haul, but he hadn't planned on house hunting quite yet. Leave it to Amy to be one step ahead.

She always was. Reliable, sharp, efficient. And annoyingly persistent, in a good way.

He smiled. Amy had been the first person to welcome him when he'd joined the team at The Riverview, back when the old mill was a skeleton of its current self, raw beams, exposed brick, and dust that clung to everything.

His phone buzzed, interrupting his thoughts. *Does she know I'm online?.*

Amy: Let me guess. You're still 'thinking' about house #3. You'll love it, trust me.

Callum worked in project management for the renovations, and though he'd initially intended to move on once the work was done, Lincoln had convinced him to stay on as their operations manager.

He stared at Amy's text a moment longer before replying.

Callum: I'll think about it. No promises.

Amy: You're impossible.

He could practically hear the exasperation in her tone. It was familiar, comfortable. They'd fallen into this easy rhythm, and though they didn't always agree, they worked well together.

A notification pinged his phone. Callum opened Instagram to see a message from an old buddy from the Army:

Brenden: Hey man, thinking of you today. OORAH. Callum's jaw tensed.

His deployments to the wars in the Middle East had ended his military career; or, more accurately, it had broken him. It was supposed to be the reset, the beginning of something new. But instead, his life had unraveled. After his failed marriage and the difficulties that followed, Callum realized he wasn't just running from the Army, he was running from everything. His past, his failures, his guilt. After replying, he got sucked into the rabbit hole, liking posts, scrolling through stories, when a handle suggestion popped up:

Instagram: Someone you may know: @Eversea_Photography

Callum's fingers drummed against his thigh, the tension in

his body coiled so tightly he felt like it might snap. He clicked on her 'new to him' profile. Months. He had spent months obsessing over getting Josephine back, convincing himself that if he just tried hard enough, if he just said the right thing, she'd remember what they had.

A laugh scraped at his throat. It was almost poetic. He stared at her landing page.

Private. He exhaled, pushing himself off the couch and making his way to his study.

Callum pasted the handle into his laptop, his lips tightening as the results populated. It didn't take long, her amateur photography page appeared in the search results, a nickname tucked neatly in the bio. He clicked the link, his mouth dry as the page loaded. The gallery was filled with her, and other women. *Boudoir. Not what he expected.*

The images of her though, not in the obvious way of influencers and models, but in the quieter, more enigmatic way she always carried herself; artful, alluring, intimate.

Every shot burned into him like a brand, reminding him of what he'd lost.

One photo stopped him cold. His dick stiffened.

Josephine, lying in soft lighting, her dark hair spilling over the white sheets like liquid. The curve of her hips, the soft shadow of her breasts, the gleam of pearls against her skin. Her lips were parted, her gaze intense, but the most painful thing was the way she was looking at someone else. Someone who wasn't him.

His head dropped back against the chair, breath shallow. His body didn't care about the anger twisting in his gut, the resentment tangled with the need. He couldn't stop himself, not when the memory of her burned so vividly in his mind.

He'd been so fucking stupid to think that he could let her go. That she could let *him* go.

His finger hovered over the screen, the temptation to

message her clawing at him. Instead, he closed the app and leaned back in his chair, his eyes closing as he thought of her.

"You're being a fucking idiot." He said aloud as he rose from his seat, casting his underwear to the floor, an exhale of relief leaving him as he moved across the living room, and into the bathroom. He turned on the shower, entering the cold stream without waiting for it to warm. Sweat beaded his brow, his mind tangled further into a mess of lust and rage. The water pounded against Callum's back, now hot enough to redden his skin, but he barely felt it.

Steam filled the bathroom, clinging to the tiles, the mirror, the glass door, as if the room itself was suffocating under the weight of his thoughts. The ache in his chest sank lower, spreading through his body like wildfire. His hand curled into a fist before relaxing. He let out a ragged breath, the steam curling around him like smoke as he leaned against the wall, his head tilting back against the slick tile.

His chest ached. His mind whirled with anger, desire, confusion. He wasn't supposed to care. He wasn't supposed to want her after everything that had happened. A guttural sound escaped his throat as he leaned back against the wall. His mind spiraled, raging, aching, wanting. He stood upright, the water dripping from his face as he turned off the shower. He hated how much he craved it, craved her. He dragged his hand through his wet hair, his fingers pulling roughly as if trying to ground himself.

The steam was suffocating now, the heat unbearable, but Callum didn't move. He stayed there, his body tense, his mind spiraling. Josephine wasn't his anymore, but she would be.

Callum got dressed, his thoughts spiraling. As he sat back down, he tried focusing on something, anything else. His friend had replied to his message, and he tapped away at a response:

Cal: Thanks man, when I find myself in North Carolina again, let's get together. Good to catch up.

He swiped out of the message, and clicked on Amy's profile from the new photo that had popped up on his feed.

Amy wasn't posing or performing for the camera the way Josephine did. Amy's photos were more effortless, more real, laughing in candid moments, caught in warm sunlight, leaning into her husband like she had no idea the whole world could see.

And for some reason, that was what made his stomach turn.

He glanced at Josephine's photography page, still open on the laptop, and then again at Amy's Instagram on his phone.

And it was almost funny.

The similarity was glaring. The way they tilted their heads in thought. The way their expressions softened when they weren't aware of the camera. The way their bodies held the same kind of delicate confidence, like they'd been carved from the same mold.

How had he not seen it before?

Amy posted an image to her grid:

An Evening with Dr. Mark Rodriguez: Book Launch and Keynote.

Callum rolled his eyes. Of all the men for her to marry, she picked the arrogant asshole. The same image, an Instagram ad was now on his feed, and he laughed, clicking it purely out of curiosity. The link took him to a professional profile, complete with a polished photo, millions of followers, and bio that reeked of self–importance.

Author.

Speaker.

Innovator.

There was a red–carpet photo of him and Amy, his arms draped around her like she was his toy. He clicked on the photo of Amy and him to read the comments. Josephine's handle stopped him dead in his tracks. He turned back to the laptop, his fingers flying across the keyboard as he searched through Mark's social media accounts scrolling through Mark's posts; the curated perfection of his life grating against Callum's nerves. Promotional shots, carefully crafted captions, pictures of polished events. And there, nestled among the thousands of likes and comments, was Josephine's handle. She had liked nearly every post. Her handle stood out against the flood of anonymous adoration. *How long had she been following him?*

Callum's fingers hovered over the screen, his breathing shallow as the pieces began to fall into place. She hadn't just been following Mark. She had been in his orbit, a constant presence beneath the surface.

Something darker settled in his stomach, something raw and electric. He clicked over to Mark's profile, and there it was, Josephine's handle, scattered through the likes and comments. Months of it. Right under his nose.

A slow exhale left his lungs, but it did nothing to cool the burn spreading under his skin.

The thought came in pieces.

Mark had taken her from him, that had to be it. The things she'd said, the mention of her therapist. It was all a fucking confession, and he had been too blind to see it.

And Amy.

Callum stared at the screen, something shifting under his ribs, something sharp. His jaw clenched, but instead of anger, something else twisted inside him, something he hadn't felt in a long time.

Excitement.

Not for Josephine, not for what they had, but for the idea of tearing it all down. The thought of taking everything Mark had.

It was so simple.

Mark had destroyed his life, so why shouldn't Callum take from him? His fingers hovered over Amy's page again, over the pictures of her and Mark, over the soft glances and quiet affection she still thought was real.

She had no idea, and that was the worst part.

Amy wasn't like Josephine. There was something sincere about her, something magnetic. Maybe that's what drew him to her in the first place. She didn't even realize that the man she was planning a future with was already miles ahead of her, dragging Josephine into their bed, into the quiet corners of both of their lives.

He could ruin Mark, expose him. Show Amy *exactly* who she was married to. It would be easy, he just needed evidence. A few messages, a few carefully placed screenshots, some photos...

Clicking back to the promotional post, he hovered over a link to purchase tickets to Mark's event. Callum stared at the glowing "Buy" button, his pulse steady but his mind racing. He clicked. The confirmation email popped up on the screen, but Callum didn't bother reading it. His eyes flicked to the corner of the desk where his phone sat, he hovered over the *Find My* app, clicking the icon as he watched the screen populate in real time. Josephine had forgotten to disable it, and he'd kept the feature active just in case. A small, twisted part of him had always known he'd need it. The thought of tracking her, knowing their every move, felt too perfect, a way to bring her betrayal into the light. But this wasn't just about her anymore.

His fingers hovered over the phone screen, lingering for a moment before swiping to the map. The Apple location feature pinpointed her last location: a small, upscale restaurant in the city. The name of the adjacent hotel sent a chill down his spine. He thought back to the night they'd fought, when Josephine had left without a word. Now, the pieces were falling into place. The map blinked on the screen, and Callum leaned forward tapping the location. His pulse quickened. This was his chance to gather more information. With a sharp inhale, Callum grabbed his jacket and stormed out of the room, phone in hand, as he began making his way to the restaurant.

△△△

As Callum entered the restaurant, and his eyes immediately traced the intricate wood ceiling, with massive beams crafted into triangular patterns. The rustic yet refined ambiance reminded him of The Riverview. The warm wooden accents and soft, ambient lighting, created an inviting atmosphere, an atmosphere that tracked for someone like Mark. The restaurant was a world apart from the chaos in his mind. The air smelled of roasted herbs, butter, and something faintly sweet, a combination so intoxicating it almost distracted him from the tight knot in his chest. Almost.

The walls were lined with bottles of wine, their labels meticulously arranged, while the soft hum of conversation filled the room, blending seamlessly with the faint strains of a band playing live music on the stage. It was the kind of place that invited intimacy, that begged for quiet moments shared over glasses of something aged and expensive. But tonight, Callum felt none of that. The atmosphere only made the ache sharper, the contrast between the restaurant's perfection and the mess in his head too glaring to ignore.

Scanning the room, Callum spotted Josephine and Mark seated at a corner table. He'd tracked her here, but he hadn't expected Mark to be with her. Their attire was notably formal; Josephine wore a tailored blazer over a blouse, and Mark was in a crisp dress shirt without a tie. To an onlooker, they could easily be mistaken for colleagues engaged in a business meeting rather than a date. This observation stirred a sense of irritation in Callum, as he had hoped to see a more personal connection between them.

Callum sat in the corner of the bar, half–shrouded in shadow, nursing a drink he'd barely touched. His attention was fixed on them. Seeing them together tore the wound wide open.

His eyes locked on the couple across the room, studying every movement. The way Mark leaned back, his body language detached, playing the game because he knew people would be watching. The way Josephine leaned in, her hand brushing against his as she tried to pull him into her orbit. It was a dance Callum recognized all too well. He had been in Mark's place once, had felt the intoxicating pull of her attention. But he also knew how quickly it could turn. How easily she could slip through fingers.

His phone hovered over the table, the camera angled just right as he snapped a photo. The tension in Mark's jaw, the flicker of frustration in Josie's eyes; he caught it all. *Evidence*, Callum thought. Not just for whatever game Mark was playing, but for himself. Proof that she was still real, still tangible. That she hadn't disappeared completely.

The flick of her hair, the way her hand lingered on the edge of her wine glass–it was a script she'd performed before. Tonight, her audience wasn't playing along. Mark's reaction was controlled, his expression barely shifting, but Callum saw it, the way his fingers curled around the stem of his glass, the way his eyes hardened for a fraction of a second. It was the kind of tension that Callum thrived on, the kind that made people slip up.

The way Mark leaned in, his expression cold and distant, said everything Callum needed to know. *So, this is how you operate*, he thought, his jaw set. *Playing her like a pawn while keeping your perfect little life intact.*

Across the room, Mark leaned forward, his voice low but sharp. Callum couldn't hear the words, but he didn't need to. Josephine's reaction told him enough. Her shoulders stiffened, her expression oscillated between defiance and fear. She was losing control, and Mark was letting her know it.

He exhaled slowly, forcing himself to look away, his gaze falling to the polished wood of the bar. The memories were too sharp tonight, cutting deeper than usual. Josephine's face, her voice, the way she used to look at him like he was the only thing that mattered, it all came rushing back in a flood he couldn't stop.

She'd been standing in the doorway, her arms crossed tightly over her chest. The fight had been brewing all night, tension crackling in the air like static before a storm. Callum could still see the way her eyes burned, the fire there not enough to mask the hurt beneath it.

"You're not listening to me," she'd said. "You never listen, Callum. You just... assume you know everything. Like I don't have a say."

He'd bristled, his jaw tightening as he tried to keep his temper in check. "That's not fair," he shot back. "I've done nothing but try to make this work, Josie. But you– you're the one who keeps shutting me out."

She'd laughed then, a bitter sound that cut deeper than any words could. "Shutting you out? Do you even hear yourself? You're the one who–" She stopped short, shaking her head as if trying to shake the words loose. "Forget it. You don't get it. You never will."

The silence that followed was deafening. Callum had taken a step closer, his hands clenched at his sides. "Then explain it to me, make me understand, because for the past month we have gone in square circles, and you won't tell me, you won't talk." his tone was rough. "Tell me what I'm missing, Josie. Because I'm trying here. I'm fucking trying."

Her eyes had softened for just a moment, but then she'd looked away, her shoulders slumping. "You made me do something I didn't want to do, Callum. And I can't–"

"I made you? Are you even fucking hearing yourself?"

"I want a divorce." She let out a shaky breath. "I said I would try, we tried, this isn't working." And then she'd turned, walking out the door without another word. He'd called after her, but she hadn't stopped. The sound of her car starting, the faint glow of the taillights as she pulled away.

The bartender's movement brought him back. Callum's grasp tensed around his glass, the ice clinking softly. *Good. Let her squirm. Let her feel what it's like to be at someone else's mercy.* His attention shifted as Josephine's composure cracked further. She drained her glass, her movements jerky, uncoordinated, a stark contrast to the practiced elegance she'd carried moments before. Mark, in contrast, exuded an air of controlled detachment, as though none of this mattered.

It mattered to Callum. He could feel the tension building in his chest, the familiar itch of knowing he was on the edge of something significant. Mark wasn't just a man with secrets; he was a man who thought he could bury them. And Josephine? She was the weak link. When Mark brushed past Josephine without so much as a glance, leaving her alone at the table, Callum leaned back in his chair, his smirk returning. She was unraveling, and he'd been there to witness every moment.

He slid his phone into his pocket and rose from the barstool. As he passed through the restaurant his view got better, lingering on her red-rimmed eyes, her fingers trembling slightly as she picked at the edge of the napkin.

Callum stepped into the crisp night air, his breath visible in the cold. The images on his phone burned in his pocket, but it wasn't enough. He needed more. He needed to understand how Josie had ended up here, with Mark. Why she'd left him. Why she hadn't come back. He drew the cool air into his lungs, mindlessly walking the streets of Albany until he came to a familiar bar. He ordered a beer as he scrolled mindlessly.

The *Find My* app blinked on his phone, her location still active. The hotel next door to the place they had dinner. Callum's lips twisted. He drained his beer before slipping out of the bar. He placed his hands into his pockets and began walking, the city lights casting long shadows across the pavement.

FIVE

Callum's Ford F150 rolled down the familiar, tree-lined streets of Hudson, a town he never thought he'd come back to. He pulled into the parking lot, as an SUV eased to a stop beside him. The Jeep Grand Cherokee was immaculate, its sleek build at odds with the rustic charm of The Riverview's weathered brick facade. Amy emerged from the vehicle, her dark waves catching the morning sun. She carried a leather portfolio and a large tote filled to the brim with swatches and samples. Callum's pace slowed instinctively.

Charlotte had hired Amy to work on marketing, and as the Event Operations manager, Callum and her would be working together on a few projects to get the word out. He noticed that Amy had a subtle wince when she shifted the weight of the bag to her left hand. His steps faltered, a flicker of familiarity punching through the cold air. *No. Amy wasn't Josephine, but damn if she didn't look like her.* His gaze swept over her olive skin, the delicate slope of her jaw, and the way her dark, almost-black eyes absorbed the light instead of reflecting it. Her features were softer than Josephine's, less severe, but close enough that it stung, that *it pulled.*

He surveyed the space from the outside, his brown eyes tracing the intricate details of its architecture. Now, it had transformed into a sleek, industrial-modern masterpiece. The building was majestically framed by the iconic Hudson River and Catskill Mountains.

The main structure was an old brick building, its red facade weathered to a soft russet over the years, with ivy creeping up one side like nature's embellishment. Tall arched windows punctuated the walls, their iron frames a deep, matte black that contrasted elegantly against the warm hues of the brick. Even from a distance, the glass gleamed, reflecting the shifting blues and silvers of the river beyond. A sloped terracotta roof crowned the structure, its edges lined with sleek metal flashing that gave a subtle nod to the industrial era. The building stretched out horizontally, sprawling yet balanced, with an annex to one side, a modern addition that hinted at the venue's versatility.

As the sun ascended, The Riverview came alive with a soft golden glow. The whole scene painted a perfect blend of timeless charm and contemporary elegance, standing proud against the endless expanse of the river and sky.

"Why are you so early?" she asked, raising an eyebrow. "I figured you'd be out celebrating with Jack. Or, you know, looking at those houses I so thoughtfully found for you."

"Celebrating what?" he replied, leaning casually against one of the tall cocktail tables. "That we're all still standing after a year of construction? Or that Jack hasn't spontaneously combusted from stress yet?"

Amy rolled her eyes. "The first one. Though if Jack's going to explode, it'll probably be tomorrow when the caterer calls with some last-minute crisis."

"Why do you say that like it's inevitable?"

"Because it is." She handed him the clipboard. "Here. I need you to sign off on this. Final vendor confirmations."

"I booked a live band for the event," she said.

Callum, leaning against a high-top table, raised an eyebrow. "Live band? Thought we were going for sophisticated and understated."

She shot him a look. "Since when do you think understated is the way to win people over?"

He smirked. "Fair point. But Charlotte signed off on this?"

She hesitated a beat too long.

Callum's grin widened. "Ah. So that's a no."

"I'll run it by her, but I ran the idea by Jack, and he is for it." she said. "But this event needs energy, not just background noise. If we want the mill to be *the* venue, we need people talking about it."

He studied her for a moment, then shrugged. "Your funeral."

Amy huffed. "You could at least pretend to back me up."

"Oh, I fully support the chaos," he said, pushing off the table. "Just let me know how it goes when Charlotte hears about the surprise budget increase."

She rolled her eyes, but a smile tugged at her lips. "Jack runs numbers more than she does, it'll be fine. You're just scared." She smirked, "and jealous you didn't come up with the brilliant idea."

"No, I'm a realist," he corrected, "and only slightly terrified of Charlotte."

Amy nudged his shoulder. "Lincoln's redevelopment project is huge, Callum. If he lands this contract, it's not just good for him, it's good for The Riverview. The media exposure alone puts us on the map in ways we couldn't pay for. We'll get a ton of corporate events, private parties. The city's investing in its future, and we'll be at the center of it."

Callum leaned against one of the high-top tables. "You've got that whole pitch ready to go, don't you?"

"Of course." She smirked, adjusting the strap of her bag. "I was thinking about telling Linc and Char about an idea. About adding an expansion project to the west side of the property, an outdoor event space, maybe convert that structure that's missing the roof into an outdoor stage. It could open up higher-end bookings, weddings, seasonal galas. And the marketing push for Lincoln's event will set the precedent for how we position ourselves going forward."

"Damn. You're really swinging for the fences."

"I don't half-ass things."

"No," he chuckled, his fingers tapping rhythmically on the side of his tablet. "You never do."

Before she could respond, the sound of sharp heels echoed through the space.

"Amy, I swear to God—"

Charlotte's voice cut through the room as she approached, her tone hovering between exasperation and concern.

Amy turned just in time to see her best friend assessing her with a sharp, knowing gaze.

"You're supposed to be in bed with your feet up," Charlotte scolded, hands on her hips.

Amy waved her off. "I'm fine, Char. And besides, I needed to see the samples in person."

Charlotte shot Callum a look. "And you let her walk around here?"

He raised his hands in surrender. "She threatened me."

Amy rolled her eyes. "I did not."

Charlotte exhaled, rubbing her temples before shifting gears. "Fine. But if you pass out in the middle of this meeting, I'm making Jack carry you out."

As if on cue, Jack strolled in, whistling to himself, his bright blue tie clashing magnificently with his lime–green collared shirt.

"Ladies, gentlemen, troubled souls," he greeted, grinning. "Tell me everything's going according to plan, because I am in no mood to deal with chaos before I've had at least three more cups of coffee."

Charlotte handed him a steaming cup. "I had them put a shot of coffee in your milk."

Jack clutched his chest. "And this is why you're my favorite." He turned to Amy, his expression shifting just slightly, the sharp gaze beneath his charm taking her in. "And you. You should be at home. Feet up. Preferably watching something trashy with a questionable amount of wine."

Amy smirked. "Noted."

Callum stood back, watching the exchange, the familiar pull of Amy's presence messing with his head. She was *here*, engaged, focused, moving through the conversation like she hadn't spent the last week unraveling. But there were cracks. The way she adjusted her stance when she thought no one was looking. The way she avoided meeting Charlotte's gaze for too long. The way she carried herself like she was bracing for something.

"Amy, did the printers finalize the order?" Charlotte asked as she checked off another item.

Amy nodded, reaching for her portfolio and flipping it open. "I've mocked up social media campaigns, influencer outreach, and a collaboration with some local artists to incorporate custom installations. The key is making this more than an event; it's an experience. Think Magnolia's Silos. We want that sort of energy, and we have it."

Callum watched her work, the way she came alive when she had a plan. It was different from the way she was with him, more controlled, more strategic. *But it was still her, and it was sexy as hell.*

Charlotte nodded. "I like it. And we can incorporate that into the expansion plans you mentioned. We get this deal, we own the luxury event market in Hudson, and I think this will bleed into the city as well, attracting all sorts of clientele."

Amy grinned. "That's the idea."

Callum smirked, his gaze flicking to Amy, who was already jotting down notes. She caught him looking, just for a second, before turning back to the work in front of her.

He exhaled, shaking his head.

Trouble.

She was always trouble.

And God help him, he wouldn't have it any other way.

Charlotte's phone rang. Hey, speak of the devil, it's Lincoln. Give me a sec. She walked to the solarium to take the call.

"Hey," she said, brushing a strand of hair out of her face. "If you're calling to tell me you're late, I'm hanging up."

Lincoln's laugh was low and easy. "Not a chance."

"Good," she replied, leaning against the wall. "What's up?"

"We got it," he said, the words settling between them, calm but heavy. "The merger's done. Manhattan's ours."

Her pulse skipped. "Wait, really?"

"Yeah. It's official. Signed and sealed."

She took a breath, feeling it settle in. "That's… huge. Congratulations."

"Thanks," Lincoln said, the quiet pride in his voice clear. "It changes everything."

Charlotte shook her head, a grin tugging at the corner of her mouth. "Yeah, I'd say so. High-profile clients, new projects, big moves…"

"I wish I could tell you this in person."

She pressed a hand to her chest. "Me too. But we're still celebrating, right? Dinner, drinks?"

"Already made reservations." he replied.

"Congrats again, I have to run, I have another meeting," she murmured, "Love you."

SIX

The two hour drive to New York City was an escape in itself. Podcasts and music competed to drown out the myriad of thoughts that consumed him. By the time Mark pulled into the hotel garage, the city buzzed with its chaotic energy. He checked in, discarded his suitcase in the room, typing a message to Amy, and then to Josie. Something about the city called him, and he inhaled deeply, his adrenaline peaking.

The elevator in the sleek, glass-walled building ascended to a floor high above the city. As the doors parted, Mark smoothed the lapel of his jacket as he checked his phone, setting it to vibrate before pocketing it.

The smell of Peppermint greeted him as he crossed the threshold of Kaitlyn Reed's office, a modern space with clean lines, and minimalism. She looked up as he entered, Mark lingered on the striking contrast of those crystal-blue eyes, a rarity with his type, but it only intensified her appeal.

She rose smoothly, extending a hand in greeting. "Mark, good to see you, please sit."

She was striking. Dark hair framed a face that was all sharp angles and soft curves, her blouse and pencil skirt emphasizing a figure that commanded attention without seeking it. Mark thought to himself, *I could fuck you on this desk.*

"Kaitlyn, you've been busy."

"Always," she replied as she shuffled some papers on her desk. Her tone was polite, her smile faint, yet her composure left no room for interpretation. She was here to discuss business, nothing more, and it pissed him off.

Settling into the chair, Mark leaned back with a casual elegance, scanning the polished surface of her desk, before he glanced at her. *Perfect tits.* "So, the podcast," Mark adjusted his cufflinks. "We need something more personal. Something raw."

Kaitlyn didn't immediately respond. Instead, she rifled through the papers on her desk, pulling out a thick folder. Mark leaned forward, his focus narrowing on her.

"We're considering a few collaborations," Kaitlyn said, finally meeting his gaze. "A joint series with a prominent relationship therapist from Chicago, someone who's building a name for themselves in unconventional therapy methods. There's also talk of a partnership with a popular dating app, a potential morning show, they're eating you up Mark, you should be proud."

Mark raised an eyebrow. *I should be eating you up.* "Hmmm. What will the series entail? Am I a guest on his show, or is this like a special that's being aired?"

Kaitlyn glanced at an email. "They want to try you out on TV, see how the banter and your personality engages the audience. He'll be your sounding board, giving balance to your more provocative viewpoints. It's about building a wider audience. You appeal to both the intellectual and the everyday person. We want both groups engaged."

He nodded, intrigued, as he scanned the documents in the folder. "The dating app angle– interesting."

"Exactly, Mark." she replied, flipping another folder open. "We're building you as the expert on the complexities of modern relationships. Something for everyone. Speaking of which, one target audience we could really focus on is families."

He leaned back, letting the thought settle. "How so?"

"Well, you've mentioned your wife's fertility struggles, we can corner that market, and if and when you start a family, the relationship dynamics of that can really add to your expertise and personal experience."

Kaitlyn's voice cut through his thoughts. "Now, let's talk about the teaser for the podcast. I've selected an excerpt from your book." She flipped to a page in her notebook and read aloud, her tone cool, her eyes never leaving him.

"In the beginning, we tell ourselves we are shaped by love. That love is simple, pure. But love, as we know, has its own rules, its own flaws. It is nothing like what we expect. Love is a battlefield, where both sides are armed, and where we must ask ourselves, what will we do when the person we trust most betrays us?"

Mark felt a spike in his pulse. The words, his words, felt different when spoken aloud. They held weight, depth, and something darker. Something dangerous. He could see it now, how it would haunt. How it would ensnare.

"This will be the hook, It's the raw, reflective piece that draws people in. It speaks to vulnerability, betrayal, and the things we fear. Perfect for the first episode."

Mark clenched his jaw, a jolt of heat spreading down his spine. That passage, it was his, it was his mind, but hearing it from her mouth, with that cool detachment, stirred something deep. His gaze flickered to her, but she didn't flinch. Her posture remained steady, professional, too damn controlled.

He leaned forward, "It's perfect," he murmured. "But it needs something more."

"More?" Kaitlyn arched an eyebrow. "Like what?"

"I need to speak about something I've lived," Mark took a sip of water. "I can talk about betrayal. But I can also show them what it means to survive it. I want them to feel every word."

"Noted," Kaitlyn's gaze lingered on him, but she quickly masked it by flipping her laptop closed.

Mark felt the subtle shift in the air between them, the heat of the moment passing as swiftly as it had come. He couldn't quite place it, whether it was the stir of attraction, or the challenge she posed in refusing to play into his hands. Either way he planned have her.

Before he could say another word, Kaitlyn had moved on. "The PR strategy is ready. We'll focus on key moments in your book, your insights on human nature, the stories that haunt you, the relationships that scar us. We'll pitch the podcast as the next chapter in your journey."

Mark felt a rush of satisfaction at her words, the thought of his ideas being consumed by listeners across the globe. He'd carved out his place in the world, and now, it was time to own it.

He stood, closing the folder and letting it rest casually in his hand. "Let's make them feel everything, Kaitlyn. Let's make them need this book."

Her resistance was maddening. Most women gave in to his attention, but Kaitlyn barely noticed the deliberate shifts in his tone, his body language. If anything, her indifference only sharpened his resolve.

He shifted in his seat, letting the silence stretch just long enough to see if she'd fill it. When she didn't, he chuckled softly. "You're a hard one to read, Kaitlyn."

"I'll take that as a compliment," she replied.

As he left the office, the hum of the city pressed in around him, a reminder of the empire he was building. Kaitlyn would fall in line eventually. They always did. For now, he had bigger things to focus on, book, the fame, a city condo he was already envisioning himself in.

SEVEN

The night air was cool, tinged with the faint scent of rain. Amy adjusted the bag of takeout in her hand, balancing it against her hip as she pushed open the lobby door to Mark's office building. Her heels clicked softly against the tile floor; the sound swallowed by the dim stillness of the space. She had spent the day running from one house tour to the next, but as evening fell, the ache in her chest nagged louder than her exhaustion.

She'd remembered him mentioning a late night, something about finishing up edits for the keynote. It had felt like an excuse at the time, another reason to put distance between them, but tonight, she had decided to close the gap herself. Maybe surprising him with dinner would remind them both of the connection they'd once shared.

Her phone buzzed in her pocket. She ignored it.

The elevator doors slid open with a soft chime, and Amy stepped out onto the quiet floor. The overhead lights cast long shadows across the carpeted hallway, and the faint hum of air conditioning filled the silence. Mark's office was at the end of the corridor.

Her footsteps slowed as she approached, the sound of muffled sounds filtering through the door. She frowned. Mark rarely took meetings this late. Still, she told herself it was nothing. Probably just a colleague.

Balancing the bag of food in one hand, she pushed the office door open with the other. The first thing Amy noticed was the sound, a low, rhythmic creak of wood straining under the weight, punctuated by muffled breaths. The room felt alive, the atmosphere charged and stifling, pressing down on her as though the air had been stripped of oxygen. Shadows danced along the walls, flickering over the dark mahogany furniture and leather-bound books that lined the shelves. The air was heavy, carrying a cocktail of polished wood, faint cigar smoke, and a hint of Mark's cologne, sharp, with musky undertones of tobacco and smoke. It clung to her senses like an unwelcome guest .For a moment, it was hard to process what she was seeing.

Something sweet tickled her nose, *Vanilla, brown sugar, maybe.* The dim lighting only added to his arousal as she lay sprawled across the desk, her body exposed in the ways that made his dick hard. He bit his lip, sliding two fingers into her. She was so wet and his dick strained against his pants as she spread her legs further apart. *Fuck.* His fingers moved in and out of her, urging her to move in rhythm with him, pushing her to the point of no return. Then he retreated, relishing in her protest as his head dipped lower, claiming her with his mouth as his gaze flicked upward to the sound of the door creaking open.

His eyes locked on Amy, *instant gratification.* The tension was so high, the urge to come almost suffocated him. She didn't know where to look. Amy's gaze snagged on the table in the corner. The wood, darker than the desk, was smooth but weathered, its edges slightly rounded. The surface bore faint scratches, barely visible unless caught by the light, and a small dent marred one corner. It looked lived-in, used in ways she didn't want to imagine.

Time seemed to still. His lips curved into a cold, knowing smile as he rose from his position, and ripped his leather belt from his pants. He hooked Josie's legs around him as he unzipped his pants, and entered her. His body kept moving, kept thrusting, the slick wetness between them only adding to the malicious heat rising in his chest. Amy's presence, in that fraction of a second, was everything. The power was unmistakable, the way she froze, the way she stood there, mouth slightly agape, as if waiting for some explanation. But he gave her nothing.

His movements were now more deliberate, harder, eliciting a spine-tingling moan from her that caused Amy to crack. It was Josie who felt the full force of his attention now. He pulled her closer, forcing her to take him deeper as he took his time, slow and controlled, his mind dark with pleasure, as his hands wrapped around her neck.

The desk groaned again, a sound that would have been harmless in any other context but now felt deafening, each creak like a crack in the facade of everything Amy thought she knew. Her stomach lurched as her gaze darted to the papers scattered beneath her, contracts and memos creased and crushed under her weight, a pen knocked to the floor, its ink bleeding into the fibers of the carpet.

Mark leaned forward, one hand sliding up Josie's thigh before gripping her hip with a possessiveness that sent a jolt through Amy's chest. His wedding ring caught the light, a fleeting glint of gold that felt like a slap.

The thrill of it washed over him, knowing that Amy was right there, powerless to do anything but watch. His smile deepened. This was more than sex. This was power. Control.

Can't he see me? The thought rattled through her mind like an alarm. Does *he want me to see this?*

Amy dropped the food she had been holding. Her dinner clattered to the floor as adrenaline took hold of her body. Mark didn't stop. His body moved with calculated purpose; his focus unyielding as though her presence was just another part of his performance. The walls seemed to close in, the room shrinking as she took in the scene that would burn themselves into her memory: the blindfold that covered her eyes, the faint bruises along Josie's wrists from restraints, the way Mark's breath escaped as he muttered something low and inaudible, the obscene contrast of their intimacy against the sterile authority of his office.

Amy's hand pressed against her mouth, the taste of bile

rising in her throat. The scene before her was wrong, twisted, yet she couldn't tear her eyes away.

This other woman was begging, pleading for him, her back arched beneath him as she responded to his every movement, each thrust making her gasp in rhythmic cadence. But Mark didn't care for her reactions anymore. His attention was on Amy as he grew closer to the edge.

"Don't move." Mark whispered, breaking the verbal silence.

Flight or fight kicked in, and Amy began to run down the hall, hitting the elevator button repeatedly as she waited for the steel doors to open. The stairs were on the other side of the building. *Shit, come on.* The tears were streaming, her heart hammering. *She was so scared.*

The elevator dinged, the sound slicing through the suffocating tension. Amy stumbled out the moment the doors opened, her legs barely carrying her as he called after her.

Amy swallowed, her vision swimming with tears she couldn't shed. The scent of that perfume, it wouldn't leave her. It clung to her, sickly sweet, weaving into the fabric of her thoughts like a suffocating web.

How could he? The words replayed in her mind, over and over, each repetition cutting deeper. But then came the louder thought, the one that churned her stomach: *Of course, he could. Why wouldn't he? You can't even give him a child.*

By the time she reached the parking lot, her hands were trembling so violently she dropped her keys twice before unlocking the door. She couldn't hold it in anymore, the sour taste reaching her mouth as her body forced her to expel the discomfort. She wiped her mouth and slid into the driver's seat, clutching the steering wheel as her breath turned into sobs.

Her mind raced. The image of Mark standing between her legs was seared into her brain. The betrayal, the humiliation, the sheer audacity of it all. Her body shook, her heart hammering against her ribcage. She couldn't breathe, couldn't think.

The edges of her vision darkened, her grip on the wheel slipping as she struggled to ground herself. *Focus. Count. Breathe.*

But the panic wouldn't let go. It crashed over her in relentless waves, each gasp feeling sharper, tighter, like she was being suffocated from the inside out. She dialed Charlotte's number, but the answering machine sounded. She ended the call, throwing the cell phone onto the passenger seat as she put the car in reverse.

She clawed at her chest, her nails digging into her skin as if she could tear the pain out by force. The sound of her own gasps filled the car, drowning out everything else as she pulled out of the parking lot.

Once home, Amy stood in the kitchen, the wine quivering in her glass. She stared blankly at the counter, her fingers clutching the edge like it could keep her upright. The darkened room felt cavernous, the faint hum of the refrigerator doing nothing to drown out the deafening loop of her thoughts. The image of him, leaning close to her, filled her mind like a curse. The warmth in his body language, the scent of her perfume, a sweetness that still clung to Amy's senses, choking her.

Her throat burned as she took another sip of wine, though it did nothing to calm the storm inside her. *How could he?* Her head dropped, gaze drifting to the counter. And then, more quietly, more painfully, *how could I not see this coming?*

Mark stepped into the kitchen, his gaze settling on her rigid back. The sharp light above the sink cast a glow over her, illuminating the trembling in her shoulders. He swallowed, his throat dry, as shame and panic wrestled for control.

You can fix this. You have to fix this. The words beat against the inside of his skull. But underneath them, a darker whisper: *If she talks, you're done.*

He cleared his throat. "Amy." His voice cracked, and he hated how small it sounded.

She didn't move.

Her grip on the counter tightened at the sound of her name. *Don't turn around. Don't give him the satisfaction.* But her body betrayed her, and she turned slowly, her eyes wet but blazing.

"What do you want me to say, Mark?" She managed through gritted teeth, "That I didn't see what I just saw?–" Her throat closed up, choking the words.

The sight of her broke something in Mark he didn't know existed. Tears clung to the edge of her lashes, her face pale and drawn, and all he could think was how she looked fragile enough to shatter. *You did this.*

She heard him exhale, a low, uneven sound that sent a wave of fury through her. He was close now, his presence looming behind her. When she looked at him, his face was pale, his dark expression looked like shame. She hated that it wasn't enough.

He stepped closer, his hands trembling. "Amy, please. Just, just let me explain."

Mark reached for her, but she jerked back. He didn't stop. He moved closer, his eyes pleading.

"Explain? How do you explain *that*, Mark?"

She felt the anger surge, but it wasn't enough to drown out her thoughts. *Maybe if you weren't so broken, he wouldn't have to look elsewhere.* The realization hit her like a punch to the gut, and her knees threatened to buckle.

"You've been distant for months, and I thought," She backed against the counter, the edge biting into her lower back. "I thought it was me. That it was because I couldn't give you a baby. That maybe, if I tried harder, you'd come back to me."

Her words sliced through him, and the tears he didn't think he could summon burned his eyes. He stepped closer, his breath uneven. "Amy, stop. Please, stop." His voice cracked, and he let it.

His hands came up, hovering just inches from her shoulders, like he was afraid to touch her but desperate to. "Amy, don't do this. Don't put this on yourself. This is my fault. All of it."

He reached for her, and to his relief, she didn't pull away. "I've been so fucking stressed, with the book, with the treatments, with us. I wasn't thinking. I wasn't strong enough, I just... I slipped." He cleared his throat. "I made a stupid, selfish mistake. It meant nothing. I swear to you, it meant nothing."

Every nerve ending was on fire as his words poured out, desperate and raw. She wanted to scream, to run, to make him feel the kind of pain ripping through her. But instead, her mind clung to the words *I slipped*.

Maybe it was just once. Maybe it really didn't mean anything. Maybe... maybe if I'd been better, he wouldn't have slipped at all.

Tears streamed down his face now, and he didn't bother wiping them away. He let the guilt twist into vulnerability, let it reshape his panic into something Amy could believe. "Amy, you're everything to me. Everything. I don't deserve you; I know that. But I can't lose you. Please. Please don't let this one mistake ruin us."

He sank to his knees in front of her, gripping her like a lifeline. Tears spilled down his face, and for a moment, she saw the man she'd fallen in love with, the man who'd once promised her forever.

"I don't know if I can," she whispered.

"Yes, you can," he reached for her "Because you're the strongest person I know. And I'll spend every day proving to you that this will never happen again."

He watched the battle in her mind play out. *Good. You're almost there.* He let another sob escape, his grip tightening on her. *Just believe me. Stay quiet. Stay mine.*

She stared at the man in front of her, broken and pleading, and hated how much she wanted to believe him. *Maybe he's right.*

Maybe I've been too focused on the baby, on the treatments. Maybe I pushed him away.

She trembled. "It was just once?"

His nod was immediate, emphatic. "Just once. I swear to you."

EIGHT

Amy fidgeted with the cuff of her sweater as she sat on the examination table waiting for her two week post–operative appointment; the small room amplifying her anxiety. Her mind was a whirlwind of dates, ovulation cycles, and desperation as she stared at the ultrasound monitor. Amy winced as the doctor moved the internal ultrasound wand from viewing her left ovary to her right.

Mark sat in the corner of the room, his phone angled slightly in his lap. She noticed his brows furrowed in concentration, his thumb moving in slow, deliberate swipes. A familiar mix of irritation and sadness rose in her chest, she knew he was posting something.

Doctor Peterson adjusted his glasses and took a few more measurements. "Alright Amy, take a breath, I'm going to remove the transducer." *Why do reproductive endocrinologists always have to be men?* She wondered as she held her breath. *The entire process is mortifying.* Her eyes flicked to the screen. And she was suddenly overwhelmed, looking at the empty expanse of the organ that was supposed to support life.

"You still have a good amount of blood in your pelvis, it can take time for your body to absorb fluid and get the inflammation under control. The surgery was successful in removing the endometriosis, but it's important to give your body time to heal. Rushing into another round of treatments too soon could be counterproductive."

Amy's nose scrunched, her hands clenching the edge of the

table as she slowly sat herself up. "But how long exactly? Weeks? Months? If we wait too long, my chances will only decrease, right? The tissue could grow back."

Doctor Peterson gave her a sympathetic smile. "It's difficult to give an exact timeline, Mrs. Rodriguez. Every case is different. We recommend at least two months before considering another round of treatments with the extent of surgery you've had."

Amy's frustration bubbled over as she leaned forward. "Two months? That's too long! Isn't there anything we can do to speed up the process? What about natural methods? Should we start trying naturally in the meantime?" she felt Mark's stare, afraid to look in his direction, she remained focused on the doctor.

Doctor Peterson sighed, his gaze steady. "Natural conception is always an option, but you need to manage your expectations. I would refrain from sexual intercourse for at least a month, again, trying to conceive should be a focus in the future. That will give your body the necessary time to heal."

Mark, sitting across from her, leaned forward, his elbows resting casually on his knees. He offered the doctor a warm, understanding smile. "Thank you, Doctor Peterson. That's really helpful to know. I've been telling Amy we need to take things slow and not push her body too hard. It's been such an emotional journey for both of us, you know?"

Amy's head whipped toward him, her brows furrowing. That wasn't what he'd been saying at all, not when she brought up trying naturally just a few days ago. But before she could speak, Mark reached over, resting a hand on hers.

"It's just been a lot," he continued, looking back at Doctor Peterson. "The surgery, the disappointment. I think we both need a moment to catch our breath, don't you agree?"

Doctor Peterson nodded sympathetically. "Absolutely. This process can be incredibly taxing, emotionally and physically. Taking time to heal is crucial."

Mark turned back to Amy, his expression softening as he squeezed her knee. "See, babe? It's not just about the timing. It's about you being okay. You've been through so much already. I don't want to see you hurt anymore."

Amy's throat tightened as guilt crept in. Was she pushing too hard? Ignoring what her body needed?

Mark's phone buzzed, and a fire emoji was sitting in the notification bar. He knew she had sent him a picture. He shifted in his seat, angling the phone away as he opened the locked google photos folder that they both had access too. The black and white image of her, naked in the bath filled his screen, and he swallowed the bile in his throat. His gaze flicked to Amy on the table, and suddenly he was back there. *His father's face inches from his, Josie sitting on the sterile table of his father's office.* He closed his eyes, trying to regain his composure, but the memory flipped through his mind like a stop motion film. *Fuck.* It was in that moment, that he understood his thought process, it made so much sense. His throat was dry, his palms sweaty. He hadn't felt this way in years, and he hated the lack of control.

"Mrs. Rodriguez, you're one step closer. Your diagnosis is great news, it means we have gained control over the issue, and my confidence in you being able to conceive is much higher than it has been. Do you have any additional questions?"

Amy shook her head. "Thanks Doctor Peterson, we appreciate your advice and the information." As he exited the room, Amy slipped her leg into her pants, pulling them up and adjusting the elastic band above her scar. In the lobby, they walked past expectant couples in the waiting room, which only added to Amy's heightened emotion.

As the door clicked shut behind him, Amy let out a shaky breath. "Mark, I–"

"Amy, listen to me," he interrupted, his tone gentle but firm. He moved closer, taking her hands in his. "I love you. And I know how much this means to you. But this diagnosis? It's a sign. We've been so focused on this one thing, we've forgotten how to just... be us. I think we need to take a step back and let things happen naturally."

Her lips parted, but no words came. His conviction made her question everything. *Maybe he was right.*

"Please," he added, running a thumb over her knuckles. "Let me take care of you for once."

Amy nodded hesitantly, the fight draining out of her. She wanted to believe him, to believe that stepping back was the right thing to do. For them. For her.

Mark and Amy walked out of the doctor's office, the warmth of Mark's hand against her back grounded her, and she finally was able to exhale fully.

Once they were in the car, Mark started the engine, putting it in reverse. He took a deep breath, his gaze lingering on Amy before he reached for her hand. The touch was warm, steady. "How are you feeling?" he asked softly.

"I'm okay," Amy replied, her fingers curling around his. She was still trying to process everything, but his hand, the familiar comfort of his touch, helped steady her.

They pulled into a nearby shopping center, and Mark cut the engine, his smile returning as he turned to her. "I've got a surprise for you."

Amy blinked, caught off guard. "What is it?"

"We'll see," Mark replied, trying to lift her spirits.

Mark slipped off his seatbelt, and opened the driver door before glancing at Amy, who was now beaming.

"You ready?" As they walked to the store, he took hold of her hand.

The door chimed as they walked inside, the store filled with the sounds of barking puppies and chirping birds. The scent of pet food and bedding wafted through the air. Amy's face lit up for the first time that day.

"Oh Babe," she whispered as she kneeled near a pen of fluffy golden retrievers. She reached in to pick up one of the puppies, and it immediately licked her face.

Mark stood back, watching. This was how he kept control, by redirecting, refocusing. The harder things got, the more he gave her something else to hold onto. And right now, that thing was a dog. He hadn't been fully on board with the idea, but watching her happiness gave him a rush. He was steering things again.

"Hi there," an attendant approached them with a friendly smile. "Looking to adopt today?"

"Yes," Mark replied, glancing at Amy. "I'm the guy who called about the goldens last week."

The attendant nodded understandingly. "Awesome."

"Have either of you had a dog before?"

Both of them shook their heads.

"Well then I have the perfect little man for you." The attendant walked past the pen of tiny puppies, and picked up an older golden retriever.

"He is six months old, he's a purebred golden, but the original owners couldn't care for him. An older dog has many benefits. He is already potty trained, and he's also taken the puppy training course." Amy watched as the yellow retriever bounced out of the attendant's arms and over to her lap.

"Mark, oh my goodness, how perfect is that?"

Mark forced a smile, trying to match her enthusiasm. "Yeah, he's cute."

The attendant smiled. "Golden retrievers are a great choice. They're loyal, friendly, and excellent with families. Do you have any specific needs or preferences?"

We just want a companion," Mark replied, crouching to rub the dog's ears. "Something to bring a little joy into our lives."

Amy beamed at him, buying every word. And that was the point.

As they walked through the store, Amy cradled the dog, her focus fully on him. Mark carried the supplies, watching as she cooed at their new pet. She leaned over and kissed his cheek at checkout, whispering, "Thank you. This means so much to me."

Mark let himself smile. "I just want you to be happy, Amy."

The drive home was quiet, Amy curled up with the puppy. Mark glanced at them, reaching over to scratch behind the dog's ears. "He's cute."

She looked at the dog, then back at Mark, with an idea. "How about we name him Maslow?"

Mark raised an eyebrow, a smile tugging at the corners of his mouth. "Maslow? As in the hierarchy of needs?"

"Yes, Maslow believed in fulfilling basic needs before we can reach our full potential. And right now, he seems to be just the thing we need to start feeling a bit more complete."

Mark chuckled, genuinely amused by her thought process. "Maslow it is, then. It's fitting."

As the car rolled into the driveway, Amy unlocked her seatbelt and opened the door. Maslow bounded out of the car, his tail wagging furiously as he took in his surroundings. "He's so cute," she mused, "Look at him go!"

Mark looked over his shoulder as he made his way around the car. "Yeah, he's quite the explorer."

As they stepped inside, Maslow hesitated at the foot of the staircase, his tail tucked nervously between his legs. Amy knelt down beside him, offering gentle words of encouragement as he tentatively approached the first step.

Another buzz snapped him out of it. This time, it was his agent: *Revisions due Friday. Confirm you're on schedule.*

Mark blinked, the weight of his reality settling back over him like a cold fog. He locked his phone and stuffed it back into his pocket, forcing the image of Josie out of his mind. *Focus. Stay in control, or you'll lose her.*

"Everything okay?" Amy's voice broke through his thoughts. She stood at the foot of the porch, Maslow tugging at her sleeve. Her cheeks were flushed, her smile tentative.

"Yeah." Mark cleared his throat, forcing a smile. He set the bags down and reached out to pat Maslow's back. "I was just thinking about everything I need to get done for the book launch."

Amy nodded, her expression softening. "You'll figure it out. You always do."

He stepped closer, moving a strand of hair from her face. "And you'll figure it out too, Amy. We've been through worse, haven't we?" His words sounded rehearsed, but she seemed to take them at face value.

Her hand brushed his briefly before she turned back toward the house. "Let's get him settled in."

Mark followed her inside, his smile fading as soon as she wasn't looking. He glanced at his phone one last time, shooting her a text:

> MARK: Keep sending photos like that, and you'll get very little sleep.

> Photographer: Don't tempt me...

The temptation of Josie's photo gnawing at the edges of his mind. It wasn't just the photo. It was her, the way she made him feel; alive, desired, understood. The contrast was suffocating. With Amy, everything felt heavy. Like he had to carry her emotions along with his own, a never-ending task of convincing her they were okay, that this wasn't falling apart.

But with Josie? She didn't ask for anything. She didn't cry into her hands at night or leave fertility pamphlets spread out on the counter like breadcrumbs leading to a dead end. She was simple. Effortless. He could almost hear her laugh, the kind that made his chest tighten.

Was it wrong to want that? To want to feel weightless for a moment? He wasn't the villain here. He was just human. He knew Josie was the right choice, he knew that she had come back into his life for a reason. But he also knew that a scandal or a divorce would derail everything he had worked for, and he felt trapped.

Shoving the thought aside, he set the bag of supplies on the counter and focused on Amy as she knelt down to fit Maslow with his new collar.

Perfect husband. Perfect life. Perfect lie.

There, she found him, his tail wagging eagerly as he explored the room off the master. Amy's heart clenched at the sight, memories flooding back of the nursery that was never meant to be.

She sank down beside Maslow, her fingers running gently through his fur as tear broke free. It had been a year since the devastating news of their molar pregnancy, but the pain still lingered, raw and unhealed.

She knew it was not the same as losing a baby. The condition caused abnormal tissue to form in the uterus, mimicking the signs of pregnancy but without the presence of a developing embryo. She was convinced she was pregnant, she had all the symptoms, her body too, thought it was pregnant, but in reality, there's only an empty sac.

Amy picked him up, her heart aching as she looked around the near empty room. Her workout equipment sat in the corner, leaving noticeable space for a crib and baby items, the few things she had purchased sat on the shelf in the closet. She imagined the room filled with baby furniture, soft toys, and the gentle coos of a newborn.

Lost in thought, she took the puppy's collar from the shopping bag in her arm and placed it around his neck. "There you go, sweet boy," she whispered.

Mark appeared in the doorway, watching her silently for a moment before speaking. "Where do you want to set up the crate?"

Amy turned to him, a smile on her face despite her melancholy demeanor. "Maybe by Christmas, this room will become a nursery."

Mark's expression softened, and he stepped forward to wrap his arms around her. "Maybe," he murmured, kissing the top of her head. His eyes held a distant sadness, a shadow of the doubt and fear that lingered in his heart.

Amy pulled out her phone and snapped a picture of Maslow, his tiny face peeking out from the inside of the closet. She sent the photo to Charlotte with a message: *Meet Maslow! Our little bundle of joy for now.*

Charlotte responded almost immediately: NO WAY! He's adorable! Can't wait to meet him, when are you free?

Amy smiled at the message, feeling a flicker of warmth despite the heaviness that still weighed on her. She looked up at Mark, who was now crouching down to pet Maslow, and for a moment, it felt like everything might just be okay.

But in the back of her mind, the emptiness of the room loomed large, a constant reminder of the dream that still felt so far out of reach.

Amy rose to her feet, stuffing her cellphone in the side pocket of her yoga pants.

"Hey, let's have Charlotte and Lincoln over to meet the puppy. Could fire up the grill or order pizza?"

Mark hesitated. "Sure, I have a few things to do for work, I'll head to the office for a bit, ask if they want to come around five. Mark turned the corner and wandered down the hall to their bedroom.

"Sounds good. I only have one client left this afternoon. I have the rest of the morning with this little tater tot." Mark popped his head in the room as he flung his loafer on his foot.

"Being a dog mom suits you." He shot her a smile before turning for the garage.

Amy looked at Maslow. *A dog mom.* It was a sweet gesture, but it somehow made her feel that much more inadequate.

In the garage, Mark slid into the driver's seat of his car, gripping the steering wheel as he sat in silence. He wasn't going to the office. Not yet, anyway. The thought of sitting alone in that sterile space, pretending to work while his thoughts spiraled, was unbearable.

He pressed the ignition button, the low hum of the engine filling the enclosed space, but he didn't put the car in reverse. Instead, he let his head fall back against the headrest, his jaw clenching.

Mark's fingers tightened around the steering wheel, a familiar ache crawling through his chest. The hum of the engine filled the empty space of the garage, but it didn't drown out the images in his mind, the ultrasound, the soft whoosh of the technician's voice, the silence that followed when they'd discovered the molar pregnancy.

Eleven weeks. Eleven weeks of pretending everything was fine, of hoping they were finally on the right path. Amy had been so excited, so certain. He'd let himself feel it too, the anticipation building with every passing day. But all of it had been a facade, shattered in an instant by a cold, mechanical diagnosis. There was nothing. There was no baby.

The room had felt suffocating in that moment. He'd tried to hold it together, tried to stay calm for Amy's sake, but inside, everything had cracked. It wasn't supposed to be like this. This wasn't supposed to happen. It had triggered something deep within him, just as Josie's photo at today's appointment, and he hated that he had no control.

The thought made him sick. He squeezed his eyes shut,

exhaling through clenched teeth, as if trying to force the memories, the guilt, the anger to dissipate. But it was always there. Always lurking beneath the surface.

NINE

The yellow cottage sat at the end of a long, narrow driveway, barely visible through the dense canopy of tall, overgrown trees. Its once vibrant paint had faded to a dull, peeling remnant of its former self, giving the house a forlorn and abandoned appearance. Overgrown hedges framed the property, their wild growth whispering stories of long-neglected care.

Callum stepped out of his truck, his shoes crunching on the gravel as he surveyed the house. The creaky wooden steps groaned under his weight, and he smiled faintly. "She's got character," he muttered to himself. The front door opened into a dimly lit living room, the air thick with the scent of cedar and dust. Exposed beams crisscrossed the ceiling, and an old brick fireplace stood proudly at its center, as if waiting for someone to rekindle its purpose.

Amy arrived moments later, leaning briefly against the door frame to sling the back of her heel onto her foot. She took a deep breath as she stepped inside, her dark eyes scanning the space with a mixture of curiosity and excitement. "It's... charming."

"Charming?" Callum echoed with a grin, glancing at her as he ran a hand over the rough wood of the mantel. "We could stage a murder in this living room without batting an eyelash. Clearly this listing was an internet vs reality situation."

She snorted. "Ha. I could totally see it. I mean, it's got great bones! Look at this fireplace." She stepped closer, her fingers tracing the brick as she shifted her focused to the ceiling. "And those beams," she sighed. "So much potential."

He watched her, his grin widening as he leaned against the doorframe. "Potential. That's the polite way of saying it needs work."

She shook her head. "This house is one of the last in the neighborhood without renovations, so the investment is solid."

"Oh yeah? Sounds like you know a lot about this neighborhood." He laughed.

"Well yeah, I live a couple streets over, it's amazing."

Amy turned to him, he flexed his biceps, just to see if he could get a rise. Her cheeks, chest, and ears were scarlet. *Yep, still got it.*

"I'm teasing," he took a step toward her, tilting his head toward the banister. "Lots of projects for sure. But this? This is the kind of project I love. A little sanding here, some polish there, and it'll shine."

His enthusiasm caught her off guard. "Do you enjoy this sort of thing?"

"Absolutely." He moved toward her, his steps unhurried as his gaze lingered on the beams above. "Woodworking, fixing up old furniture, building things—it's satisfying. Gives me something to focus on."

Amy's interest piqued despite herself. "You make furniture?"

"Sometimes," he shrugged as if it weren't a big deal. "Tables, shelves, even made a bed frame once." She blushed an even darker shade of red, *do that again, Ames.* "Never anything fancy, but I like it. There's something about turning raw materials into something solid, something that'll last."

Her lips curved into a small smile. "That's impressive. A lost art."

He tilted his head, his gaze dipping briefly to her lips before snapping back to her eyes. "What about you? You seem like the type who's good with her hands. *Shit, why did you say that? Recover!* "Like, you enjoy crafting, perhaps?"

"I don't know about that," she found herself laughing nervously as she stepped away from the fireplace. "But I do love the design process, choosing colors, rearranging furniture, finding ways to make a space feel like home."

Callum followed her. "Then you get it. That feeling when you see it all come together. It's addicting."

"It is," she admitted, glancing at him with a shy smile. Her pulse quickened under his steady gaze, and she forced herself to turn back to the room. "The kitchen," she waved, motioning toward the next space. "Let's check it out."

He gestured for her to lead the way, his lips twitching with amusement as she hurried ahead.

Amy gestured toward the built-ins. "Callum, look at these, your first project! These could be incredible. If you stripped the paint and restored the original finish–"

"I'd leave it natural," he interrupted, stepping closer. "Let the grain show through. Maybe add some custom shelving here." He pointed to a bare patch of wall, his shoulder brushing hers.

Amy instinctively stepped back, her heart racing as his proximity sent a jolt through her. She cleared her throat, hoping he didn't notice. "That's... a great idea."

He noticed.

"So, "how's Maslow?"

The question caught her off guard, but her face lit up. "He's the best. Total goofball, but so smart. We're still working on not eating every sock in sight, but he's getting there."

"A retriever with a sock habit? Shocking," he teased.

She laughed, her shoulders relaxing. "He's only six months, still a baby, give him some grace. He follows me everywhere and loves cuddling."

Callum raised a brow, a faint smile playing on his lips. "Retrievers make great running partners, that'll be good for you."

Amy paused, her brows narrowing as she tilted her head. "How do you know I run?"

There was a flicker of something in his eyes. "I've seen you at Hudson Park a couple times, I run too. Training for a marathon this fall."

Her suspicion softened, and she gave a slow nod. "Huh. Small world, that's awesome."

He smiled, pleased she didn't press further.

Amy's eyes widened. "You notice a lot, don't you?"

He smirked, stepping closer again, his presence filling the space between them. "It's hard not to." He paused. *With you...* his thoughts trailed. She didn't need to know he made it a point to notice where she was, like the way he'd timed looking at this house, knowing the proximity to hers, knowing that he could keep an eye on both her and Mark. "Maybe I'll see you on the trails."

Her blush deepened, and she turned back toward the built-ins, feeling somehow desperate to change the subject. "So, thoughts? Want to put in an offer?"

"I think so, I trust your judgment."

Amy focused on her phone, tapping away as she tried to regain her composure.

Callum stayed where he was, his gaze steady and contemplative. There was something about her, something magnetic, even in her flustered attempts to keep things professional. He knew she felt it, too, even if she wouldn't admit it. As the heat in her cheeks lingered and her voice took on a breathless edge, Callum felt a quiet satisfaction.

He didn't know exactly what it was yet, but he had a feeling it was more than just chemistry. It was the way she looked over her shoulder, like she was caught in something she couldn't quite escape. The way her voice softened when she mentioned Mark, as if she was still tethered to him, even though she didn't want to be.

Callum's jaw tightened, but he kept his face neutral. The

man had a grip on her, a hold that was hard to shake. He didn't need to know the details to understand that much. But one thing was clear; he wasn't about to let Mark get away with this. Not while she was still here, not while there was something between them.

He took a slow step forward, letting the space between them shrink without rushing it. He knew better than to push. But he also knew when to stand firm. And right now, all he wanted was to make sure she understood that she wasn't alone in this.

For now, he'd let Amy keep pretending she wasn't affected, but as long as Mark was out there, Callum would be right here, standing between them. He wouldn't let her face whatever this was on her own. Not if he could help it. Not if she'd let him in.

TEN

The doorbell rang. Checking her watch, she noted that they were much earlier than anticipated. She made her way through the living room, adjusting one of the cream pillows on the leather sofa before making her way to the front door. The heavy steel door swung open to find her mother, a familiar knot of anxiety tightening in Amy's stomach. She forced a smile as invited Marady inside, who was holding a few dishes of food.

"Hey, Mom, I wasn't expecting you." Amy greeted, stepping aside to let her in. *Why does she always do this?* she thought with an exhale.

Marady, with her usual air of composure, gave a curt nod. "Hello, love." She stepped inside, her ebony eyes scanning the spotless kitchen as she passed through the steel archway. "I brought some food. I thought you might need it after your surgery."

"Thanks, Mom. That was thoughtful of you," Amy replied, taking the dishes from her mother and setting them on the granite island. She traced the stone with her finger, its gold bronze veining in cream stone accentuating the expresso cabinets.

"Where's Mark? I saw his car in the driveway." Marady's lips pursed slightly as she began to wipe down the already spotless counter.

"He's on a call in the office, we have company coming over in a few minutes." Marady shot a glance at Amy with a nod. "Lincoln and Charlotte? Oh, that little Genevieve is just the cutest. I hope you have a girl one day; a granddaughter would be such a blessing."

Amy started preparing a salad, her hands moving methodically as she tried to keep her nerves in check. "I'm doing really well," Amy replied, trying to shift the conversation. "The appointment was positive. Now that we have a diagnosis, I can finally breathe knowing it's not my fault." Amy's mind echoed. *It's not my fault.* The words felt like a shield, but also a victory. For years, her mother refused to acknowledge there was anything wrong with her fertility.

"Yes, well, it's good to hear you're feeling better, it's such a relief, trying naturally without all these treatments is always the best way to have a baby. It's likely just been those drugs all along causing your body strife." She passed Amy a dish from the dishwasher, and Amy placed it in the drawer with a clang.

"Mom, endometriosis is an *actual* medical diagnosis, it's not just stress. Amy turned to the island and began vigorously chopping the vegetables, feeling the cords of her neck tighten.

Marady cleared her throat, dismissing the statement with a wave of her hand. "I just worry, you are getting older. You should have started trying sooner. But let's not dwell on the past. It's good to hear you should be able to conceive naturally," she passed the salad bowl to her. "Mixing medicine with conception is not the way of things. It disrupts the natural order. This is how it should be. Trust it." Marady continued cleaning, her actions methodical and precise, as if wiping away invisible imperfections.

Trust it. The words echoed in Amy's mind. How could she trust a body that had betrayed her so many times before? The excitement in Marady's words felt like a double-edged sword, cutting through Amy's hopes with every condescending remark. Amy forced a smile, feeling the weight of her mother's disapproval mixed with a flicker of hope.

"Yes, we're hopeful too," Amy's eyes fell to the vegetables on the cutting board. Amy felt trapped between her mother's expectations and her own reality. The state-of-the-art kitchen, with its sleek lines and modern fixtures, felt like a sterile battlefield. Every utensil handed over, every dish passed, was a silent struggle for validation.

"Alright, I need to get going! I hope you have a wonderful time with your friends tonight, it was good to see you." She kissed her on the cheek and dismissed herself.

As her mother's car faded into the distance, Amy stood still, the silence in the house swallowing her whole. The sting of her mother's words clung to her. She couldn't fix it, couldn't be what they wanted her to be.

She glanced at the office, noting that the door was still closed, the vibrations of Mark's voice evident behind the door. She took a steadying breath and climbed the stairs, unlatching the crate. Maslow stretched, his soft fur gliding against her fingers as he stepped out, his tail sweeping in a wag.

She sank onto their bed, pulling him into her lap, his weight grounding her in a way no words could.

Her fingers ran through his caramel fur, the motion soothing, almost automatic, as her thoughts spun in a blur of doubt and frustration.

"I can't do it, boy," she whispered. "I can't give him what he wants." Her hand stilled, fingers clenching into the soft fur. Maslow's brown eyes met hers, his presence unspoken but somehow louder than anything her mother had said. He nuzzled her, pushing against her with quiet insistence.

"I don't know how to fix this." She kissed his head. *I'm scared he'll leave, scared I'm not enough. I don't know how to give him what he deserves.*

Amy scratched Maslow behind the ears. "I can't keep up." She sighed, her hand stilling in his fur, then reached for her phone on the counter.

A new notification flashed across the screen:

We're having a baby! Due this Christmas. We're so excited to start this journey together.

The picture was textbook perfect: Lila glowing in a sunlit field, her husband kissing her temple as she cradled a bump just big enough to make Amy's chest tighten.

Amy locked the phone quickly, but it buzzed again. A wedding announcement this time. *Another one.*

She closed her eyes, inhaling deeply, but the ache settled stubbornly in her chest. Her fingers twitched, hesitating before she unlocked her phone again, her feed stalled on an old photo.

It was from college, someone had posted a throwback to a party. She smiled despite herself, the memory coming back vividly.

The music had been obnoxiously loud, the air thick with cheap beer and bad decisions.

"Come on, Amy!" Lincoln's voice boomed from across the room. He was already setting up for beer pong, a cocky grin plastered on his face. "This one's yours."

Amy rolled her eyes but grabbed Charlotte by the arm. "Let's go embarrass him," she'd said, pulling her reluctantly toward the table.

"Oh no, not a chance, Amy, I don't do beer pong." Charlotte protested.

Amy rolled her eyes. "How else would you like to get to know him? Come on, he's great."

Lincoln had waved a tall guy over to the table. "Amy, meet my best friend, Mark. Ride or die since middle school." His warm stare hit her like a freight train, but she was over boys. Over the drama, over the sex, over the incessant need for them to get into her pants.

Amy glanced at Mark, unimpressed, and typed a quick text to Lincoln under the table.

Amy: Not another match. You have a terrible record.

Linc: Well, you could've dated me, but noooo.

Linc: Pls, he's only here for break, what could possibly go wrong?

Amy: beer + puke = death

Linc: He thinks you're hot, and we all know he's right. ;)

Linc: LETS GO.

Amy bit back a laugh, her tipsy brain filing his response under 'not serious enough to think about' and moving on.

They lost. Miserably. Charlotte spilled half a cup of beer on her shoes, and Amy had managed to miss every single shot, except one, which ricocheted off someone's head.

Mark had walked her to her dorm that night, steadying her when she stumbled over a crack in the sidewalk. He was charming in a quiet way, and by the time she crawled into bed, she realized she'd been smiling the whole time.

Now, years later, she couldn't ignore the irony.

She glanced down at Maslow, her fingers curling into his fur. "How do you fix something when you can't even figure out where it broke?" His tail thumped softly in response as she nuzzled his face. In that simple, unwavering gesture, she felt the bond between them, unspoken, pure, and more constant than anything else in her life.

Amy closed her eyes, feeling the steady beat of his heart. For the first time in a long while, she didn't feel so alone.

Maslow's ears perked at the sound of movement outside, he jumped off her lap, barking as he bounded toward the foyer with Amy in toe. When she opened the door, he tumbled down the porch stairs, ears flapping behind him as the creamy ball of fluff flew past Amy.

"Oh my gosh, he's even cuter in person!" Charlotte exclaimed, bending down to pet him. Maslow planted sloppy kisses all over her face.

'Where's Evie?" Amy asked, looking for Charlotte's daughter.

"Oh, mom came over to baby sit, figured an adult only night would be better, especially." She caught herself. "You know, with the mill and everything."

"Bummer, I got her some new coloring books and a couple toys. Next time."

Maslow wagged his tail furiously, soaking up the attention. Lincoln laughed as Maslow jumped up his leg. "He's a ball of energy, isn't he?"

Amy nodded. "He's been keeping us on our toes, that's for sure."

They all settled in the living room, chatting and laughing as they watched Maslow play with his new toys. For the first time in a while, the house felt warm and filled with life. Mark slid the door open from the patio with a beer in hand, smoke from the grill wafted into the house. His eyes were on his phone as he looked up.

"Hey man, how's it going? Can I grab you one?" Mark tilted his bottle towards Lincoln with a nod.

Lincoln smiled, throwing his thumb over his shoulder toward the kitchen. "I'll grab one. Need me to bring anything out?"

Mark nodded. "Yeah, I have a platter on the top shelf of the fridge for the grill. Should be heated up enough."

Lincoln threw a thumbs up, disappearing around the island before stepping onto their expansive screened–in patio.

The stone fireplace was ablaze, casting a warmth that was necessary this time of year. Lincoln swung the door open with his hip as he joined Mark near the grill.

"A puppy, eh? Big move for you." Lincoln playfully slapped his shoulder.

Mark shook his head, a bitter smile playing on his lips. "At least he's a cute little bastard," he muttered, bending down to peer inside the wine fridge of their outdoor kitchen. He retrieved a bottle of whiskey and a couple of glasses, pouring the amber liquid with practiced ease. He reached for the ice maker, plopping a couple of large cubes into each glass. Mark's jaw clenched as he slid the glass towards Lincoln.

"Double fisting tonight, must have been one hell of a week." Lincoln exchanged his unopened beer for the whiskey, knowing that Mark only bought top shelf.

Mark checked the incoming notification on his phone again, his expression hardening momentarily before he continued. Mark leaned back, running a hand through his hair. "You know, this book deal... it's bigger than I ever imagined, and the buzz around this book is insane. Media interviews, endorsements rolling in. The launch is going to be massive."

"For sure, I'm proud of you." Lincoln clinked his glass against Mark's.

Mark nodded appreciatively. "My agent wants to focus on our fertility struggles, how she managed to get that narrative out of me is a miracle. Meanwhile, Amy, she's still stuck on the same thing. It's the next round of treatments, the next doctor's visit, like that's the only thing that matters anymore." He took a heavy sip from his glass, exhaling with relief as the liquid burned a warm trail down his throat.

Lincoln swallowed. He knew the strain trying to conceive had put on Mark, having had this conversation a few times already. "I hear you; Amy can be a bit much. I think this will be good for her, she can focus on the puppy and recover, you can focus on your book. At least you have a diagnosis, perhaps things will be different now." He pushed his glasses up his nose as he slipped into the nearby barstool.

"But you know her. *Fuck*, I'm done." He pulled out a cigarette and lit it, drawing it into his lungs.

Lincoln hesitated, glancing over his shoulder. "Done with trying?"

Mark nodded, taking a sip of whiskey. "Yeah."

"Have you told her?" He raised an eyebrow. "When did you take up smoking again?"

Mark sighed. "It's the stress." He offered the box to Lincoln, who waved it off. "Do you know how expensive this all is? Fertility treatments and appointments are not covered by my insurance."

"She doesn't see me anymore. She doesn't see what this is doing to me. She's so focused on getting pregnant that she's blind to everything else. Maybe not having a kid is the best thing for us. Maybe it'll give me room to breathe... room to focus on something that matters. You get it, right?..." he exhaled another plume of smoke.

"I need to focus on my book, on this whole damn thing blowing up, but she's just caught in the idea of the next treatment, the next round. It's exhausting, man."

Lincoln hesitated. He wanted to say something. Instead, he leaned back processing Mark's words. "I get it, but there's got to be a middle ground. You can't just walk away from everything. You've been trying to make it work for years. You're not just going to throw that all out the window."

Mark's eyes darkened. "I'm not throwing anything away. I'm making a choice. I've made my choice." He grabbed the tongs, flipping the burgers. "Her diagnosis actually cemented my decision. I can't do it anymore. I can't just keep giving in, pretending it's all okay."

Maslow bounded over, nuzzling Mark's leg, and he reached down to scratch behind his ears. "Dinner's ready, let's head inside. Please don't mention this to Charlotte, the first thing she will do is tell Amy, and you know what a disaster that will be. It will work out, thanks for letting me vent." Mark straightened himself, grabbing the tongs to place the patties and sausages back onto a platter.

△△△

Inside, Amy meandered around the kitchen, preparing fixings for the burgers. Charlotte set some plates on the table, then moved back to the kitchen to help. "What's up? You look flustered."

Amy huffed, her frustration bubbling to the surface. "It's my mom. She's just... so overbearing. Every visit turns into a lecture about how I should be living my life, especially when it comes to having a baby."

Charlotte nodded, understanding. "That sounds rough. What did she say this time?"

Amy rolled her eyes. "The usual. 'You need to relax more, Amy. Stress is why you're not pregnant yet.' And then, of course, she tags me in my cousin's pregnancy announcements, as if the five hundred announcements I see about pregnancies and births on my own page is not enough." With a mock sigh, she threw her hands up. "Oh, how I wish I had a grandchild to spoil."
"It's bullshit."

Charlotte squeezed Amy's arm gently. "I'm sorry. That must be really hard to hear."

"It is," Amy uncorked a wine bottle, and tilted the neck against the glass. She then cracked a can of ginger ale, pouring the fizzing liquid in the other glass. "She just doesn't get it. It's not like I'm *not* trying. Every time she talks about it, it just makes me feel worse." Charlotte gulped, eyeing the wine glass. *Does she know?* The thought made her stomach flip.

"Speaking of posts, did you see the throwbacks Chad posted on Facebook from that college party?" Charlotte tried to shift the conversation as Amy slid the glass toward her.

Amy sipped her ginger ale, forcing herself to focus on the

bubbles tingling against her tongue. "Yes, I almost died. That was one hell of a night. I'm surprised either of us could remember it." Amy laughed. Her thoughts trailing once more as she started to laugh. "You practically drowned your shoes in beer."

Charlotte groaned, burying her face in her hands. "Oh God, don't remind me. I think I still have the stain on my old sneakers somewhere. You are terrible at beer pong, by the way."

Amy smirked. "I wasn't the one who spilled an entire cup on myself, thank you very much. Besides, I had a better distraction."

Charlotte raised an eyebrow, a grin tugging at her lips. "You mean Mark? The tall, broody one who practically swooped in like some knight in shining armor when that guy grabbed your ass?"

"Yeah, him," Amy rolled her eyes, though a soft smile crept onto her face. "He was so cocky, calling me his girl to scare that guy off. I couldn't tell if I wanted to punch him or kiss him."

"And you went with the second option," Charlotte teased, her laughter light and familiar. "Meanwhile, I was over there locking lips with Lincoln. He was so smug about it, too. Like he'd planned the whole thing."

Amy chuckled. "He probably did."

Charlotte grinned. "But look how it turned out. You're married now, so technically, Lincoln was right."

"Don't give him too much credit," Amy shot back, sipping her ginger ale. "He's already insufferable enough as it is. But yeah, I guess I owe him for that one."

Charlotte leaned back in her chair, her eyes softening. "It's kind of crazy, isn't it? That one night changed everything. I never would've guessed that spilling beer on myself and making out with Lincoln would lead to... well, this."

"To what?" she took another sip of soda. "What's that look for?" Amy's smile faded just a touch as her gaze shifted to her glass. Charlotte hadn't touched it.

"You know, it's your favorite wine, what gives?" Amy's

stomach flipped as she glanced up, and her friend's flushed cheeks told her everything before she even spoke.

"I'm pregnant."

For a second, Amy's hand froze around her glass. The words reverberated in her mind, sinking into her like stones in deep water. *Pregnant.* Her throat was dry as she forced herself to swallow, turning quickly to the sink, desperate to hide her face.

"That's… that's amazing news, Char. Really," her voice was stretched thin. *Why her? Why now?*

She heard Charlotte's response, yet they felt muffled, distant. *A life that wasn't hers. A future she couldn't seem to reach.*

She forced a smile, searching for something to occupy herself. Reaching for the utensil drawer, she began sifting through forks and knives. How many weeks are you?"

"Eight." Charlotte cleared her throat. "I wanted to tell you sooner, but I…"

Amy waved it off with a reflexive gesture. "Honestly, it's fine. You don't need to walk on eggshells around me. I can handle it, Char." The words slicing before she could catch herself. The quiet that followed felt raw, stretched tight between them.

"It's amazing news, truly." She forced down the saliva that filled her mouth.

She cleared her throat, grounding herself with the one sliver of hope she had left. "Actually, I think I'm about to ovulate any day now." She let the words linger, her fingers curling around her glass as if she could squeeze her way into the future she so desperately wanted. "Maybe we'll get lucky, and you and I can be bump buddies. They say you're more fertile after these procedures, right?"

Charlotte's smile faltered, her brow creasing with worry. "Amy, it's only been two weeks since the surgery. The doctor said–"

"Please." The plea escaped harsher than she intended. "I've waited *so–* long– Charlotte." She held back tears. I can't let this chance slip through my fingers." *Can't let another month, another failure, just swallow me whole.*

"I understand how much this means to you, but–"

"Forget it." She cut Charlotte off, jaw clenched tight. "It probably won't happen anyway; we don't have your– that kind of luck." She held a bitterness she could no longer hide.

Amy couldn't bear to look at her. *The sympathy. The careful words.* None of it filled the gnawing emptiness, the years of waiting, hoping, and losing. The cracks she'd kept hidden widened, threatening to spill over. She sighed. "I'm happy for you, I really am." She fixed the salad, unable to make eye contact as she felt the tears brim. *If I take that test now, if it showed even the faintest glimmer of hope…*

The sliding glass door opened, and Lincoln and Mark walked in. Amy was so relieved.

"Hey boys, almost ready here."

Charlotte started walking toward the stairwell. "Hey, is the bathroom down here up and running or do I need to run upstairs?"

Amy smiled, wiping her hands on a dish towel. "Nope, they're still working on it," she joked, casting a playful glance at Lincoln. "Maybe you could hop in and finish the job, Linc. Just use the one upstairs, Char."

Charlotte laughed, nodding as she made her way to the staircase. "Thanks."

As she climbed the stairs, Maslow darted past her, running into the room across the hall from the bathroom. "Maslow, what are you up to?" she whispered, curiosity piqued. She followed the dog, wondering what mischief he was getting into.

Before she could call out to Amy, Maslow emerged, dragging a tiny onesie still on a hanger. Charlotte's heart skipped a beat.

"where'd you get that?" she murmured, bending down to pick up the baby item. Instead of bothering Amy, she decided to return it herself. She rounded the corner into the olive toned room.

What she saw made her stop. The closet was filled with baby items. A table next to a basket of baby clothes caught her eye. On it, an ultrasound photo lay on its surface, seemingly pulled out from a file folder adjacent to it. Charlotte picked it up, her fingers trembling.

Amy's name and date of birth were printed on it, but the image showed an empty sac. No baby. The date was from last year. Charlotte's heart sank.

Why didn't she tell me? Charlotte thought, feeling a wave of sadness and guilt wash over her.

She glanced around the room, darting once more to the baby items stuffed in the closet. She could see where the basket went, as there was an empty space of those dimensions on the shelf. The sheer number of baby items was overwhelming. From this vantage point, she realized Amy had been preparing for a baby, hoping, dreaming, and yet, she never mentioned any of this to her.

Tears welled up as she gently placed the onesie back on the pile of clothes, and slipped the ultrasound picture back on the table where she'd found it. She took a deep breath, trying to compose herself before returning downstairs.

As she headed back to the dining room, Charlotte couldn't shake the heavy feeling in her chest. She had missed so much. Amy had been carrying this silent burden, and Charlotte felt a pang of guilt for not knowing, for not being there for her friend. The questions swirled in her mind, heavy and unrelenting. She blinked back tears, determined not to let anyone see her upset.

△△△

The evening continued, the conversations weaving between work, personal lives, and future plans. Amy excused herself to the bathroom. The dinner plates were nearly empty, the remnants of a hearty meal scattered across the table. Conversations had started to dwindle, replaced by the soft clinking of cutlery and the occasional burst of laughter. Mark, however, was noticeably drunk, his movements a bit more animated and his laughter louder than usual.

Lincoln grinned, nudging Charlotte as he observed Mark trying to pour himself another drink. "Looks like someone's had a bit too much fun tonight," he joked, raising his eyebrow.

Charlotte chuckled, glancing at Mark. "He's going to have a wicked hangover tomorrow."

In the bathroom, Amy sat on the toilet, her heart pounding with anticipation and uncertainty. She clutched the ovulation test, the dark pink line confirming her suspicions. She didn't think she'd ovulate, and with it this positive, they'd already missed a key window. A lump formed in her throat realizing this was it. She winced as she rose from the seat, pulling her underwear carefully over her scar as she adjusted her dress. At the sink, she ran the water, allowing it to pool before she dabbed a napkin with the cool fluid on her beaded forehead.

As Amy returned, "Well, it's getting late, we should probably start wrapping things up."

Mark waved dismissively, slurring slightly. "Nah, the night's still young!" He attempted to stand but swayed, catching himself on the back of his chair.

Lincoln stood up, giving Mark a pat on the back. "Alright, buddy, I think it's time we head out. Don't want you falling asleep on us."

Everyone laughed, and Mark chuckled along, albeit a bit unsteadily. "Fine, fine. You're probably right."

Charlotte began gathering their things, pulling Amy into a hug. "Thanks for having us over, Amy. I love you so much, girl."

Amy smiled, a bit more genuinely this time. "Love you, too. Thank you for coming. It was great having you."

As they stepped outside, the cool night air sobered the

mood. "We should do this again soon," Amy tapped her shoulder. "Give Evie kisses for me."

"Absolutely," Charlotte replied. "Take care, lady."

As Lincoln and Charlotte walked down the street to their home, Mark leaned heavily on Amy, who was struggling to keep him upright. "Come on, time for bed." she said.

"Nope. Not ready for bed." Mark shifted heavily from one foot to the other as he made his way to the kitchen. He leaned against the island, taking another sip from the glass Amy wasn't sure was his.

He flopped down, a groan escaping his lips. "I had fun tonight," he mumbled, his eyes half-closed.

Amy sighed, sitting next to him, she handed him a large glass of iced water. "Mark, we need to talk."

He opened one eye, looking at her with a mixture of confusion and fatigue. Taking the glass, he swiftly gulped back the water, setting it back down with a large thud. "Talk about what?"

"I took an ovulation test and it's positive." Amy's fingers skimmed Mark's sleeve, hesitant yet seeking, a whisper of a touch that lingered. Mark stumbled forward with a heavy sigh, his words slurring as he rose from his seat, struggling to maintain his composure. "We've been through this, the doctor said—"

"I know what he said, but—" her voice rose and Mark shot her a stern glance.

"No. Amy, don't." He took another sip of his drink. "We *just* got a fucking dog. Why isn't that good enough?" He took a step away from her, his body now tense.

Amy held her breath, her heart pounding with a mixture of hurt and anger. "How can you say that?" she countered. "We've been trying for years. You know how much it means to me." She started to cry. "Charlotte is pregnant. Did Lincoln tell you?"

Mark's eyes flashed with frustration as he pulled away from her, his movements unsteady as he walked toward the sofa, spilling a bit of his drink. "No, he didn't but probably for this fucking reason, because you–" He sighed. "I can't do that again, Amy. Last year almost broke me." The truth came out of nowhere, and she felt her heart jump. He steadied himself against the wall, placing his empty glass on the side table.

All I care about is having a baby? His accusations mingled with his confession, fueling a surge of emotions. She knew she wanted more than just a baby. She wanted Mark, the man who had once been her everything.

The last shot hit him hard. As Mark leaned in, his words disjointed, His mind raced, his palms sweaty.

Amy noticed the sudden shift, how the relaxation swept his entire body, he swayed a bit, and she closed the gap between them, her hand drifting to his waist as she inched closer to his groin. She leaned in, her breath warm against his ear as she whispered, "You know how much I want this, but it's not just about a baby. It's about us, about the way you make me feel."

Mark's eyes flickered with a mixture of confusion and desire as he struggled to focus on her words. He was so drunk, so vulnerable, and Amy knew that she had him right where she wanted him.

She leaned back slightly, her seductive gaze locking with him as she continued, "I miss *us*. I miss the way you used to look at me, the way my body feels when you touch me." She slipped his hand between her legs. He sighed, his eyes rolling back in his head as he captured her mouth with his. Amy's proximity sent a jolt through him, her scent like a heady perfume that clouded his senses. He tried to steady himself, to maintain some semblance of control, but her allure, or the alcohol, proved too potent to resist.

"You miss us?" He knew this dance all too well, the push and pull of their relationship made worse by her unyielding desire for a baby, an imaginary being she put above him.

Amy's posture was laced with motive as she leaned in. "More than anything," she murmured, "I want you." She lured as she palmed his dick, eliciting the reaction she wanted as she pulled him toward the stairs.

Mark's body fell heavily against the mattress. Amy's mind was elsewhere, consumed by a single, overwhelming thought, *the positive ovulation test*. It clawed at her insides, a relentless ache that overshadowed everything else.

Amy's heart raced with desperation as she struggled to undress Mark, his drunken protests echoing in the dimly lit room.

"Amy, get off." He complained, each syllable slurred as his head bobbed from side to side. Each push away felt like a blow to her hopes, to her dreams of motherhood. She couldn't bear the thought of another missed opportunity, another chance slipping away.

She kissed him, drawing his whiskey breath into her mouth, pulling him against her as she tried to tilt his focus to sex. Her scar throbbed. Tears welled as she fought against the waves of guilt crashing over her. She knew what she was doing was wrong, but the longing for a child consumed every thought, blinding her to reason.

Her hand grasped him tightly, moving in a rhythm to get him going. When it didn't work, she lowered herself to his pelvis, drawing him into her mouth as she worked to excite him. She tried not to look at him, his face, his chiseled body, the way he looked right now voided that charisma. She closed her eyes as she pushed through, trying to avoid his blank state as he slipped in and out of coherence.

He grunted, a limp arm flailing against her as he tried to push her off him. In his intoxicated haze, Mark was barely conscious of what was going on, but on the inside, his mind fought against the sensations he was feeling, and while the disconnect from his thoughts to his physical being kept him from pushing back, he found himself in a dance with desire, and repulsion.

As she straddled him, her mind raced with doubt and uncertainty. *Is this truly the right choice?* The question gnawed at her conscience, but the pull was too strong to resist.

She pushed herself off the mattress, straddling his hips as fast as she could. Once she had positioned herself against him, she felt his muscles tense. Drawing closer to him she whispered "I love you baby," She moved faster, frustration mounting at how difficult it was to keep him erect. She wanted it to be over, trying everything to get him to come as fast as possible. Finally, she pushed him to the point of no return.

Her breath came in shallow swoops, the tingling sensation of anxiety gnawing at her fingers and toes. A sense of calm rushed over her when it was over. She carefully shifted off of him, quickly laying on her back as she placed a pillow under her hips, hoping to pull the semen in the right direction. She choked on bile as she realized the gravity of what she had just done.

They hadn't had sex since the last cycle, a cycle she forced on him, pressuring him, once again, that those three days during ovulation were the most important. She guilted him with the things she had to do to her body in order to give him a baby, the symptoms, the side effects, all of it could *not* be for nothing.

Her thoughts drifted to the pain in his voice when he brought up the molar pregnancy. *This would work*, they had found the problem, and now, she just had the two–week wait, a wait for something that they had wanted for years.

ELEVEN

Mark woke up to a pounding headache. He shifted onto his stomach, wincing with discomfort as he looked at the time on his phone. His legs were heavy as he swung them over the bed, glancing over his shoulder to find that Amy was already awake. His eyes were fixed on the sheets, Navy blue, freshly washed, the scent of detergent still lingering. She'd washed them yesterday, like she did every Friday, a mindless ritual he hadn't paid attention to until now. His gaze followed the sharp crease of the fabric, settling on a pale stain, glaring against the deep blue. It stretched out from the middle of the bed, unmistakably creeping toward her side.

His pulse raced, each second dragging him deeper into a suffocating rage. His jaw locked as his fingers twitched, hovering just above the bedspread, resisting the urge to tear the fabric apart. His heart hammered against his ribcage. *What the fuck?*

He pinched the bridge of his nose, trying to pull the night back into focus. *His head was pounding.* Bits and pieces flickered in and out, a patchwork of moments, fractured, distorted. *He could taste the smoke from the barbeque, and could feel the warmth of the fire. There'd been too many drinks; the glass sweating against his grip. The laughter of their friends, blurred voices rising and falling, their argument.*

His knuckles cracked as he strained to remember. Her face, contorted with frustration, swam before him. Their argument slipped out of reach. All he remembered was the anger rising in him, the need to escape.

Then, the bedroom.

The sheets beneath him had been cool, his body sinking into the mattress, exhaustion seeping into his bones. He could feel her beside him, his hands on her, pushing her away. He'd told her to stop. And then... nothing.

His mind clawed at the edges of that blank space, but it remained stubbornly empty. Only the taste of bile rose in his throat, a cold knot forming in his gut.

He could hear the shower as he crossed the threshold, making his way to the bathroom. The tile was cold against the soles of his feet, the sensation momentarily shifting the tension in his body. His mind was churning with a storm of emotions. Rage boiled beneath the surface, a seething anger fueled by the realization of Amy's manipulation, her *audacity* to take advantage of him.

Her skin was slick and wet as he entered the shower, pulling her against him with a force that made her wince.

"Do you want me?" He lowered his face toward her ear, his hand sweeping up to the nape of her neck. She could feel his erection against her back as he moved the weight of his body against hers, pushing her to the wall. Amy inhaled sharply, the pain of the tile hitting her abdomen from his abrupt advance took her by surprise. A moan escaped as she arched her back against him.

"Yes."

Mark's eyes darkened, pulling her slick hair away from her back, winding the strands tightly around his fist, wringing out the water. He spun her to face him. He was towering over her now, and he noticed a shift in her demeanor. She was not excited, she was afraid. *Good.*

Amy felt his anger, she sensed his tension, the way his veins popped out of his neck, his jaw clenched, his body rigid. She gulped, the realization hitting her like lightning. *Does he remember what happened?* She began to panic, her mind racing as she tried to calculate the best way to handle this. She lowered herself to her knees as she submitted herself to him.

He shook his head, pulling her from her feet by her hair. *I don't think so.*

Through clenched teeth, he guided Amy to the bed. He pushed her onto the mattress. He was over her now, forcing himself into her. She gasped as he moved his hand over her mouth, pushing against her with an intensity that caught her breath. Mark's intense gaze was locked on her, his jaw clenched so tight, she could hear his teeth grinding against one another. He shifted all of his weight onto her, exerting his control, feeling a thrill of satisfaction for the pain he was inflicting. She was still his, still bound to him.

She couldn't breathe.

In his crate, Maslow growled, his nails scratching against the sides, desperate to get to her. The sound reverberated through the house, echoing like a warning. But it was too late. The tension had already snapped, and Amy was pinned beneath him.

She clawed at his pecs as his hands tightened around her neck, his grip tightening as spots filtered her vision. He pulled away from her, and she gasped, inhaling air that was starved from her lungs. He flipped her over so she was on all fours as he took her from behind. He purposely moved the blankets, exposing the sheets beneath it and her focused zoned in the stains.

He knows. Bile filled Amy's throat as she realized what was going on. *Is he turned on by this?* She reached between her legs to stroke him; to show him she loved him, that she did this *for* him. She quivered when he slapped her hand away. She felt his breath hot against her ear, sweat dripping off him and onto her back as he slowly pulled out.

"Turn around," he ordered. She did as she was told, fear anchoring her to his words. Her skin prickled with adrenaline as his steel gaze pinned her in place, her body nearly paralyzed beneath its weight.

"Mark…." She tried to speak, but the lump in her throat prevented another word from escaping. He was standing over her now, one arm pinning her to the bed, the other stroking himself. She felt the hot liquid spill over her stomach and she shut her eyes, tears escaping. She let out a cry as his hand swiped her face with blunt force. Her ears were ringing, her body shaking as she instinctively shielded herself from him.

A chill spread through her as Maslow's barking turned frantic, almost as if he could sense the danger. The way his growls mixed with the sound of Mark's breath, the weight of it all pressing down on her, suffocating her.

Mark's chest heaved with fury as he stood over her, his eyes dark and cold. "You think this is how you win me back?" His tone was rough, like it had been dragged over broken glass. "You've got no fucking clue what you're doing, Amy."

His words hit her like a slap, but they were nothing compared to the rage in his eyes. She tried to shrink back, but there was nowhere to go. She was trapped, both in the room and in this sick, twisted game they were playing.

He leaned over her, his breath hot against her skin. "You can't just pull me back with a fucking move like that. You think I'm going to forget everything? Think again." His hands gripped her arms roughly, and he shook her, the action harsh and demanding.

"Don't ever try to control me like that again," he spat, trembling with rage. His face twisted with disgust as he let go of her arms and stepped back. "Fuck with me like that again, Amy, and you'll regret the day we met."

Without another word, he stormed off, his footsteps heavy and relentless as he barreled into the bathroom, slamming the door with such force that the house seemed to shake.

Amy was frozen, her body trembling with a mix of fear and guilt. She pulled her knees to her chest, her arms hugging herself like a lifeline. She knew he'd exited the master through the adjoining laundry room, and that running after him would make things worse.

Her breath was ragged, uneven, her vision fading in and out. Everything was spinning. She felt like she was drowning, like she couldn't breathe, couldn't think straight. What had she done?

She couldn't help it. Her mind raced, desperation clawed at her chest. *How do I fix this? How do I make it right?*

Her stomach churned, her skin cold and clammy as the silence between them stretched longer than she could bear. *He was right.* She knew he was right. He had the power. She was the one who had overstepped, who had messed things up. *What the fuck did I do? He won't forgive me.* She couldn't bear losing him, even if he didn't want her anymore.

And then, the unmistakable sound of metal scraping against metal jolted her attention, and the low thud of paws against wood was followed by a sharp bark. The door to the bedroom creaked open. Amy's pulse quickened, heart slamming against her ribcage. She blinked, confused for a moment, then realizing he had managed to get out of his crate.

Maslow's fur bristled along his spine as he leapt onto the bed with a force that sent the blankets shifting. His body pressed against her, warmth and softness flooding her senses. His head burrowed into her chest as he curled into her side, his whimpers soft but persistent.

His breath was fast, uneven, the tremor of his body a silent echo of the tension still hanging in the room.

Amy reached out, shaking, and she pulled him closer, feeling the steady rhythm of his heartbeat against her chest, his body warm and solid, a small anchor in the chaos of her emotions. He nuzzled against her, his soft fur damp with her tears.

"What have I done?" She whispered.

The tears came harder now, the dam crumbling. Amy clung to Maslow, her fingers running through his soft fur, grounding herself in the sensation of him, the only steady thing she had left.

TWELVE

Amy adjusted the fit of her sneakers as the early morning sun painted the Hudson River in warm streaks of gold. The past couple of weeks had been tense, and the trails had become her sanctuary during these morning runs, a place to focus her scattered thoughts before the chaos of the day began. She felt alone, unable to process her thoughts, unable to share what she was thinking or feeling with anyone. The isolation felt even greater than the distance he had put between them, and she understood it, she deserved it.

The crisp air carried the faint smell of water and earth, a grounding scent that mingled with the sound of her rhythmic strides on the gravel path. Amy's eyes followed the river's edge, its surface glinting like shards of glass, and she found herself drawn toward the sprawling space. It wasn't her usual route, but something about the quiet invitation of the path beckoned her.

She rounded the bend, the faint hum of traffic from the Rip Van Winkle Bridge blending into the background. Her breath puffed visibly in the cool air as she slowed to a jog, allowing her surroundings to seep into her senses. The park's neatly trimmed lawn stretched toward the water, dotted with benches and trees that lined the river.

Amy paused near a cluster of tall trees, stretching out her calves as she let the calm of the scene settle her restless mind. It had been a sleepless night, her thoughts tangled in the complexities of Lincoln's upcoming merger event and the tension that had been simmering at home with Mark. Her phone buzzed in the pocket of her running jacket. Pulling it out, she glanced at the screen.

> Charlotte: We need to finalize the table arrangements for tonight. Call me when you're on your way, No rush.

Amy exhaled sharply, stuffing the phone back into her pocket. Work was always waiting, no matter how far she tried to run from it. But she couldn't complain. Charlotte had entrusted her with a significant portion of the event planning, and tonight's merger announcement was a career-defining moment for Lincoln's company.

As she turned back toward the path, a figure caught her eye. Callum stood by the railing near the water, his forearms resting casually on the metal bar as he stared out at the river. His sleeves were pushed up, his usual polished appearance softened by the relaxed posture, and running attire. She hadn't expected to see him here, not this early, and certainly not looking so untethered.

Her stomach tightened involuntarily, the unexpected sight of him stirring something she wasn't ready to examine. She debated slipping away unnoticed, but as if sensing her hesitation, he turned his head. Their eyes met, and a faint smirk tugged at the corner of his mouth.

"Morning, Ames," he called out.

Amy forced a smile and closed the space between them. "Hey, didn't expect to see you here."

He shrugged, his gaze shifting back to the water. "Needed some air. Thought I'd clear my head before tonight."

"Same," she admitted, leaning against the railing beside him. The chill of the metal seeped through her jacket, grounding her. "The merger's got everyone on edge."

Callum glanced at her, his expression unreadable. "You seem different this morning. Everything okay?"

Amy hesitated, pinching the bridge of her nose. "Yeah, just… a lot on my mind, I guess. Nothing I can't handle."

"You sure?" he pressed. His eyes lingered on hers, searching for something she wasn't sure she wanted to reveal.

"Positive," she replied quickly, straightening up. "We've got a lot to do before tonight, and…just getting a run in to clear my head."

Callum studied her for another moment before nodding, a faint smile softening his features. "Alright, if you say so. But if you need to talk… you know where to find me."

"Thanks," she replied, her voice quieter now.

He pushed off the railing, his presence lingering even as he stepped away. "See you at work later."

Amy watched him go, his figure blending into the waking city as the morning light bathed the world in warmth. She exhaled slowly, turning back toward the Riverview, the stress starting to mount as she turned around and ran back to the house.

After showering, she made her way to work, adjusting her blazer as she stepped into the mill, the faint scent of wood polish and fresh coffee greeting her. The steady click of her heels against the floor softened as her steps faltered. Her gaze swept the space, not so much taking it in as moving through it, landing briefly on details before darting to the next.

Callum was the first thing she focused on for more than a second.

He stood by the bar, his sleeves rolled up, revealing strong forearms that flexed as he adjusted the coffee grinder. His hair was tousled, like he'd been running his hands through it in frustration or thought. Something about the sight tugged at her, though she couldn't name why.

Chris Stapleton's *Tennessee Whiskey* drifted through the room, the soulful melody lingering in the air. It had a way of filling the quiet, making the space feel warmer, richer. It also made her pause just a little longer than she should have.

Callum looked up then, catching her mid-step. His brows

lifted slightly, a flicker of curiosity crossing his face before he smiled. "Morning, Ames."

The name struck a chord with her, and her heart fluttered. "Morning." Her voice sounded thinner than usual, even to her own ears.

"How was the run?" he asked, his tone light but watchful.

Amy nodded quickly. "Great, yours?" she gestured toward the speakers. "Didn't know we were hosting a concert today." Her smile was genuine this time.

He chuckled, leaning back against the counter. "Dito on the run," he nodded toward the speakers, "Keeps the mornings interesting."

Amy moved past him, heading toward the table where their meeting materials were spread. Her movements were precise, like she was focused on controlling every gesture.

Callum watched her as she reached for a stack of papers, her fingers trembling slightly before she steadied them. Her blazer was perfectly tailored, her hair pinned back neatly. She looked polished, together, but something was off.

She wasn't herself.

Amy's jokes usually came with an easy smile, her laughter rich and full of life. Today, though, it all felt mechanical, like she was playing a role. Even the way she spoke, it was quick, efficient, as though she was trying to avoid giving too much away.

He glanced down at his tablet, trying not to overthink it. People had off days, and maybe that's all this was. But then he caught her fidgeting with a pen, twisting it between her fingers like she needed something to focus on.

"You sure you're okay?" he asked, keeping his tone casual. He instinctively took a step closer.

Her head lifted, and for a brief second, her mask slipped. There was something in her eyes, hesitation, exhaustion, something heavier than he'd expected. But she recovered almost instantly, tucking the pen into her notebook and flashing a quick smile.

"Of course. Just busy. This event, the two couples coming in, the printers messed up my last set of flyers, *and* a design project in the works." She turned back to the papers, her voice steady but distant. "Well, the design project, I am actually stoked for."

Nodding, Callum didn't press her. He knew her well enough to recognize when she didn't want to talk.

She was trying, that much was obvious. Trying to seem fine, trying to stay focused, trying to hold herself together.

It was the trying that worried him most.

"Impressive," he reached over her to grab his own folder. "Though, if you're trying to outshine me as the mill's MVP, I should warn you, it's a tough competition."

Amy shook her head, ignoring the flutter in her chest as she grabbed her clipboard. "Don't tempt me. I'm not above sabotage." She nudged him.

"There it is, got you to smile." He shot back with a wink.

Before Amy could respond, Charlotte appeared, tablet in hand and a determined expression on her face. "There you two are. "Lincoln's event just got even bigger." She glanced at the text on her phone. "The mayor just approved Lincoln's firm taking on the city redevelopment project. We've got a few more last-minute guests. I updated the Excel file," she said, glancing at Amy. Amy nodded. "Everyone from the mayor's office to the state planning board will be watching him tonight." Amy slid into a seat as she opened the file. "I finalized the catering details and confirmed the guest list. No changes besides yours, but I'll keep an eye on RSVPs in case anyone decides to show up unannounced."

Charlotte nodded, scrolling through her tablet. "Good. Callum... Audio, visual, and security?" she looked up at him.

"Already locked down," Callum replied, his tone confident. "Lighting, sound, cameras, all tested twice. Security team is briefed and in position."

Amy didn't look up from the tablet she'd grabbed. "And for your next trick?"

Callum's lips curved. "I could juggle, but I'd hate to outshine your efforts."

Amy tilted her head. "That's cute, Callum. Remind me to get you a participation ribbon later."

He chuckled, leaning back against the table. "Please do. It'd pair nicely with the gold star I already earned for saving the day on the floorplan, I like this much better." He handed her the blueprint of the table arrangements.

Charlotte raised a brow, glancing between the two. "You two are cutesy, pairing well in your positions of power." She laughed a little too loud at her own joke.

Callum didn't miss a beat. "Looks like it. Very *demure*." They all laughed.

He glanced at Amy, raising an eyebrow. "Ames, you dropped the ball." Watching her smile widen. *There she is.*

"How so?"

Jack's voice echoed as he strolled in. "VERY MINDFUL, come on girl, you're killing me." "Ladies and gent, the brains of this operation has arrived! Please, save your applause."

Amy glanced toward him as Jack held a tray of coffees in one hand and a bag of pastries in the other. "I come bearing caffeine and carbs, so I expect undying gratitude," he announced, setting everything on the bar.

Charlotte laughed. "Jack, we need help with hanging these garlands, and I have no idea where you put the ladder."

Jack threw a thumb over his shoulder. "Um, just have Callum stand under the arch, he's about 7 feet tall, just sit on his shoulders." Amy choked on her coffee.

"Hold on, *there's* an idea." Jack turned to Amy, lowering an octave, but everyone could still hear him. "Never mind, I volunteer as tribute."

Amy shook her head, "You three are ridiculous."

Jack gave Callum a once-over, nodding in approval. "Tailored suit, rolled sleeves, just enough brooding." He flicked his wrist. "It's very hotshot lawyer who secretly has a heart of gold energy."

Charlotte arched a brow. "That's oddly specific."

Jack shrugged. "If this were a rom-com, he'd be the guy who pretends he hates Christmas but secretly donates to an orphanage."

Callum shook his head, already turning away. "I'm leaving before this gets worse."

Jack called after him, grinning. "Denial is step one, my friend!"

△△△

From his office, Callum sat in shadow, his gaze fixed on the monitor streaming live footage from the main hall. The camera tracked Amy as she moved between tables, unpacking candles while Charlotte adjusted chairs nearby.

He leaned in, jaw tight, watching the way her shoulders stiffened. She was trembling–just enough to give her away. She was holding it together, trying to stay polished, but here, away from the noise, the strain was starting to show.

His brows knit together. There was something in the way she held herself, her defenses barely hiding the tension and emotion beneath. It was the kind of mask he knew too well, one that said *don't look too closely*, but he was already seeing past it. *Poor Amy*, he thought, his fingers brushing the edge of the desk. *She is caught in a cycle, too tangled in Mark's control to even realize she is suffocating.*

Then her phone rang, slicing through the air and pulling her from her conversation with Charlotte.

"Hey, give me a minute. I'll be right back." Amy excused herself, tucking her phone to her ear as she stepped outside.

In his office, Callum adjusted the controls on the security system, switching the camera feed to the side exit as Amy stepped outside. His fingers hovered over the audio dial before turning it up, the faint crackle giving way.

"Hey," Amy's voice was shaking. She wrapped her arm around herself, pacing a few steps before stopping.

"Hey," Mark's voice came through, clipped and cold. "I need to stop by the house later today," Mark continued. "Left some files I need for work."

Amy shifted, her free hand clenching at her side. "Okay. What time?"

"Probably around noon. I won't be long."

Callum frowned. *Of course, it's him.*

She hesitated, and even without seeing her face up close, Callum could sense the conflict in her body language. "Maybe we could talk when you're there? I could meet you, and we–"

Mark's sigh cut her off. "Amy, we've been over this. I just need time to think. Space to breathe."

Callum leaned forward, watching as Amy froze. Her pacing stopped, and she stood still, like she was bracing herself.

"I know," she whispered, quieter now. "I'm so sorry, I know I don't deserve–."

Mark's reply came quick, with that same tone Amy had heard too many times before. "Amy, you're the one who made things complicated. Not me. I'm doing what I can to get through this, and the last thing I need is you pushing."

Callum clenched his jaw, his hands tightening on the console. *He doesn't even hear her.*

Amy was pleading. "I'm not trying to push. I just... I want us back, Mark. I want us to be okay."

And there it is. The hope she shouldn't even have to beg for. Callum's jaw clenched.

Mark's sigh crackled through the feed, softer this time. "I want that too, Amy. But you've got to stop making this harder."

The silence that followed stretched thin, and Callum could almost feel the ache radiating off her.

"I'll be by the house at noon, I'll take the dog for a walk." Mark hung up.

Callum stared at the screen, his chest tightening as Amy lowered her phone, staring at it like it might somehow undo what she'd just heard. She didn't cry, didn't break down. She just stood there, looking so damn small.

Mark's a coward. A selfish, clueless fucking coward. Callum thought as he realized his hands were now fists.

Amy turned back toward the building, her pace slower now, her shoulders hunched just slightly. By the time she reentered the main hall, she'd forced her head high, blinking rapidly to hide the redness in her eyes.

She's wearing it again. That mask. The one she puts on for everyone else so they don't ask questions.

But it didn't fool him. Not for a second.

Mark doesn't see it, what he's doing to her. How much she's still fighting for him. And the bastard doesn't even deserve it. Callum leaned back, his hands steady on the console despite the anger simmering. He doesn't deserve her. But she'll never see that as long as he keeps dangling just enough hope to make her think there's a chance.

But I see her. Air escaped though his clenched teeth. He watched her meet up with Charlotte.

She moved to the bar, fidgeting with the candles, though

the tremor was harder to hide.

Charlotte looked up from her tablet with concern as she gripped Amy's arm. "Hey, were you crying? Your mascara is smudged."

Amy quickly wiped her eyes before she lowered her voice, leaning in slightly. "Mark left. We had another fight about having a baby. I think I pushed him too far this time."

Charlotte's brow furrowed as she pulled a chair out and motioned for Amy to sit. "He walked out?"

Amy nodded, her throat tightening. "Packed a bag and left. It's been two weeks, Char. I don't know what to do." The words came out in a rush, desperate and heavy. "I just talked to him, tried to reason with him, but he's still so upset. This is all my fault."

Callum's brows narrowed as he studied her reaction. She was unraveling. He could feel it. The weight of the space between them, the absence of Mark, was like a vacuum pulling her closer to the edge. And she didn't even realize how much she was leaning into Charlotte; how much she was opening up to her.

But why Charlotte? Why not me? Callum thought, his fingers tapping rhythmically on the desk.

Charlotte tilted her head. "Oh, I'm so sorry. I know how much this means to you both."

Amy wiped her eyes. "I don't know what to do. He's so cold. It's like... he's just... gone now. I've never felt so alone." Her fingers twisted around the candle, the delicate flicker of the lightbulb almost mocking her brokenness.

Callum's jaw clenched. *Alone? She wasn't alone. Not anymore.* He could feel himself shifting inside, the hunger growing. He was right here, watching, waiting for her to let him in. She needed someone to see her, to understand the pieces of her that Mark had neglected.

His fingers gripped the edge of the desk, his knuckles turning white as Amy continued speaking.

He watched her exhale deeply. "Hey Char? I'm going to head to the store to pick up a few things we are missing. Do you need me to grab anything else while I'm out?" Charlotte rose from her seat.

"No, I think we're good. but if I think of something, I'll text you." She hugged her. "Mark is many things, but he is not stupid. He will come back to you; you just need to give it time."

Callum's gaze darkened. She was a thread hanging by a single strand, ready to snap, and he wanted to be the hand that she reached for.

△△△

The minute the words "two weeks" left her mouth, Amy knew she needed to go to the store. It wasn't even a conscious decision, her body reacted before her mind could argue otherwise. Sweaty palms. Racing heart. A hitch in her breath she couldn't quite ease.

She hadn't thought about that in a while. At least, not directly. But standing there, frozen in place, it hit her all over again; the molar pregnancy last year. The memory hit her like a visceral wave, like a wound that had never fully closed.

It had started with two pink lines. She could still see them, clear as day, sitting on the edge of the bathroom sink. The rush of disbelief. The way her hand shook as she'd called for Mark, holding the test out like she wasn't sure it was real.

He hadn't been on board with the idea of kids, not at first. Too busy. Too much responsibility. But something shifted when he saw the test in her hand. He'd stared at it for a long moment, his face unreadable, before his lips curved into the smallest smile.

And then everything changed.

He'd held her hair when she puked, rubbing circles on

her back even when he was running late for work. He'd stopped by her favorite bakery after meetings, bringing home warm soup or soft pretzels just because. And when she'd teased him about needing to buy a baby name book, he'd surprised her by rattling off a list he'd apparently been keeping in his head.

"*Josephine for a girl, maybe. Or what about William, if it's a boy. Something timeless.*"

She could still hear his voice when he said it. Still see the way he'd touched her stomach when he thought she wasn't paying attention, a tenderness in him she'd never seen before. For the first time, he seemed all in; present and protective in a way that made her feel grounded. Safe.

Until she wasn't.

The memory of that night clawed at her chest, threatening to unravel her.

The cramping. The blood. The sterile coldness of the hospital room and the look on Mark's face when the doctor said, "It's not a viable pregnancy."

He hadn't cried, not in front of her. But his quiet retreat in the days that followed had felt worse than any outburst. She'd wanted him to rage, to blame the universe, to say anything to prove he cared. But instead, he'd folded in on himself, slowly pulling away piece by piece until she'd barely recognized him.

That's when the loneliness began.

Amy swallowed hard, forcing herself back to the present. Her palms were damp as she opened the purchased box at Walgreens, and made her way to the bathrooms at the back of the store.

Mark had been different when they thought she was pregnant, different in a way she desperately missed. She wanted that version of him back. Wanted the hope, the tenderness, the promise of something more to cling to.

Her hands trembled as she locked the door behind her, the thought finishing itself before she had the strength to stop it.

If a baby was the only way to feel whole again, she had to try.

She sat on the edge of the toilet; the room dimly lit by the soft glow of the bathroom light. She was shaking as she glanced once more at the pregnancy test, its positive result glaring up at her. Her thoughts raced, replaying the night they had conceived. She reached for the test once more, running her fingernail along the joint where the two pieces of plastic came together so she could snap open the test to get a better view of the strip. She clutched her stomach, a mix of excitement and anxiety churning inside her. This was the moment that she'd waited so many years for, and somehow, this was the worst day of her life.

Oh my God. How do I tell him?

THIRTEEN

The Riverview took on an entirely different aura as the evening light and chatter bathed the venue in a soft, enigmatic glow of moody darkness and natural elegance. Mark moved through the crowd, his polished demeanor masking the war waging inside him. He couldn't lose control. Not tonight. Mark stood near the bar, scanning the room. This wasn't about them, it was about appearances, and despite this being Lincoln's event, the buzz of his book launch meant it was for him, too, and he needed to play the fiddle. Everything had to be perfect. He needed Amy to stay in line, to be the partner he could present in front of everyone. Mark took a long sip from his glass, the whiskey burning a trail down his throat.

Amy was standing near the hearth, the flickering flames dancing in her eyes. Before he could take another step toward her, she moved, walking toward him with that cautious grace of hers. Her black dress hugged her frame, the kind of dress she used to wear when she wanted him to look.

"Amy," he greeted her in a controlled but warm tone. He could smell the faint trace of her perfume, mingling with the heavy scent of the whiskey in his glass. The heat between them should've been familiar, but instead it felt wrong. She felt off tonight, just like he did. She was unraveling, just like everything else in their life.

"I'm glad you came," Amy started.

He gave her a dry smile. "Why wouldn't I be here? Or do you have plans to fuck up my friendships too?" The words stung more than he intended, but he needed her to realize who was in control.

She reached for him, and for a moment, he saw her

desperation "Can we talk? Please."

There it was again, the crack in her armor, the plea that made him want to pull away and pull her closer all at once. She was slipping, and it was maddening. He sighed, looking around to make sure no one was listening in. "Amy, this isn't the time or place."

"I want to fix things. I know I've made mistakes, but we can work through this."

She still didn't get it. "We've been through this, Amy. You don't get to just decide when things are okay."

She swallowed hard, and he felt a sick satisfaction at the tears brimming. She was vulnerable. She was his.

"I know, I know I pushed things too far," she cleared her throat, "I thought it was what we needed. I don't know what I was thinking. I just wanted us to have a chance."

She didn't know what she was thinking? That was the problem. She'd stopped thinking about him long ago. It wasn't just about *her* anymore. It was about *them*. The way she'd pushed him, the way she had betrayed him, he'd never forgive her for it.

His hand moved to her shoulder, pressing her down into the seat by the fireplace. He watched her closely, forcing her to look at him, to feel his control. He focused on the flames, the warmth of them flickering against the coldness of his tone.

"You really believe that?" He gripped her chin, his nails digging into her skin, as he pulled her face toward his.

"I don't want you to leave, Mark," she whispered.

Too late for that, Amy. Her tears spilled over, and he felt that familiar pang of something. What was it? *Guilt?* No. It wasn't guilt. It was something else, something darker. He didn't want her to have that power over him, either.

"I'm sorry," she whispered.

She clung to him, desperate, pleading. It made him feel powerful, needed, aroused. He had always been the one who had to hold it together. Now, she needed him to fix this, and that's exactly what he wanted.

The guilt, the anger, the thrill, it churned in him, mixing with the need to maintain control. He couldn't give her what she wanted, but he wanted her to believe that he could. There was a part of him that wanted to hold her, that wanted to tell her everything would be fine, and he hated that.

As Mark glanced around, he saw Charlotte with Lincoln. He was supposed to be at the top of his game tonight. He was at the top. All of this, his book, his career, everything depended on the image. And Amy? Amy was just part of that image.

She couldn't fall apart. Not now. He planted a kiss on her forehead, his gaze briefly softening. "Let me get my things tonight, I'll swing by tomorrow after work, we can talk then." Mark said, allowing her to relax. "Stay here, I'll be right back."

He turned toward the bar, needing a drink to settle the storm inside him. "I'll take an old fashion, and a cabernet." He returned to Amy's side, handing her the glass. She grasped the stem. He slowly brought the glass to his lips, taking a sip.

"You're not drinking," his tone was casual, though the accusation was barely veiled.

Amy's eyes flicked to the glass, then to her lap. "I'm not really in the mood."

Not in the mood? Mark's expression shifted. She loved wine. His fingers curled tighter around his own glass.

"Right." He let the silence linger, his gaze heavy on her.

Her fingers fidgeted, brushing the stem of the untouched glass, but still, she didn't raise it.

Mark inhaled deeply, forcing his tone lighter. "Let's get some air," He reached for her arm, his grip firm as he guided her outside. The crowd thinned as they moved through the venue, the air cooling as they stepped into the night.

The patio was quiet, the faint glow of string lights casting soft shadows across the space. The rush of the river hummed in the distance, a sound Amy might have found calming on another night. But tonight, it only amplified the weight pressing on her chest.

Mark guided her across the vast stone patio, the river's murmur growing louder with each step. The firepits flickered in the distance, their glow stretching toward the water's edge. As they neared, the flames cast a warm, shifting light over his sharp features, shadows flickering across his face. The heat from the fire barely touched her skin, her nerves too frayed to register its warmth.

Her gaze dropped to the ground, her silence fueling the tension radiating from him.

Then it hit him.

Mark's stomach churned, the thought clawing its way through his mind.

His jaw tightened, the disgust curling inside him. He stared at her. "You think you're pregnant."

Amy's head jerked up, her wide eyes betraying her. She didn't even need to say the words, her face said it all.

A sharp, humorless laugh broke from his throat. "Unbelievable," he muttered, shaking his head. "You actually think one night, one fucking night, was enough?"

"Mark, please…"

"Pathetic," he snapped as he stepped closer. "Do you hear yourself? You're clinging to some desperate fantasy, Amy. God, it's embarrassing."

She flinched, her trembling hands clutching at her arms as if she could hold herself together.

Mark lifted the wine glass from the table, the dark liquid swirling as he held it up between them. "Drink it," his cold gaze locked on hers.

"What?" Her throat constricted.

"Drink it," he repeated, shoving the glass toward her. "Prove to me you're not completely out of your mind. That you're not delusional enough to believe this could even be possible."

She shook her head, her lips trembling. "Mark, I don't want to–"

"Of course, you don't," he cut her off, his sneer deepening. "Because that would mean admitting nothing's changed. That you're exactly where you've always been... grasping at something that's never going to happen."

Her chest heaved, a quiet sob choking back in her throat. She stared at the glass, her fingers curling weakly around its stem as he pressed it into her hand.

"Enough, Amy," he said sharply, "Drink it. Now."

Her hand shook as she raised the glass, her movements slow and hesitant. She took a small sip, her gaze fixed on the ground.

Mark's anger flared again, "The entire fucking glass, Amy."

Tears pricked her eyes as she obeyed, tilting the glass to her lips and forcing herself to swallow.

The moment she finished, Mark's demeanor shifted. His posture relaxed as if shaking off the heat of his outburst. He scoffed softly, a hollow laugh escaping him. "Jesus, Amy," shaking his head. *I didn't mean the whole damn thing in one go.* And just like that, he had her again. He could see the way she shrank just enough, waiting for his next move, the way she wanted so badly to believe this was just another misunderstanding. She was always so quick to smooth things over, to convince herself that if she could just anticipate what he wanted, she could avoid setting him off.

He leaned forward, capturing her lips in a kiss that caught her off guard. The sudden warmth of his tongue brushing against hers startled her, and for a moment, she leaned into him. His hands rested lightly on her waist, his touch a calculated reassurance.

"I've missed you." Mark said as he pulled back, his expression had softened, his tone almost teasing. "You've been off all evening," his thumb grazed her cheek. "Relax, okay? We'll figure this out."

The tenderness in his tone was enough to make her believe him, even as her heart twisted painfully.

"I love you, so much." She repeated and allowed her hand lingered on his. "I'll be right back, I need to use the restroom," Amy stood up, to return to the crowd.

His stomach twisted. He didn't like letting her out of his sight, especially now. "Okay," He cleared his throat. "Meet me by the bar, can't not dance with you tonight, you look incredible."

She nodded and moved toward the hall leading to the restrooms. "Okay, see you in a bit." He tracked her, an unease settling in his chest.

Amy pushed the restroom door open, grateful for a moment to breathe. She stepped to the sink, turning on the water, and let the cool rush wash over her palms. The mirror reflected her emotions of the evening and the faint flush from mingling in a room full of guests.

The door opened again, and the soft click of heels followed. Amy glanced up in the mirror as a woman in a crimson dress entered. Her dark braid fell over one shoulder, and she carried herself with an effortless grace that immediately drew attention.

Amy offered a polite smile, stepping aside as the woman approached the sink beside her.

"Lovely event," the woman's tone was light and conversational as she began lathering with soap.

Amy nodded. "It really is. Charlotte and Lincoln put so much work into it."

The woman's lips curved faintly, though her hazel eyes remained focused on the mirror. "Are you close with them?"

"Charlotte's one of my best friends," Amy replied, grabbing a hand towel. "Do you know them?"

"Not directly," she replied, tilting her head slightly. "I'm here with my father. He's a big supporter of Lincoln's firm." She paused, her gaze drifting to Amy in the mirror. "And you? Who are you here with?"

"My husband, Mark." Amy smiled softly.

The woman's expression brightened with what seemed like genuine admiration. "Mark Rodriguez? The therapist?" She let out a soft laugh, shaking her head. "What a small world. So excited for his book to launch, I follow him online. He has such a way with people, doesn't he?"

Unease prickled at Amy's skin. "He's very passionate about what he does."

The woman leaned slightly against the counter, folding the paper towel carefully. "Passionate, mmm. He really knows how to make people feel seen. Understood. It's rare, that kind of gift." Her gaze lingered on Amy.

Amy forced a polite laugh, brushing a strand of hair behind her ear. "He works hard at it."

The woman nodded slowly, her smile taking on a sharper edge. "You must be proud. It's not easy being married to someone like that. So many people vying for his attention, but you're the one who has it all." She straightened, tossing the paper towel in the trash. "That's something special."

Amy's mind snagged on the strange weight of the words, and all she could muster was "Thanks."

The woman stepped toward the door, glancing back. "You're lucky. He's quite the catch."

The door closed with a soft click, leaving Amy standing there, her pulse thrumming in her ears.

△△△

Mark sat at the bar, waiting for his drink when he saw her.

Josie emerged from the restroom, her red dress clinging to her like a second skin. Her expression was unreadable as she stepped into the hallway. And then, Amy followed.

Mark's entire body stiffened, a cold sweat breaking out across his back. Amy's gaze lingered on Josie, her brows knitting together. It wasn't recognition, not entirely, but something shifted in her expression, *a realization.* His stomach plummeted as Amy hesitated for a fraction of a second. Mark's heart pounded in his chest, his mind screaming at him to move, to say something, to stop this before it spiraled.

But then, Amy simply looked away, as Josephine stepped aside so she could exit the bathroom.

Mark exhaled shakily, relief flooding him, though his pulse didn't slow. Josie, who had paused in the hallway, was scanning the room. He watched her pull out her phone.

His phone buzzed. She hadn't noticed Amy. Or if she had, she didn't care. Posture was rigid as he watched her start to walk toward him.

Photographer: Your car is here? Are we at the same place?

He couldn't let her and Amy cross paths again. Not tonight. Not ever. He made a subtle adjustment as he stood from the bar, closing the distance between him and Josie. His drink swayed slightly, the ice clinking against the glass. He downed the last of it as he approached her.

"Josie," he hissed under his breath when he reached her. "What are you doing here?" He eyed the brick partition, a wall that divided the entertaining space from the honeymoon suite. "Walk with me." Mark demanded.

Her hazel eyes locked onto his, her lips curling into a smile that was equal parts bitter and amused. "I told you dad had an event, mom wasn't feeling well, he asked me to come." She paused. "You said *you* were going to a work thing." She stepped closer, the scent of her perfume weaving into his senses, pulling him in. "But now I see why you lied."

Mark's jaw clenched as he glanced toward the bathroom, then back at Josephine. "Not now."

Her words were edged with steel. "You mean it's not the time or place because *she's* here?"

"Keep your voice down," he growled, as they made their way toward the back of the venue. He scanned the room. No one seemed to be paying attention to them, but that didn't ease his nerves.

Josie's smile vanished, replaced by something darker. "How do you even stomach it? Pretending everything is fine–"

"Stop." Mark didn't let her finish. He pushed open the suite door, his hand firm at her lower back as he guided her inside. "You're not doing this. Not here." The weight of his words left no room for argument.

The suite was breathtaking, a space meticulously crafted for romance. A canopy bed dominated the room, its frame carved from dark, polished wood and draped with soft white chiffon that billowed gently in the faint breeze from the air conditioner. The bedding was lush, layers of silk and velvet in deep, airy shades of white and ivory, inviting anyone who entered to sink into its embrace.

The walls were painted a soft, warm blush, complemented by the flicker of candlelight from elegant sconces mounted above. In one corner, an upholstered chaise lounge beckoned for stolen whispers and intimate moments, while a small, ornate table held a silver bucket with an unopened bottle of champagne and two crystal flutes.

The air was lightly perfumed, a blend of rose and sandalwood, subtle but heady, wrapping around the senses like a lover's touch. Above the bed, a delicate chandelier cast a golden glow over the room, the light refracting through strands of crystal and dancing across the surfaces.

Everything about the suite whispered of passion, of desire, of moments meant to be remembered. Mark barely noticed. He walked in with the same casual indifference he might have carried into a sterile hotel room, his movements sharp and unhurried. He gripped Josephine's wrist as he led her inside, but there was no tenderness in his touch, only control.

Mark took another swig from his glass, toying with an ice cube in his mouth. Stepping closer, he reached out to touch her trembling hands, his musky scent enveloping her as she moved closer. "Small world I suppose, the host is my best friend, technically it's *his* work thing." He watched her breasts rise and fall with each uneven breath, the sight stirring a primal longing. "We've been through this, Josie," he stroked her cheekbone dotted with freckles, adding an unexpected innocence to her otherwise sultry appearance. "You know I can't just leave Amy, not now." he countered, his mouth forming a hard line. He knew he shouldn't be here, shouldn't be entertaining her advances, but he felt a sense of power washing over him, a reminder of the hold he had over her.

Her expression flickered with pain, but she quickly masked it with defiance. "Then when, Mark? Tell me. Where do I get to do this? When?"

Mark's fingers danced along the curve of Josie's jawline, a possessive grip guiding her gaze to meet his. "You're all that matters," he sliced through her doubts, each syllable a command she dared not defy. "This is most definitely not the place for you and I to be together." He took her mouth with his, transferring the melting ice cube into her mouth as his frigid tongue stroked hers. She could taste the whiskey in his mouth, and she sucked on the tip, biting it softly as a moan escaped. In his embrace, she felt her resistance melt away, swallowed by the overwhelming force of his will, as he claimed her with nothing more than a whispered promise.

Mark raked his fingers through his hair, his jaw clenching as his cold fingers trailing her exposed spine. He was drawn to her silhouette, the curves of her figure accentuated by the soft glow of candlelight, his touch lingering with an intensity that made her shudder.

"Josie," he murmured, "This dress…" he traced the embroidery that hemmed the back, enticing the unusual feeling of movement as the pad of his finger flexed against the bumps of the beadwork. "So sexy."

Josephine's resolve faltered as she felt the weight of guilt settle over her, her anger giving way to a sense of resignation. "I just want us to be together, I'm tired of this. It should be me out there with you, not her. I want to go to events like this, to be yours, just us." Her gaze darted from his mouth to his pelvis and back as she felt his muscles tense against her, giving her a sense of satisfaction that he was responding to her.

She leaned into him, igniting a fire she knew she could control. Mark's gaze traced over her, as he pulled her in, leaving no space between them. "Eyes on me," His lips moved along her neck, then her chin, before claiming her mouth. His teeth grazed her lip, then bit down. She winced as the metallic taste of blood touched her tongue.

One finger traced her thigh, creeping beneath her dress slowly, the thrill in his expression sharpened by something darker. His fingers pressed into her, possessive, as his gaze darted to the window, always careful, always in control. He reached up to close the curtains, locking out the world and locking her in.

He pushed her shoulders down, unzipping his pants as he pinned her against the wall by placing his leg in between her thighs. He wound his fingers around her braid, pulling just enough to make her gasp. "Sit on your hands." He commanded. He stared into her, causing every ounce of her body to tense as he tilted his hips forward, his dick slowly grazing the side of her cheek as she drank in the sight of him. Her body was on fire, every nerve tingling, every inch of her willed to him. She parted her lips, as he stroked her tongue with the head, releasing all tension as she moved her mouth rhythmically against each thrust. His head flung back, a sharp exhale escaping as he let her linger, feeling the vibrations of her moan as he pushed himself against the back of her throat, then slowly withdrew. Her hands moved to wrap around his legs, but he caught her wrist, pushing it to the floor as he shook his head. She had no control, and she found herself trying to suppress the reflex to gag as he grasped the back of her head.

His grip was firm, possessive, holding her in place while taking in her surrender with a faint, almost dangerous smile. She couldn't look away; she didn't want to. She was lost in the heat of him, in the promise that he'd take her to places no one else ever could. He pulled her from the floor, eyeing a bowl of condoms on the nightstand, he reached for one, ripping the package as he spun her around.

"You belong to me," he murmured, savoring the way her breath came in quick, shallow bursts. "You're the best thing that has ever happened to me, Josie."

The tension mounted as he shifted her against the couch, bending her forward with a force that made her shiver. He moved in sync with her, driving her further into that consuming, disorienting passion he always elicited, until there was nothing else, not even herself, only him. And he knew it.

He moved against the friction of her, his hand closed around her throat, holding her just on the edge, the pleasure laced with a dangerous thrill. There was a strange calm in his movements, a sense of mastery as he brought her to the brink of an orgasm, she could feel her muscles begin to tighten around him, and she arched her hips against him, trying not to make noise, holding her breath as her body began to spiral, and then he came, his body jerking against hers. He pulled out, giving *just* enough, never more.

"Fuck, the things you do to me." He spun her around, tilting her back into the sofa. He lowered his head the apex of her thighs as his tongue ran the length of her. She was so wet, her frustration almost maddening that he didn't let her climax, and she watched as he smiled, relishing in the feeling, a feeling that he no longer got with Amy.

"Stay if you must, but please keep your distance. I will see you later tonight." He pulled up his pants, and zipped them, leaving her flushed and out of breath. "I love you." He kissed her freckled cheek, and picked up his glass, as she composed herself.

"I love you too."

He nodded. "You go first, I'll be out in a minute, I need to calm down." He watched her slip out of the room.

Moments later, he slipped out of the back door leading to the patio, only to have Lincoln inches from him, his presence filling the quiet space. Mark lit a cigarette, taking a slow drag as it smoldered between his fingers, his gaze fixed on the river as if it might offer answers.

"What the fuck man, and here I was going to give you the benefit of the doubt. He gestured toward the door to the suite.

"I saw her," Lincoln cut straight to the point. "I came this way so it wouldn't make a scene.

Mark's shoulders stiffened, but he didn't turn. "And?"

"And you need to tell me what the hell you're thinking." Lincoln crossed the patio, his muscles tense. "Because if this blows up, it's not just you who'll pay for it. You know that, right? Amy was fucking looking for you. You are lucky I know you better than you know yourself."

Mark exhaled a long plume of smoke. "It's under control."

Lincoln scoffed. "Under control? Josephine's not some loose thread you can just tie off. She's back, Mark. Here. In the same city, breathing the same air as you. You think that's a coincidence?"

Mark finally turned, his muscles tense. "What do you want me to do? Pretend she doesn't exist?"

"I want you to think," Lincoln shot back. "About Amy. About the life you've built. About what happens if Josephine decides she's done keeping quiet."

Mark flinched, the words hitting home. He stubbed the cigarette out in the glass ashtray with more force than necessary. "She won't."

"You don't know that." Lincoln's tone softened, but the edge remained. "She's a wildcard, and you know it. She always was. You've spent years burying this, and now it's clawing its way back to the surface."

Mark sank onto the bench, taking another hit of his cigarette. "I didn't ask for this. She just showed up."

Lincoln's voice dropped, quieter but no less intense. "Yeah, and now she's here, dragging everything you've been running from right back into the light. Don't tell me it doesn't rip you apart to see her."

Mark's jaw clenched, but he didn't respond.

Lincoln stepped closer, his tone softening. "Look, I get it. I know what she represents. The baby, the life you lost... hell, the person you were before it all went to shit. But you can't...Not now. Not when you've finally put the pieces back together."

Mark whispered, "She's the only one who knows. The only one who–"

Lincoln cut him off. "She was there, yeah. But she's also a walking reminder of the choice you didn't get to make. The life you didn't get to live. And if this gets out, if Amy even gets a whiff of what happened back then, it's over."

Mark's head dropped into his hands. "You think I don't know that?"

Lincoln crouched down in front of him, forcing Mark to meet his gaze. "Then act like it. I know this is dredging up every ounce of guilt and anger you've been burying for years. But Josie being here? It's not a chance to fix the past. It's a chance to burn everything to the ground."

The air fell silent, the weight of their shared history pressing down on them both.

Lincoln stood, his hand on the door. "I'm telling you this because I care. You've got too much to lose, Mark. Don't let her take it from you."

Mark didn't look up. "She's not taking anything. Amy already did."

"What the hell are you talking about?"

"I can't do this. You don't understand. Another time, I'll explain everything, for now, just know, I have it under control. Trust me."

Lincoln lingered for a moment, "I trust you, I do, you're like my brother, but you better catch me up to speed, because I'm not covering for you, this entire thing is fucked up. Your wife is waiting for you near the bar." He walked off, shaking his head.

△△△

As evening waned, Amy navigated through mingling guests, her thoughts consumed by the weight of her conversation with Mark earlier. She found herself in the quieter patio area, seeking a moment of solitude amid the lively event.

Mark followed her discreetly from across the room. His emotions were a tangled mess of desire and guilt as he approached her, a glass of whiskey in hand. The hint of vanilla and brown sugar clung to him, blending with the musky air of the venue. She felt like she was going to puke.

"Amy," Mark's voice was low, a mixture of restraint and longing.

Amy turned to face him, her stomach churning with anticipation. "Oh, there you are, they've started serving dinner."

Mark led Amy toward the dance floor, her silhouette bathed in the warm glow of the string lights overhead. She clutched her glass of sparkling water tightly, her fingers tense around the delicate stem.

"Amy," he murmured as he reached her, the whiskey softening his edges as he brushed his knuckles against her cheek. He took hold of her hand. "Dance with me."

Her brow furrowed slightly. "Now?"

"Now," he repeated. "We'll make an impression. It's what we do best." He winked at her.

Amy hesitated, her gaze flickering to the milling guests inside, then back to him. Reluctantly, she placed her hand in his, and he led her toward the dance floor. The murmur of chatter and clinking glasses faded as the opening chords of *Mayday* by Wild Rivers spilled from the speakers.

Mark's hand settled possessively on the small of her back, pulling her closer than she wanted. His fingers clasped hers tightly, not leaving room for her to dictate the movement. She followed his lead out of muscle memory, her body responding while her mind flailed against the constriction.

All eyes were on them, as he wanted, and it only made her feel smaller.

The song washed over her like a tide, each note carving through her defenses. The weight of the melody hit deep, pressing into places she didn't want touched. She leaned her head against his chest, trying to make herself invisible. His grip tightened, his movements measured and calculated, as though each step was a statement: *I own you.*

Mark's face was unreadable, a mask of calm composure, but Amy knew him too well. The tension in his jaw, the slight edge to his smile—it was all a performance. A message for the room as much as for her.

He bent down and whispered, "I know I was angry, but I've missed you. So much." His lips brushed her ear, and her stomach fluttered. Her mind whiplashed. Was she imagining it? Seeing something that wasn't there?

As they swayed, her gaze drifted, catching on the figure leaning casually against the bar. *Callum.* His presence was magnetic, impossible to ignore. The sharp cut of his suit accentuated the rich brown of his eyes, making them seem even darker. The tailored fit highlighted his defined figure, every clean line drawing attention to his broad shoulders and narrow waist.

It was as if she were seeing him for the first time. Her pulse stammered as his gaze locked onto hers. His jaw clenched, muscles flexing with restrained intensity. He wasn't dressed to match the pretension of the evening, yet somehow, his quiet confidence outshone the tailored suits surrounding him. His stance–steady, assured–made him seem unshakable, a sharp contrast to the man currently holding her.

Callum's fingers flexed around the tumbler in his hand, the amber liquid catching the light. *Protective. Assessing. Dangerous in a way that made her feel safe.*

The song swelled, the rawness of its lyrics settling in her chest like an ache. Her gaze lingered on Callum. She felt the pull of his unspoken question, the demand in his stare: *What are you doing?*

Mark shifted, pulling her attention back to him with another kiss.

Amy blinked, her chest heaving as the song pressed deeper into her ribs, wrapping around the moment like a vice. Her lips parted, but she couldn't find words. Her body moved with Mark's, but her mind was miles away, tethered to the quiet storm in Callum's posture.

Mark leaned in again, his lips grazing her ear. "We're still a team, Amy. No matter how hard you try to pull away."

The words coiled around her throat, her pulse pounding in her ears. She stiffened, her feet faltering slightly, but he adjusted effortlessly, tightening his hold.

Her tears glistened as Mark twirled her, his smile sharp and knowing. She forced herself to mirror his expression, to keep the façade intact for the audience around them, for fear that if she let him go, she would lose everything. But her heart betrayed her, each beat pounding a name she couldn't say aloud.

As they passed, Callum moved into the crowd, his presence unnoticed by Mark. He watched them with a burning intensity, his jaw tight, his breathing shallow. Mark didn't know he was there, didn't know who he was, and Callum planned to keep it that way.

The way Amy shrank under Mark's touch, her shoulders stiffening with every step. The way Mark leaned into her space, his movements calculated, just enough to appear affectionate, but with a precision that sent shivers down Callum's spine. It wasn't just proximity; it was dominance. Control. He brushed Amy's arm, then her back, as though marking territory he thought was still his. Callum's stomach churned.

Then he saw Josephine, her back was to his, and he made it a point to keep it that way. Slipping to his office, he watched through the screen as Josephine lingered near the dance floor, her silhouette caught in the glow of the chandeliers and the brick fireplace. Her movements were restless, her gaze darting between Mark and Amy. Something in her posture was off; hesitant, almost frantic. She knew. She saw it too. But instead of stepping in, she waited. *He had a hold on her, too.*

Amy was slipping further under Mark's influence, and Josephine was trapped in a web she might not even realize was strangling her. Callum's knuckles grazed the rough brick wall against to his desk as he slammed his fist against it, frustration and fury boiling over. Stepping into their orbit, tangling himself in Mark's chaos, would only make things worse for Amy. For now, all he could do was watch, the tension coiling tighter with every calculated move Mark made.

FOURTEEN

Josephine opened the bathroom cabinet, her fingers brushing past the rows of neatly arranged bottles until they found the slim foil packet. She slid it free, flipping it open, and sliding out her birth control. A single pill fell into her palm, but it carried a weight she could feel in her chest.

Filling the glass at the sink, she stared at her reflection in the mirror, her cheeks flushed from the text that Mark had sent earlier. She flicked the pill into her mouth, the water chasing it down in one smooth swallow.

But her chest stayed tight, her fingers gripping the counter as her mind drifted.

The waiting room had been silent except for the faint hum of fluorescent lights and the rustle of paperwork. She sat on the edge of the chair, the clipboard in her lap, fixed on the ink that formed her name.

She twisted her wedding ring absently, the metal cold and heavy against her skin.

Josephine had told herself it was the right choice. She was still in nursing school, her future stretched out in front of her like an unfinished map. A baby wasn't part of the plan, not yet.

But her reasoning felt hollow in the face of what had led her here.

"You don't need it anymore Josie," Callum noted, as he leaned against the bathroom doorway.

The birth control packet was gone, the drawer empty where it had been the night before.

"Don't call me that, never call me that." Her breath caught, at the emotional slip as she turned to him, her throat tight. "Where is it? This is not the right time Callum; I have one year left." Callum didn't know about Mark, about the baby, about the past she tried so desperately to run from.

He stepped into the room, his presence as heavy as his words. "I threw it out. It's time for us to start a family, Josie."

Her protest had come too late, swallowed by his mouth as he closed the distance between them. "You're my wife," he'd murmured, his lips brushing her temple. "I want you to be a mother, to carry our baby..." His arms circled around her waist, Leaning her into the wall, his breath hot on her neck... In that moment, the weight of what she had been through came crashing down, and suddenly, she wanted what she'd lost, if only for a moment.

At the clinic, Josephine shifted in her seat, the words still ringing in her ears. She signed her name at the bottom of the page, the pen trembling slightly.

It's a miscarriage, she rehearsed silently, her lips forming the words without sound. *'It just wasn't the right time. We'll try again.'*

She palmed her wedding ring as her name was called, the weight of it suffocating.

She had rehearsed the plan over and over:

"It's a miscarriage. It wasn't meant to be."

Her words had felt hollow, but they were her lifeline. She'd clung to them, convinced he'd accept them, that he'd hold her and tell her it was okay. That they could try *again later.*

But Callum found out.

And everything fell apart.

There had been more to it than readiness. She wasn't sure she could explain heaviness in her chest every time the thought of having a child crossed her mind, the way it dragged her back to a sterile room, the cold weight of the table beneath her, and the steady, emotionless presence of his father. She never told Callum, told anyone about that night, and she never would.

She gripped the counter now, her breath uneven. Mark's father had forced it. She had been too young to argue, and too scared to ask for anything different. He'd called it the right thing to do. His voice echoed in her memory, calm and authoritative, like it had been some lesson in practicality. She knew within herself that having a baby at that age would have broken them, would have changed them, but the way it happened? That broke her more.

She thought she'd buried that part of herself long ago. But the past had a way of slipping its fingers into the present.

She thought back to how she'd found Mark.

Instagram's algorithm had placed him there, and for a moment, she wasn't sure if it was him. His eyes, his face, the same, yet different. She focused on the jagged scar that snaked down his neck, which hadn't been there many years ago. His last name was different, his wedding ring. She'd scrolled through his feed, catching glimpses of his life. She lingered on his beautiful face, the way his muscles flexed when he rolled his sleeve up of his tailored shirt. The business trips, where she imagined herself having dinner with him. The therapist videos disguised as thirst traps, where she found her hand slipping between her legs as she imagined him inside her. But it was the reels that caught her attention; short, magnetic bursts of his presence.

One auto-played as her thumb hovered over the screen.

"Love isn't about finding someone who completes you," Mark's voice was smooth, drawing her in like a whispered confession. "It's about finding the strength to rebuild when everything else falls apart."

She froze, glued to the screen. His features were sharper now than they had been years ago, more defined, more commanding. The way his dark eyes locked on the camera made it feel as though he was speaking directly to her, cutting through the years and the distance.

"Loss teaches us who we are," he continued, his tone softening just enough to send a shiver through her. "It strips us down to our core, shows us what we're capable of surviving. But love...love is the thing that reminds us we're still alive."

Josephine leaned back against the headboard. It was infuriating, how effortless he made it seem. How he could sit there, looking into a camera, and make her feel seen.

Her core tightened, heat blooming low in her stomach. She hated the way her breath caught, the way her chest ached with something between yearning and regret.

The reel ended, looping back to the beginning, and she forced herself to pause it.

What was she doing? But the truth was already there, unspoken but undeniable: she'd never stopped wondering about him, wanting him. What his life had become, if he ever thought of her, if he remembered the nights they'd stayed up whispering about dreams they were too young to believe in. The news of his mother and father had shattered her, it was all over the news.

And then it hit her. That's why he changed his name. That's why she could never find him.

Before she could stop herself, she clicked to message him. Her thumb hovered over the keyboard, hesitation prickling her skin.

Her gaze flicked back to his profile picture. That smile. It made her heart stutter, and before she could talk herself out of it, she typed the words:

Eversea_Photography: I can't believe I found you. Long time.

The message sent, breaking years of silence. She set the phone down quickly, her fingers trembling. It was reckless, impulsive. But when her phone buzzed only minutes later, her stomach dropped.

DRMARKRODRIGUEZ: Wow, Josie. Didn't think I'd ever hear from you. How's life treating you? You went into photography?

She got a notification for a friend request. Her lips parted, a soft exhale escaping. She glanced at her wedding ring, and saliva filled her mouth. She stared at the screen, her mind whirring as memories flooded back, his laugh, the way he'd looked at her like she was the only thing that mattered. She clicked accept.

Eversea_Photography: Ha, no. I am a nurse. Photography is a hobby.

DRMARKRODRIGUEZ: Josephine, these photos...

[Dr. Mark Rodrigues turned on vanish mode.]

The chat background turned dark, signaling that messages sent in vanish mode would disappear after they're seen and the chat is closed. Josephine's heart jumped.

And just like that, Mark was back in her life, drawing her into his orbit with the same magnetic pull he'd always had. It had started innocently enough. Small talk, catching up. But soon the conversations had stretched into the night as she lay in bed, staring at the ceiling. Mark had always had a way of making her feel seen, even from miles away. It was intoxicating, like the version of her he reflected back was brighter, freer, untouchable.

But as she stood here now, waiting for him to arrive, her anxiety mounted with the weight of everything he stirred in her. The good, yes, but also the guilt, the grief, the questions she didn't know how to answer.

The sound of her phone buzzing pulled Josephine back to the present. She blinked, her chest heaving with a breath she hadn't realized she was holding.

Mark: I'm on my way.

Josie stepped out of the bathroom, the silk clinging to her curves. The deep slit whispered open with each step, revealing glimpses of bare thigh, while the plunging neckline hinted at what lay beneath. The sash cinched loosely at her waist, a fragile barrier between her and temptation. Her breath wavered as she moved through the hush of the house, the cool air teasing against her exposed skin. The faint buzz of her phone on the counter barely cut through the lingering heat of her thoughts.

Once in the living room she settled herself on the sofa. She didn't want to seem like she was waiting.

When Mark walked in, the air in the room thickened, and her pulse raced. She hated how much she felt for him, even when she was angry. Josie wanted to hold onto her anger, to let it ground her, but the moment her eyes met his, it wavered. He looked like he always did; put together, controlled, but the loosened tie, the faint crease in his brow, made something in her chest tighten. Her body betrayed her first, softening before she could stop it, before she could remind herself of the way the night had unraveled.

She clenched her fingers at her sides, willing herself to remember why she was mad. But then he stepped closer, and that familiar gravity pulled at her, unraveling her resolve thread by thread.

"You're home late, do you still want to watch that movie?" Josie asked, as she glanced at the clock.

Mark placed his keys on the counter. "Sorry, the event took longer than anticipated."

Her brows furrowed. "I wouldn't know. I didn't get to stay at the event long enough to find out." She took a sip of her wine.

Mark tensed, his arm resting on the counter. "We're doing this now?"

Josie stood; her arms crossed tightly over her chest. "Why not? You've spent every other night here, telling me this is what you want. Then you act like I don't exist."

He sighed, turning to face her, his expression weary. "I told you, Josie. The book launch is important. Lincoln's event was about appearances. It's too risky, I spent half the night trying to avoid your father." His eyes fell on her as she shifted into a barstool, her legs perched up on the footrest.

"Because I don't fit into your perfect little picture, is that it? I'm good enough to fuck, but not good enough to be seen? I was there with my dad, Mark. I had every right to be there, but because I didn't fit in with your narrative, I had to sit in the back like a good little girl."

"It's not like that," Mark's tone slipped into something softer, more measured. He crossed his arms as he leaned against the bar. "You're overthinking this."

Josie instinctually pulled away. "Don't. I watched you with her. You were all over her."

"This isn't about Amy," he cut her off.

A sharp tsk escaped her lips. "It's *always* about her. She's what you want, isn't she? The doting wife, the perfect image. What am I to you? What are we even doing here?"

Mark's jaw clenched, and he closed the distance between them. His hands found her shoulders, grounding her, holding her in place. His gaze bore into hers, sharp and unrelenting. He reached into his jacket pocket, producing a small velvet box and set it on the counter between them.

Josie eyed it warily. "What is this?"

"Open it."

She hesitated, then flipped it open. Inside lay a delicate gold chain, a single diamond pendant catching the light. Simple. Elegant.

She swallowed hard, lifting her gaze to his. "Mark..."

"You think I don't see you?" His fingers brushed against her jaw, tilting her face toward him. "I see you everywhere, Josie. You're in every damn thing I do. You think I don't want to be next to you, that it doesn't kill me to have to play this game?" He paused, turning into her. "I need you to believe in me."

She inhaled shakily, her resolve cracking.

He took her wrist, pressing her palm flat against his chest, right over his heartbeat. "I've already made arrangements. A week. Just us. No pretending, no hiding." He paused, gauging her reaction. "I booked the flight this morning."

Her lips parted, but no words came.

He slid his fingers into her hair, his touch slow, hypnotic. "I don't just say things, Josie. I do them. I fucking prove them." He traced the column of her throat, dragging his thumb along the pulse fluttering beneath her skin. "I want you in my bed, in my arms, where you belong. I want you waking up next to me, not wondering if I'm coming back."

A tear slipped down her cheek.

Mark caught it with his thumb, dragging the moisture across her lips before dipping his head, letting his mouth replace the touch. Soft at first. Then harder, more possessive.

She should have held onto her anger, should have made him work for it, but when he stepped closer, her body betrayed her, drawn to the pull of him like always. He brushed a knuckle along her jaw, a touch so familiar it weakened something inside her. His silence was calculated, letting the weight of his presence do the work, and she hated how easily it did.

"Josie," he murmured, his voice laced with something that felt like regret, like a promise she'd fallen for too many times. Her throat tightened, her hands curling at her sides, but when he reached for her, she didn't pull away.

That's it. He lifted the necklace from its box and fastened it around her neck.

She froze, unable to draw in a breath.

"You think Amy compares to you?" he continued, his thumbs brushing against her collarbones as her breast fell out of its silk restraint. "She's a placeholder. A face for the public." She felt the roughness of his palm against her skin, and her resolve melted as his touch grew more certain. "But you? You're mine. You're what I need." he lowered his lips to her neck.

She exhaled, the fight in her wavering as she pressed against him to create some distance. "Then why does it feel like we have not moved an inch from where we started?"

Mark's jaw clenched before he leaned in, his lips brushing her ear. "Because you don't trust me. You don't see the bigger picture." He gripped her waist, pulling her closer, his erection pressing into her parted legs. "But I do. I see us, what we can be."

Tears welled, blurring her vision. "I just want to feel like I matter to you."

"You do," he whispered, his lips brushing hers. "Let me show you."

Taking a deep breath, he turned his attention to his briefcase. She adjusted her gown with a confused expression as he clicked it open, the snap jolting Josie's nerves. He handed her a large envelope. "Don't ever tell me that I do not love you, that I do not care for you. If I didn't, I wouldn't be getting a divorce." He inhaled sharply trying to contain his rage. "You need to trust me, Josie."

His hands tightened around her waist, lifting her onto the counter as he stepped between her thighs. His grip was unrelenting, his touch branding. When she broke the kiss, gasping for air, he murmured against her lips, "Tell me you trust me."

"I don't know if I can."

His fingers dug into her hips. "Then let me remind you."

The moment cracked, tension spilling over. He didn't give her another second to doubt. His hands slid beneath her robe, dragging the silk apart as he pressed his mouth to her throat, down the curve of her collarbone. When he kissed her again, it wasn't slow. It wasn't careful.

"You're everything," he exhaled, "You're what keeps me sane, Josie. Don't you see that?"

Outside, Callum's fingers flexed around the camera as he watched through the lens. The light in the living room flickered, shadows casting long shapes across the walls.

Mark's hand was on Josephine's face now, cupping her jaw as he tilted her head back.

Click.

The camera captured her tear-streaked face, her lips parting as Mark leaned closer.

Click.

Mark's body pressed into hers, gripping her waist as his fingers glided to his zipper, and Josephine removed her gown.

Click.

He carried her to the leather chair, hitching her on its arm rest as he spread her legs, sliding himself into her with such force, her body flung into the seat of the chair, leaving her hips tilted as he pushed further.

Click.

This is what you chose, Josephine, he thought bitterly, lowering the camera. And I'll make sure you regret it.

As Callum watched, Mark's expression softened, his hand lingering on Josephine's cheek. Callum's stomach churned with jealousy. The intensity of his emotions left him conflicted, as he watched them, he saw Amy, and suddenly, he felt even more disdain for Mark, his heart pounding in his chest. He wanted to be the one touching her, comforting her, loving her. He couldn't make out the paper that Josie was holding, but based on the thickness, he assumed it was something work related, or coveted divorce papers. He watched as Josephine's wide smile crossed her face. *Has to be the divorce*, he thought.

FIFTEEN

The smell of grilled burgers and hot dogs hung in the air, mingling with the cheerful hum of neighbors chatting and kids darting between tables laden with potluck dishes. Amy stood near the edge of the party, absently stirring her lemonade as she skimmed the crowd. Mark's absence felt heavier than usual tonight, but the cheerful atmosphere was a stark contrast to the empty house waiting for her.

"Where's your hubby? Or is Maslow your date?"

His deep voice penetrated her. Amy turned, to find Callum standing a few feet away, holding a beer. He dressed in dark jeans and a fitted Under Armor T-shirt that accentuated his muscular frame. His posture was relaxed, but his eyes, those were something else, sharp and unsettlingly focused on her.

Amy sighed. "Mark is in the city, a publicist thing. Charlotte bailed on me, Evie's nap time."

He smirked, stepping closer, his presence more commanding than the casual way he held his drink. "Smart to hang back, can't let the neighborhood gossip wear you down too fast."

"Is that why you're hiding out back here too?" she countered, feeling the corners of her mouth lift.

"Something like that." He glanced around, his tone dropping. "Figured I'd find the one person here who wouldn't launch into unsolicited advice about lawn care or school districts."

Amy snorted. "Fair point. Though I don't know how much better I am. I'm the one who sold you on your house, remember? Pretty sure that makes me the neighborhood enabler."

Callum's smirk deepened. "Then I guess I owe you one. But don't expect me to start handing out thank-you muffins or whatever it is they do around here."

He tilted his head slightly, studying her. "Speaking of the neighborhood," he took a swig of his beer. "Which one is yours so I can bring Maslow some snacks, and sneak in some puppy time. I'm only half kidding here." He winked, as he bent down to pet the dog.

"Ha, that's all part of Maslow's master plan. Step one, bat those eyelashes, step two, make you his personal chef." They both laughed.

"Clearly."

She jabbed her thumb over her shoulder. "The one behind me. We finished construction a few months ago. Now I'm having fun with the decor."

Callum focused on the home. It boasted clean lines of cedar, steel, and glass made a striking statement to the old-world charm of the neighborhood surrounding it, and with the time of day, an eerie reflection from the fog danced upon the grandiose panes of glass.

"Wow, it's impressive." Maslow was now curled up by Callum's ankles, and he bent down to pet him. "Since we're on the subject, I've been meaning to ask you something."

"Let me guess," she cracked a smile, raising an eyebrow. "You found something weird in the basement, and now you want me to play real estate therapist."

"Not quite," Callum crossed one foot over the other, "The place is a blank slate; good bones, bad personality. I've been staring at the same empty rooms for weeks now, and I realized I have no idea where to start."

"You want design help?" she asked, surprised.

"Help. Guidance. A miracle." He shrugged. "Call it what you want. I've got that bedframe I told you about." He found himself picturing her in his bed.

He shifted, with a knowing smile. "Oh, and a half-stocked kitchen, and a house that looks like it came straight out of an episode of SVU. Figured if anyone could fix it, it's you."

Amy hesitated, caught off guard by the mix of his candidness and the weight of his gaze. She'd worked with plenty of clients, but this felt different, they worked together already.

"I am by no means an expert." *Ouch, what the fuck was that?* She immediately gripped her stomach. The pain hit first. A cramp, sharp and intense, doubling her over.

"Hey are you okay? You look a little pale." Callum took a step closer.

She gasped, struggling to breathe as the world seemed to tilt off balance.

Callum was at her side, his earlier ease disappearing. "Amy? Are you okay?" His hand landed on her shoulder. Maslow began to whimper.

She tried to steady herself, but the pain came again, and she felt the warmth spreading between her legs. *No. No, not this. Please.*

Her vision blurred, dizziness creeping up on her. Callum's words became muffled as she staggered forward, trying to move toward the garage, her body failing her.

"Callum, I..." she started, but then the rush came, a sudden flood of panic. Her legs felt weak as she gripped his arm, the blood soaking through her clothes, and she collapsed against him. "Callum, I need help," she managed to gasp.

He was silent for a moment, the weight of her fear settling into his chest. His eyes went dark, sharp with instinct. "You're bleeding, fuck this is a lot of blood." The words came out jagged, like this was something far worse than they could deal with. Callum reacted on instinct, picking her up. He sprinted toward the house, with Maslow in tow. The garage door was open, and he opened the door of her SUV.

"Wait here. Where are your car keys?"

"Hook by door." She managed through ragged gasps as panic gripped her.

Callum raced up the steps and into their house, searching the wall before pulling the keys, and the hooks off the wall. He grabbed a kitchen towel on the counter as he unhooked Maslow's leash, before sprinting back down the garage steps, and into the car.

He started the ignition, the car roaring to life. The pool of blood in the seat startled him as he placed the towel between her legs.

"Shit, Amy, are you pregnant?"

Amy nodded, unable to speak as her head bobbed against the window, her face pale and withdrawn as she tried to control her breathing.

Another cramp ripped through her. She felt and heard a gush of liquid and the wave of panic intensified. Her heart raced as she looked down, her breath catching as she began shaking uncontrollably. A growing sense of dread and numbness overwhelmed her as her vision tunneled.

She was having a severe panic attack. Callum, recognizing the signs, pushed down on the gas.

"I –tried –to– tell –him– so many– times." She couldn't catch her breath.

Amy's breathing was rapid and shallow, each gasp growing more frantic. "Amy, you need to calm your breathing," he tried keeping his voice steady. "Focus on me. Slow, deep breaths."

Amy's eyes were wide with panic, her chest heaving. She was becoming hypoxic, her skin growing pale as her bloodstream strangled with high levels of carbon dioxide and not enough oxygen. Callum glanced at her, fear clawing at his chest as he saw her begin to lose consciousness. "Hang on, Amy." *Shit.* "Hang on," he urged.

He pushed the car faster, the engine roaring as they raced toward the emergency room.

Images of losing control, of losing herself, flashed before her. The fear of the unknown, of what was happening to her was all consuming. She tried to focus on Callum, but the panic tightened its grip, squeezing the air out of her lungs, making her chest ache with the effort of each breath.

She felt Callum's hand on hers, his touch grounding her in the chaos. Part of her wanted to apologize, to assure him she was fine, but the panic was relentless, overwhelming any rational thought. Tears streamed down her ashy face, the scene before her spotty. She was losing control, losing herself to this dizzying storm raging inside her as her head flung violently into the window.

He counted, "One, two, three. *In.* One, two, three. *Out.*" His own breath matched the rhythm he was trying to set for her.

As they neared the hospital, Amy's breathing began to slow, her chest rising and falling more evenly. Her head was pounding, and her hands and feet felt like tingling ice blocks. Callum felt a surge of relief, but his fear for her was still sharp. The urgency of their situation left a raw need to protect her, to ensure she was okay.

He pulled up to the emergency room, slamming his foot on the brakes. "Stay here, I'll get a wheelchair." Before she could say anything, he was out and running inside.

"I need a wheelchair; my wife has lost a lot of blood and is having a severe panic attack." His voice was louder than he wanted it to be, and he realized that he was feeling a lot more emotional than he thought he would.

As he opened her door, a nurse helped her out of the car. "We're not too busy; we can take you right back." She replied, as they wheeled her inside.

Callum stayed by her; his fingers entwined with hers. "You're going to be okay," he whispered, "We'll get through this."

The hospital lights flickered overhead as they moved through the corridors, the sterile smell of antiseptic stinging his nostrils. His mind was a storm of emotions, the need to protect her battling with his anger at the situation they were in.

The doctor and nurses worked quickly, starting an IV protocol for blood transfusion and soon, Amy was stabilized. Callum stood back, watching as they prepared her for tests.

A doctor had ordered a urine test and an ultrasound to assess the situation. The oxygen mask provided immediate respite from the clawing need for air as she lay on the hard examination table, her heart pounding as the technician prepared the ultrasound machine.

The dread that filled Amy as she sat there waiting for the inevitable news filled her. *I deserve this, I am in this situation because of what I did.* The coldness of the room enveloped her. Even with a heated blanket, she could not stop shaking. The beeping of nearby machines heightened her anxiety. Callum held her hand, his own heart racing, his mind filled with a torrent of thoughts and fears.

The ultrasound technician walked in. "Do you want me to leave?" Callum searched her face.

She shook her head. "No, stay, please stay." She whispered. As the ultrasound began, the room was filled with tense silence. Callum's focus was glued to the machine, despite the fact that the technician had it turned from both of them. His mind was battling with the fear that this was more than just a pregnancy loss. The emotional ups and downs he felt were getting the better of him.

Then, the sound of a heartbeat filled the air, a steady, reassuring rhythm that caused Amy and Callum to lock eyes, frozen in shock. The technician turned the screen towards them. It was a tiny, flickering pulse of life. Callum's heart dropped. It wasn't the fact that she was pregnant, it was the fact that she was pregnant, with that jackass' child.

The doctor, who was now standing next to the technician,

examined the screen carefully. "You're approaching nine weeks gestation," he remarked. "Your due date is November fifteenth. The placenta forms around weeks eight to nine, heavier bleeding can definitely be attributed to this." He paused. "It looks like you have post-surgical bleeding here." His grip tightened involuntarily, making Amy wince, but she was too focused on the screen to react. He struggled to maintain composure, to mask his inner conflict.

The doctor shifted the ultrasound wand slightly, bringing a clearer view of the dark area in her uterus. His gaze flicked between Amy and the screen, his posture rigid.

"Mrs. Rodriguez, I want you to understand the seriousness of what's happening here," the doctor's tone was soft but firm. "This isn't a typical pregnancy complication. When you had surgery to remove the endometrial lesions, they needed time to heal fully. The doctor side eyed Callum. *What the hell man, it wasn't me!*

"But because you conceived so soon after, the growing uterus has been placing a lot of pressure on those healing areas."

He pointed to the large dark spot on the screen. "One of the lesions that was removed burst due to that pressure, causing the hemorrhage you're experiencing now. The bleeding you've been dealing with isn't just from the pregnancy itself; it's from this wound reopening. Pregnancy causes increased blood flow, and internal bleeding like this is absorbed through the uterus, and expelled, which is why you are bleeding."

Amy gulped. The implications of her choice felt like a weight pressing against her chest. "But the baby… the baby is okay, right?" she stuttered, her focus glued to the flickering heartbeat on the screen.

The doctor hesitated, choosing his words carefully. "The baby is stable for now, but this situation is delicate. Any further strain could increase the risk. That's why I need you to understand the importance of rest. Even minor exertion could lead to more bleeding or even worse complications. I don't think it is going to require surgery to fix, but we will monitor you closely to ensure it clots, and the bleeding stops."

Amy's fingers curled against the thin hospital sheet, her guilt settling like a stone in her stomach. She'd wanted this so badly. She wanted to make it happen, to fix what felt broken. But now, knowing her actions had led to this, she felt a pang of desperation mingled with remorse.

Callum's own emotions twisted in conflict. *What the fuck did Mark do to her? He pushed her to have sex this early?* The anger raised his blood pressure. His heart was pounding so hard, his ears were throbbing.

The doctor turned to Callum, as if sensing the gravity of his silence. "Mr. Rodriguez, I need you to help her take this seriously. No stress, no physical strain, this will need to be a team effort. It's critical."

Callum, ignoring the clear implication of him being her husband, again, nodded stiffly, his jaw clenched, a new urgency simmering beneath his seething anger.

Amy nodded, still shaken but feeling a small sense of relief. The doctor handed her a single photo.

Amy clutched the ultrasound picture, staring at the tiny jelly bean on the black and white image. Her fingers traced the soundwave on the bottom of the picture, and she internalized the memory of that incredible sound she was not prepared to hear.

"We'll keep an eye on your hormone and blood levels to make sure the baby's development remains stable and that your body is coping with the demands. Once we're confident that the bleeding has stopped and your levels are where they need to be, we can discuss discharging you with strict instructions for modified bed rest at home. But for now, staying here is the best way to ensure both your safety and the baby's."

Amy nodded, and began to cry. He stood, taking hold of her hand as the doctor finished up writing his notes.

Once in her hospital room, Callum's gaze lingered on Amy's

face, his expression unreadable. He masked his turmoil through stoic support, silently grappling with the repulsion for Mark and the growing protection he had for Amy.

"I can take Maslow for you if you'd like. Would you like me to get a bag ready for you?" *Shit, too strong man, she's going to think you're fucking nuts.* Callum shifted in his seat, his gaze both steadying and raising her heart beat. "Or, I can call Charlotte, catch her up to speed, if that would make you more comfortable."

Amy exhaled, her breath coming out with a ragged shake. "Callum, I'm so sorry I roped you into this. I'm–" he cut her off.

"Don't, don't be sorry. I'm happy you're safe, you're okay."

"I'll call Mark, he can bring me a bag, take care of the dog. He's supposed to be back tonight."

Of course he is. "Of course. Please let me know how you're doing. Congratulations, Amy." He rose to leave. "I'll leave your keys on the counter, and let the dog out. Please let me know if you need anything else."

"Thank you, again, for everything." She exhaled. "I'll let you know. Also, Since I'll be in bed for the foreseeable future, I'll work on your design plans. Expect some emails."

He nodded, his tone steady. "Looking forward to it. Chat soon." He bent down to kiss her. *Wait, shit. No.* Then quickly recovered by dropping his keys.

Later that evening, Mark opened the door to her room, to find Amy sitting in the bed, her eyes puffy from crying. His focus shifted to the picture she was holding, and his jaw clenched, he closed the door, locking it.

Fuck, the ultrasound, she was holding the picture. *WHY is it in my hand?*

"Well, well." His voice was smooth, "What a surprise." He walked toward her, stretching out his hand as she gave him the photo.

Amy's stomach dropped. "Mark, I–"

"Don't," he interrupted, his tone sharp. He leaned over her, invading her, his face an inch from hers. There was nowhere for her to go.

"You're scared," he murmured. His hand brushed her cheek, making her flinch. "Good. You should be."

Tears welled, but she held her breath, in hope they would not fall.

"You thought you could trap me, didn't you?" Mark continued.

"You thought you could take advantage of me, and there wouldn't be consequences. But you're wrong, Amy. Dead wrong."

Amy's mouth ran dry as his he gripped her chin, forcing her to look at him.

Her heartbeat was rapid, as she tried to curl her fingers around his, but he pushed it away.

"You'll be a good little wife now," he continued, his lips brushing her ear. "You'll play along. You'll smile and nod and do exactly what I tell you to do. Or I will ruin you. Completely. Publicly. You'll lose everything; your reputation, your business, your friends, your life as you know it. What would people think if they knew you were a rapist? It's an interesting angle, isn't it? This baby proves it. You went against the doctor's advice. Charlotte was there when the doctors told you to wait, and you begged them to try sooner." he crossed one leg over the other. "Charlotte and Lincoln were both there that night, and they saw how drunk I was. You've dug such a big hole."

Amy's tears spilled over now, silent but uncontrollable, her body trembling under the weight of his threat.

Mark's hand dropped to her neck, his grip firm enough to make her flinch. "Do you understand me?"

She nodded weakly, unable to muster words. "You're going to go to my events, play along, as soon as everything settles, as soon as it's set in motion, you'll be free. We will sign a little NDA,

I'll draft the divorce papers, we will make it fair, clean break. If you don't, things get messy." He took her hand in his, running her finger down the jagged scar along his jaw. "You know what happens when someone tries to play me, Amy? They pay."

"Mark, we can work on th–" She gulped.

"Don't. Fucking don't. I'll see you at the event." He pressed a kiss on her forehead before rising from his seat. *This could not have happened at a better time.* She watched him retreat as a reply from Charlotte pinged her phone. She felt like she was suffocating. When he left, the dam broke.

She glanced toward the window, where weak sunlight filtered through the blinds, casting striped shadows across the floor. She wanted Charlotte there, more than anything, and based on the last text that came through, she would be here any minute. Her fingers instinctively rested on her abdomen, though the gesture brought her little comfort. The baby was safe for now. That should've been enough to calm her, but it wasn't.

A few minutes later, a knock at the door startled her. She looked up to see Charlotte stepping in, a tote bag slung over her shoulder, her expression somewhere between concern and relief.

"Hey," Charlotte closed the door behind her.

Amy forced a smile. "You didn't have to come all the way here."

"Of course I did," Charlotte replied, setting the bag down by the bed. "What kind of friend would I be if I didn't?"

"What's in there?" Amy asked.

"Comfort essentials," Charlotte grinned. "Snacks, magazines, some herbal tea I'm pretty sure they won't let you have, and…" She pulled out a small, stuffed teddy bear. "For the little one."

Amy's anxiety mounted as she stared at the bear, its soft fur and tiny stitched nose an almost unbearable reminder of everything at stake.

Charlotte sat in the chair beside the bed, studying Amy carefully. "How are you holding up? Really?"

Amy hesitated, her fingers fidgeting with the edge of the blanket. "Callum took me to the hospital. What a shit show, let's have my coworker turned neighbor see me in a bloody mess. It was mortifying. He was calm the whole time, which helped. Everything's fine now, I guess. The baby's fine, thank God." She paused, "Mark just left, I'm glad you missed him."

Charlotte's brows furrowed. "What did he say? Is he so excited? Minus the scare of course."

Amy hesitated, the memory of Mark's visit still fresh and raw. "Things between us have been broken for a long time, Char. I don't think this is going to fix anything, but that's why I am in this mess, I thought having a baby would bring him back."

Charlotte reached for her hand, giving it a reassuring squeeze. "You don't have to go through this by yourself. I'm here for you."

Amy swallowed hard, her free hand moving instinctively to her stomach. "I'm scared," she admitted, "I don't even know if I can do this. I don't even know *how* to do this."

Charlotte gripped her. "You're stronger than you think, and you're not alone, no matter how much it feels like it right now."

SIXTEEN

The pool room felt like a hidden gem tucked into the bones of the old mill. Exposed brick walls stretched high, lined with antique industrial fixtures that paid homage to the building's history. Wooden beams, weathered with age, crisscrossed the ceiling, and large, iron-framed windows let in the faint glow of the moonlight reflecting off the river below. The soft lap of water against the mill's foundation could be heard faintly through the walls.

Lincoln had outdone himself with the renovation. What was once a crumbling relic of another era now buzzed with new life as an event space, each room a perfect blend of history and modernity. The pool room was no exception. Its centerpiece was a mahogany bar, polished to a shine, flanked by plush leather chairs that invited lingering conversations. Behind the bar, shelves were stocked with carefully curated bottles, their labels catching the warm glow of Edison bulbs.

Mark stood at the bar, sleeves rolled up, pouring Whiskey into two heavy glasses. The muted clink of ice against glass echoed in the quiet space. Lincoln leaned against the pool table, the green felt untouched, his arms crossed as he watched Mark in silence.

Lincoln hesitated, then crossed the room and picked up the glass. "You're making it sound like I'm gonna need it."

Mark's lips pressed into a thin line. He looked down, swirling the Whiskey in his glass, before lifting his eyes to Lincoln. "You are."

Lincoln stared at him for a long moment, then took a sip.

"All right. Let's hear it."

Mark stared at the pool balls on the table, their surfaces gleaming in the multicolored light. He didn't move to set them up yet, instead gripping the edge of the table as if it could ground him. *How do you start a conversation that could unravel everything?*

"Did you ever have a moment," Mark started, "where you thought, this isn't how my life was supposed to go?"

Lincoln's brows lifted slightly, but he didn't answer, letting the silence press on Mark.

Mark sighed, finally picking up a cue. He moved to the other side of the table, rolling the balls into the rack without meeting Lincoln's gaze. "Amy's pregnant."

Lincoln froze, the only movement the faint flex of his hand around the cue. His expression didn't shift, but his silence felt heavier.

"Yeah," Mark scoffed, half-laughing to fill the space. "Not what you were expecting to hear, I'm guessing."

"Not really," Lincoln paused, "I thought? Last we talked about this–"

Mark snorted, shaking his head as he tightened the rack. "It's like fate decided to screw with me." He set the rack aside, watching as the balls shifted slightly under the lamp's light as he drained his glass. "I don't even know how to tell you this." Lincoln straightened up, setting the cue against the table as he too, drained his glass.

Lincoln clapped him on the shoulder. "All right, Mark. Out with it, rip the band aid off, I'm here for you, man."

Mark hesitated as he poured another shot, swirling the amber liquid in his glass. The overhead light caught the edge of his profile, sharpening the tension etched into his features. "That night. The one when you and Charlotte came over. After you left, Amy…" He trailed off.

155

Mark's voice dropped. "I was blackout drunk, I remember the argument, her wanting to try again, I said no, she didn't take no for an answer."

The words hung in the air like a stone dropped into still water. Lincoln's grip on his glass tightened. "She—*what? What the actual fuck?*"

"Don't," Mark cut him off sharply, his fingers tightening around the glass. "It's exactly as it sounds; she knew what she was doing. I woke up the next morning and… and now she's pregnant." He laughed. "What are the fucking odds. We've been trying for years and then BAM and I wasn't even trying." He shot back the rest of this drink.

Lincoln froze, his expression darkening as the weight of the revelation settled over him. "Shit. This is…"

Mark let out a bitter laugh, rubbing a hand over his face. "What can I do? She's having the baby whether I like it or not. Even though I don't want it now, it's bringing up all the shit I thought I buried. About the past. About Josie."

Lincoln didn't respond immediately, letting the silence linger. His gaze pinned Mark, unyielding.

Mark's frustration bled into every word. "And Josie…" He trailed off, his gaze flickering to the plaque above the fireplace. "Josie coming back into my life has…" He broke off again, shaking his head.

"Has what?" Lincoln's tone was sharp now, cutting through the tension.

Mark's jaw tightened. "Complicated everything. I thought I was over her. I tried to be, but…" His voice cracked, just enough to betray him. "I still love her. I always have."

"I don't even know what I'm supposed to do with this," Mark muttered. "How the hell do I explain this to anyone? To myself?" His thoughts spiraled as he spoke.

That night. That goddamned night. It always came back to

it, no matter how far he ran or how deep he buried it. Josephine, her tears, the chaos of it all, it was still there, etched in his memory.

Lincoln's jaw flexed, a flicker of tension breaking through his calm.

Mark pressed on. "You remember how bad it got. What my father, what happened then." His words stopped short, but the implication landed. He didn't need to say it. He couldn't. "It's not just about me. This is about keeping everything contained. For everyone's sake."

"Contained." Lincoln echoed the word, his tone unreadable. "What are you really saying?"

Mark's grip on the cue tightened, his knuckles paling. "You know what I'm saying. You know how things spiral when you lose control of the narrative. I can't let that happen."

Lincoln's jaw tightened, his silence urging Mark to continue.

Mark looked up, "This isn't just about Amy. It's about what happens if the wrong people find out. About her. About that night, about Josie." He let the words hang in the air, heavy with implication.

Mark leaned on the table. "I need you to understand. This isn't just a mistake I can fix. It's a fire I have to contain before it burns everything down."

The silence stretched between them, the colors from the lamp shifting as Lincoln straightened. "You're asking me to lie for you."

"I'm asking you to protect what matters," Mark corrected sharply.

Lincoln's gaze flicked to the lamp, its intricate patterns throwing ribbons of light onto Mark's face. "And what's that?"

Mark didn't answer. He sent the cue ball rolling with a calculated flick of his wrist, watching as it struck its mark with quiet finality. Then, without so much as a glance in Lincoln's direction, he set the cue down and headed for the bar.

△△△

The next morning, Callum leaned into the glow of the monitor, the room around him dark and still. His hand hovered over the mouse as the security footage played, the timestamp ticking forward. The sound was patchy, cutting in and out, but the images were clear enough, Mark and Lincoln near the pool table, their movements tense.

He adjusted the volume knob, hoping for clarity, and caught a snippet of Mark's voice.
"...Amy...pregnant..."

The words landed like a dull thud in Callum's chest. He leaned back slightly, his gaze narrowing on the screen. For a moment, he wondered if she'd told Mark before anyone else. The thought irritated him more than it should have.

The audio cut out again, static filling the silence as Callum rewound the footage, trying to decipher what he'd missed. His frustration mounted when the feed stuttered back to life.

"...Josie...coming back..."

He clenched his teeth. "Coming back? What the fuck does that mean?" He leaned forward, his elbows digging into the desk as he toggled between the two men on screen.

The sound cracked and fizzled, the words slipping through in fragments.
"That night... You remember how bad it got. What my father... what happened then."

Callum stilled, his pulse quickening as the words burrowed into his mind. That night. What the hell had Mark been talking about? And why did Josephine's name come up like that, like she was tangled in their past in a way Callum hadn't known?

He rewound the footage again, his jaw tightening as he strained to hear more.

"...About her. About that night. About Josie."

The edges of his vision blurred, his focus narrowing to the monitor as the words looped in his mind. Mark's tone wasn't casual, it was weighted, heavy with history. History Callum hadn't been privy to.

Josephine was his. She had only ever been his. That certainty had been a cornerstone of his belief in their connection, their history. He thought that he had let it go, but this conversation stirred so much emotion.

The audio dipped into static again, but Callum barely noticed, his mind racing. Mark and Josephine, how far back did they go? His stomach churned at the possibilities. The way Mark had said her name, the deliberate drop of *"that night,"* wasn't something one said about a passing acquaintance.

His hand curled into a fist on the desk. Josephine hadn't just belonged to him. She'd been tied to Mark, too. The realization hit with a sharp, bitter edge, twisting something deep in Callum's gut.

He moved the footage forward, catching another snippet of Mark as the audio cut back in.
"This isn't just a mistake I can fix. It's a fire I have to contain before it burns everything down."

The monitor flickered, then went dark, leaving Callum staring at his own reflection in the blank screen.

A fire.

That's exactly what it felt like. A blaze igniting in his chest, consuming every rational thought and leaving behind nothing but raw, seething anger. Mark thought he could manipulate everyone; thought he could twist the past and control the present. And Josephine? She'd let him. She'd been a part of Mark's life, of his secrets, long before Callum had ever entered the picture. It made him sick.

His hand slid off the mouse, and he pressed his palms flat against the desk, the tension rippling through him. He thought of

Josephine's touch, her words, the promises she'd made that now felt like lies.

Mark wasn't the only one playing games.

Callum stood, the chair scraping against the floor. His reflection in the monitor stared back at him, cold and unyielding.

His thoughts drifted to Amy, how innocent she was in all of this, so naive to the monster she had married. Amy wasn't a part of Mark's past. She was part of Callum's future. And no one, not Mark, not anyone, was going to rewrite that.

SEVENTEEN

Amy drove slowly up the long gravel driveway, her tires crunching against the stones as the house came into view. She barely recognized it. The once-faded yellow exterior was now painted a deep forest green, with a natural wood porch stretching across the front, framed by new railings and hanging planters filled with trailing ivy and bright blooms. The transformation took her breath away.

Her hand lingered on the steering wheel for a moment before she parked. A faint smile tugged at her lips as she stepped out, the warm air brushing her cheeks. Callum's truck was parked to the side, its bed filled with lumber and tools, hinting at his latest project. She glanced at the house again, marveling at how it radiated warmth and life now, just like its owner.

Callum met her at the door, his presence filling the space as he opened it wide, his lips curving into a slow grin. "You're finally here," he stepped aside to let her in.

"Yeah, and I almost didn't recognize the place," Amy replied, stepping inside. The smell of fresh wood and paint greeted her, mingling with the faint scent of coffee. Her eyes widened as she took in the refinished banister, gleaming with a rich stain that highlighted the grain of the wood. The built-ins along the walls had been stripped and restored, their natural tones contrasting the terrible choice of faded wallpaper.

"You've been busy," she ran her fingers along the smooth edge of the banister.

"Had some time on my hands," he leaned casually against

the doorframe.

Amy tilted her head as she inspected the details. "Some time? This looks like a year's worth of work, and you hired me because?"

He arched an eyebrow. "Don't look too closely, the rest of the house is the same. Amy, you should have left this in the car, I would have gotten it. His biceps curled around the box she was carrying.

"Not to worry, that's load one. Only a hundred more in the back of the car. Let's go, muscles."

In the weeks leading up to this moment, they'd coordinated furniture deliveries, paint samples, and every detail for the house. Amy's modified bed rest had kept her grounded, but now that she was cleared to move around, she was a storm in motion.

They worked on positioning furniture, rearranging items, and unrolling area rugs. Callum hadn't believed the house could look this good, but she had an eye for it. Suddenly, Amy's mark was everywhere. He couldn't help but think, *I fucking love this.*

She stepped onto the staircase, tilting her head as she examined a handful of swatches. "This staircase might need reinforcing. It creaks, just watch that step."

Amy leaned against the banister with her arms crossed. "Sturdy, huh?" She shifted her weight, and the wood groaned under her. "Sounds trustworthy." Amy laughed, holding up two swatches. "What do you think? Green or blue?"

"Blue," he replied without hesitation, stepping closer to her. "Green feels too safe. Blue's bold."

"Oh, look at that, the student has learned!" she side eyed him, smiling.

Callum leaned against the wall, watching her with amusement. *She is beautiful.*

Amy stepped back, oblivious, holding the swatch up to the wall. She had the slightest bump, accentuated by the tank top she was wearing with an opened button up floral top. The way she carried herself despite everything, it made his throat dry.

"You know, you have a lot of opinions for someone who doesn't live here. When are you moving in?"

Amy shot him a look. Callum's laughter escaped. "You hired me for my opinions. You are *welcome*."

"Here, Let's throw it on and see how it looks. She opened the can, and dipped the brush, taking a step up to balance herself. As she dipped the brush into the jar, Callum tilted his head. "That's dark. Hold on, let me step back. He pursed his lips together, crossing his arms across his chest. "Never mind, I like it, it looks great."

"Um, of course it does, do you want your house to look amazing or not?"

"I want my house to not look like it belongs to a serial killer. Amazing is a bonus."

Amy rolled her eyes again, stepping forward to swipe some paint on the wall of the stairwell that didn't have direct lighting. "Well, lucky for you, I don't do serial–killer chic."

Amy shifted her weight on the stair, the wood groaning ominously beneath her. "That's weird," she shifted on her feet, bending down to inspect it.

"This isn't the step you–" The next creak came too fast. Before either of them could react, the stair splintered under her. Amy gasped, the sudden shift causing her arms to flail as she stumbled backward.

"Shit!" Callum lunged forward as her back fell against him. He reached around to stabilize her.

The impact knocked the wind out of him, but his grip was firm, steady. She landed against his chest, her hands clutching his thighs as his arms anchored her securely. For a moment, the world stilled, the only sound the rapid pounding of his heart in his ears.

He swallowed hard. *Why'd you have to grab her boob?* He

quickly shifted that hand to her waist.

The heat of his body seeped through her blouse, his scent, a mix of soap and something ruggedly masculine wrapped around her, holding her in place. She could feel the steady rise and fall of his chest, the solidness of his arms. And... *oh, no.*

"Oh my God," she blurted, her voice laced with mortification. "I'm so sorry–I didn't mean to–"

"Relax," he said, his tone laced with amusement. "You're fine." He focused on the smell of her perfume.

Except she wasn't fine. She was very aware of just how close they were. And then she realized something else.

Her stomach dropped, her entire body was pressed against him, his hands were on her.

Don't think about it.

Don't acknowledge it.

STOP.

But her brain betrayed her, and the thought screamed in neon: *He's big.*

Oh my God, Amy, why are you thinking this?!

Her cheeks burned as she tried to step forward, but Callum's grip on her waist kept her steady. "Easy," he said, his tone dropping slightly. "You almost went flying."

She forced a laugh, but her mind was racing, her heart was pounding, he could feel her heartbeat through her stomach.

Callum's mind raced, and for a moment, he couldn't focus on anything except how soft she felt in his arms, how her body fit against his. *God fucking damn it, she's making me hard.* He hoped his expression didn't match his thoughts.

"I–I'm good now," she stammered, forcing a laugh that sounded anything but natural.

But she wasn't. Not in the way she should have been. *Not when he's so close.*

His hand had drifted to her stomach as he helped her get her footing. His palm gently resting against her bump. *So, this is what it feels like.*

She pushed off of him, which only made the heat spread. "We, uh, might want to add the stairs to the repair list," she said, unnaturally loud.

He leaned casually against the banister, his gaze steady on her. "And here I thought you were just falling for me."

Her jaw dropped. "Excuse me?"

He grinned, his dimples deepening. "Relax, I'm kidding."

Amy let out a nervous laugh, but inside, her brain was screaming. *Relax? Relax?!*

She turned away again, trying to regain her composure. "Well, *you* wish," she muttered under her breath, her cheeks blazing.

Callum chuckled, shaking his head as he reached for the paint brush. "You're something else, Ames."

She ignored the warmth that spread through her chest at his words, focusing instead on the paint samples. *Get it together, Amy. You're here to work, not… whatever this is.*

But as she stole a glance at him out of the corner of her eye, she knew she wasn't going to stop thinking about the way he'd felt against her anytime soon. She stepped onto the *not* broken stair, and continued to paint the wall. "I like it. What do you think?" *Just look at him! You're making this awkward.*

"I see you," he said suddenly.

Amy paused, looking up. "What? You mean the color? Yes, what do you think?"

"I see how much you carry," his tone was earnest, "How much you give. You deserve someone who sees that too. Who doesn't make you feel like you're not enough."

She found herself holding back tears, and for a moment, she

couldn't respond. Her heart fluttered, and she hated how much his words affected her.

But Callum didn't push. He just smiled, handing her the paintbrush. "Blue is perfect." He paused. "Perfect."

EIGHTEEN

Amy's phone buzzed on the counter, "Husband" flashing across the screen. The sight of it sent a wave of hesitation rippling through her. She wiped her hands on the dish towel and took a breath before answering. "Hey."

"Amy," Mark's tone was unusually soft, disarming. "I've been thinking about us, about everything."

Her grip on the phone tightened, her pulse quickening. "Okay…"

"I'm sorry," his tone carrying just enough weight to make her pause. "For everything. For how I've treated you, for the things I've said. I wasn't fair to you. Or the baby."

The words hit her like a tidal wave. "Mark…"

"No, let me finish," he interrupted gently. "I've been selfish, and I see that now. I want us to work, Amy. I want us to get through this, for the baby, for us."

She blinked, her throat tightening as she struggled to process his sudden change.

"I've rented a condo in the city for the weekend," he continued, "It's pet–friendly, so bring Maslow. They've got this whole setup for dogs; it's really nice. I thought it could be a fresh start. Just you and me, away from everything. We can talk, really talk."

Her heart wavered, torn between caution and a flicker of hope. "Mark, I don't know…"

"Please, Amy," he pressed, pleading. "Let me prove to you

that I mean it this time. I've missed you."

She swallowed hard, glancing at her reflection in the window. "When do you want me there?"

"I'll send you the address," he replied quickly. "Pack a bag, and bring that red dress I love, for the event. You always look so beautiful in it."

"And Amy," he added, "I do love you. I know I haven't shown it the way I should, but I do. More than anything."

Her hand trembled as she set the phone down after he hung up. The words played over in her mind, filling her with an uneasy mix of longing and doubt.

He sounded different, but she knew how easily his words could cut both ways. Still, the part of her that yearned for the man she'd fallen in love with clung to the idea that maybe this time would be different.

She exhaled shakily, brushing a stray tear from her cheek. Packing a bag felt like a step forward, but the sadness she felt reminded her how far they still had to go.

The line went dead before she could say anything more. She set the phone down and looked back at her reflection, feeling a pang of sadness. She wanted so desperately to fix things, to be the family she had envisioned, they had envisioned, for so many years. And now, she was stuck, alone, and caught between the disgust she felt for his betrayal and for *her* treachery, and what the past few weeks meant for both of them.

Tonight's event was an opportunity, perhaps a last chance, to mend the growing rift. If she was there to support him, perhaps he would forgive her, and she could find it in her heart to forgive him too. The soft hum of the extractor fan was the only sound as she continued to examine her reflection.

Her hands gently traced the curve of her stomach, now showing a subtle roundness. At nineteen weeks pregnant, her body was changing in ways she both marveled at and feared. Her breasts were fuller, her belly more pronounced, and even her gait had shifted, a subtle sway she couldn't ignore.

In the walk–in closet, Amy ruffled through her wardrobe, searching for something suitable. Most of her clothes were now too tight, hugging her new curves in ways that would undoubtedly draw Mark's disapproval. She finally settled on a flowing dress, formal enough for the event but loose enough to hide her growing belly, but glanced again at the red dress he wanted her to bring. It was form fitting, and would definitely draw attention to her midsection. She shook her head, not understanding why he wanted her to bring it, but she pulled it off the hanger, and packed it anyway.

△△△

The interstate stretched before her, cloaked in morning mist as Amy's car cut through it. Her phone screen glowed in the console; his new podcast episode's title bold against the dark background: *In Our Darkest Moments*.

The idea of listening, of being pulled into Mark's carefully crafted world, felt like a betrayal of her own mind, the feeling that kept telling her something was amiss, while her heart told her otherwise. She pressed play anyway, longing to feel close to him.

Mark's enigmatic voice emerged, his measured pauses and inhales creating a false sense of intimacy. *"There are times in life,"* he began, *"when the people we trust most fail us. When even love becomes a weapon."* He paused, and she could picture him sitting in the studio as he layered each word with his hidden agenda. *"What I've come to learn, though, is that the darkest moments can guide us to a new kind of strength, a way forward."*

Amy's grip on the wheel tightened, a chill moving through her despite the car's warmth. Maslow's cold nose brushed her elbow which was resting on the center console. She looked at him in the rearview mirror.

"What you doing, boy?" She angled her arm backwards so she could pet him, and he lunged forward, jumping from the back seat into the passenger side of the car, and rested his head on her lap.

"Dude, you're going to get us killed." She laughed, as he curled into a ball on the seat next to her with a huff.

Her thoughts focused again on his episode, and she exhaled heavily, tapping the steering wheel as he concluded his segment. This was what he did best: taking shards of their life together and arranging them into a pattern that cast him as both victim and teacher. The subtlety made it even worse. He never called her out directly. Instead, each word was laced with implication. She felt trapped by it, by how completely he owned their story now. She glanced at the steering wheel, realizing that she had left her wedding ring on the bathroom counter. *Shit, rookie move, he's going to be pissed.*

By the time she hit the congested streets of New York City, her nerves were frayed. The city's towering buildings and the noise of traffic should have distracted her, but Mark's words lingered, winding themselves deeper into her thoughts.

Amy arrived at the address Mark had sent her. Twenty stories in the air, the condo felt sterile, an almost eerie emptiness that no amount of modern art or freshly stocked kitchenware could erase.

Mark was already on the phone when she walked in with Maslow, the conversation smooth, confident, as if he owned the city itself. The instant she closed the door behind her, his attention flickered toward her, just enough for him to pull her into the conversation without ever truly letting her go.

"Yes, the Discovery Health team is on board. They love the concept of resilience and family dynamics, it's exactly what we discussed," Kaitlyn said on the other side of the line.

Amy didn't interrupt. Instead, she moved to unpack Maslow's bag, hoping to focus on something tangible. Mark's attention flickered toward her, a quick glance, before he turned back to the conversation.

"Of course, Kaitlyn, I agree. Framing it as a journey, not just mine, but ours, makes it relatable. That's the angle that will resonate." he continued.

Amy gave Maslow a pat and crossed to the sliding glass door, pulling it open to step outside. The cool breeze offered a reprieve from the stiffness inside. She leaned against the railing, gazing at the bustling city below, her thoughts too tangled to settle on any one thing.

Mark watched her for a moment, his expression unreadable, before returning his focus to the call. "We'll finalize the pitch later. Let me know when the producers are ready to discuss timelines– I want this to feel seamless," his voice dropping just enough to suggest something he didn't want overheard.

She walked toward the balcony, sliding open the door as the sterile breeze of the city washed over her. There was a contained space on one side of the balcony with turf for Maslow to do his business, and she was excited for not having to use the elevator every time he needed to go.

But even as he spoke, the air felt thick. Amy's stomach churned. She couldn't ignore the shift, how his presence had gone from suffocating and cruel to comforting. The tension from before, the threats, the control, it was still there, beneath the surface. She could almost taste it, like a lie half–told.

The idea of it, a weekend in the city, just the two of them, felt strangely appealing, but something about it didn't sit right. Her hand brushed her purse, remembering the drive down, the way Mark's presence had filled the car as she listened to his podcast episode. She'd tried to push his words aside, but they'd stuck, their meaning creeping beneath her skin. It was as if he'd recorded it just for her, a message carefully wrapped in vague terms, barely masked resentment, and pointed references. She'd switched it off halfway through, but the words echoed, lingering in her mind.

She studied the way he leaned back, casual, but with that same undercurrent of unease as she walked toward him. Mark had ended the call.

"You know," she hesitated, "This makes no sense, you said… Why?"

Mark's expression softened instantly, the way he always did when he wanted to disarm her. He moved closer, his tone smooth, comforting. "It was a shock Amy– it was a visceral reaction. You took away my ability to choose this baby. I was angry, part of me still is." He reached for her hand, his fingers brushing gently over hers. "But I have thought about it, we have wanted this for years. I want to support you. It's my baby too."

Amy pulled back slightly. There was something about the way he was making it sound too good to be true, too controlled. "It just seems sudden. Like, I didn't even know you were looking at places in the city. Was this your idea, or your agent's?"

He sighed, as if the weight of her resistance was somehow an inconvenience. "Amy, I'm thinking long-term. The baby deserves stability. You deserve stability. Everything that's building with my career means a life in the city is best."

Her jaw flexed. "Don't use the baby as an excuse. You've been anything but stable, Mark."

His gaze hardened for a fraction of a second before softening, a shift so quick it left her doubting herself. He took a step closer. "I've made mistakes. I won't deny that. But everything I'm doing now is for you. For us. Can't you see that?"

Amy shook her head. "You don't mean that. You're doing this for your agent. For the magazine spreads and podcast ratings. What happens when the shine wears off? When you decide you don't need us anymore?"

Mark took a sip before setting his glass down. "Is that what you think? That this is all for show? We've been married for six years, Amy."

She didn't reply, the lump in her throat threatening to choke her words. His proximity was suffocating now, the faint scent of his cologne triggering a cascade of memories.

"You're the only person who's ever really known me, Amy," he paused, "Do you honestly believe I'd throw that away?"

Her silence was his answer, and he took it as an opening. His hand brushed her arm, a touch that sent an involuntary shiver up her spine. "I was angry, but can't lose you," his fingers trailed down to intertwine with hers. "Not now. Not ever."

Her resolve wavered as he drew her closer, his other hand resting gently on her bump. He kissed her temple, then her cheek, her neck. She turned her head slightly, and his lips found hers. He was intentional, his tongue stroking hers, his fingers caressing her neck. She felt herself relax into his embrace.

When he pulled back, his finger brushed her bottom lip. "Come with me," he whispered. "Let me prove to you that this can work."

Amy closed her eyes, her breath shaky. Every rational part of her screamed to push him away, to remind herself of his lies, his betrayal. But his touch was too familiar, too intoxicating. Her heart, still tethered to the boy who had once been her everything.

Mark kissed her again, deeper this time, as if the answer didn't matter. As if he'd already won.

Amy blinked rapidly, the past few weeks catching up with her. His words wrapped around her like chains disguised as warmth. She had to admit, there was something in his gaze that tugged at her heart, something real, something almost tender. But then the words from their last conversation hit her like a slap. *You'll be a good little wife now. You thought you could trap me.* That memory seared her.

This is my fault, and he's trying, why am I being such a fucking idiot? She wove her fingers with his, wrapping her arm around him.

Mark seemed to sense her hesitation, and he picked her up, causing Amy to squeal as he shifted her so that her body was square on his. He guided her legs to curl around his waist. "I know it's a lot to ask, but I'm here. I'm all in. For both of you." *This isn't just about winning her back. It's about control. About making sure she's tethered to me, no matter how much she doubts.* He thought.

"Amy, I wish you could see yourself right now."

She looked at him, "What do you mean?"

"You're beautiful. Even when you're mad at me. *Especially* when you're mad at me." He drew her hand from his chest, and kissed her knuckles. "But I hate seeing you upset, I hate being away from you."

He noticed her bare left finger. "Where's your ring?"

Amy blushed. "I accidentally left it at home." Mark shook his head.

His hand cupped her ass, and her defenses rose like clockwork. "Don't. You don't just–"

"Just what?" he interrupted, "Love you? Want you? I do, Amy. God, I always have." he slipped his pinky ring off, crafted from polished gold, its bold, rectangular face housing a sleek black onyx stone. The sharp contrast between the deep, inky black and the radiant gold created a timeless sophistication, a hallmark of someone who commanded attention without trying.

He slipped it onto her left ring finger, the coolness of the metal pressed against her skin.

Mark didn't touch her, but the proximity alone was enough to make her falter. "You're tired," he paused, "You've been fighting me, fighting everything, and I don't blame you. I've made this harder than it needed to be. But right now, I just want to take care of you."

Her lip quivered, and he saw the crack in her armor. *There it is. She wants to believe me, even when she knows better.*

He lifted a hand, brushing a strand of hair from her face.

"Let me show you how much you mean to me." he murmured. His thumb traced her cheekbone, his touch feather–light but intentional. "No strings. Just you and me. Can I do that?"

She didn't answer, but she didn't pull away either. That was all the permission he needed.

Mark guided her to the edge of the bed, his hands sweeping her stomach. "I've missed this," he murmured, kneeling before her, his hands resting on her knees as he spread them apart. He looked up at her, his expression unreadable. "You. Every part of you."

Amy swallowed hard, she tried to speak, but no words came. Mark took her silence as an invitation, leaning in to kiss her thigh through the fabric of her leggings, his lips lingering, his breath was hot as he pulled both garments down.

"You deserve to feel everything," his voice was thick, "No distractions. No doubts. Just us."

Tonight, will be the thing she remembers. Not the threats, not the lies. Just this. His thoughts curated every move.

Mark made it a point to linger, drawing soft gasps and quiet whimpers from her as his tongue explored her. He spoke between each kiss, each touch. "You're perfect." A kiss. "I don't deserve you." Another touch, reverent and slow. "But I'll spend the rest of my life trying to."

Amy's body responded to him in ways that made Mark's chest swell with triumph. She was his again, if only in this moment. But as she reached for him, he took her wrists gently, pinning them above her head.

"Not tonight," he paused, "Tonight is about you."

She looked at him, startled, her breath uneven. "Mark…"

"You're so perfect like this," he whispered, his tone laced with awe. He lifted his head as he met her gaze. "Do you even know how much you mean to me?" His hands slid to her hips, steadying her as he leaned in closer. "Let me show you."

This wasn't just seduction, it was strategy. Mark knew

exactly where to touch her, how to move, what words to say. His lips found the softest part of her belly, just below her navel, and he pressed a kiss there, lingering long enough to make her tears well. "Every part of you," he vowed, "I love every part of you."

Amy felt weightless under Mark's touch, his words sinking into her like anchors. It wasn't just the way he touched her; though the deliberate press of his fingers on her, and the slow drag of his lips across her skin felt like nothing she'd ever experienced before. It was the way he looked at her, as though she was the only thing that mattered. The way his voice cracked just enough to sound sincere.

Her body arched into his hands and mouth; every nerve alive with sensation. She wanted to drown in it, to believe the promises he whispered. But as his hands explored her, her thoughts stirred again. *Why does this feel so perfect now?*

Mark's hands moved with intent, every touch a whispered promise, as he traced the curve of Amy's breasts, of her stomach. His fingers lingered just enough to make her breath catch. *I've got her.* Mark's thoughts churned beneath the surface, even as he murmured words of devotion. *This is what she needs. This is what keeps her tied to me.*

She felt it, the patience and emotion he rarely showed. It wasn't just desire. It was worship, as though he were memorizing her, reclaiming her inch by inch.

Mark silenced any doubt with his gaze. Dark and unwavering, it pinned her in place, holding her in a space that felt like coming home. "You don't even realize, do you?" he murmured, his lips brushing against the shell of her ear as he shifted to his knees, his legs bracketing her hips. His breath was warm against her skin.

"How much I need you." He entered her slowly, angling his hips against hers.

Amy's fingers clawed at his shoulder blades. It hurt. She hadn't had sex in months, the feeling of him sliding into her gave her a wave of pleasure, and anxiety. The tension in her body began melting under the weight of his body and his words. She wanted to believe him, to let herself fall into the safety he was offering. Her mind fought to keep up, but Mark's lips traced down her collarbone, and suddenly, thinking felt impossible. His touch was disarming, each kiss and thrust crafted to unravel her piece by piece.

Mark felt the moment Amy gave in, her body yielding beneath his. It wasn't just submission, it was trust, the kind he'd lost and was determined to regain. *You'll never question me again, not after tonight.* He dragged his lips lower, taking his time, his hands following the path his mouth had traced. Every flicker of her breathless response fed his resolve.

Mark's lips returned to hers, soft but insistent, and the question dissolved in the heat of the kiss. "You're everything to me," his words were thick with emotion, "everything, Amy, I'm sorry."

She didn't answer, not with words. Instead, she kissed him back, hard enough to silence whatever doubts still lingered. In that moment, he was hers. And she was his. Completely.

As Amy relaxed beneath him, Mark's mind shifted. He studied the way her body reacted to his touch, the way her breathing quickened and softened in rhythm with his movements.

When she finally shattered, her cries muffled against his shoulder, Mark held her tightly, cradling her as though she were the most precious thing in the world. He brushed his lips against her temple, "I'll never let you go, Amy. Never."

She didn't hear the undercurrent in his words, the subtle possessiveness that seeped into his tone. But it was there, laced with the kind of finality that made his promises feel less like declarations and more like bindings.

You'll stay, Amy. You always stay. The thought alone made him come, and he pressed as far into her as he could, making her cry out his name as her muscles tightened around him, she finally surrendered completely, her body trembling. His final kiss possessed her, a kiss that made her believe this was real.

And for a moment, maybe it was.

△△△

The Marriott Marquis lobby seemed alive with grandeur, its towering atrium reaching endlessly upward, lit by the soft glow of suspended chandeliers. But tonight, the space carried something more, something intangible and haunting. David Kushner's voice spilled through the air like a whispered confession, *Skin and Bones* wrapping the room in its melodic agony. Each note seemed to echo off the polished marble floors, swelling in the vastness and weaving a spell over everyone within earshot.

Amy moved beside Mark, the deep crimson of her dress slicing through the muted elegance like a heartbeat. It clung to her every curve, accentuating her bump, a bold declaration of both vulnerability and power. Her heels clicked softly against the marble, a rhythmic counterpoint to the music.

Mark's hand remained firmly on the small of her back, his touch possessive yet reverent, like she was both a prize and a fragile treasure. He leaned in close, his lips brushing the shell of her ear as they walked. "Every man in this room is going to hate me tonight," his voice pulsed through her.

Her laugh was quiet, almost swallowed by the haunting refrain of the song. "Why is that?" she asked, though the answer already burned in his gaze.

"Because I'm the one holding you," his words weaved seamlessly into the aching beauty of the lyrics. His hand slid from her back to her waist, pulling her just a fraction closer as if to prove his point.

The music swelled as they reached the center of the lobby, its lyrics cutting through the air with raw vulnerability. Amy's steps faltered for a moment, caught in the gravity of it all, the song, the space, and the man who held her so tightly she could hardly tell where his grip ended and her own longing began.

"You okay?" Mark asked, his brow furrowing slightly as he tilted her face toward his with a gentle touch.

"Yeah," she whispered. Her gaze flicked toward the glowing ballroom doors ahead, then back to him. "It's just... this feels like a dream."

Mark's smile was small but sure, his confidence grounding her. "If it is," brushing his thumb over her hand, "I'm never waking up."

The melody lingered in the air as they reached the gilded ballroom doors, each note resonating in Amy's chest like a second heartbeat. Mark leaned in again, his lips finding her temple in a lingering kiss that felt more like a promise than an affection. For a moment, she let herself believe it, that this spell he had cast wasn't a trap, but a new beginning.

And as the doors opened, bathing them in the warm glow of the waiting crowd, the music faded into the background, leaving behind its haunting imprint. *Skin and bones*, she felt stripped down to hers, yet Mark's presence made her feel whole.

Guests mingled amongst the auditorium as they waited for Mark's presentation to begin.

The event was everything he'd wanted. Hosted in a historic venue in Manhattan, every detail gleamed with the kind of understated elegance that made people lean in and admire. Glasses clinked, laughter filled the air, and attendees whispered as they took their seats. It was an audience filled with journalists, literary figures, and influencers who would each hang on his every word.

Amy could feel her own unease mounting as she navigated the crowd, before taking her place by his side, as he pressed a kiss to her forehead. They walked hand in hand to the carpeted entrance, where a photo backdrop of his book launch stood, with a professional photographer ready to take shots. Mark positioned himself adjacent to her, tilting her hips toward his as if to hide her bump, and then he did something she didn't expect, he shifted behind her, placing his hands on her stomach, his palms accentuating her pregnancy as the camera flashed. Amy swallowed hard, pressing a smile to her lips as the flashes blurred her vision.

The launch party hummed with the low chatter of journalists and influencers. Amy sat in the front row, trying to steady her breath, though her chest felt too tight. Her emotions had been so volatile today, and it suddenly caught up to her.

"Mark's about to speak," She looked up to see his agent, Kaitlyn, standing at the edge of the row, clipboard in hand. Her face was all business, a practiced smile just barely covering the sharpness in her gaze.

"Hey, Amy. Can I talk to you and Mark before we start?" she asked, head turning to where Mark was mingling with a group of guests.

Amy nodded, "Of Course."

Kaitlyn grasped her hand. "Congratulations, Amy. You look amazing."

Amy swallowed hard. It made sense for Mark to tell her, but it felt invasive. "Thanks."

She followed Kaitlyn to the corner of the auditorium near the stage entrance, and Mark caught up to them. Kaitlyn smiled as she handed Mark a thick envelope.

"Congratulations, Mark! First off, you've been nominated for the *Ambies* and *iHeart Radio Podcast Awards*. It's huge–the recognition from the industry is well deserved. Your last episode really resonated with people." She paused, waiting for him to react. Mark's lips pressed into a thin smile, as he opened the envelope.

Kaitlyn continued, "And also, big news– I have already told Mark about it, But Amy, *Parenthood Magazine* wants to do an interview. They're eager to feature you two in a special article on relationships and pregnancy. They'd love to know your thoughts on the importance of support in these early stages, and your struggles with infertility, what got you to this point. I'm sure it'll be a huge boost to your image, Mark."

Amy froze, her stomach knotting at the words. *Support?* Her skin prickled, and she felt the weight of his hand on her stomach earlier, the flashes from the camera burning into her memory. That shift, so subtle, was calculated. *He's using this. He's using me.* Her body went cold.

She glanced up at Mark, searching for some sign of self-awareness, some glimmer of guilt, but all she found was that same polished, perfect expression—the one he wore for everyone else. Her muscles tightened with the effort of keeping her composure, her mind racing.

Before she could say anything, Kaitlyn went on, "And, Mark, you've also been sent a platinum *YouTube* plaque for your channel's subscriber milestone."

Amy barely heard the last part. The words blurred as her thoughts collided. *A plaque for... what? For all the people he's deceiving with his perfect little narrative?* Her lips parted, but nothing came out. She wanted to scream, to slap the smile off his face, but the weight of his presence, of his control, suffocated her.

Mark gave Kaitlyn a terse nod, his hands casually slipping into his pockets, his gaze shifting back to the crowd. "Thanks, Kaitlyn. Appreciate it." He acknowledged Amy with a kiss, is hand lingering on her stomach. *Or was it just a demand for a reaction?*

Kaitlyn's smile lingered as she stepped back. "Alright, show time. I'll set up the details for the magazine interview and the awards ceremony next week."

Mark didn't even acknowledge her departure, his focus already on his next conversation. Amy, feeling the heavy weight of the moment, slowly turned her back, retreating to the edge of the room. She needed air, space—away from him. Away from this world he had so carefully crafted.

Her fingers gripped her dress, the fabric cool against her skin. *Everything is a performance for him. And I'm just a part of the script. A pawn in his perfect narrative, or does he really mean it?* The lump in her throat grew as she fought the urge to run from the conflict that was burning a hole into her chest. She sat down in the front row, her attention intensely focused on Mark as he readied himself to begin.

The crowd settled into an eager silence as Mark moved to the podium, book in hand, the pages carefully held between his fingers like an offering. With his refined, confident posture, he seemed to know exactly what they wanted from him. The lighting caught his features in a flattering way, amplifying his carefully curated image; suave, introspective, and charismatic. Amy could feel the attention of every woman in the room shifting toward him.

Mark opened to a marked passage, cleared his throat. He knew precisely which words would resonate, which lines would be quoted and remembered.

"In my field," he started, drawing out each word, "We aim to understand the depths of human experience, the complex motivations that drive us, and the hidden desires that often lead us astray. But the most challenging part isn't the research itself, or even the writing." He paused, glancing at his captivated audience. "It's the reflection. Seeing the truth of ourselves in the shadows of our subjects, finding echoes of our own flaws, our vulnerabilities, in the lives we analyze."

A soft murmur moved through the crowd. Amy watched as Mark shifted his stance, letting his gaze sweep over the room as if he were speaking to each person individually. The energy felt intimate, magnetic, calculated.

He continued, reading with a precision that Amy knew was no accident. "Sometimes, we come face to face with aspects of ourselves we'd rather forget. But to do the work well, to be honest about the human condition, we must be willing to stare into that mirror without blinking. To ask ourselves, what drives us? What are we truly capable of?"

A few women near the front leaned in with a fascination that bordered on awe. It was the kind of attention Mark thrived on, a subtle power he wielded with ease. Amy could feel the tension tighten within her; a reminder of the Mark she knew versus the version he was selling now.

"Love is not a sanctuary," Mark echoed, rich and measured as he read aloud, "It is a battlefield, a place where vulnerability becomes a weapon, and trust is the very thing that can destroy us. In the beginning, we are drawn to one another by an invisible thread, a shared need, a deep-seated craving for something we cannot name. It's the magnetism of our weaknesses, the pull of our own unspoken desires that keeps us tangled in each other's lives. But here's the truth we rarely speak: It's the lie we choose to believe that keeps us in the game."

Mark paused, his gaze drifting over the room, his words hanging in the air like smoke.

"We think we control the narrative. We think we choose who we love, who we trust. But love, in its rawest form, is nothing more than a negotiation. We make bargains, sacrifices, and sometimes," He took a sip of water. "Sometimes, we offer our very soul in exchange for affection that isn't even ours to claim. Love thrives in the shadows of manipulation, in the spaces between what's spoken and what's felt. To love is to give power away, to bend the narrative until it becomes something darker, something more dangerous."

He let the words settle, his breath slowing, his chest rising with the weight of what he had just revealed. The room was silent, the energy thick. He could feel it, the tension, the pull of his own words twisting in the air, wrapping around everyone present.

"The truth is," Mark's cadence now softer, "we all love because we want to be loved. But somewhere along the way, we lose sight of the line between affection and control. We are all desperate to write our own stories, to play the hero, the victim, the lover, the betrayer. But the most powerful love is the one we can manipulate, the one we can shape with our hands, our words, our desires. It is not the love that chooses us–it is the love we choose to create."

His gaze flickered toward Kaitlyn, who stood across the room, her arms crossed, her lips pressed tightly together. For a moment, something unspoken passed between them, a recognition, a challenge. He knew exactly how his words had landed.

"What happens then?" he asked, "What happens when you see the truth behind the mask? When you realize that love was never about connection, but about the control you thought you had? And when that illusion breaks, when the narrative slips out of your hands... that's when you discover what you're truly capable of."

Mark let the last sentence hang in the air, its implications sharp and cutting, and then he closed the book with a snap.

As he finished the excerpt, Mark looked up, his attention briefly catching Amy's in the crowd. For a second, there was something sharp in his gaze, something unspoken but unmistakably pointed. Then, with a practiced smile, he acknowledged the room's applause.

When questioning opened, a man rose among the sea of faces. Amy froze, her gaze landing on Callum, seated toward the front row, his demeanor steady, challenging. The air seemed to thin as he spoke.

"You talk about betrayal and trust," Callum's voice carried through the crowd, "Would you say that taking control of the narrative is its own kind of power? How would you do the work, when *you* cannot see your own flaws?"

Mark's smile faltered for the briefest moment before sliding back into place. *What a prick. You're out of your depth.*

He offered a practiced smile, as if deflecting the barb with grace. "I think anyone who's been through hardship understands the importance of owning their story," he replied, his tone warm but guarded. "It's not about power, it's about survival."

Callum leaned back in his chair. *Survival? Is that what you tell yourself? Fucking dick.* He wanted to grill him, to lay every lie on the table for all to see, but the next question was asked, and Mark pivoted.

As the event wrapped up, Mark moved to greet admirers, his agent hovering nearby. Amy lingered near the refreshments, avoiding the crowd but watching Mark with a quiet intensity.

Callum stayed seated, biding his time. He watched as Mark leaned close to a guest to take another picture. His charm was seamless, but Callum saw the cracks. *He thrives on this. Strip it away, and what's left? A piece of shit without a compass.*

Amy took it all in, glancing around the lavish hall while Mark signed books. Despite the polished space and carefully placed flowers, the air felt thick, almost stifling. She knew this launch meant everything to Mark, yet the unease that had been building within her all day clung even tighter here, each elegant detail somehow magnifying the tension beneath.

Callum appeared, moving toward the line with a calm that only sharpened the restlessness in Amy's chest. He watched Mark, then stepped forward when it was his turn.

Mark's polite smile faltered when he recognized Callum from the audience. But Callum didn't give him time to react. He leaned close, lowering his voice so that only Mark could catch the words.

"Congratulations, you've certainly crafted a compelling story. Though, it's hard to tell which parts are inspired by real life. Do you think anyone will be able to?"

Mark's smile returned, but there was a stiffness to it, a recognition of all that was wrong in this moment. And yet, he did nothing. He stayed where he was, eyes locked on Callum.

Amy, who was standing near the table watched Callum leaning slightly forward, his presence unmistakably tense.

"That's a good question." Mark twisted the cap off the pen. "Who do I make the book out to?"

Callum placed his hands on the table, his knuckles cracking against the wood.

"Josephine." He watched Mark's focus shift toward him, the pen gliding smoothly across the page. Callum could almost sense the weight of his thoughts, the icy resolve radiating from him.

Callum stiffened, the prickle of awareness crawling over his skin as his eyes met Amy's for a fraction of a second. *Shit. How much had she heard?* The air between them thickened, the tension coiling tighter. Mark broke first, turning his attention to the next guest in line. "Next," his tone clipped.

Callum straightened, stepping back slowly. He tilted his head, gesturing for her to follow. She looked away quickly, noting Mark's absorbed state, and exhaled, walking toward him as he tentatively walked away from the crowd, and out of Mark's orbit.

Moments later, Amy found herself at Callum's side, his presence both grounding and unsettling. She took a sip of her sparkling water, her gaze flickering nervously around the room before settling on him.

"How'd you like the event?" she asked.

Callum paused before answering. "Honestly? I wanted to see him in his element. I wanted to understand what makes someone like him tick."

Her brow furrowed. "Why would you care about that?"

He didn't answer right away. Instead, he motioned toward a quieter corner of the room, a hallway that led toward a more isolated part of the hotel. "Come with me for a second."

Amy hesitated, but something in his expression made her follow. They moved through the crowd, the hum of conversation fading as they slipped away. When they reached a quieter spot,

Callum turned to face her.

Callum closed the door behind him. "We need to talk." The firmness in his tone startled even him.

Amy straightened, bracing herself. "Is this about the wedding? I already said I'd–"

"No, it's not about that," he interrupted as he paced. "It's about Mark."

Her shoulders stiffened, but she didn't respond, her fingers tightening around the edge of the cocktail table.

"I don't know how to say this," Callum admitted, "I've been sitting on it for weeks, trying to figure out if it's even my place. But I can't keep quiet. Not when I see what he's doing to you."

Amy's lips parted, then closed; her silence only encouraged him to continue.

"The night of Lincoln's event, I saw him." He stopped pacing and turned to face her fully, his jaw tight. "I saw him with a woman. They went into the honeymoon suite together. I didn't think much of it at first, but I walked around, checked the lot, and before he pulled the curtains, I saw enough to know what was going on."

Amy looked down, "You're sure it was him?"

"Amy, I wouldn't be standing here if I wasn't," his tone was softer now, almost pleading. "I know it's not my business. I was going to tell you, and then you were pregnant, and I– I know I'm walking a fine line here, but you deserve to know. You deserve better than this."

"Better?" She finally met his gaze. "I already know, Callum. At least, I thought I did. He swore it was just one time. A mistake. And like a fool, I believed him."

Callum took a tentative step closer, his hands hanging at his sides, unsure if he should reach for her or keep his distance.

"He's lying to you, hiding behind excuses because he's a coward. And you're stuck trying to make sense of his mess while carrying his child."

Amy flinched at his words, her hand instinctively going to her stomach. She shook her head, biting back tears. "Don't. Don't make this about the baby. I've waited years for this."

Callum's jaw clenched, his emotions warring inside him. "And you think staying with him is the way to do that? Amy, he's not going to change. He doesn't deserve you or your loyalty."

Her cheeks flushed with anger, but there was pain there too. "You think I don't know that? You think I haven't told myself the same thing over and over? But it's not just about me anymore." She looked away, her chest heaving as she struggled to keep herself together.

Callum's expression softened, unable to hold back anymore. "I'm not saying this because I want to hurt you. I'm saying this because I care about you, Ames. Because since we met, I've watched you, seen how strong you are, how you carry the weight of everything he's thrown at you, and I–" He stopped, swallowing hard. "You shouldn't have to do this alone. You don't deserve to be treated like you're second to anything. You and that baby deserve someone who will fight for you."

Amy stared at him, her lips trembling. "Callum... I appreciate what you're trying to do, but you don't understand. Mark, I can't–I can't drag you into this."

"You're not dragging me into anything," he shifted toward her, taking her hand. "I'm here because I want to be. Because I can't just stand by and watch you go through this. You don't have to trust me completely, but at least trust me enough to let me help."

Callum's vulnerability caught her off guard. Amy felt the walls she'd carefully built around herself start to crack. "You don't know what you're offering," she whispered, "This isn't your fight."

He smiled faintly, though there was sadness in his expression. "Maybe not. But that doesn't mean I'm going anywhere. And for what it's worth, I'm not just doing this because it's the right thing. I'm doing this because I care about you, Ames, both of you. "You don't need to say anything, just know that you're not alone in this. Whatever happens, I'm here."

She nodded slowly, her tears finally spilling over. For the first time in months, she felt like she wasn't drowning. She looked up at him, and something in his gaze made her gulp, a protectiveness, a steadiness she didn't realize she needed until now.

"I'm sorry, I can't. Callum, we work together. You're a good friend, please let me have that."

She raised a hand to touch him, then let it drop.

"I have to go, good night, I'll see you Monday. Thank you." she forced a smile before returning to the gala.

△△△

Amy stood in the kitchen, her fingers tracing the edge of the counter, her thoughts a chaotic storm. The condo was too quiet, the kind of silence that made every breath feel heavier. She didn't turn when she heard the door open, nor when Mark's footsteps crossed the room behind her. She'd hailed a cab when she was no longer needed, using Maslow as an excuse to get out of there.

"Long day," He dropped his jacket onto the back of a chair and loosened his tie, his movements unhurried. "You should be in bed."

She turned slowly, her arms crossed. "We need to talk."

Mark's hand paused on his tie, his brows narrowing slightly before his expression softened into a practiced smile. "It's late, Amy. Can it wait until morning?"

"No," she said firmly, "I need answers, Mark. And I need them now."

He sighed, stepping toward her with exaggerated patience. "If this is about the past–"

"It's not just the past!" she snapped, cutting him off. Her hands trembled, but she kept them pressed against her arms. "How long, Mark? How long have you been lying to me?"

His jaw tightened, the mask of calm slipping for the briefest moment before he caught it. "I told you," He replied, "It was one mistake. A single lapse in judgment."

She shook her head, her throat tightening with anger. "Don't insult me by pretending it was one time. I know better now. And I know you've been using me, for your career, your image, your perfect little narrative."

Mark's eyes darkened, and he leaned against the counter, crossing his arms as he tilted his head. "What exactly is it you think you know, Amy? Because it sounds like you're letting your emotions get the better of you." He tipped the whiskey bottle into a glass, pouring himself two fingers worth.

The dismissal hit like a slap, but she didn't back down. "I know you don't care about me," she seethed, "You care about what I bring to you. The baby. The story. The perfect picture of redemption and resilience. That's all this has ever been to you, hasn't it?"

His lips curled into a faint smile. "And why shouldn't it be? Do you have any idea what we've been through together? What we've built?" He closed the gap between them, his voice softening as if he were reasoning with a child. "You're looking for problems where there aren't any, Amy. You need to stop sabotaging yourself."

"Sabotaging myself?" she repeated, her voice rising. "You've been sleeping with someone else for God knows how long while parading me around as your devoted wife. You didn't want this baby until you realized what it could do for your career. And now you want me to just play along? Pretend everything is fine for the cameras?"

"Yes," his tone was devoid of warmth. "Because that's what's best for all of us. For the family. For the future. You're not thinking clearly, Amy."

She took a step back, her stomach twisting as his words sank in. "You're unbelievable."

Mark straightened, his face hardening. "You need to understand something. Everything I've done, I've done for us. For you. Without me, you'd still be the woman everyone pitied. The one who couldn't give her husband a child. I gave you purpose. I gave you a chance to matter."

Her breath caught. "You don't get to decide my worth," she swallowed hard.

He tilted his head. "Don't I? Think about it, Amy. Everything you have, everything you've become, it's because of me. And now, you want to throw it all away because of some misguided need to stand on your own? It's laughable."

Her vision blurred with tears, but she blinked them back. "I can't do this anymore."

Mark's expression darkened, and he leaned in close. "Oh, you'll do it. You'll smile for the cameras. You'll say exactly what needs to be said. Because if you don't, I will destroy you. Do you understand me?"

She froze, her heart pounding so loudly she thought it might break free from her chest.

"You'll be the one they pity again. The one who couldn't keep her family together, the one who sabotaged her own marriage, her husband's trust, her own morality for something that wasn't even guaranteed, that wasn't medically approved in the first place. The unstable woman who made herself the villain in her own story. I'll make this all a positive for myself, my career. So, if I were you, I'd think very carefully about what you say and do next." He pressed a kiss to her cheek. "Love me, Amy, love me the way you always have, and I will give you the world." He took a measured step toward her, "But know, that it will always be on my terms."

NINETEEN

Callum stood near the entrance to the tasting room, he shifted his hair away from his eyes as he leaned over, his attention divided between his phone and a stack of papers resting on the counter.

Amy stepped inside, the chill of the autumn morning still clinging to her cheeks. She paused for a moment, taking in the warm ambiance before her gaze landed on Callum. His head lifted, his expression softening when he met her gaze.

He tilted his head, scanning her from head to toe. "Good morning, Ames. You're glowing today. No, really, like, annoyingly radiant. It's almost offensive."

Amy laughed, shaking her head. "Offensive, huh? That's one I haven't heard yet. I'm heading out for my anatomy scan. Picking up Char."

His heart jumped into his throat. *She isn't wearing her ring.* "Big day," Callum set the clipboard aside. His tone shifted slightly, the humor still there but layered with sincerity. "Excited?"

Amy glanced down, fiddling with the cap of her water bottle. "Nervous. But yeah, excited too, I guess."

He leaned back against the counter, flexing his arms as he crossed them. "You team blue or team pink?"

"I'm team yellow, actually. I don't think I want to find out."

"Old fashioned, I like it. Well, whatever happens, you let me know if I need to order pink or blue decorations for your shower. I have a very good eye for these things."

She raised an eyebrow, amused. "Do you, now?"

"Absolutely. Streamers, balloons... Maybe a cake shaped like a baby bottle. Really leaning into the theme."

Amy snorted, shaking her head as she twisted off the bottle cap and took a sip. "Wow, special. You should probably stick to operations management."

"Fine," Callum conceded, smirking. "We'll keep it classy. But seriously, Ames, let me know how it goes, okay?"

The warmth in his tone settled over her like the sunlight streaking through the room. "I will," she replied softly, her grip tightening on the bottle.

"Charlotte's upstairs," he added, gesturing toward the wide wooden staircase. "She's been asking about you all morning. Oh, and before you go–" He reached for a stack of papers on the counter, spreading them out. "Tell me if this layout makes sense for the next event. The bride's plan is making me rethink my career choices."

Amy leaned over the counter, the scent of coffee mingling with the faint cedar from Callum's cologne. She scanned the diagram, her brow furrowing. "Move these tables closer to the bar, people always cluster there anyway. And put the desserts near the windows so the guests can linger. That way, they're out of the servers' way."

Callum arched an eyebrow. "Why didn't I think of that?"

"Because you're not me," she added, flashing him a grin.

"Don't I *know* this." He tapped the papers against the counter, his smirk softening into something more genuine. "Good luck, Ames. You've got this."

Her smile faltered, but only for a moment. "Thanks, Callum." She turned toward the stairs, her heart lighter despite her nerves.

As she disappeared up the staircase, Callum leaned against the counter, his gaze lingering on the empty space she'd left behind. The room buzzed around him, but for a moment, all he could hear was the faint echo of her laugh.

Amy got into the driver's seat, slipping the seatbelt across her body as she readied herself for the appointment.

"So, are you ready? I'm so excited. The anatomy scan is always the one where the baby actually looks like a tiny human." Charlotte's voice was bright, but her gaze flicked toward Amy, sensing her hesitation. Here, I was going to go a gender reveal thing, but I can't hold it in anymore. We had our twenty week ultrasound, but the baby had their legs closed, so I had to go for another scan." She handed her the photo. "It's a boy."

Amy took the photo in her hand, beaming. "Awe, one of each, this is amazing! Congratulations. This is awesome, now I can really start working on your shower."

Charlotte beamed. "I'm so excited to see what you're having. I feel so bad that Mark had to miss this. Why didn't you just reschedule?"

Amy managed a smile, but it quickly dissolved into a shaky breath. "Mark isn't away because of work…" She glanced at Charlotte, her words barely audible. "I'm going to do this on my own."

Charlotte tilted her head, her brows knitting together as she studied Amy. "What do you mean?"

Amy's hands clenched the steering wheel, her knuckles white as the leather gave beneath her fingers. "Mark's been having an affair."

The words hung in the air, sharp and unrelenting, shattering the fragile calm between them.

"What?" Charlotte's reaction was sharper than she intended, her face a mixture of shock and anger.

Amy nodded, tears slipping free despite her best efforts to hold them back. "I walked in on them. In his office. It was a few months ago. He swore it was just one time, and then I got pregnant, and that put so much strain on us. He told me he didn't want kids anymore." She inhaled shakily. "But then he changed. He asked me to stay with him in the city. He talked about starting over, having this baby, and…" Her voice broke as the tears came faster. "We had sex. And he was so gentle, so… different. For one night, I believed every word. He made me feel like I was the only person in his world, and I let myself believe it."

Charlotte reached over, squeezing her arm. "Amy…"

Amy shook her head. "And then at his event, Callum told me he saw Mark with another woman. At the mill, in the honeymoon suite. I knew it was true. I could smell her perfume on him when he asked me to dance."

Charlotte shook her head, her anger rising. "Amy, that's not on you. That's on him."

"It is on *me*," Amy scoffed bitterly. "*I* pushed him. I made him want something he didn't."

"Stop it." Charlotte turned to face her fully. "Do you hear yourself? You didn't make him cheat, Amy. He made that choice, not you. Don't let him make you carry the weight of his mistakes."

The car pulled into the parking space, and Amy cut the engine. Her hands trembled as she reached for her purse, her chest tightening with a mix of shame and sadness.

"I don't know how to move forward." she whispered. "I have feelings for Callum. I shouldn't, but I do. And I still love Mark, even though I shouldn't. I don't know how to make sense of any of this."

"Holy shit, Callum? Really? You haven't…" She raised an eyebrow.

"Fuck you, *no* I haven't." She slapped her shoulder, knowing she was trying to cheer her up.

"Well too bad, because he's fucking hot, and it would serve Mark right." Charlotte unbuckled her seatbelt and stepped out of the car, circling to Amy's side before she could open the door. She pulled her into a tight hug. "It's okay to not have all the answers right now. You're allowed to feel messy, to feel everything. But you don't have to make any decisions today. Just take care of yourself and the baby, one step at a time."

Amy let herself sink into Charlotte's embrace, her tears soaking into Charlotte's shoulder.

When they finally checked in, Amy was ushered back to one of the suites. Charlotte settled into the chair near the bed, "Make sure you take off your pants, they always get the gel everywhere."

"Don't I know it, they use more lube than a porno." They both laughed.

"You're stronger than you think, you know. No matter what happens, I'm here. We'll figure this out together."

Amy met Charlotte's gaze. For the first time in weeks, she let herself feel the smallest flicker of hope. "That's because you're an amazing person."

"Well, duh. And an amazing aunt, this baby is so loved."

Amy nodded as she looked around the room, trying to ground herself.

The ultrasound suite was a blend of clinical precision and comforting touches. Soft, pastel-colored walls were adorned with framed black-and-white photos of various stages of embryonic development. A state-of-the-art ultrasound machine stood beside the large examination chair, which was covered in soft, sanitized padding.

Megan, the technician, entered, her bright demeanor a balm against the tension. "Good afternoon, Amy. Ready to see your little one?"

Amy nodded; her throat tight. "Yes, can't wait." She squeezed Charlotte's hand so hard; her fingers were starting to tingle.

Megan moved efficiently, prepping the equipment and spreading the warm gel across Amy's lower abdomen. Amy flinched slightly.

The soft hum of the machine hummed through the stillness of the room. Megan adjusted the wand, and the screen came to life with a flickering grayscale image.

Amy nodded weakly; her throat too dry to speak. She settled onto the table, the crinkle of paper beneath her loud in the stillness.

The gel was warm, but still, she shivered as the probe pressed against her abdomen. The technician's brow furrowed slightly, her movements slowing as she adjusted the machine.

Seconds stretched into an eternity.

Amy's heart raced, her chest tightening as she watched the technician leave the room without a word. The silence she left behind was suffocating, each second stretching unbearably long.

Her stomach twisted, nausea rising sharp and fast. Panic clawed at her throat, her pulse pounding in her ears. She felt Charlotte shift beside her, the weight of her presence suddenly unbearable.

"I'm going to be sick," Amy blurted out. She clutched the sheet draped across her lap, trying to keep her composure. "Charlotte, please go."

Charlotte leaned closer, her tone soft and steady. "Amy, it's okay. I'm here. You don't have to go through this alone."

"No, Char." Amy's voice cracked as she turned to face her friend. "Please. Just wait outside."

"I'm not leaving you like this." Charlotte's brows knitted together, her concern evident. "You're scaring me. Whatever's going on, we can handle it together."

"Together?" Amy snapped, the word a bitter echo on her tongue. Her hands fisted the sheet, her body trembling. "You don't understand, Charlotte! You can't. Look at you. You're glowing and perfect and *pregnant*."

The last word came out like a slap, and Charlotte froze.

Amy's chest heaved as the words kept spilling, sharp and relentless. "You're ten weeks ahead of me. Ten weeks. You already have the answers, your pregnancy is viable. You've already felt your baby kick. You get to walk into every appointment and see nothing but smiles and hear everything is *fine*, and I'm sitting here waiting for the other shoe to drop!" she was hyperventilating. "YOUR baby will live, and mine." She couldn't breathe.

Charlotte's hand went to her belly reflexively, her mouth opening and closing as she tried to find the right words. "Amy, honey–"

"Just go!" Amy's voice broke, the sound cutting and raw. Tears streaked her face as she looked away, ashamed of the resentment boiling under her grief. "I can't do this with you here. Please, just leave me alone."

Charlotte hesitated, her own eyes glistening. She reached out, then pulled back, unsure if her touch would soothe or shatter. "Okay, I'll be right outside."

The door closed behind her, and the silence came rushing back.

Amy collapsed against the exam table, her head in her hands. Her whole body shook as sobs wracked through her. She hated herself for snapping, for pushing Charlotte away, but she couldn't stop the crushing weight of it all.

He's not going to live. He's not going to be okay.

The thought hit her like a blow to the chest, stealing what little air she had left. Her hand trembled as it moved to her stomach, her fingers barely brushing the curve there.

When the doctor finally entered, his expression grim, Amy didn't even flinch. She had been preparing for this moment from the second the technician left the room, but no amount of bracing could make the words hurt any less.

The doctor nodded, placing the probe back on her stomach. "I'm sorry Mrs. Rodriguez, but there is no heartbeat."

The words didn't register at first, floating in the air like a foreign language. When they finally hit, they came with the force that knocked the wind out of her and the weight of the world seemed to press down on her chest.

"No," she whispered, shaking her head. "That's not possible. I just... I just felt him move."

The doctor placed a hand on her shoulder. "I know this is hard to hear. But I need you to know that none of this is your fault. Sometimes these things happen, and we don't know why."

Tears streamed down her face as she clutched her stomach, a raw ache tearing through her.

"We need to address this soon. Your blood pressure is dangerously high, and it's putting your health at risk. You also have a hydropic placenta. There are cysts that have formed in the tissue, and with your blood pressure being as high as it is, there's a possibility your body is mirroring what is wrong with the baby. I recommend inducing labor through the hospital."

Inducing labor.

The words made her stomach churn, the finality of them suffocating. She nodded weakly, unable to form words.

"Is he a boy? I thought he was a boy." Her shattered sobs barely made the sentence audible.

The doctor nodded, squeezing her hand. "I'm so sorry Amy, I really am. I'll made a call to labor and delivery."

Once dressed, she met Charlotte in the hall. She couldn't look at Charlotte, who stood there stunned, unable to do much more than hold her hand. But the thought of Charlotte, pregnant, glowing, untouched by the unfairness of it all, ignited a spark of resentment and anger Amy hadn't anticipated.

Why her? Why always her?

Alone. She would do this alone.

Charlotte didn't say anything, she just pulled her into a hug.

"I need you to just drop me off," Amy replied. The words came out colder than she intended. "I can't have you in the room, Charlotte. Not when you get to keep your baby, and I have to say goodbye to mine."

Charlotte froze, the words stinging more than she could have anticipated. She took a step toward Amy but stopped, her face etched with confusion. "Amy, please, I'm so–"

"No, those words better not come out of your mouth." Amy interrupted. "He's dead, Charlotte. Please, just... go. This is something I have to do alone."

Charlotte didn't argue, didn't fight back. She swallowed hard. "I understand Amy, I do. Should I call–"

"No, I don't want him to know, are you fucking insane?" Amy clenched her fists at her sides, a wave of guilt rushing through her as Charlotte pulled her toward the car. The car ride was silent as Amy sat with her thoughts, a storm of anger and heartbreak churning inside her.

"I'll be right here, Amy. If you need me, I'm just six minutes away. I love–" But Amy slammed the car door and made her way to the labor and delivery entrance.

△△△

Charlotte's steps faltered as she entered The Riverview. Her face was pale, shoulders slumped as if she carried Amy's grief along with her own guilt. She started to cry.

Callum, leaning against a table immediately straightened.

His expression hardened. "What the hell happened?" he asked.

"She's in labor and delivery. The baby didn't make it." Her hand rested on her stomach, tears streaming down her face.

Charlotte froze, startled by his sharp tone. "She told me to leave," she paused. "She didn't want me there."

Callum moved toward her; his jaw tight. "And you just *left*?"

"She was adamant," Charlotte snapped, defensive now. "You don't understand, Callum. She—"

Callum's anger flared. "You should've stayed. Fought for her, no matter what she said."

"I know her better than you do!" Charlotte shot back, her voice rising. "You think she'd let anyone stay after everything she's been through? She needs space!"

Callum scoffed, "You don't get it. You don't know her at all." His gaze darkened. "You don't know what it's like to feel completely alone, to carry everything because no one gives a damn. That's Amy. That's what she's been doing for years."

Charlotte flinched. "And you do?"

Callum's gaze flicked to her. "Yes, I do, I love her."

Charlotte froze.

He swallowed hard, his tone a mix of guilt and regret. "I should've made her see it, made her know she's not alone."

"Callum..." But he cut her off, shaking his head.

"No," he reached for his jacket. "I'm done standing by while everyone fails her. You can sit here and wait for her call. I'm going to the hospital." He glanced at her. "Give me Amy's keys."

"What? Why?"

"Charlotte, just—" His frustration broke through, sharper now. "Listen for once." She threw him the keys.

"Wait, let me come with—" She started. He was out the door before Charlotte could stop him.

Charlotte's phone buzzed again, the notifications from Jack were rapid fires. She glanced at the screen: another photo of Mark kissing a woman, the headline reading:

Famous Relationship Guru Caught in the Act

Her stomach twisted as she quickly scanned the texts.

Jack: Holy shit, have you seen this?

Jack: Mark's in the news. With another woman.

Jack: How the hell is this not a bigger deal?

Before she could even respond, Lincoln appeared in the doorway. His eyes flicked to her phone, and he swallowed hard, stepping closer.

"I–I saw," he said, "I came as soon as I read it. We need to talk."

Charlotte stood still, her fingers ran cold, the expression on his face told her everything. "How long did you know about this?" She crossed her hands over her chest.

Lincoln took a deep breath, his gaze dropping to the floor for a moment before meeting hers. "I didn't want to tell you, Charlotte. I didn't know how to say it. It's so much more complicated than it seems."

She blinked. "What do you mean? How could you *not* tell me?"

His voice lowered as he shifted uncomfortably. "This goes deeper than you think." He hesitated, a conflicted expression crossing his face. "Mark and Josephine, they have a complicated history. They were together when they were young. Long before Amy. They were each other's first real love." He paused, weighing his words. "When she came back into his life, well, it stirred things up for him. I thought it was just once."

Charlotte's heart raced as she processed his words. "So, you knew? You knew about the affair? And you didn't tell me?" Her face was scarlet.

Lincoln's face softened with regret. "Amy also has a hand in this, their problems stem from Amy's decisions too. She needs to come clean with what's been going on, and I don't even think I have the right to share that with you, you need to speak with her about it. I feel like shit for not telling you, but it wasn't my place."

Her breath caught in her throat. "What the *hell* could Amy have done to deserve this Lincoln?"

Lincoln swallowed, pain flickering across his face. "Honey, I'm not excusing it. I don't condone what Mark's done. It wasn't just an affair. It was, it was *her*." He exhaled. "Mark and Josie were together when he was eighteen, but she was fifteen. He got her pregnant, and his dad found out. It was a big deal, a huge mess. Mark moved in with us for a few months afterward. Only I know this, Char, you cannot tell anyone."

"What? So, he has a baby with this woman?" she was seething.

"No, Mark's dad made her get an abortion, he nearly beat Mark to death that night." Lincoln's shoulders slumped. "I'm sorry. I really thought he would fix this. I didn't think it would go this far."

Charlotte felt the weight of his words, but it only made the anger burn harder. "You could've told me. You should've told me, Lincoln. I'm not *his* wife, and you're my husband." Charlotte sighed. "this is a lot to unpack, I need a minute." She squeezed her eyes shut. "Amy won't let me at the hospital, Callum just confessed his love for her, and–" she exhaled. "I need to sit down."

TWENTY

The elevator dinged softly, but Lincoln barely registered it. His pulse pounded in his ears as he stormed through the sleek corridor of Mark's office building. The receptionist glanced up, startled, but didn't say a word. One look at his expression, and she wisely stayed silent.

Mark was seated behind his massive desk, phone pressed to his ear, when Lincoln shoved the door open. The force sent it slamming against the wall, startling Mark enough to drop the receiver. His eyes darted up when he saw Lincoln.

"Do you have any idea what the hell you've done?" Lincoln seethed as he strode forward.

Mark stood slowly, adjusting the cuffs of his shirt with maddening nonchalance. "Hey man," he greeted evenly, "What's this about?"

"Don't play dumb with me, Mark. I'm not in the mood for your bullshit."

Mark leaned back against the desk, arms crossed. "You're going to have to be a bit more specific."

Lincoln didn't bother with a reply. He crossed the remaining space between and grabbed the front of Mark's shirt, shoving him hard against the edge of the desk. Papers scattered to the floor, but neither man looked at them.

"Josephine?" Lincoln growled, his face inches from Mark's. "What the hell were you thinking? You promised me, Mark. You swore you'd cut it off. There are multiple events photographed, it wasn't a onetime thing."

Mark shoved him back with a sharp movement, adjusting his shirt where Lincoln's grip had wrinkled it. "And what? You thought I'd just drop her? Like she didn't mean anything?"

Lincoln stared at him, disgust tightening his features. "You're married, Mark. You don't get to pull this 'poor me act' like you're some lovesick teenager. You had a choice, and you chose to blow up your life."

Mark's lips curled into a smirk. "Blow up my life? You mean Amy's life, don't you? Let's call it what it is. She's the one you're really here for."

"Don't." Lincoln shook his head. "You don't get to talk about her. You're fucking sitting here while—"

He cut Lincoln off. "Oh, but you can?" Mark shot back, stepping closer. "Let's not pretend this is about morality, Lincoln. You're pissed because I got her and you didn't. Because no matter what you did for her, she chose me. That's what's really eating at you, isn't it?"

Lincoln's fist collided with Mark's jaw before he even realized he'd swung. Mark stumbled back, catching himself on the desk, his hand flying to his face.

"She's in the fucking hospital, and you're sitting here, in your office, as if it doesn't matter, as if she doesn't matter. You're a spineless piece of shit."

"You son of a bitch," Mark snarled, straightening up. "You really think you're some kind of hero, don't you? Riding in here like the white knight, ready to defend poor Amy's honor. Newsflash, Lincoln. She's not so perfect. She didn't even tell me about the hospital, what the fuck are you talking about?"

Lincoln froze, his chest heaving.

Mark rubbed his jaw. "She didn't call me, when did it happen? What kind of woman hides something like that from her husband? What does that say about her?"

Lincoln's fury tangled with uncertainty. "She's in the hospital," his voice was raw. "She just lost your child."

Mark shook his head slowly, his expression shifting to something softer, almost pained. "You think I wouldn't want to be there?" He let the words hang in the air before continuing. "She didn't tell me. She's been... erratic lately. Shutting me out. The mood swings, the way she's been acting, God, I didn't even know... Do you know how that feels?"

Lincoln hesitated, his anger cracking under the weight of Mark's words.

"She's grieving, Mark. She just lost—"

Mark cut in, "She didn't give me a chance to grieve with her, to be there for her. She didn't trust me, Lincoln. She hasn't for months. I don't know how to fix this if she won't even let me in."

Mark's shoulders sagged, and he looked down, running a hand through his hair. "I'm not saying I'm perfect. God knows I've made mistakes. But Amy... she's not okay, Lincoln. And I've been doing everything I can to hold it together, for her, for us. Maybe you don't believe me, but I love her. I want to make this work."

Lincoln's jaw tightened, the doubt creeping in. "You think she's unstable?"

Mark sighed heavily, walking to the window. "I think she's going through something she won't talk about. And if I push too hard, it's only going to make it worse. You saw her after her dad died, she spiraled. It feels like we're back there again."

Lincoln said nothing, his fists were still clenched, but the fire in his eyes had dimmed. Mark turned back to him, meeting his gaze with a calculated vulnerability.

"I'm not your enemy, Lincoln. You think you're helping her, but the more people crowd her, the harder it is for her to cope. She needs time and space. And maybe, she needs me more than you realize."

Lincoln's face hardened. "You're going to fix this. You're

going to come clean to Amy, to the press, to everyone. And if you don't, I swear to God, I'll ruin you."

Mark waited until the footsteps faded before sitting at his desk. He picked up the scattered papers, his hands lingering on the photos of him and Josephine. The headlines were brutal, but he could spin them, just like he'd spun Lincoln. All it took was the right narrative.

He sat down slowly, smoothing the creases from his tie as he stared at the mess. His mind worked quickly, calculating. Josephine was already taking the brunt of the fallout, and if he played his cards right, Amy would too. The hospital would shield her for now, but once the press got wind of her silence about the baby, the narrative would shift.

He tapped his fingers against the desk, his smirk returning. He wouldn't go to the hospital, not yet. A public display of grief could be staged when it would serve him better. For now, there were fires to put out, alliances to manage, and blame to shift.

Mark leaned back, his smile sharp as he reached for his phone. Both women would fall before he did. He'd make sure of it.

TWENTY ONE

The woman at the window looked Amy over. "Ma'am, regular appointments are done in the OBGYN office across the street, this is labor and delivery."

"Yes, I'm very aware of what this place is. She pushed the paper toward the nurse. My doctor has called about my admission."

She read over the paper. "Oh my, I'm so sorry Mrs. Rodriguez, yes, right away. I need you to come back for vitals and we will get you changed. Do you have anyone here with you?"

Amy shook her head, inhaling as much air into her lungs as she could muster. She held her breath, trying desperately not to lose her shit. Once they had taken her vitals, Amy locked herself in the bathroom. The walls were painted a moody green, the soft ambient lighting casting shadows across the wall. She looked at herself in the mirror, tracing the firm roundness of her belly. She wanted to imprint this moment, trying to remember what it felt like, what she looked like. She couldn't bring herself to take a picture. She pulled her shirt over her head, the arctic chill of the air conditioner causing her to shiver, though the adrenaline was pumping so fast at this point, that every nerve ending was on fire.

The world around her blurred into a chaotic whirl of colors and sounds. As she settled on the bed, the curtains did little to drown out the sounds of women chatting about meeting their babies, of nurses asking if they were having a boy or a girl. She felt like punching her fist through the wall.

The student nurse arrived with her mentor, her face red,

tears streaming. Amy looked up at her. Jesus fucking Christ, I have to have this one with me? Feeling sorry and losing her shit even more than I am, Great.

The doctor came in and assessed her, he was tall with a gentle demeanor. He performed an ultrasound, noting that she had no amniotic fluid.

"Amy, we can do this one of two ways. We can give you a cervical dilation medication, its inserted into the cervix and will work to open and dilate the body so that you can deliver him naturally. The other option would be for me to take you to the Operating room." He sighed. "While it is your choice, With the operation, I will not be able to deliver the baby intact, so you will not be able to say goodbye." She felt numb, not truly being able to grasp the gravity of his words.

She shook her head. "No, he does not deserve that. I'll go through labor." She choked on each word.

"I'll try to make this as painless as possible. We can set you up with an epidural, and–"

"No, I already feel nothing. I want to experience this fully."

The doctor squeezed her hand. "I'm here, in whatever way you need, Amy. Truly."

△△△

Pain came in endless waves, each one more intense than the last. It felt like her entire body was on fire, each breath sending fresh agony through her chest and limbs. She couldn't pinpoint where it was coming from; her head throbbed, her stomach churned, and her lungs felt like they were being crushed. She tried to breathe slowly, but the sharp ache hit her again, fierce and unrelenting, radiating from everywhere and nowhere at once. Her head pounded with each heartbeat, her stomach twisting, her legs feeling heavy and numb as if caught under an unbearable weight.

She couldn't tell where the pain ended or began, only that it was everywhere, relentless, pulling her under. She could hear the distant sound of her own heartbeat on the monitors. In every birth situation, it would be her baby's heartbeat she would be hearing, but his heart was still, the cold reality of her situation settling in. She chose to do it without medication, she wanted to experience this, but the strength of the induction medication, coupled with laboring with no amniotic fluid, caused a ceaseless torment that left her gasping and crying out. The smell of antiseptic filled the air, mingling with the feeling of a gush of fluid. She was confused, the doctors had told her that he had no amniotic fluid, that the placenta was hydropic, meaning, it was filled with fluid filled cysts.

Panic was overtaking her as she pushed the call button. A metallic tang of blood flooded her, and she looked down to see that the entire mattress was soaked from her hips down. The pressure was suddenly intense, and she called out, as the nurse came rushing in. "I–can't breathe– help."

She took one look at Amy, rushing over to her to give her oxygen as she simultaneously tapped the small badge clipped to her scrub pocket. "Doctor Lee to Room 304, now." The device emitted a soft chime, confirming the message had been sent.

"Okay honey, he is going to be born feet first. You need to push now." She positioned herself with a towel, and as the pressure quickly as it happened, he was born. Slipping between her legs in a shattered breath. Amy's heart pounded louder in her ears as her vision clouded with the breath of oxygen against the mask. She felt trapped, and the realization brought a fresh wave of panic. Tears streamed down her face as she struggled, the desperation giving her a last surge of adrenaline. Her body stilled as she turned toward the nurse, who had clamped the cord and taken the fetus to the other side of the room. Doctor Lee was at the foot of the bed.

"Call for the OR cart." He placed his goggles on his face as the nurse gowned and gloved him. "Amy, your placenta is coming out in pieces, there are pieces stuck in your uterus." His hand gently slid into her, but the blunt force of his fingers scraping inside her body knocked the wind out of her. "I need to clean out as much of it as quickly as possible, or you could lose a lot of blood. He was pushing against her pelvis with such an intensity, she thought she was going to pass out. The contractions were even more intense, and she gasped for breath, tears streaming against her tingling skin. The nurse prepped a metal instrument with gauze, and as quickly as his hand came out, the instrument went in. She saw stars, she was shaking violently now, unable to control any aspect of what was going on, unable to process what was being done to her. One hand gripped the nurse's, feeling her fingers crack against her grip. She felt something hot seep into her vein, like an acid that slowly creeped up her arm, and she let out an agonizing sound that was bitter, feral.

What the fuck is happening. Her eyes rolled back into her head as she tried to focus. She arched her back against the mattress, trying to ground herself, trying to feel something else, *anything else.*

The pain was so overwhelming that she couldn't think straight. Her mind was a blur of fear and confusion.

And then it stopped.

The doctor began to talk to her about the baby, she heard "Small, fragile, bruised." She tried to speak, but nothing came out.

She didn't think she could look at him, that she could face the loss head on. She turned her head over the side of the bed, as the contents of her stomach projected from her mouth to the floor. She was alone, and she had never felt more broken.

TWENTY TWO

Josephine's shoes clacked against the linoleum as she walked past the nurses' station, she scanned the whiteboard for nurse assignments so she could give report. Familiar names and patient details blurred together until one stopped her cold.

Amy Rodriguez. DOB: 11/16/1991. DX: Mirror Syndrome, Fetal Demise, Induction.

She's pregnant. Her stomach twisted. She stared at the board as if the letters might rearrange themselves into something less devastating, less final. But they didn't.

Josephine adjusted her grip on her clipboard as she turned to the nurse she needed to debrief.

That was when she heard it. "We need an OR cart!" She stood, and as if on instinct, stood, making her way down the hall to grab it.

"What room?" she called out on her communication device."

"304."

Josephine's blood ran cold.

When she returned from the room, she didn't bother changing out of her scrubs. She took her stethoscope off her neck, and hung it on the wall before grabbing her bag from her locker.

The moment she turned the corner, she leaned against the cool wall, her heart pounding. Her hand trembled as she pulled out her phone and typed a quick message.

Photographer: Where are you?

The reply came almost instantly:

Mark: At the office. Long day. I'll call you later.

Her face burner as she stared at the words. *She's alone, Mark. Alone.* The thought repeated itself, each time sharper, angrier. Her phone started rattling off notifications.

Her fingers hovered over the screen, then she shoved the phone into her pocket. She couldn't breathe. She couldn't think. Turning on her heel, she stormed out of the hospital, her pulse racing as the cold night air hit her skin.

The city lights blurred together as Josephine gripped the steering wheel. Mark's voice echoed through the car speakers, smooth and practiced, as his latest podcast episode played.

"…infidelity is never black and white. It often stems from deep emotional voids, unmet needs, or even the complexities of human connection. It's not about blame but about understanding what drives people to make these choices. I've experienced this firsthand in my own life…"

Her jaw clenched as she listened, each word heightening her anger.

"…what began as support for a client going through a painful divorce evolved into something more. It was wrong, yes, but we were both in difficult places, and sometimes, in moments of pain, we seek connection in the wrong ways…"

Josephine's grip on the wheel faltered as she swerved slightly, the words cutting through her like shards of glass. He was framing himself as a victim, a man who had merely stumbled into infidelity out of human frailty.

"…and while I deeply regret the hurt I've caused, I hope sharing my experience will help others understand the complexities of relationships and forgiveness."

She slammed the off button, her breathing ragged. *Forgiveness? Was he serious?*

Her foot pressed harder on the gas as she navigated toward the city, her mind spiraling. By the time she reached Mark's office, she was shaking, her emotions a volatile mix of fury and betrayal.

TWENTY THREE

Mark's mouth formed a hard line as his fingers flew across the keyboard. He had a lot of fires to put out, and was working on every aspect of damage control as he fought the barrage of emails and notifications. Every notification that lit up his phone added another log to the fire raging in his chest. Photos. Screenshots. Accusations. His affair wasn't just a rumor now; it was trending.

The damage control wasn't enough.

And Amy.

His jaw clenched at the thought. She was the only one who knew the intricacies of his private life, the only one capable of orchestrating such a targeted attack, only *she* knew. She had waited for the perfect opportunity, waited until the peak of his exposure, everyone was talking about him, everyone wanted him.

His eyes remained fixed on the stream of incoming emails and notifications, every alert a new variable in his carefully crafted equation. In his mind, he catalogued each message with a clinical detachment: *One more threat to neutralize, one more opportunity to spin the narrative.* The neatly arranged family photos and meticulously clipped news articles weren't tokens of sentiment, they were instruments in his arsenal, each waiting to be deployed in his strategic comeback.

The sound of hesitant footsteps disrupted his concentration. Mark's gaze flicked upward as Josie entered, her presence a sudden, uncontrolled burst of emotion that sliced through his calculated calm. Her fists trembled at her sides, and her eyes shimmered with raw grief and barely contained fury, a stark contrast to his own measured detachment. *Perfect fucking timing.*

"You're here," he stated flatly, not bothering to hide the cool calculation behind his eyes as he continued sorting through his documents. Internally, he noted, *her arrival isn't a setback; it's a variable. I can use this... if I play my cards right.*

He opened his drawer, and stood, handing her an orange bottle. "Here, before I forget, you left these at the hotel." *He knew it would come in handy, which is precisely why he took them.*

Josie's lips trembled as she stuffed them into her bag. "Don't you dare act like this is just another Tuesday, Mark." Her words cracked under the weight of betrayal.

She stepped closer, her eyes desperate and pleading. "My shift just ended at the hospital," she managed, "Did you know Amy was pregnant? Did you know she lost the baby?" The words tasted bitter, like bile rising in her throat. The papers on the desk, the same ones Mark used to plan his next move, mocked her. Mocked *them*. "Why are you here? Do you even care?"

Mark paused, relief suddenly flooding him. His fingers hovered above the keys as a cold calculation took over. *Amy's loss... not an irreparable tragedy, but an opportunity to pivot the narrative.* Outwardly, his expression was neutral.

A shift in the chessboard. He leaned back slightly, the clinical detachment never faltering as he replied, "Yes." The word was flat, stripped of any human warmth. *Exactly as he wanted to deliver it.*

Josie's eyes searched his face, desperate for a flicker of remorse or concern, but found nothing. "How can you not care?" Her anguish was palpable.

His eyes met hers, but there was no warmth, no acknowledgment of the grief she carried in her chest. "What would you like me to say, Josephine?" he asked, using her full name on purpose, "Would it help if I cried? If I pretended to care?" His tone far too calm.

The way he said her name, and in that tone, hit her like a slap. She staggered back, the anger welling up inside her until she was shaking, her whole body trembling with a rage that was only just beginning to form. *He's not even pretending anymore.*

"You're an asshole," she spat.

His expression was cold, a thin veneer that covered the rot beneath. "No, I'm a realist," he paused, "The baby complicating things is no longer an issue. That's all this is, one less problem to deal with." *That blow will push her over the edge.*

One less problem. The words echoed in her head, hollow and unforgiving. She wanted to scream, to shake him until he understood what he was saying. He was dismissing everything; Amy's grief, her pain, her loss, and reducing it to just another inconvenience. There was a sudden shift in her, she felt like Amy, transported back in time, to her fifteen-year-old self.

Josephine couldn't breathe. She was choking on the reality of it all. "You don't even see her as a person anymore, do you? Or me, for that matter." The words slipped out before she could stop them, but they were true. And somehow that made it worse.

Mark sighed. He stood, slowly, angling his phone toward her. "Here," he began flicking through the screen. "Take a look."

There were comments from the news sites covering the affair, each one more cutting than the last. The words blurred together, a stream of venom directed at *her*, at him, at anyone caught in the storm.

Typical homewrecker.

The poor wife. What kind of woman sleeps with a married man?

Whore.

Mark is a God.

Let me play therapist next, Dr. Rodriguez.

The comments blurred, merging into a sickening wave of hate and judgment, each word piercing her chest. This wasn't just a scandal. This wasn't just about her anymore. This was about everything she had become, everything Mark had turned her into.

Her eyes flicked up to him, searching for something, anything, resembling remorse. But there was nothing. Just that cold, calculating look. The one that always made her feel small, insignificant.

"Do you see now?" his voice softened. "Do you see how easy it is for people to believe what they want to believe?"

Josephine's heart pounded. She wanted to fight back. She wanted to break the mask he wore, to claw through his indifference and force him to feel something, anything. But all she could do was stare, frozen in a horror that no words could capture.

She had fallen too far. And now, standing here, watching the man she thought she loved crumble everything around them, she realized that she had always been just another casualty in his war.

"This is what *you've* done. You leaked it, didn't you?"

Her mouth opened, but no sound came out.

"Don't lie to me, Josephine." He was so close, he could feel the heat radiating off her body. "This is your fault. All of it. The mess, the backlash, the destruction of my career. You've ruined everything."

She shook her head as her back found the wall. "I didn't leak anything."

Mark laughed, cold and humorless. "No? Then who did? Because it sure as hell wasn't me. You think you're the victim here, but you're not. You're a liability. A mistake."

She staggered back, her hands gripping the edge of his desk for support. "I gave up everything for you," she was trembling. "My marriage. My life. For what?"

"For nothing," he replied bluntly, his tone devoid of emotion. "You were convenient. A great fuck, that's it. I've moved on."

Her breath came in short, ragged gasps, the walls closing in around her.

His brows narrowed. "You know, you remind me of my mother." his head tilted toward a picture on his desk.

Josephine focused on the old photograph. She knew the story well, and bile filled her throat.

"She was a fighter, too," he continued, stepping closer. "Always standing up to my father, always trying to protect me. But you know what she taught me? That fighting only makes things worse when you are dealing with a smarter, more powerful opponent."

Josephine froze, the implication in his words raising her blood pressure.

"She liked to push back," he murmured, almost thoughtful. "Loved to challenge him. Thought it made her strong." His gaze darkened, pinning her in place. "But all it ever did was prove how weak she really was. Because desperate people? They don't fight, they flounder. They grasp at things that were never there to begin with." His head tilted, almost pitying. "And that's when they start making mistakes. Not the kind you can come back from. The kind that ruin everything."

Mark leaned in. "This is the price of your choices, Josephine. You made this bed, and now you get to lie in it. Alone."

She flinched at the word, her mind spiraling as his words sank in. *Alone.* She had no one left. She'd run so far from him, but could never let go. What they had was special, and she thought his father was the cause of their pain, the reason they didn't start a family, a life together. She had blamed everyone but Mark, but it was then, she realized, that Mark had become the same man.

Josephine didn't move. Her gaze darted around the room,

searching for something, anything, that might tether her back to reality. But all she found was emptiness.

As she stumbled toward the door, Mark called out, "Oh, and Josephine? The cameras in this building haven't worked for years."

Her shoulders stiffened, but she didn't turn around. She walked out of the office, the door clicking shut behind her, the sound echoing in the empty hallway.

Mark sat back in his chair, a satisfied smirk playing on his lips. He took a sip from his glass of whiskey, staring at the dim glow of the city outside his window. His mind raced. *Grief: useful for redirection; sorrow– manageable collateral damage. Use her despair to bolster the narrative of a man wronged by circumstance rather than the villain of his own story.*

He'd posted the photo of her and Amy earlier that day, knowing that Josephine would see it. He reached for his phone, scrolling through the chaos of the comments online, his reputation hanging in the balance. But that didn't bother him. He'd already won. This was a shit show he would need to reign in, but he had a plan, he just needed her to put it in motion, and this conversation was step one, even if it broke him to lose her again.

△△△

The heavy thrum of her heartbeat drowned out the sound of her car's engine as she killed the ignition. Mark's podcast still echoed in her ears, his carefully crafted words turning over and over in her mind.

"I made a mistake, yes. But it was born of two broken people trying to find solace in a difficult time. Amy and I were struggling, and Josephine... well, she was enduring her own heartbreak."

He made it sound so noble, so tragic, as if the affair had been an unfortunate but inevitable consequence of life's cruelty. Mark's voice on the reel was smooth, calculated, every word perfectly chosen to craft his narrative. He had painted himself as the flawed hero, a man who had succumbed to emotional vulnerability, caught in the grip of a failing marriage. It had *just happened.*

Josephine's stomach churned as she parked her car in the dimly lit garage. Her hands trembled against the steering wheel, nails pressing crescents into her palms. The cool leather offered no comfort, no grounding.

She reached for her phone, her fingers fumbling as she unlocked it. The images hit her like a physical blow; grainy but unmistakable. She couldn't look away. Mark's face was perfectly visible in every shot. His smirk, his hands, his body, every damning detail captured with merciless clarity.

And her? None of the photos showed her face.

Josephine swallowed hard; her throat tight with panic. There she was, her naked body exposed, her hair a curtain shielding her features. In one image, she was blindfolded, her hands gripping the edge of a desk as Mark loomed behind her. The intimacy of it, the brutality of having her vulnerability stripped and displayed for the world to dissect, made her feel sick.

Her hands shook as she scrolled further. The captions beneath the photos were worse.

Power dynamic, much?

She's fifty shades of slutty.

Mark's the man. She's just another notch.

A sob clawed its way up her throat, but she swallowed it back. Mark had done this; he'd reduced her to nothing but a blurred body in a scandal. And then, on his reel, he'd said her name.

He *knew*. He knew the photos didn't show her face, and yet he had spoken her name. He'd thrown her to the wolves to shield himself, to control the narrative.

Her thoughts wavered as the realization sank in. It wasn't

enough for him to survive this unscathed; he needed someone to blame, and she was the perfect scapegoat. The world wouldn't pity her. It would shred her, chew her up, and spit her out.

Josephine's grip on her phone tightened, her breath hitching as tears blurred her vision. It wasn't just the photos. It was the way he had framed everything. He had been careful, oh so careful, to twist the story in his favor.

"Josephine," he had said, "She was an old friend. She was going through some marital troubles. I tried to be there for her, to support her, but I made a mistake. We both did. I take full responsibility, but I wish things hadn't gone this way. It's a lesson I'll carry with me forever."

He made it sound like he had saved her, that his actions had been a momentary lapse of judgment. He had erased her pain, her choices, her humanity, leaving only his carefully curated narrative.

She thought back to the first night they reconnected in person. She wanted to hold onto that memory forever, of how it made her feel, of how she still felt.

She leaned back in her chair, the candlelight flickering across Mark's face. He had aged well, a little more rugged around the edges, but the same sharp eyes and half-smile that once unraveled her. Her gaze drifted to his hand resting on the table, and there it was. The ring. His pinky ring, a small onyx stone encased in gold that she had given him years ago, before everything fell apart.

"You still wear it," she'd said softly, tracing the rim of her wine glass with her finger.

Mark glanced down at his hand, a wry smile tugging at his lips. "Of course I do. It's the only thing that ever felt permanent."

Her breath caught, but she masked it with a sip of wine. "That was a lifetime ago."

"Doesn't feel like it."

The words hung heavy between them. Josephine felt the pull of nostalgia, the warmth of familiarity mingled with the ache of what they had lost. She'd reached out to him impulsively, a simple message on social media, and now here they were, sitting across from each other after all these years. She'd told herself it was just curiosity. Closure. But now, watching him pour her another glass of wine, she wasn't so sure.

"You're still a terrible influence," she teased, nodding toward the wine bottle.

"Or an excellent one," he countered, his smile more pronounced now. "Depends on how you look at it."

She laughed softly, feeling the edges of her resolve blur. She hadn't laughed like this in months. Years, maybe.

Mark tilted his head, studying her. "What?"

"Nothing," she lied, shaking her head. But it wasn't nothing. It was everything; the way he looked at her, like she was the only person in the room; the way his voice dipped when he said her name, as if it still meant something to him.

"You're a terrible liar," he leaned forward. "Tell me what's on your mind, Josie."

The nickname hit her like a jolt, a tether to a past she'd tried to bury. She reached for her glass, more for something to do with her hands than anything else. The wine was rich, bold, and dangerously smooth, much like the man sitting across from her.

"I was just thinking about how strange this is," she admitted. "Seeing you again. It's... surreal."

"Good strange or bad strange?" he cocked an eyebrow, and she felt her muscles tense.

"Both," she replied honestly. "I didn't think–" She stopped herself, unsure if she wanted to finish the thought.

"Didn't think what?" his arms flexed as he leaned forward, resting his chin in his hands.

She sighed. "I didn't think it would still feel like this."

His eyes darkened, his expression unreadable. "Like what?"

"Like..." She hesitated, the words sticking in her throat. "Like no time has passed at all."

Mark's gaze held hers, unflinching. "It hasn't, not really. You're still you. Still the same woman who..." He paused, "Who made me believe in something bigger than myself."

Her mouth filled with saliva, the weight of his words pressing against her ribs. She hadn't expected this, this raw, unfiltered honesty. She'd come here looking for answers, but all she found were more questions.

"Mark..." She started, but he cut her off.

"Do you ever think about it?" he asked, "About what we had? What we lost?"

She looked away, unable to meet his gaze. "Of course I do," she admitted. "How could I not?"

"I'm sorry," his sincerity made her chest ache. "For everything. For what I put you through. For not fighting harder to keep us together."

her throat tightened, memories flooding back in vivid, painful detail. The nights she cried herself to sleep, the guilt and shame that consumed her after the termination, the way they drifted apart until there was nothing left but silence.

"It wasn't your fault, it wasn't mine," she exhaled.

"We both... let go when we shouldn't have, but what happened, I couldn't find it in myself to–."

Mark leaned back; his expression troubled. "And now?"

She shook her head, trying to ignore the way her heart raced. "Now we're different people, in different lives. You're married... I'm married. This..." She gestured between them. "This is just two old friends catching up, right?"

His smile was bittersweet. "Is that what this feels like to you? Just catching up?" he took a sip of whiskey.

She didn't answer, she couldn't. The truth was too dangerous, too real. Instead, she drained the rest of her wine, the liquid burning its way down her throat.

Mark watched her, his gaze steady and intense. "Josie, I need to tell you something."

"What?" she asked.

"Amy and I..." He paused, swallowing hard. "We've been trying to have a baby. For years. But I can't. Every time I think of her, pregnant, I think of you..."

The admission hung in the air, heavy and unspoken. She felt a pang of guilt, a flicker of regret.

"I'm sorry," and she meant it, "That must be so hard."

"It is," he admitted. "And I feel like I'm suffocating. Like I'm stuck in this life that doesn't even feel like mine anymore. The only time I've felt alive in years is right now, sitting here with you."

She thought about Callum, about his desire to start a family, a dream that felt more like a noose around her neck. She'd never told Callum about Mark, about the pregnancy, about the termination, about the fear that still haunted her. *How could she? How could she explain that she didn't want to have a baby with him, that she couldn't see herself being a mother at all?* She saw a mirror in Mark, as if she was staring at the same person, and for the first time, she felt seen, truly seen for who she really was.

"Mark," her voice was trembling. "We shouldn't..."

"Shouldn't what?" he asked, leaning closer. "Feel something? Want something? Josie, if there's one thing I've learned, it's that life is too short to pretend."

She looked at him, really looked at him, and saw the man she'd fallen in love with all those years ago. The man who'd kept the pinky ring still wrapped around his finger, a token of a love that had never truly died. Her resolve cracked, the weight of her emotions too much to bear.

"I can't stop thinking about you," she admitted, "I never stopped."

Mark's hand brushed against hers, a tentative, electric touch that sent a shiver down her spine.

"Then don't." he said simply.

And just like that, she leaned in, her lips finding his in a kiss that felt inevitable, like the closing of a circle they'd been tracing for years...

Her tears fell freely now, hot streaks tracing her cheeks. She stared at the photos again, at her body on display, at the sneers and judgments of strangers. The air felt too thick, the walls of the car pressing in on her.

And now? Now the world thought it *knew* her.

Her pulse was roaring in her ears. *No safety net. No future. I'll have to quit my job. How am I supposed to face anyone after this?* The thought clawed at her, relentless. And Mark? Mark was untouchable. He'll rebuild everything, piece by perfect piece, while I have nothing left.

Josephine let her phone slip from her fingers, the screen landing face-up on the passenger seat.

Josephine's vision darkened at the edges, her grip on reality slipping. She thought of her empty apartment, the cold silence waiting for her there. She thought of Mark's face, smug and untouchable. She thought of her name being whispered in judgment by people who didn't know her.

And then, she thought of the lake.

TWENTY FOUR

The room seemed to blur around her as the reality of the loss washed over her in waves. She couldn't breathe. It felt unreal–none of it made sense. Her body shook with silent sobs as she looked down. His body fit in the palm of her hand, the weight of him was tangible, but her mind betrayed the reality of the citation, fluctuating between what she thought was real, and what felt like a fantasy.

The conflict churned in her mind: he was real, a tangible weight in her arms, yet what she held was the heartbreaking truth, a preterm baby, too small to survive, with all the fragile details of life but none of its promise. It felt like a blessing, and a curse. She ran a finger over his hand, no bigger than the pad of her pinky. She focused on his tiny lips, his perfect fingers, his little toes. Every part of him was there, and every part of him was gone. The grief washed over her intensely, the gravity of her reality suffocating every aspect of her being. She was so blind sighted by the pain that it forced the air out of her lungs, and she squeezed her eyes shut, trying desperately to inhale, but unable to draw in a breath. It didn't make sense, but it was the truth she had to face, she would never hear his cry, never see him grow. She would only hold him, small and still, in her arms.

"This isn't real," she whispered, shaking her head. "This... none of this is real." She'd held him until he ran cold, and as they moved her in a wheelchair down the maternity ward, she had asked the nurse for a blanket to keep him warm.

The room was quiet, except for the faint beeping of the monitors and the occasional muffled footsteps in the hallway. Amy sat propped up in the hospital bed, staring blankly out the window. The sun had dipped below the horizon, leaving the sky an eerie mix of orange and gray. A small, crocheted blanket rested in her lap, her hands twisting the edges into knots.

Her phone sat on the tray table, untouched. She hadn't looked at it all day, unwilling to face the well-meaning messages or the deafening silence from those who didn't know what to say.

She tucked her knees under her chin. "Okay Google, play some music."

The soft glow of the setting sun filtered through the curtains, casting long shadows across the room. Plumb's *I Want You Here* filled the air, the haunting piano melody weaving through the stillness.

Of all the fucking songs to play. But she didn't turn it off. It made her feel something. Her hands trembled as she held the mug of tea, the warmth seeping through her fingers, grounding her. The singer's voice carried through the room, raw and aching, each note pressing into wounds she had no way to close.

The door creaked open. Maslow trotted in first, his nails clicking against the hardwood floor, followed by Callum. His jacket was slung over one shoulder.

He hesitated, one hand still on the doorframe, his brow furrowing. The song's lyrics hung heavy in the air, speaking of loss, absence, and a grief that never quite faded.

"Ames," he muttered quietly, stepping inside.

She didn't look up, her gaze still fixed on the window. The music filled the silence between them, carrying the weight of everything she couldn't say.

As the last notes faded, she finally turned to him, her eyes glassy. For a moment, neither of them spoke, the energy between them louder than any melody.

Maslow moved around the room, his nose twitching as he took in the unfamiliar smells.

"Maslow?" Amy's voice was cracked and raw.

Callum's expression was carefully neutral, but his expression was dark with worry as he closed the door, and unclipped Maslow's leash.

"Before you protest, I didn't break in, I took your keys from Charlotte. I hung out in the lobby for a while, and then decided to drive home to get Maslow, I thought he might help." He paused, glancing at her before closing the door. "He's been restless since you've been gone." Amy glanced at the face of the screen, pushing pause on the track as she took them both in.

Maslow's tail wagged briefly, but his attention was already elsewhere. His nose dipped to the floor, sniffing intently as he wandered toward the corner where the bassinet had been. He paused, his tail stilling as he circled the empty space. A soft whine escaped his throat before he turned sharply, focusing on Amy.

The sight of her on the bed, the blanket clutched tightly in her lap, made him rush forward. He leapt up, his front paws landing gently beside her as his nose pressed against the blanket. He sniffed it frantically, then whined again, his large, warm head dropping into her lap as if trying to comfort her.

Amy's composure shattered. Her shoulders shook, her hands twisting harder around the blanket as the sobs she had been holding back broke free. Maslow licked at her trembling hands, his tail wagging softly as if to tell her he was there, that she wasn't alone.

Callum placed a vase of flowers on her night stand, as he watched the dog nuzzle her, trying in his way to piece her back together. A tear slipped down Callum's cheek, and he quickly wiped it away, but the lump in his throat only grew.

Finally, he moved toward her, setting the leash down on the chair as he reached her side. He didn't say anything, there were no words for this kind of pain. Instead, he wrapped his arms around her, pulling her gently against his chest. She didn't resist; she folded into him, her sobs muffled against his shirt.

She pulled away then, with a desperate need to tell someone, anyone the weight of what she was holding. She looked at him, exhaling a shaky breath. "I need to tell you something."

He froze, his hands stilling as he turned to face her. "Okay."

She looked down at her hands, her fingers twisting in the blanket. "I've never told anyone this. Not Charlotte. Not anyone. And I don't even know why I'm telling you now, but... I need to."

Callum's expression softened, and he sat down beside her, his weight shifting the mattress. "Take your time."

For a moment, she thought she might choke on the words, but then they came, tumbling out like water from a broken dam.

"After my surgery, they told me I couldn't try to get pregnant. Not yet. My body wasn't ready." She gripped the blanket tighter. "But I didn't listen. I couldn't. I knew Mark was having an affair, and then Charlotte announced her pregnancy, and it pushed me over the edge. It was all I could think about, having a baby, filling the emptiness, trying to fix why he didn't want me."

Callum's brow furrowed, but he stayed silent, his attention on her.

"One night, Mark got really drunk. He was completely out of it, didn't know where he was, what he was doing. And I..." She covered her face with her hands. "I took advantage of him."

The silence was deafening. When she finally looked up, Callum's expression was unreadable, shock, pain, confusion.

"I knew he didn't want to," she continued, "But I told myself it didn't matter, that I deserved to have this one thing, even if it meant..." She trailed off, her words dissolving into tears.

Callum let out a long breath, his hand running through his hair. "Amy..."

"I deserve this," she inhaled. "I deserve to lose him, to lose the baby, to lose everything. I've been lying to myself, to everyone, pretending I'm the victim, but I'm not."

Callum reached out, his hand brushing her arm. "Stop," he said quietly. "You don't deserve this."

Her head snapped up; disbelief etched into her features. "How can you say that? I–"

"Because I know what desperation does to people," he grasped her hand. "I know what it's like to make choices you regret, to hate yourself for them. But that doesn't mean you're beyond redemption."

Her shoulders shook as she sobbed, and when he pulled her into his arms, she let herself collapse against him. His hands smoothed over her back.

He took a deep breath, the weight of his own confession pressing on him. "I know what it feels like to break someone you care about. I won't let that happen to you."

For a moment, they sat in silence, their shared pain filling the space between them.

Maslow leaned into her, watching her with quiet understanding. Callum rested his chin lightly on her head, his own tears slipping silently down his face as he held her.

Once Callum left to take Maslow home, the room was suffocatingly quiet. Amy sat in the rocking chair, its creak breaking the stillness as she swayed forward and back, the motion more habit than comfort.

Her arms ached to hold him. The phantom weight of a baby she would never cradle again pressed against her chest. She exhaled, her fingers curling over her lap as if she could conjure him there. *Her son.* She imagined his face–round and soft with the smallest nose, his sleepy eyes, and his mouth opening in that perfect newborn yawn.

But he was gone.

Amy reached for the table by the chair and grasped the keepsake card. Tiny handprints were stamped on one side, the nurse's careful writing beneath them: *Baby Rodriguez, 11 oz. He fit in my hand.* Her finger traced the edges of the card as tears blurred her vision. She sobbed silently, a deep, guttural ache that left her shaking, clinging to the card like it might tether her to him.

Her body betrayed her. Her breasts were swollen and beginning to harden, a cruel, painful reminder of what should have been. The engorgement was a physical echo of her grief, her body had prepared itself to nourish her child, but there was no child to feed.

She stood on shaky legs and walked to the bathroom; her breath shallow as she turned the shower knob all the way to hot. Steam filled the room, and she stepped in, letting the scalding water cascade over her skin.

When the stream hit her chest, the warmth triggered a letdown. She gasped as colostrum dripped down her body, mixing with the water a hollow relief coursing through her. She pressed her hands to her breasts, willing the pressure to ease even as she hated herself for the relief it brought. She knew it would only make the milk come in stronger, but it was the one thing she had left of him, one reminder of the life she'd longed for.

Her knees buckled, and she sank to the shower floor, blood pooling around her feet, her sobs rising to a primal scream. It wasn't just the aching breasts, her hollow abdomen, it was all of it. The finality of her son's absence. The life she had imagined for him, for them, stolen before it could begin. Her cries turned to gasping breaths as her forehead pressed against the slick tile, water streaming down her back as if to wash her grief away. But it couldn't.

The sharp sound of the phone ringing startled her. She stayed on the floor, her body shaking, before forcing herself up. Wrapping herself in a towel, she stumbled into the room, the cool air prickling her wet skin.

The screen of her phone glowed in the dim light. *Husband.* She needed to change his name immediately. *Asshole was a better title.* And she made a note to change it later.

Amy stared at the screen as the phone buzzed in her hand. She let it ring until it stopped, but almost immediately, the screen lit up again. This time, it was a text.

Husband: Amy, answer. Please.

She typed a response.

Amy: Text or call me again, and I will get a restraining order. Your divorce papers will be mailed, Leave me alone.

She threw the phone onto the bed and pressed the heels of her palms to her face, willing herself not to cry again. But the tears came anyway. She tightened her robe around her waist and curled into the uncomfortable bed, the room feeling even more cavernous than it ever had. She opened the *Zillow* to flip through listings. Listings that could get her as far away from this god forsaken town. The idea of leaving, of starting over started taking root. Her thoughts then shifted to Callum, and her stomach flipped.

TWENTY FIVE

Mark stepped into Kaitlyn's office, scanning the space with practiced indifference, even though the sight of it stirred something in him. The sleek, minimalist furniture, clean lines, polished wood, served to highlight the pristine gallery of accolades on the wall. Her bestselling book covers were framed in silver, every inch of the space exuding success and control.

Kaitlyn sat at her desk; her posture as sharp as her gaze. A file lay in front of her, the papers inside scattered across the glass like a calculated mess.

"Sit down, Mark." Kaitlyn tapped her finger against the file, then slid it toward him, the images inside staring up at him like accusations.

Mark's gaze flicked over the contents—the photographs of him and Josephine, the explicit messages, the transcript of his speech on manipulation.

He'd been expecting something like this, but the timing? The leak? It felt deliberate. A disgruntled client, a former patient. He couldn't place who. But he was sure this was no random accident.

He opened the file, scanning it quickly, his mind already racing for a way out. "The room was quiet except for the faint hum of Kaitlyn's assistant typing furiously in the adjoining office. Mark sat across from her, his posture deceptively relaxed, one leg crossed over the other. Yet, his presence was anything but calm; it felt charged, like a coiled spring ready to snap.

Kaitlyn leaned forward. "You wanted my help, Mark. So,

talk. Tell me why I should care."

For a moment, he didn't respond, letting the silence thicken. He ran his thumb along the edge of the scar on his jaw, a habit so unconscious it seemed part of him. Then he leaned forward, resting his elbows on his knees.

"Do you know what it feels like to be nothing?" he asked, his tone devoid of pretense.

Kaitlyn's brow furrowed slightly, but she didn't answer.

"To have everything you are, everything you could be, reduced to someone else's fists?" He traced the line of his jaw again, his gaze darkening. "My dad, if you could even call him that, used to tell me that scars were lessons. You know what my lesson was?" He tilted his head, "That people will hurt you, not because of what you've done, but because of who they are. Because they can."

"My father was charming," Mark continued, his gaze distant, as if looking back through time. "Everyone loved him. A respected surgeon, the kind of man people trusted implicitly. But at home..." He trailed off, his fingers tracing the edge of the desk as if grounding himself. "At home, he was a monster. He tore her down piece by piece, until there was nothing left of her but fear." Kaitlyn's composure faltered for a fraction of a second, her eyes flicking to the scar.

"Thirty stitches," Mark continued. "He laughed when I hit the stairs. Laughed like it was the funniest thing he'd ever seen." He leaned back in his chair.

Mark exhaled, rising from his seat.

"When I was eighteen, I was involved with a girl. She was fifteen, and she got pregnant. Dad caught us, and when I told him about the pregnancy, he lost his shit. He made her abort it, forced her that day to take the pills to end it. I told my mother, and when he realized the gravity of what he had done, of what the true implications of it was, he did it–"

Kaitlyn's composure broke. Tears fell.

"You remember the Doctor Morales case, don't you?" Mark continued. Kaitlyn nodded.

Mark exhaled, his fingers running cold. My last name is not Rodriguez, that's a name I chose for myself shortly after he–. "We went home, and while he was getting the mail, I got out of the car and ran ahead to tell my mom what had happened. He was not far behind me though. He locked me in the basement..." The shift was subtle but undeniable. The present blurred with the past as he recalled the day with haunting clarity.

He ran a trembling hand over his face, unable to look at him. Mark's father stopped at the mailboxes at the end of the cul–de–sac to check theirs.

"I'll walk home." Mark slid out of the car, his steps increasing into a run as he made his way through the front door.

He let the door crack against the wall as he stumbled inside, his cheeks streaked with tears. His chest felt tight, each breath sharp and uneven.

"Mom!" he shouted, "Mom!"

She appeared from the kitchen, a dish towel in hand, her face creasing with worry the moment she saw him. "Mark, what is it? What happened?"

Mark's legs buckled beneath him as he fell to his knees, his hands gripping his hair. "He made her, he made her take it," he gasped, his words tumbling out in a rush.

"What?" she asked, rushing to his side and kneeling down. She grabbed his shoulders, forcing him to look at her, her eye glazed with purple undertones, hidden beneath her concealer. "Mark, slow down. Made who, take what?"

"Josie," he choked out. "She's pregnant, Mom. And Dad... he took us to his office. He forced her to... to end

it. He wouldn't let me stop him. He wouldn't listen!"

Her face paled, the dish towel slipping from her fingers. "Oh my God," she whispered. "He did what? Josephine is–?"

Mark tried to speak, but the words caught in his throat, his sobs making his whole body shake. She pulled him into a hug. "Tell me everything. Start from the beginning."

He nodded, pulling back to wipe at his face. "We–"

But the sharp click of a closing door cut him off.

"Mark."

The low, venomous tone made both of them whip around. Doctor Morales stood in the doorway, his face an icy mask of control.

"What are you doing, Mark?" His eyes flicked to his wife, narrowing on them both. "You're telling her?"

Mark shot to his feet, putting himself between his parents. "She deserves to know what you did!" he yelled, "You had no right."

"Enough," his father barked, striding toward him.

"You're a monster," Mark spat. "You ruined everything! You–"

Before he could finish, his father grabbed him by the shirt, hauling him forward with an almost effortless force.

"Let him go!" his mother cried, lunging for Mark, but Doctor Morales shoved her back with a cold, commanding glare.

"Stay out of this, Lucia," he warned. "This is between me and him."

He dragged Mark through the hallway, past the kitchen, and down the stairs to the basement.

"Dad, stop!" Mark struggled against his grip, his feet skidding against the hardwood floor. *"You can't do this!"*

"Oh, I can," his father snapped, wrenching the basement door open, the blow to his jaw blind sighted him, and for a moment, the world spun as the click of the deadbolt sent a chill down his spine. Mark stumbled, unable to catch himself as his body flew back, his head making contact with the wood, and then repeatedly, down the stairs.

"FUCK!" his jaw was on fire, as he brought his hand to his face, the warmth of his blood gushed over the palm of his hand. He braced himself against the wall, his hand tightly clamped over his jaw as he slid up the hard surface, trying to steady himself. He looked around in the dark, allowing his eyes a moment to adjust, his hand searching for the downstairs switch.

Shaking, he made his way to the bathroom, where he looked at his jaw in the mirror. A jagged gash ripped through his skin, running the length of his jawline and down his throat. Blood was pumping in cadence with his rapid heartbeat, and his mouth went dry. He shook as he pulled the hand towel from the wall before opening the medicine cabinet to find something to secure the wound.

This needs fucking stitches. He thought as the screaming upstairs intensified. There was nothing but a box of Band-Aids and some gauze, so he unfolded the squares to cover as much ground as possible, then made his way to the toolbox near the laundry room to find some duct tape.

Mark flew back up the stairs, pounding his fists against the door. *"Let me out!"* he yelled as he rapped on the door, the sound echoing through the cold, unfinished space. *"You can't keep me in here!"*

Mark's breath came in ragged gasps, his chest tight with something that felt too much like panic, too much like heartbreak. He couldn't move, couldn't speak, only listen to the broken sounds that echoed from behind the door. His mind raced, trying to process, trying to put together what had just happened, what had been torn from them, what they had lost in one single night.

He forced his hands to open the door, the cold metal of the crowbar still gripped in his fingers. His mind was reeling with anger, fear, helplessness, every step towards the stairs felt like a mistake. Like the weight of his father's cruelty was pushing him further down a hole he couldn't crawl out of.

Upstairs, his mother's voice was a jagged whisper. Mark could hear her muffled sobs from down the hall, the sound breaking him even more. He thought about Josie. About the look in her eyes when his father's shadow loomed over her, how she didn't even fight back. She had shut down, completely.

Everything about her was gone. The fire, the life, suffocated. And Mark hadn't been able to stop it.

His chest tightened with a grief so raw it was almost unbearable, and he slammed his fist into the wall. The echo of the impact was nothing compared to the scream building in his throat. His blood pulsed in his ears as it trickled down his head. His thoughts spiraling.

She didn't want it. We didn't want this. But his father had destroyed her, erased her choices.

And I did nothing.

His father had never been a man to show love. He had buried that a long time ago, wrapped it in arrogance, wrapped it in control. Mark had thought, had believed, that he could change things. Everything Mark had thought he understood about love, about right and *wrong, had been ripped from him.*

Josie had been the only truth he'd ever known. Now, it felt like that was gone. He was nothing but the remnants of the man his father had shaped him into.

Tears blurred his vision as he looked down at the ground, the pain rising within him in a thick tide, filling his throat until he couldn't breathe.

His thoughts spiraled back to the moment in the office, the look on Josie's face as she swallowed the pills, her body trembling like a leaf in a storm. It would never leave him. That moment would follow him, haunt him. He had been helpless. They had been helpless.

Mark ran his fingers through his hair, pacing back and forth across the room. His mind spun like a carousel, memories mixing with his shame, with the screams that still echoed in the silence of the house.

As he closed his eyes, the tears finally came. They were slow at first, like a trickle, but soon, they became a flood, rushing over him as the storm within him finally broke free.

Mark bolted down the basement steps, his mind racing as fast as his legs. He skidded to a stop, eyes darting around the dimly lit room. Tools. Something heavy. Anything to break the door. His gaze locked on an old crowbar leaning against the wall. Grabbing it, he turned and sprinted back upstairs, nearly tripping in his desperation.

"Mom!" he shouted, slamming his fists against the door. "Mom! Open the door!"

From the other side, muffled voices reached him. His father's tone was low, every word heavy with menace. He could hear his mother, sharp and frantic, but he couldn't make out what she was saying.

Then came the crack.

It wasn't just a sound, it was a thunderclap that stole the air from his lungs. Mark froze, the crowbar slipping from his fingers and clattering to the floor, and down the stairs. His hands remained pressed to the door as the sharp thud buried itself deep in his chest.

"Mom?" His voice broke, his knees buckled, and he leaned into the door to keep himself upright.

Silence.

The kind of silence that swallows everything whole.

Mark's thoughts began to swim, panic clawed at his chest, and he pounded on the door, harder this time. "Mom!" His fists burned with every strike, but he didn't care. He bent down to retriever the crow bar, this time, successful in prying the door open.

Mark slammed his shoulder into the basement door, over and over, until the latch gave way. The house was eerily quiet as he stepped into the house, the sound of his own breathing deafening in his ears. He heard his father.

When he reached the living room, he stopped dead in his tracks.

His mother lay motionless on the floor, her eyes open but unseeing. A pool of blood spread beneath her, soaking into the carpet.

Doctor Morales sat in the armchair, a glass of whiskey in one hand and a lit cigar in the other. He looked up at Mark, his expression unreadable.

"What did you do?" Mark trembled, his chest heaving.

"She pushed me too far," Doctor Morales had said calmly, taking a slow drag from the cigar. "I couldn't let her ruin us. She was becoming a liability."

"You... you killed her." Mark stood frozen, unbelieving of the scene in front of him. His hands shook as he reached for the phone in his pocket.

Doctor Morales' eyes followed the movement, his expression darkening. "Put that down."

Mark's thumb hovered over the keypad. "I'm calling the police."

"You won't."

Mark's gaze snapped to his father, defiance burning in his eyes.

Doctor Morales reached for the gun on the table beside him.

Mark stumbled backward, He looked up just in time to see his father's face before another shot shattered the silence.

"This ends here."

He shot himself after he killed her. The fucking coward couldn't bear to live a life where he wasn't in control."

Kaitlyn's expression was unreadable, her knuckles gripping the arm of her chair. "And that's why you went into psychology," she murmured.

Mark nodded slowly. "I needed to understand. To make sense of what he did, what she endured, what I went through. And more than that, I needed to make sure I never became him." The vulnerability in his gaze was so convincing, it could've been real. "That's why I study relationships, why I write about them. To help people see the warning signs, to break the cycle."

He exhaled sharply, his jaw tightening. "Amy. She didn't just push, she manipulated me. Took my trust, my... my need to believe someone could want me for me, and twisted it. Used me."

Kaitlyn's sharp intake of breath was audible, but she didn't interrupt.

"She pretended to care, but all she really cared about was her obsession with having a baby. I told her no, Kaitlyn. I told her I wasn't ready. That I wasn't sure I could ever be a father after where I came from. But she didn't care. She waited until I was black out drunk, pretty sure she served me most of the drinks I had that night, and took what she wanted."

Mark swallowed hard as he pushed through. "Do you know what it's like to wake up and realize your body has been used against you? To know someone you loved, thought so little of you, they made you a pawn in their fucking plan?" he pointed at the incriminating photos. These were taken after she fucked me, all of them, time stamped. She's pregnant, you know. Having a child, a child conceived through rape. Funny how those tables are turned? Isn't it?"

He drew a cigarette before lighting it. "And in an even more fucked up and twisted turn of events, we tried to make it work, as you can see with her at the event."

He rose from his seat, pacing the floor as he continued. "Josephine, the woman in the photo," he nodded toward the scattered images. "She's the same girl, Kaitlyn. She had moved, but when I went viral, she recognized me and came back. I couldn't lose her again. And now this."

Kaitlyn exhaled slowly, shaking her head "Why haven't you told this story before?"

He let out a humorless laugh. "Because it's not about me. It's about the work. But now..." He focused on her, "Now, people are tearing me apart. Painting me as a fraud. A liar. And for what? For one mistake? A mistake that was warranted."

She leaned forward. "This isn't just about the affair, Mark. It's about betrayal, the hypocrisy. You built your brand on trust and intimacy, and now that's what they're targeting."

The room seemed to contract around them, the weight of his words pressing in from all sides. Kaitlyn sat back, her expression unreadable, her mind clearly racing.

"Mark," she tapped her pen against the desk. "This... this is dark. It's messy. But it's raw. Authentic. People will eat this up, but only if we control the narrative."

"I need you to help me," Mark exhaled, "Not just to salvage my career, but to make them see who I really am. To remind them why they listened to me in the first place."

She tapped a message on her phone. "We need to move fast. A podcast could work, intimate, confessional. We will do that in the studio right now, but we'll need visuals, too. Late night show. I can pull some strings. A documentary angle, maybe. Something raw and unfiltered."

Mark's expression softened, his lips curling into something almost like relief. "Stages, releasing this story in stages will make it better."

Kaitlyn smirked. "Mark, with the right angle, we don't just clean this up. We make you untouchable."

Mark allowed himself a small, satisfied smile. "Then let's get to work."

TWENTY SIX

Josephine looked at the photo of Mark and Amy at his event. She was radiant, beautiful, his hands were cradling her bump, and her hands were on top of his. Her stomach flipped.

His ring, the one she gave him, was on Amy's left finger. She felt the bile rise as she threw the phone on the floor, the screen making a loud crack. *I'm nothing to him, I've never been anything.*

The sun dipped below the horizon, casting the trail in a wash of orange and purple hues. The water was calm, mirroring the fading light as if the world were holding its breath. Josephine walked slowly along the trail, her shoes crunching against the gravel. Each step felt heavier than the last, her breath shallow, her mind a whirlwind of thoughts.

You're nothing but a whore.

The air smelled of wet earth and fading summer. She could hear the gentle lapping of the lake against the rocks, the only sound in the stillness. It should have been peaceful, but the quiet made her feel more alone than ever.

She stopped at the edge of the trail, her gaze falling to the water. It stretched endlessly, dark and vast, like the void she felt. Her fingers curled into fists, her nails biting into her palms.

Why did I come here?

But she knew. This was where Mark had brought her once, years ago, the day he'd told her he loved her, the night they'd conceived. She could still hear him echoing in her ear, could see the way he'd looked at her like she was the only thing that mattered. A *lie, like everything else.* Her thoughts returned to the photo he had handed her. *She remembered Amy's face at the hospital.*

She stared out at the water, the stillness pulling at her.

The podcast played in her mind, twisting the truth into something palatable for the masses.

"Josephine was a friend. She was struggling, and I tried to be there for her. I take responsibility for what happened, but let's not forget the toll this has taken on my family."

Every muscle in her body tensed. He sounded so noble, so gracious, even as he threw her under the bus. The comments had been worse:

She's disgusting.

Poor Mark, having to deal with someone like that.

What did she expect? He's a married man.

She bit back a sob, her breath leaving her body in ragged iterations. They didn't even know her face. They didn't have to. Mark had made sure of that, leaving her to bear the brunt of it all while he came out unscathed.

"You're the reason this happened, Josephine," Mark's words lingered, a memory or an invention, she didn't know anymore. *"You remind me of my mother...."*

Josephine walked slowly, each step crunching against the gravel, her breath shallow, her mind replaying memories she wished she could silence. He reminded her of his father, and she wasn't sure that he wouldn't come after her.

Her anxiety surged as her thoughts circled back to that day, the day Mark's father handed her the pills. She remembered his cold, calculating stare, the way his words sliced through her resolve. *"You'll do as you're told,"* he'd said. Mark had stood behind him, his face pale, his hands trembling. Mark hadn't stopped it, he hadn't even tried.

Her nails bit into her palms as she walked, her fingers

curling into fists. She could still hear him, hoarse and pleading, after it was over. *"I couldn't save you, Josie. I couldn't save us. He would've destroyed you. Don't you see?"*

She'd seen it. She'd seen the fear in his eyes, the way he caved under the weight of his father's shadow. But that fear hadn't erased the betrayal. It hadn't healed the emptiness she'd carried ever since. Now, all that emptiness felt sharper, more vivid.

"Your parents would disown you." Mark's father's words echoed in her ears, overlapping with the cruel comments that had flooded the internet after the podcast.

Josephine stepped closer to the water, the edge of her shoes brushing against the wet stones. She slipped them off, letting her bare feet sink into the cool mud, the sensation was grounding, a fleeting tether to the earth before she let it go.

Her mind returned to Mark, that mix of regret and cowardice in his tone. *"You'll find someone better, Josie. Someone who can give you the life you deserve. A family, when the time is right."*

She'd given too much of herself to Mark, to men like him, men who saw her as something to be used, then discarded.

She thought of Callum, of his silence, of the way he'd looked at her in those last moments they'd shared. His anger, his distance, it was all the same. She'd spent her life bending for men who only wanted to break her.

"You did it without telling me? Without–" *He staggered back, like the air had been sucked from his lungs.* *"Why, Josie? Why would you do this?"*

She had folded her arms tightly across her chest, a futile attempt to hold herself together as her stomach churned. She couldn't tell him the truth, the truth about finding Mark, that it wasn't fear of the future or uncertainty that had driven her to it, but a quiet, desperate act of rebellion. Against him. Against the life they'd built, one suffocating step at a time.

"It wasn't the right time," she'd said, her tone clipped, rehearsed. "I didn't see a way forward for us."

Callum's laugh was hollow, more a sharp exhale of disbelief. "You didn't see a way forward, or you didn't want one?"

Josephine flinched, her composure slipping. His words, his scrutiny, carved into the parts of her she'd tried to keep hidden. He always did that, saw too much, demanded too much. It was suffocating.

"I made the choice," her voice rising, "And I won't apologize for it."

"You don't get to decide this alone!" Callum thundered. The tears in his eyes betrayed his anger. "You've taken everything from me, Josephine. You don't even care what it's done to me, do you?"

Her throat tightened, the sight of his pain hitting harder than she'd anticipated. But she couldn't back down. Not now. "I care," she said, softer this time, but it only seemed to enrage him more.

"Then fix it," he pleaded, stepping closer. "We can fix this. I'll forgive you, Josephine, for all of it. I just need you to stay. I can't lose you."

His desperation sent a shiver down her spine. It was everything she should have wanted, his willingness to fight for her, to salvage their shattered marriage. But all she felt was a crushing sense of finality.

She reached for the divorce papers she'd left folded on the edge of the dresser and held them out between them like a barrier. "I can't do this anymore, Callum."

His face twisted in anguish, but beneath the pain, she saw something darker flicker. Possession. Control. The same things she'd been running from since the beginning. He snatched the papers from her hand, his grip so tight she thought he might tear them in two.

"You think you'll be free of me? This doesn't end with a signature, Josephine. It doesn't end with you walking away."

Her breath caught, the intensity of his words chilling her. But she forced herself to stand firm. "It ends with me choosing the life I want, and it's not this."

The truth weighed on her, a truth she could never admit to him. Not then, not now. It wasn't just about Mark, though he'd been her future when Callum was still her present. It was about the life she couldn't have with Callum. A life where she wasn't always looking over her shoulder, wondering if she belonged to herself or to him.

Her fingers brushed against her pocket, where her medications once sat, she'd thrown the empty cartridges in the trash can a few yards back.

She waded into the lake, the cold biting at her now heavy legs, her arms, her chest, until it surrounded her completely. It was startling at first, then numbing. She floated on her back, her arms spread wide, her eyes fixed on the darkening sky.

Her thoughts drifted to the moment she walked into Amy's room with the OR cart.

The room had smelled of antiseptic and iron, the chaos pressing in as the doctor worked frantically to stop the bleeding. The fetus in the nurse's hand had looked so small, too small. The sight of it had twisted something deep inside her, something she thought she'd buried long ago. He didn't look real. Her gaze drifted to Amy's pale state. She was alone, she was terrified, she was on the precipice of death. There was so much blood, her blood pressure was dangerously low, and her doctor's demeanor was frantic as he pulled pieces of placenta out of her body, a usually whole organ, was riddled with cysts, resembling ground beef beneath his fingertips... And then she thought of the day she lost her own baby, the only baby she ever wanted...

The first stars appeared, tiny pinpricks of light that felt impossibly far away. She let out a shuddering breath, the tension in her body ebbing away as the water held her. She thought of her career, her choices, the reactions, messages, calls. She hadn't been able to quiet the storm, it only pulled her deeper into darkness.

The water lapped gently against her face, her hair fanning out like a dark halo. Her mind quieted, the noise fading until there was only the stars, the water, and the cold. She thought of Mark, of Callum, of her life.

This will be my peace, she thought.

TWENTY SEVEN

The Riverview gleamed under the midday sun, its wide windows capturing the golden light and spilling it across the polished floors. Inside, the space was a flurry of pastel balloons, delicate floral arrangements, and carefully arranged tables laden with finger foods and desserts.

Charlotte walked in with Genevieve perched on her hip, her cheeks flushed with excitement. Jack trailed behind her, carrying an oversized diaper cake that he carefully placed on the gift table.

"All right, everybody!" Jack called as he clapped his hands to call attention. "Welcome to the baby shower of the century. Drinks are over there, snacks are over here, and if anyone touches the cupcakes before the games, you'll have me to answer to."

Laughter rippled through the room as Charlotte rolled her eyes, leaning over to whisper something to him that made his grin widen.

Amy stood near the entrance, taking it all in. She adjusted the hem of her dress, her fingers smoothing over the soft fabric, a nervous habit, something to do with her hands when the weight in her chest became too much. She wanted to be here. She wanted to celebrate her best friend, to throw herself into the joy of it all. But the ache hadn't eased, no matter how hard she tried to push it down.

Today, Charlotte was thirty–two weeks pregnant. Amy should have been twenty–four. Viability. A milestone her baby never reached. It had only been a month, but it felt like an eternity.

The thought wedged itself into her ribs, sharp and

unyielding. Twenty-four weeks meant a chance. It meant doctors would try. It meant incubators and steady beeping monitors and tiny hands gripping fingers. It meant something other than an ending. *Maybe he would have survived whatever complication caused his death.*

She swallowed hard, blinking against the warmth stinging her eyes.

Charlotte spotted her and waved, her smile lighting up her face. "Amy! You made it!"

Amy forced a smile, stepping forward. The hug was careful, like Amy might break, though she knew Charlotte didn't mean it that way.

"Of course I made it. Wouldn't miss it for the world." The words tasted hollow, but she hoped Charlotte wouldn't hear it.

Charlotte pulled back, her eyes scanning Amy's face with quiet concern. "How are you feeling? Everything okay?"

Amy's smile thinned. "I'm fine, Charlotte. Really."

Charlotte's brow furrowed, her free hand resting lightly on Amy's arm. "You sure? You look a little pale. Have you been eating enough? Drinking enough water?"

Amy hated this. Hated the way grief made her something fragile, something people tiptoed around.

"I'm fine," she repeated, stepping back to put a little more space between them. "Seriously, Charlotte. Stop worrying about me. This is your day."

Charlotte hesitated, her expression flickering with uncertainty before she nodded. "Okay. Just let me know if you need anything, all right?"

Amy nodded, forcing another smile as Charlotte was swept away by another guest offering congratulations.

She exhaled slowly, gripping the edge of a nearby table to steady herself. Around her, the party carried on; glasses clinking, soft laughter threading through conversations, the distant hum of music.

It was beautiful. It was everything a baby shower should be.

And it was everything Amy had lost.

Upstairs in the security office, Callum leaned back in his chair, focused on the video feed from the event below. The cameras offered a clear view of the room: Charlotte chatting with guests, Jack cracking jokes, and Amy standing off to the side, her expression guarded. *She's trying so hard to hold it together, but they're suffocating her. Can't they see that?*

He zoomed in slightly, his attention narrowing on Amy. She moved through the crowd with a forced grace, her smiles quick and fleeting. The way her fingers gripped the stem of her champagne flute–not drinking, just holding it–told him everything he needed to know. *She needs a way out. Someone to give her space. Someone who understands.*

He stood, stretching his shoulders as he made his way downstairs. The chatter and laughter of the party grew louder as he approached, but his focus remained on Amy.

Amy had just escaped to the refreshments table, her smile slipping as she poured herself a glass of sparkling water. She felt a light tap on her shoulder and turned to find Charlotte there again.

"Are you sure you're okay? You can take a break if you need to."

Amy gripped the glass. "Charlotte, I'm *fine*."

Charlotte blinked, taken aback. "I just want to make sure–"

"I said I'm fine," Amy interrupted, her tone cutting now. She set the glass down harder than she meant to, the sound making a few nearby guests glance their way. "Can we not make this about me for once? This is your baby shower, not my therapy session."

Charlotte stepped back, hurt flashing across her face before she masked it with a tight smile. "Of course, I'm sorry."

Amy exhaled, guilt already creeping in as Charlotte walked away. She pressed her fingers to her temple, willing herself to keep it together.

"Hey, I lit the fire pits. Want to join me?"

Amy turned at the sound of Callum's voice, her shoulders relaxing slightly at the sight of him. He stood a few feet away, his hands in his pockets.

"Yes, dear lord, thank you." She let out a shaky breath, this time grabbing her full glass of champagne and she followed him through the mill and onto the patio. Callum gestured for her to sit. The smoky flames caught the breeze as her gaze fixed on the raging river.

"What are you thinking about?" Callum leaned forward, resting his forearms on his thighs. His hair fell against the reflection of the flames dancing in his eyes.

"Just Charlotte being Charlotte," Amy muttered, picking up her glass again. "She's so busy worrying about everyone else, she forgets this is supposed to be her day."

Callum nodded, inching closer. "She means well. Too much fuss can feel like a shit show, I get that."

Amy huffed. "That's one way to put it." and as carefully as she tried to keep herself composed; the dam broke.

Callum tilted his head, studying her for a moment before standing. "Come, I'll drive you home. Let's take Maslow for a walk."

She looked at him, her defenses softening slightly. "That... might not be the worst idea."

"Good, because I've been having withdrawals from spending time with both of you." he winked as he extended a hand to help her from her seat.

Amy nodded, some of the tension easing from her shoulders. "Thanks, babe," she swallowed hard. "I mean–."

He put up a hand. "I know, I know, I'm hot. Deal with

it." His dimples appeared and her tensioned eased, partly from mortification, largely from the effect he had on her.

Later that afternoon, Amy found herself walking alongside Callum on the winding trail near the neighborhood. Maslow trotted ahead, his leash loose in Callum's hand as the dog sniffed curiously at everything in sight.

The crisp air was a welcome contrast to the crowded stuffiness of the venue, and Amy found herself breathing a little easier.

"Feel better?" Callum asked, glancing at her.

"Yeah," she admitted, "I just... needed to get out of there."

"I figured, you don't have to be the one to hold everyone together, Ames."

Amy nudged his shoulder. "You're not wrong, it's my kryptonite."

"I think a dog is the next step for me, I need the company, thoughts on breeds?"

Amy's demeanor shifted, smiling for the first time in weeks. "Maslow is the best thing that's happened to me in a long time, he's the cutest, I totally think you should go for it."

"Alright, from your mouth, to God's ears. You shall be coming with me to pick out all the accessories, because I have no idea what I'm doing."

"Noted. Fair warning, rage cuddles are a thing, and you will be subjecting your fur baby to them daily."

"I've already picked a name."

She glanced at him, raising an eyebrow. "For your imaginary dog?"

"Uh huh, Bloom." Callum's gaze shifted between the dog, and Amy's animated gestures as she walked. He handed her a bottle of water.

"Bloom?" Amy repeated, twisting the cap off the bottle.

"Okay, it's kind of earthy. I like it." She took a sip, eyeing him over the rim like she was waiting for more.

"Yeah." He raised an eyebrow, waiting for it to hit.

"Stop. The psychologist?" her smiled widened.

"Yep, and here's the kicker." He sighed dramatically, shaking his head like he was already regretting his own joke. "So that when we go for dog walks, I can say that Maslow came before Bloom."

The second the words left his mouth, Amy choked mid-sip. Water sprayed out of her nose, her hand shooting up to shield her face as she gasped for air.

Callum grinned, tapping her on the shoulder. "There it is, I think that means we've officially reached second base."

Amy wheezed, still coughing and clutching her stomach, the water bottle forgotten in her hand.

"And now you're choking," he continued, his tone unrelenting. "Which means we definitely can't make it to third."

She glared at him, her face still red as she tried to catch her breath.

"Breathe, Ames," Callum's smirk widened, "Because if you die right now, that would absolutely ruin this relationship."

Amy finally managed a ragged inhale, her laughter breaking through the coughing fit. "Excuse–me, sir. Are you–trying–to–add murder, –ahem– to the list this evening?" She cleared her throat again, "I almost died."

"And yet, here we are," he snorted. "You, alive. Me, hilarious. Maslow, officially outdone by Bloom."

"Stop, I'm crying." She gasped through a fit of laughter.

They walked in companionable silence for a while, the crunch of gravel underfoot the only sound.

Amy tapped his shoulder. "Thanks for this, I didn't realize how much I needed it."

Callum shrugged; his gaze fixed ahead. "To laugh? Oh, I have more of those jokes. Let me know when to start firing."

"No, for this. For you." She slowed as they came to the end of the path, with the river sprawled out in front of them.

"Sometimes it takes someone on the outside to see what you need."

"Callum, Can I make you dinner?"

Callum's expression lifted, "I would love that."

"Good." She smiled. "My place, or yours?"

"That depends on you, Ames." He took her hand in his.

"Come to my house, I know where everything is."

"What do you want me to bring?" he asked, his dimples flashing.

"That smile."

TWENTY EIGHT

Amy glanced at him from across the table, the candlelight softening the sharp lines of his face. She gulped at his sincerity, her fork stilling over her plate. She didn't say anything, but the look she gave him spoke volumes. For the first time in a long time, she didn't feel completely alone.

She gathered the plates, standing before he could object. "Desserts in the fridge if you want it," she called over her shoulder.

"Didn't realize this was a full-course affair," he replied, leaning back in his chair, his gaze following her movements.

"Only the best for the guy who saved me from my mental spiral today, she winked as she carried the dishes to the sink.

"Want help?"

"Nope. I've got it." She rinsed them off before placing them in the dishwasher. He watched her intently, sipping his drink as Maslow plopped himself at his feet.

When she returned, Callum was by the fireplace, glass in hand, his free arm resting on the mantle. The firelight flickered across his forearm, highlighting the tattoo there. She sat on the couch, the warmth from the fire seeping through her fingers.

Her gaze lingered on the ink on his forearm, curiosity finally pushing the words out.

"The tattoo, what does it mean?"

Callum glanced down at his arm, his thumb running absentmindedly over the coordinates. For a moment, the flicker of the flames was the only sound between them. Then he turned

259

toward her.

"It's a place," he began, sinking into the chair across from her. "The rifle and helmet, they're part of a battlefield cross. It's a symbol for a fallen soldier. A friend." Callum glanced at her, then down at his arm. "My best friend, Max. The coordinates mark where he died."

The silence stretched, but it wasn't uncomfortable. Amy studied his expression, the firelight casting shadows on his face, the usual edge in his demeanor softened by something deeper. She gripped her knees, "I'm sorry."

Amy's muscles tensed, the weight of his words sinking in. "That must have been hard to experience."

Callum leaned back; his gaze fixed on the flames as his expression hardened. "We were on patrol. I was lead. It was my call to push forward." His voice grew quieter. "I missed something. A tripwire. He stepped on it."

Amy's hand instinctively moved to her mouth. She wanted to say something, anything, but the depth of his pain held her silent.

"I watched him die," Callum continued, his jaw tightening as he stared into the fire. "One second he was right there, cracking some dumb joke. The next..." He dragged a hand through his dark hair, exhaling sharply. "Nothing I've done since has made up for it. And it never will."

"You can't blame yourself," Amy paused. "Even if you want to."

He looked at her then, his expression heavy with guilt. "Try telling that to his wife. To his kid. To the men who trusted me."

Taking a sip of wine, she shifted off her spot on the sofa, and walked over to where he was sitting. His gaze locked onto hers. "I've been there, Amy. I've made choices I regret, choices that hurt someone I loved. You're not the only one who's done something they can't take back."

She nodded, tears welling. Clearing her throat, she asked. "Any other tattoos?"

"Yes, one other."

"Well, where is it?"

"I'd have to take off my–" he laughed at her expression, and cleared his throat, "What about you?"

She pointed a finger at him, laughing. "Deflection! Fine, I'll show you mine first, but then I wanna see your other one." She turned her back to him, then reached over, pulling her long hair over her shoulder. Her scent was intoxicating, and he felt a surge of excitement trail his body. On the back of her neck was a small tattoo in white ink. There was a feather shaped like the letter "J" with its quill spelling 'ames' and two small birds flying away from the 's.'

"James?" Callum questioned.

"Mhmm, My dad. He called me Ames, because it tied his name to mine." Her lips rose into a smile. "Funny."

"What's that?"

"Callum, you're the only other person I've ever let call me that." Her cheeks flushed.

Callum's gaze lingered on the tattoo, the delicate white ink catching the light. His fingers itched to trace the design, but he stayed rooted in place, swallowing hard. The intimacy of the moment wasn't lost on him, and the way she said *his name* made him want her more.

"Only me, huh?" his tone dropped. A playful smile tugged at his lips.

Amy shrugged, her fingers idly twisting a strand of her hair. "Well, maybe you kind of remind me of him. A little."

"Your dad?" His brows furrowed slightly, his grin softening. "I hope that's a compliment."

Her eyes flicked to his, a smirk playing at her lips. "Don't push your luck."

He laughed, the sound warm and easy. His focus, on her. "It's beautiful, Ames," the nickname now carrying weight, "He'd be proud."

The way he said it, so sincere, so sure, made her stomach flutter. She turned quickly, trying to hide how much his words had affected her.

Callum's fingers brushed over Amy's shoulder as she leaned into him, her back against his chest. She could feel his heartbeat against her as his hands soothed her. But when they grazed the faint discoloration near her shoulder, he froze.

His thumb moved lightly over the spot, as if testing its reality. The bruise was faint, yellowed at the edges, but unmistakably shaped like fingers. His expression shifted.

"Amy," he hesitated, "What happened here?"

She stiffened, her body tensing beneath his touch. "It's nothing," she uttered quickly, her tone dismissive. "Just bumped into something."

"Bumped into something?" Disbelief edged his voice as his gaze swept over her. She shifted, pulling the blanket tighter around herself. "It happens," she shrugged.

He leaned back slightly, as he tilted her chin gently to meet his eyes. "Amy, this isn't just 'nothing.'" His hand hovered over her shoulder, brushing the bruise again, he kissed it.

She pulled away. "He didn't mean to," she murmured.

The weight of her words hit him like a freight train. Callum's expression hardened. "Mark," his tone was sharp, "What did he do?"

She shook her head. "He was angry," she admitted. "He thought I leaked the affair. I didn't, but... he thought I did. He just..." she trailed off, her hands trembling in her lap.

"He just what?" Callum pressed, his tone sharper now. "Amy,

what did he do to you?"

She swallowed hard, her gaze dropping to the floor. "He grabbed me, shoved me, maybe, I don't know. It wasn't... it wasn't as bad as it sounds."

Callum stood abruptly, pacing the room as his fists clenched at his sides. "As bad as it sounds?" he repeated, "Amy, that bastard put his hands on you."

She looked up at him, her tears spilling over. "It's my fault," she whispered. "I made him angry. I–"

"No," Callum interrupted sharply. He knelt in front of her, his hands gripping hers tightly. "Listen to me. None of this is your fault. Not one damn thing. Do you understand me?"

Her lip quivered as she nodded, but the shame in her eyes told him she didn't fully believe it.

"You deserve better," his hands cupped her face. "You deserve someone who loves you, who would never hurt you."

I love you, Ames. I love you more than anything. The thought was so loud, he felt like it had escaped his lips.

"And I can't stand by and watch you think you're not worth the world. *Fuck,* I'm going to kill him."

Callum's hand curled into a fist against his knee. "Amy, you need to get a restraining order."

Panic flashed across her face. "I can't, you don't understand. He'll find a way to turn it around, to make it worse."

Callum leaned closer, his hand brushing against her arm. "I *do* understand," he paused, "and that's why you need to do this. To protect yourself. To protect your future."

She looked at him, her tears spilling over again. "I don't know if I can."

"You can," he exhaled. "Because you're stronger than you think. And you're not alone in this. I'm here, and he will never fucking touch you again."

Her stomach fluttered as she met his gaze. The moment was heavy, teetering on the edge of something neither of them could define. Then Maslow barked, his nails clicking against the floor as he nudged Amy's leg with his nose.

Callum eyed him. "See? Even Maslow is pissed."

"Ha, no, he just wants to go outside."

Callum chuckled. Right, I'll take him out. "Up next on the to-do list, fencing in the yard for the goofball."

Amy let out a broken laugh, trying not to cry. Maslow barked again, more insistent this time.

She stood, but Callum caught her wrist gently. "No," He looked down at Maslow. "Let's go, boy."

Amy's heart twisted at the sight of him, his protective nature shining through even in the smallest moments. As Callum grabbed the leash and headed for the door, she leaned against the counter, her hands trembling as she wiped away her tears.

Callum walked back into the house, the brisk evening air still clinging to his jacket. "Your boy has too much energy," he joked, hanging up the leash.

She motioned for him to join her on the couch. "Okay, you think you got away with it, well guess what? Your turn," She waved her hands up.

Callum chuckled, shaking his head. "You're bossy, you know that?"

"And you're stalling," she shot back, crossing her arms.

With a dramatic sigh, he tugged his shirt over his head, revealing the lean muscles of his chest and the tattoo inked across his left rib cage. Amy let herself stare. His body, his muscles. The definition of his pecs. Heat trailed her cheeks. The design was intricate, a black–and–gray Celtic knot with a date inside it.

She leaned closer without thinking, her hand reaching out to touch the tattoo. Her fingers barely brushed his skin, but the contact sent a jolt through both of them.

"It's... beautiful, what's the symbolism? The date?"

"The Celtic knot is for my heritage. I'm Irish and Scottish. The date is a reminder of something else I lost."

Her brow furrowed, confusion flickering across her face. "What?"

He ran a hand over his face, the weight of his words pressing down on him. "My ex–wife." He hesitated, "She didn't want kids. She was in nursing school, trying to build her career. But I... I wanted a family. And I pushed her into it. I stopped respecting her choice, her autonomy. I threw out her birth control, initiated sex more, trying to get her to see that this was the next step."

She held her breath.

"When she got pregnant, she was devastated. And I told myself it was for the best, that she'd come around. But she didn't. She terminated the pregnancy." He looked away. "It broke us. I broke us."

The room was suffocatingly silent. Amy stared at him; her own pain momentarily eclipsed by the weight of his confession.

"I'm telling you this because I know what it's like to carry that kind of guilt," he ran his hands through his hair. "To feel like you've ruined everything. But you're not beyond redemption, Amy. You're not beyond forgiveness."

Tears blurred her vision, but she didn't wipe them away. "And you? Do you forgive yourself?"

He let out a shaky breath, his gaze falling to the floor. "I'm trying."

Her lips parted, but no words came. The weight of his words pressed against her chest, making it hard to breathe. She felt the pull of his gaze, the quiet strength and vulnerability beneath it, and it unraveled something inside her. A single tear escaped, tracing a hot line down her cheek.

Callum didn't flinch, didn't look away. The silence between them was thick, heavy, yet oddly grounding. For a moment, she let herself feel it, the pull, the ache, the comfort of someone seeing her, truly seeing her.

His gaze dropped to where her hand lingered on his ribs, and then back to her face. "You're beautiful," the words slipped out before he could stop them.

Amy blinked, her cheeks flushing. "Deflection," she noted.

"Honesty," he corrected, he leaned in, closing the space between them.

Her lips parted in surprise. She didn't move, didn't pull away. When his hand cupped her cheek, his thumb brushing lightly against her skin, she felt the world tilt.

"I can't, Ames." he murmured, his breath warm against her lips.

His gaze dropped to her mouth, lingering, unreadable. His fingers flexed against her skin, like he was holding himself back. Then, just when she thought he might pull away, he kissed her.

It wasn't tentative. It wasn't careful. It was deep and slow, a kiss that unraveled her, piece by piece. Her hands found his chest, fingers curling into the fabric before slipping up, winding around his neck, tangling in his dark waves.

He let her pull him closer. Let her feel the restraint in the way his lips moved against hers. It wasn't tentative or uncertain, it was deep and slow, a kiss that unraveled her piece by piece. Her hands found their way to his chest then curled around his neck as she wound her fingers through his dark waves.

"Well," a teasing smile broke through the tension, "that was unexpected." He chuckled. "Well not really, I've wanted to kiss you for months."

She laughed. "Yeah, *totally* didn't see that coming."

"You're bossy *and* sarcastic, funny, and beautiful…" he said, brushing a strand of hair from her face. "This might be dangerous."

"Dangerous?" she repeated, arching a brow.

He grinned, the playfulness returning to his tone. "You're making me fall for you, Ames. That's a pretty dangerous game."

Her smile faltered, but she didn't pull away, not when his arms felt so safe, so sure.

She brushed the tear away quickly, managing a small, shaky smile. "Well, tonight deserves some ice cream. You want Jimmy Fallon or Stephen Colbert?"

Callum leaned back, pulling his shirt back over his head. He wanted her, fuck. He could take her then and there, but he knew that if he did, it would push her to do something she wasn't ready for. He smirked. "Always Fallon. No contest."

TWENTY NINE

Amy stood at the kitchen counter, slicing strawberries for Genevieve's breakfast. She moved mechanically, her mind tangled in the weight of the date. Three months ago, to the day, she had given birth. And now, Charlotte's due date landed on that same day; the day her son died. It came so much faster than she had anticipated, but it also felt like she lost her baby yesterday. Charlotte had made every excuse in the book to try to get Amy out of watching Genevieve today, and it hurt. She was strong enough, capable enough to watch their daughter. She was damned if she was going to let Charlotte take this away from her, the ability to be the friend she should be.

She knew it would be a difficult day, but she also wanted to prove to herself, prove to everyone that she is okay. *I am okay? Right?*

Genevieve bounded into the kitchen, her hair wild and her face alight with a smile. "Can we play outside after breakfast, Aunt Amy? Maslow loves when I throw the ball!"

Amy forced a smile, ruffling Genevieve's curls. "Of course, sweetie. Finish your toast first, okay?"

She set Genevieve's plate on the table and watched as the little girl dug in with the kind of unbridled enthusiasm only a child could muster. Amy's stomach churned, but she ignored it, focusing instead on the small moments of joy she could cling to.

The yard was alive with the sound of Genevieve's laughter and Maslow's excited barks as the morning wore on. Amy sat on the porch steps, her arms wrapped around her knees, her gaze fixed on the little girl as she chased Maslow across the lawn.

The rhythmic thud of running footsteps drew Amy's attention, and she looked up to see Callum jogging up the driveway, his shirt damp with sweat and his breathing steady. He slowed when he saw her, his gaze narrowing slightly as he approached.

"Morning." His breathing was uneven as he placed his hands on his knees.

She returned his smile, feeling a warmth spread through her chest. "Hey, Cal, are you stalking me now?"

"Nah, I'm just stalking your dog." He bent down to ruffle Maslow's fur, kissing him on the forehead." *Oh my god, that was so cute.* Amy thought.

The collar of his shirt was ringed with sweat, his skin dewy, giving off a musky aroma that drew her in.

"Only if you promise to give me more attention than Maslow, honestly, I'm a bit offended." she replied, grateful for the company, *for his company.* He settled on the step next to hers. Amy tilted her head, raising an eyebrow. "Did you run all the way here?"

"Figured I'd stop by, see how you're holding up." His eyes met hers, and something softened in his expression. "Genevieve keeping you busy?"

"She's a whirlwind," Amy hands gestured toward the yard. "Maslow's loving it, though. I think they're conspiring against me."

Callum smirked, stepping closer to ruffle Maslow's fur as the dog bounded up to him. "Well, I'm here for Maslow, obviously. He's the star of the show." He pressed a dramatic kiss to the dog's head, earning a delighted bark.

Amy laughed despite herself. "And here I thought you were here to check on me."

Callum straightened, his tone carrying a seriousness that made her throat jump. "You're not wrong."

Her smile faltered. "I'm fine, Cal."

She's not fine. Callum thought. He could see it in the way her hands fidgeted, the way her shoulders curled in just slightly. But he didn't call her on it. "I know you are," he replied instead, "But it doesn't mean it's not hard, or that fine can't become great."

Amy looked away. "Charlotte didn't even want me to watch Genevieve. Like I'm not capable or something."

"She knows you're capable," Callum brushed against her shoulder. "She's just trying to be thoughtful and considerate, that's all."

Amy's throat worked as she swallowed. "I just... I need to prove to myself that I can handle this. That I'm not..." She trailed off.

Not broken, Callum finished silently, his stomach twisting. He sat beside her on the steps, careful to keep a bit of space between them.

"You're here. You're doing it. That's what matters."

She let out a shaky breath, her arms tightening around her knees. "What if, what if it's too much, Cal? What if I can't be happy for her? For her baby?"

Callum's heart twisted. "It's okay to feel however you feel," he drew in a breath. "No one's expecting you to be anything other than what you are."

Amy turned to him. "And what am I?"

Strong. Resilient. Beautiful. The words rose to his lips but stayed trapped behind his teeth. "You're human," he responded with instead.

A silence settled between them, heavy but not uncomfortable. Amy looked back at the yard, watching Genevieve toss a ball for Maslow. "You always know what to say," she murmured.

Callum's lips quivered into a faint smile. "Not always. But I try."

She glanced at him, her gaze lingering. It made his pulse quicken, his hands curling into fists against his knees.

Amy broke the moment first, exhaling softly. "Thanks for coming by, it means a lot."

"Anytime," He stood, brushing off his hands. "You've got this, Ames. And if you don't, it's a short jog away." He said, then gestured to his sweaty state.

She nodded, her gaze lingering on him as he walked back toward the driveway.

△△△

Amy and Genevieve were knee deep in a game of Jenga when Lincoln texted that the baby had arrived. They made their way to the hospital. Amy sent a text to Callum.

Amy: Baby time, wish me luck. I feel like I'm going to puke.

Callum: I know it sucks, but you've got this.

Amy stepped into the hospital room, the sterile scent of disinfectant and faint antiseptic soap assaulting her senses. Her stomach churned as her eyes darted to the bassinet beside the bed, where Charlotte lay cradling her newborn, her face glowing with joy despite her exhaustion.

Genevieve's small arms coiled around Amy's neck, her warmth grounding and yet unbearable all at once. Amy clung to her like a lifeline, her heart hammering against her ribs. Every step forward felt like wading through quicksand.

"Aunt Amy!" Genevieve wriggled excitedly, "I see the baby!"

Lincoln turned at the sound, his expression softening as they met Amy's. He moved toward her, his smile kind but weary. "Hey," he said gently, reaching out for Genevieve. "Come here, kiddo. Let Aunt Amy sit down."

Amy hesitated, her arms tightening instinctively around

Genevieve before she released her into Lincoln's waiting embrace. The moment Genevieve was gone, the weight of her absence felt unbearable. Amy's arms fell limply to her sides as she stumbled to a plastic chair in the corner, as far from the bassinet as the small room allowed.

She couldn't bring herself to look at Charlotte or the baby. The faint coos and tiny sounds emanating from the bassinet felt like daggers, each one slicing through her composure. She clenched her hands together, her nails digging into her palms. Outwardly, she was still, numb, composed. Inside, her heart was breaking into a thousand jagged pieces.

"Come meet him," Charlotte motioned for her to come closer.

Amy's lungs felt like lead as she forced herself to meet Charlotte's gaze.

Lincoln approached with the baby swaddled in a soft blue blanket. "Here," He placed the baby in Amy's arms.

The weight of him was unbearable. The warmth of his tiny body seeped into hers, threatening to undo her completely. She couldn't look down, couldn't bring herself to see him. She held her breath, and it took every ounce of willpower not to shatter right there in front of them.

"He's perfect," She finally forced herself to glance down. The baby's dark hair, his tiny, delicate fingers curled into a fist, it was too much. Something inside her cracked, a silent, agonizing fracture.

She stood abruptly, careful not to jostle him as she approached Charlotte. "He's perfect, Charlotte," she felt her throat tighten. "I'm so happy for you."

Charlotte reached out, taking her son back into her arms. "Thank you for everything today."

Amy nodded, blinking rapidly to keep the tears at bay. She felt the saliva thicken, her stomach twist. "You need your time together," she said, her words clipped but gentle. "I'll call to check in later."

Without waiting for a response, she turned and walked out of the room. The moment the door clicked shut behind her, the composure she had fought so hard to maintain shattered. She broke into a run, her sneakers echoing against the polished floors as she fled down the corridor. Her vision blurred with tears, her chest heaving with silent sobs.

By the time she reached the hospital's main exit, her legs were trembling, she was gasping for air. She didn't see him at first, but then Callum was there, his tall frame a steady presence amidst the chaos in her chest.

"Ames," he said softly, pulling her from the brink.

Her body moved of its own accord, collapsing into his arms. His embrace was firm and unwavering, his scent warm and familiar. The dam broke, and she crumbled completely, her sobs muffled against his chest as he held her tightly.

"It's okay," he murmured, his fingers stroking through the silky strands of her hair. "I've got you. Let it out."

And she did. Every ounce of pain, every shard of heartbreak poured out of her, her body trembling against him. She let herself be vulnerable, let herself be seen.

He walked her to the car, ushering her into his truck as he rounded the vehicle and jumped into the driver's seat.

"I'm going to drop you off, so that you can have a relaxing bath while I grab some dinner. You think you can handle being alone for thirty minutes?"

Amy nodded.

Amy sat curled on the couch, Maslow resting at her feet, his soft snores breaking the silence. Her phone dinged, and she looked at it to see a message from Callum. *Didn't know what to get you, stopped at two places.*

As she was about to tap a reply, a low growl escaped Maslow

as he huffed off the couch, the sound of his claws clicking against the wood floors filling the room. There was a slight knock, and the front door creaked open. Callum stepped in. "Figured thirty second warning would give you no time to protest." he held up two takeout bags.

Amy glanced up, exhaustion clouding her features. "If it's not soup, I don't want it."

"Lucky for you, it's miso. Extra tofu, but I hit the drive through for Mexican, just in case you wanted a bit more spice."

He made out a faint smile. That's cute actually, how does he do it? She thought.

Callum smiled, setting the bag down. He slid into the sofa opposite her, his sharp gaze softening as he took in her pale face.

"You don't have to keep doing this," Amy murmured, adjusting the blanket over her lap.

Callum shrugged. "You need someone, and I'm someone. Deal with it."

A faint smile tugged at her lips, but it faded just as quickly. She stared down at the table, her fingers absentmindedly picking at the fraying edge of the blanket. "It's been–" she let the air out of her lungs.

"I know," Callum leaned back against the couch, "You've been through hell, Amy. No one expects you to just... be okay."

She nodded faintly, her gaze fixed on the steam rising from the soup container. "It's not just the grief," she said after a moment. "It's this house. Every corner of it reminds me of him...of them." Her hand trembled as she gestured around. "The nursery upstairs. The stupid mugs we bought together. I can't do it anymore."

"I just... this is too much." Her breath rattled her chest.

"I know, Ames. But you did it, the worst of it is over." He placed his hand in hers.

Callum's brow furrowed, his hands resting lightly on his knees. "Would it be helpful if I packed the nursery for you? You will use those things at some point, but it may be better to have it put away."

Amy glanced at him, her lips pressing into a thin line. "Yeah, maybe." She sighed. "I signed the divorce papers. Mark doesn't care about this place. It was always mine to begin with." She paused, swallowing hard. "I've been looking at listings. Vermont, maybe. I just need to get out of here."

The words hung in the air between them, heavy with finality. Callum's expression was unreadable. He nodded slowly. "If that's what you need, then you should do it."

She searched his face. "I built a life here. A life that fell apart. How do I even begin again?"

He didn't answer immediately. Instead, he reached out, his fingers brushing hers lightly where they rested on the edge of the blanket. The touch was barely there, but it steadied her. She hadn't realized how much she needed something, someone, solid to anchor her.

"You don't have to figure it all out at once," he said softly. "One step at a time. And you're not alone in this, Ames. I'm here."

The weight of his words pressed against her chest, and she let herself lean into the moment. The heat of his hand against hers was grounding, and she clung to it like a lifeline.

"I don't know what I'm doing," she admitted, "I keep thinking I should feel something...anger, relief, anything. But all I feel is this emptiness."

Callum shifted closer, his knee brushing hers. "That emptiness will pass. Maybe not today, or tomorrow, but it will. And until then, you just keep going."

Amy blinked back tears, his words sinking deep into the hollow places inside her. She turned her hand over, her palm brushing his. It was impulsive, but the warmth of his touch calmed her in a way she didn't fully understand.

"Callum..." she began, but the words caught in her throat. She shook her head, "This is ridiculous. I'm being ridiculous. You don't need to keep showing up, I'm sure there are countless things you could be doing."

He tilted his head, his lips curving into a faint smile. "Maybe, but I want to."

His honesty made her stomach flip. She looked away, focusing on the frayed threads of the blanket again. Her mind wandered to all the nights he'd checked in on her, the meals he'd dropped off, the times he'd just sat with her in silence when the weight of the world felt unbearable.

And now, the thought of him not being here scared her more than she cared to admit.

She glanced back at him. "You're not going to let me push you away, are you?"

"Not a chance." The look in his eyes betrayed something deeper.

Her thoughts were spinning. *It was too soon. It had to be too soon.* But as he shifted slightly closer, the space between them narrowing, she wondered if it was just her grief making her hesitate–or something else entirely.

The silence stretched between them, heavy with possibilities, until Callum broke it with a soft chuckle. "Your soup's getting cold."

Amy exhaled a shaky laugh, her lips curving into the faintest smile. "God forbid."

He leaned back, his gaze lingering on her for a beat longer before reaching for his jacket. "I'll let you get some rest," he said, his tone gentle. "But Amy–if you need anything, you call me. Anytime." He kissed her lightly, and her stomach did a summersault.

As he stood, she hesitated, watching him move toward the

door. "Callum," she called after him.

He paused, turning back. "Yeah?"

"Thank you." The words felt inadequate, but they were all she could manage.

His smile was small but warm. "Anytime," he said again.

And then he was gone, leaving the room feeling somehow both emptier and lighter all at once. Amy curled back into the couch, pulling the blanket tighter around herself. For the first time in months, the crushing weight of her grief felt a little less suffocating. And she wasn't sure if it was because of the soup, or the man who had brought it. She rose from the seat, throwing a few things into a bag before grabbing Maslow's leash, his food and bowl, pausing for a moment to look at Maslow, but she couldn't focus. She then tapped her leg, and led him to the car.

THIRTY

Amy contemplated the idiotic idea of showing up, with a packed bag and the dog for five seconds, before she bounded up the steps. She knocked on the door. When he answered, Callum's heart twisted at the sight of her. Her face was pale, her eyes rimmed red, but there was a steeliness beneath the exhaustion, something holding her together even as she unraveled.

"I leave you for five minutes, and now you're moving in?" She started to laugh, and then immediately cry, her chest rising and falling as she fought to steady her breath. The weight of the past days had hollowed her out, leaving her raw and alone. She didn't know why she'd followed him home, or maybe she did. She couldn't face her own walls, couldn't let the silence swallow her whole again.

She didn't move at first, her gaze fixed on the floor. Then, with a slow nod, she stepped forward. The door clicked shut behind her, and the weight of the silence pressed in.

The house was dimly lit, the soft glow of a lamp casting warm light over the worn wood floors. Amy stood inside the doorframe; her arms wrapped around herself as if holding in everything she couldn't say. Her bag hung limply at her side, Maslow's leash dangling from her fingers.

She looked up, and something inside him cracked. He let out a heavy breath.

"No," she said abruptly. "No talking. Just... I need..."

Her words trailed off, and before he could respond, she

reached for him. Her fingers curled into the fabric of his shirt, pulling him closer, her lips brushing his with a tentative desperation that sent a jolt through him.

"Ames," he breathed, his hands instinctively landing on her waist. He didn't pull her in, didn't press her further.

Her eyes met his, wide and pleading. "I just want to feel something other than this. I can't sleep at home, I can't be alone." She sighed. "but when I'm with you…"

Her vulnerability tore through him. He cupped her face with one hand, his thumb brushing a tear from her cheek. "Then let me take care of you."

The words hung between them. She nodded, her chest shuttering as he dipped his head, capturing her lips in a kiss.

It wasn't rushed. It wasn't frantic.

He kissed her like she was something sacred, something fragile. His lips moved against hers with a tenderness that unraveled the walls she'd built around herself. Her hands slid up his chest, her fingers curling into his shoulders as he deepened the kiss, his tongue sweeping across hers in a way that deepened what she felt for him.

His lips broke from hers, his forehead resting against hers as they both caught their breath. "Come on," he murmured.

"I have something to show you." He knit his fingers with hers, drawing her to the back of the house, where the glow of the patio illuminated the dark living room.

Amy stepped onto Callum's back patio and stopped in her tracks. Soft string lights crisscrossed the space, casting a warm glow over the cozy conversation set arranged on an outdoor rug. A bubbling hot tub sat in the corner, its cover slightly ajar, steam hinting at the warmth waiting within.

"You've been busy," she said, turning to him with a smile.

Callum shrugged, his lips curling just enough to suggest he was proud of himself. "Thought it might be a nice surprise.

Honestly, I was about to text you to come over, you must have ESP."

"It is," She took in the thoughtful details. The intimacy of it all made her stomach flutter. "But I didn't bring a bathing suit."

His gaze lingered on hers, heat building as he stepped closer. "That's not a problem, you can borrow one of my shirts, or–"

She cut him off. "Or you can help me out of this."

"Can I?" his hand traced the back of her neck.

She nodded. "Yes."

Reaching for the zipper of her dress. His fingers grazed the bare skin of her back as he worked the fabric free. The garment slipped from her shoulders, pooling at her feet. She was standing in front of him in a lacy black bra and matching panties.

He bit his lip, a thumb circling her shoulder as he kissed her neck. Her eyes darted to his pelvis, and she could see that he was already ready for her, which made her gulp.

Amy shivered, not from the cool air but from the way his hands followed the curve of her waist, the way his touch burned a path down her arms. His lips teased further, leaving her wanting more.

He stepped back, giving her a lingering look before pulling his phone from his pocket. A tap on the screen, and the hot tub hummed to life, water swirling invitingly. "I'll grab some wine and snacks," he said, "Make yourself comfortable."

Amy nodded, watching him disappear into the house. Glancing at the JBL speaker, she reached for her phone, and slid into the hot tub. She opened *YouTube Music*, found her 'likes' playlist, and pressed shuffle.

Missy Elliot's *Get Ur Freak On* started to play, at full volume.

"SHIT." She dropped the phone.

"Oh yeah, Ames? You trying to set the mood?" He called out with a laugh, from the kitchen.

"*Automatic* playlist, Callum." She yelled back. *Oh my god, this is mortifying.* She clicked 'next', only to have *The Kind of Love We Make* by Luke Combs begin its familiar melody.

She palmed her face. Callum's laughter was echoing through the space.

"No, leave it, Ames." He called out. "This is fucking perfect." She laughed, shaking her head as she settled into the hot tub.

The warmth enveloped her, intoxicating and soothing all at once. She sank lower, letting the water ripple over her shoulders as a contented sigh escaped her lips. Drawing her arm out, she watched the steam rise from her skin, marveling at how perfect the moment felt.

The sound of the sliding door brought her back, and she turned to see Callum stepping onto the patio with Maslow trotting beside him.

"You're not allowed to be Maslow's human," Amy teased. "He's mine."

Wet Dreams by Artemas started playing, and she felt an immediate response to his hard stare, she could feel how turned on she was by his presence. He stood there, shirtless in a bathing suit. Her eyes trailed the muscles on his chest, his arms, his abs, he was beautiful, but not in an over the top way. He wasn't ripped, he had just the right amount of definition, an understated allure that was even more appealing.

And now, she felt herself staring.

Callum set the tray on the edge of the tub. "I'm not trying to steal him. I'm just here to elevate his quality of life. Consider me his executive assistant."

Amy snorted. "Executive assistant? That's rich. You're going to make him even more of a Prema donna."

Callum shrugged. Amy's cheeks flushed watching his muscles flex as he descended into the water, her brain playing it in slow motion. Her nipples constricted, and she felt a familiar pang of longing.

He gestured to Maslow, who was now sprawled on the outdoor rug, tongue lolling. "Clearly, he's thriving."

"Still, you can't be his favorite." she chuckled, shaking her head.

"No, that spot is reserved for you." he shot back with a wink, raising his glass.

She laughed, accepting the wine. The water lapped at the edge as he settled in, his arm brushing against hers. They sipped their wine in companionable silence for a moment before he turned to her, his expression softer now.

"What's going on in that head of yours?" he asked.

Amy looked into her glass, considering. "I think..." she sighed. "So many things. I'm having a hard time sleeping, every time I close my eyes I see James." she admitted. "It's been a long time since I've been able to just relax."

Callum gulped. She'd never shared his name, and the connection, the weight of it made his throat dry. He shifted closer, his hand finding hers under the water, and her heart jumped into her throat. "Let me be the person who makes sure you do."

Her stomach fluttered at his sincerity, her heart both aching and swelling in equal measure. "You're doing a pretty good job so far," she mused.

Amy sank deeper into the steaming water, letting her head rest against the cushioned edge of the hot tub. The gentle jets kneaded her shoulders, but her thoughts refused to loosen. She stared at the stars scattered across the inky sky; her stomach flipped.

Why am I so nervous? It's Callum, for God's sake. He's been nothing but...

She glanced at him across the tub, his head tipped back, eyes closed, as if the weight of the world didn't exist. The warm glow from the string lights above highlighted the sharp angles of his face, his damp hair curling at the edges. She swallowed hard, her gaze trailing down his neck to the faint scar cutting across his collarbone. It felt intrusive to stare, but she couldn't look away.

And yet, it's still him.

"You're staring," he murmured, cracking one eye open with a knowing smirk.

Her cheeks flamed, and she quickly turned her attention to the water rippling around her fingers. "No, I wasn't." *Heaven* by Kane Brown started to play, and she started to swoon. *The song, it was definitely the song.*

"Liar." He shifted closer, the water swaying between them. "What's on your mind?"

"Nothing," she said too quickly, but the tilt of his head told her he wasn't buying it. She sighed. "I just… I don't know. It's been a long time since I–"

"Since you let yourself relax?" he finished for her.

"Yeah, something like that."

He didn't push her to explain, didn't offer clichés or solutions. Instead, he reached over and gently tugged her foot into his lap, his thumbs pressing into her arch. She was startled at first, but the sensation eased her resistance.

"What are you doing?" she asked.

"Helping you relax." His grin was easy, teasing. "Stop overthinking everything."

She rolled her eyes but didn't pull away. As his hands worked over her foot, she allowed herself a rare moment of indulgence, sinking back against the tub and letting the tension seep out of her body.

He leaned forward, bending her leg toward her body as he pushed off his seat, the water rippling against her as he closed the distance. His lips brushed hers softly at first, then deepening as the kiss grew. She stood up, water dripping down the lace of her bra as she pressed him against the seat. His lips met hers, softly at first, then deeper, his other hand gripping her waist beneath the water.

Amy exhaled against his mouth, threading her fingers into his hair, her body pressing against his instinctively. Callum groaned, his grip tightening as she slid onto his lap, feeling the firm line of him against her.

He's hard.

The realization sent her heart racing, and heat pooling between her thighs.

Instead of hesitating, she pushed further, grinding subtlety against him, testing. His breath caught, his hands shifting, his fingers pressing against her bra before slipping a finger beneath the wire, tracing the curve of her breast.

Callum pulled back just enough to search her face, his restraint visible in the way his jaw clenched, the way his fingers flexed.

"Ames," he murmured.

She pressed closer, her lips tracing the scar on his collarbone, her hands roaming over his shoulders. *He feels so good.*

But when she reached for the strap of her bra, his hand shot up, catching hers.

"Not here." His voice was strained, low.

Frustration swirled through her, but beneath it, something deeper. *He wasn't stopping because he didn't want her.*

He was stopping because he did. The thought sent another rush of desire through her, making her want to push him just a little more. Before she could lose herself completely, a wave of water hit her back. Maslow jumped into the spa, happily panting as he took Amy's seat. His tail began wagging furiously, sending water everywhere.

"Maslow!" Amy exclaimed, half laughing, half exasperated.

Callum groaned, "Guess he didn't want to share his mom." *Cock block.* He ruffled his ears.

"See? This is what happens when you spoil him," Amy teased, standing to help lift the dripping dog out of the water. "Oh my God Maslow, you weigh five hundred pounds. She pushed him. GET OUT."

Callum smirked, *her ass was perfect, the way her cheeks peaked out of the black bottoms that framed her perfectly.* He shook his head, trying to focus on the soaking dog as he grabbed a towel. "I'll handle him. You stay here and enjoy yourself, but not too much." Her cheeks ran scarlet.

By the time Amy got upstairs, she tightened the towel before grabbing her kindle from her bag. The hot tub fiasco already felt miles away as she started scrolling through her TBR pile.

She padded toward the bathroom door, which had been left ajar, and peeked in. The sight stopped her. Callum had Maslow in the shower, the dog completely foamed up with soap, his golden fur sticking up at odd angles.

"You know you can just hose him off, right?" she teased, leaning against the doorframe.

Callum glanced at her over his shoulder, water dripping down his neck. "Not when he smells like a wet dumpster. He's getting the full spa treatment."

He glanced at her through the doorway, she was sitting on the bed which was parallel to the bathroom, giving him the best view. He arched a brow. "What are you reading?"

Amy was as mortified as she looked. "It's called *Lights Out*. Dark romantic comedy. Apparently, it's a vibe."

He chuckled. "Dark and comedy seem contradictory." He called out from the bathroom. "Maslow, SIT STILL."

She opened to the trigger warnings, skimming the list before gasping. "Oh my God," her laughter filled the space. "This list."

"What's the list?"

She began reading aloud, skipping a few for fear of dying of embarrassment. "Contains graphic violence, dubious consent, and breath play." She stopped, her eyes widening. "What the hell is *breath play*?"

Without missing a beat, Callum smirked. "That's an easy one. Come here." *Her stomach fluttered.* He closed the shower door, and leaned over her, his face so close it was all she could see. Then he blew air into her face.

Amy jerked back, startled, before bursting into laughter. "What the hell?!"

He cocked an eyebrow. "Huh, not having the indicated effect?"

She swatted at him, amused. "I can't with you."

Callum kissed her cheek. "Maslow wasn't as cooperative as I thought. I'm going to finish up in here. You good?"

Amy smiled, stepping in closer. "Do you need anything? A drink or–"

"Actually, yeah. Can you turn off the Bluetooth on your phone?"

"What?"

"Your phone is still connected to the speaker." his posture and tone held a casual confidence she'd come to find maddeningly attractive.

She tilted her head but did as he asked, grabbing her phone from the bed and swiping the Bluetooth off.

"Thanks." He turned back to the shower and said, "Hey, Google, play *My Home* by Myles Smith." He winked at her, and a smile cracked.

The familiar melody filled the bathroom a moment later, the kind of song that made you stop, listen, and feel. Callum's hands slowed as he rinsed Maslow, and Amy caught the faintest shift in his expression, a vulnerability she wasn't used to seeing from him.

Then he started singing along, his voice low and unpolished but somehow perfect.

Amy's chest tightened as the song unfolded, each line hitting deeper than she wanted to admit. She leaned against the counter, arms wrapped loosely around herself as she watched him.

Callum glanced back at her, his eyes locking on hers as he sang the last line.

The moment lingered, the air between them thick with something unspoken.

Maslow shook, sending droplets everywhere, and Amy startled, breaking the spell. Callum laughed, grabbing a towel.

Amy shook her head. "Sorry about the mess. He's a drama queen." She hesitated, still caught in the moment. "Callum," she started, but the words caught in her throat.

He turned toward her, still holding the towel. "Yeah?"

"Was that–" Her voice faltered, and she cleared her throat. "Was that your way of telling me something?"

His gaze softened, a small smile tugging at the corner of his mouth. "Maybe."

Before she could overthink it, she crossed the space between them, placing a hand on his chest. "Say it again."

Callum set the towel aside, his fingers brushing against her damp arm. "You're my home, Amy."

For a moment, the world outside the steamy bathroom ceased to exist.

"You're dripping," she finally managed, her voice shaking.

"So are you," he murmured, his hand trailing up to her neck. "We should fix that."

Her breath hitched as he led her into the shower, warm

water cascading over them. Maslow had already been ushered out, the door shut behind him, leaving only the two of them.

Callum's hands found her waist, pulling her against him. She didn't protest. *Couldn't.*

"You're ridiculous," she murmured, her lips brushing his.

"And you're impossible."

The kiss started slow, exploratory, before deepening into something neither of them could pull away from. Water ran between them, mingling with the heat building in the tiny space.

Callum's fingers traced her spine, sending shivers in their wake as he reached the clasp of her bra. He hesitated, his breath warm against her cheek, before undoing it with careful precision. The straps slid down her arms, and she resisted the urge to cover herself.

He noticed.

His lips brushed her temple, then lower, murmuring against her skin, "You're beautiful."

Amy swallowed hard. *He means it.* But the weight of her own insecurities pressed against her ribs. The softness of her stomach, the subtle changes that still lingered after the stillbirth, it all felt magnified in the intimacy of his gaze.

But Callum wasn't looking at her like she was broken.

His hands skimmed lower, to the waistband of her underwear, his thumbs hooking the fabric. He slid them down, inch by inch, his knuckles grazing her thighs as he dropped them to the tiled floor.

Amy's breath came unsteady as she let her hands wander, fingertips ghosting over the scars on his abdomen, as she pushed his swimsuit down. He tensed at first, but as her touch softened, tracing each line, his body relaxed beneath her hands.

She met his gaze. "You've never talked about these."

His fingers curled under her chin, tilting her face up to him.

"We all have scars we carry."

The weight of that truth settled between them.

Then Callum kissed her again, deeper this time, his hands sliding back up her body, memorizing every dip, every curve. He turned her, pressing her back against his chest, his erection hard against her lower back.

"You're not close enough," he murmured.

Her pulse pounded as he reached for the shampoo, lathering it between his palms before threading his fingers through her hair. A soft moan escaped her lips as he massaged her scalp, his movements unhurried, indulgent.

"Mmm, don't stop," she whispered, her eyes fluttering closed.

He didn't.

Callum rinsed the suds away, his touch lingering, mapping every part of her like she was something to be cherished, not hidden.

When he turned the water off, he didn't let go. Instead, he lifted her into his arms, a startled giggle escaping as his lips caught hers, she felt herself sliding against him, the slickness of both of them being wet making it impossible for her to stay in one place. The feeling of her body against his, of how he made her feel, her mind was spinning, her heart hammering.

This time, she didn't hesitate.

As he closed the distance to the bed, he pinned her wrists gently to the mattress, his weight hovering above her as he blew air down her collarbone. He cocked an eyebrow.

"About breath play…. Let me try again." His breath was now against her neck, hot and cold at the same time.

Her laughter filled the room, her cheeks flushed. "Callum, stop!" she said through fits of laughter, "I'm really ticklish." She snorted.

"So sexy, do that again."

His playful tone shifted; his movements slower. He brushed his lips against the hollow of her throat, his breath warm against her skin. Her laughter faded, replaced by a soft, involuntary gasp.

"Still funny?" he murmured, his lips now grazing her jawline.

Her pulse quickened, her hands no longer fighting his hold. "Not… really."

"Good." The sound vibrated against her stomach as he let go of her wrists, his hands sliding to her waist. "Let's see where this goes."

He pushed himself off the mattress before kneeling in front of her, his hands trailing up her thighs, as he shifted her body to the edge of the mattress, pausing to look at her. Her body naturally arched toward his touch.

"Tell me if you want me to stop," his voice was steady but thick with restraint.

She exhaled sharply as his mouth found her inner thigh, His warm breath trailing a line from her knee cap to the apex of her thighs. She raked her nails across his forearms as a moan escaped. He focused his hot breath in a circular motion around her clit, and she saw stars, the sensation only heightening how vividly and painfully turned on she was.

His hands moved to her waist, then circled around her back, leaving a trail of goosebumps as his lips found her navel, her breasts, her nipples. Pressing warm kisses along her skin as his hands explored, his touch both gentle and firm. He took his time, peeling away every layer between them, revealing every inch of her as he slid his fingers between her legs, coating them with her excitement.

"You're beautiful," he rasped.

Her lips trembled, and she swallowed hard, unable to speak.

He kissed the faded scars on her abdomen, the places her body had endured so much, his touch a silent acknowledgment of her strength.

"Callum…"

"I'm here," he murmured against her skin, his hands bracing her hips as he moved lower.

She gasped, her back arching as his mouth found her, every stroke coaxing a response from her body that she hadn't felt in years, hadn't felt ever. He took his time, building her up, bringing her back down. Sweat was dripping off her body as he moved over her, his eyes locking on hers as he slipped a finger into her, and then another. She could feel how hard he was and she held her breath, unsure about taking him. "Don't worry, I've got you."

When he finally sank into her, his movements were careful, slow. She felt the resistance, a burn that aroused her even more. She inhaled sharply, taking all of him, her hands clutching his back as he stilled, giving her time to adjust.

When he kissed her again, it was slower, reverent, as if he were taking the time to memorize her. Her hands moved over his shoulders, down his back, gripping him. His skin was warm, grounding her when she felt like she might shatter under the weight of her own emotions.

Her tears began to spill. She couldn't stop them, couldn't hold them back, and the vulnerability of it left her breathless. But Callum didn't stop. He didn't pull away or question her. His hand, his thumbs brushing away the wetness as he kissed her cheeks, her forehead, her lips.

"It's okay," he murmured against her skin.

Her body ached in ways she hadn't known it could, the physical pain of her still-healing wounds mingling with the emotional scars she carried. But his touch was careful, his hands guiding her as if he understood the weight she bore.

How could this feel so raw, so beautiful, after everything? she thought.

She took his mouth with hers, and for the first time in

days, the weight in her chest lifted. It wasn't just the physical connection, it was him, grounding her, pulling her back from the edge she'd been teetering on. She could feel every sensation, every inch of him as he moved inside her, filling her so completely, so perfectly. *He is perfect.*

"Are you okay?"

Tears spilled down her cheeks, but she nodded. "Yes."

They moved together, their breaths mingling, their bodies finding a rhythm that felt like coming home and falling apart all at once. Every touch, every kiss, every whispered word was a reminder that she was still alive, still capable of feeling something other than pain.

Amy's heart raced as Callum's lips found hers, soft but insistent, pulling her into the moment. Her fingers trembled as they slid into his hair, the dark strands coarse and familiar against her skin. She inhaled his musky scent, The world seemed to fall away, leaving just the two of them suspended in the quiet intimacy of his touch.

It wasn't just the first time since her divorce; it was the first time she'd let herself feel this exposed. The thought made her hesitate, her lips faltering against his, but Callum didn't push. He pulled back slightly, his breath brushing her skin.

"You're here, with me," he whispered, as if he could sense her thoughts unraveling.

She'd told herself she'd never let anyone this close again, that she was too broken, too raw to let someone see her like this. And yet, here he was, patient and unwavering, as if he saw every jagged edge of her and wanted them anyway.

Amy closed her eyes, swallowing hard. *It's just a moment*, she told herself, though deep down, she knew it wasn't. This was more. It was everything.

His breath was ragged as he moved with her, matching her rhythm. She felt her body tremble beneath his, her cries muffled against his shoulder as she finally let herself go, the release overwhelming and all–consuming.

Callum followed her, his body shuddering as he stilled. He whispered something, words she couldn't fully hear but felt in the way he held her, in the way his hands trembled against her skin.

Afterward, he didn't move away. He didn't leave her to collect herself or try to fill the silence with meaningless reassurances. Instead, he pulled her against his chest, his arms wrapping tightly around her as if to shield her from the weight of the world.

Amy pressed her face into his shoulder, her tears soaking his skin. The ache of loss, of longing, of grief, mingled with the fragile hope that maybe, just maybe, she could start to let go of the pain she carried.

Callum's hand moved against her back, his touch gentle and unhurried. She could feel his heartbeat beneath her cheek, steady and reassuring, as if it were telling her she wasn't alone anymore.

Her mind raced with everything she'd been trying to bury, the pieces of herself she thought were gone forever. But here, in his arms, she let herself feel it all. The pain. The connection. The quiet, unspoken promise that somehow, she might heal.

For the first time in years, Amy let herself believe that she wasn't broken beyond repair. That maybe, in Callum, she'd found something she never thought she'd deserve again.

Peace.

"I love you." his lips were warm against her neck.

"I love you too."

THIRTY ONE

Callum's eyes fluttered open at the sensation of something soft brushing his leg. His body stirred to life before his brain fully caught up, the lingering haze of sleep melting into awareness. Warmth radiated beside him, her scent, a warm and spicy burst of bergamot and papyrus, and something uniquely Amy, wrapping around him like a tether. His lips curved faintly, memories of the night before rushing in, each one more intoxicating than the last.

Her fingers, featherlight, trailed up his thigh, teasingly close but maddeningly not enough. He let out a quiet groan, low and rough, his hips shifting instinctively toward her touch.

"Morning," she whispered, the vibrations against his thigh immediately waking him up.

His hand found her wrist, brushing her skin as he looked at her. She was propped on one elbow, her hair falling in soft waves over her bare shoulders.

"Do you ever sleep?" His grin was lazy as he tugged her closer, his fingers tracing slow patterns along her spine.

"Not when I have better things to do," she murmured, as she slid on top of him, her lips grazing his jaw, just below his ear.

He hummed, the sound more growl than anything else, as her kisses drifted lower, her mouth mapping a slow, torturous path across his chest before dipping to his pelvis. Every nerve in his body seemed to spark to life, anticipation coiling tight as he reached for her, ready to shift the playful morning into something much more.

The bed jolted beneath them as fifty pounds of fur and energy launched itself into their bubble. Maslow landed on the bed, nudging Amy away from Callum, tail wagging like a propeller, his big brown eyes beaming with uncontainable enthusiasm.

"What the–" Callum sat up, his head whipping toward the dog now happily licking Amy's arm.

"Maslow!" she squealed, laughter bubbling from her lips as she tried to dodge the onslaught of wet kisses.

Callum groaned, flopping back against the pillows as the dog turned his attention to him, shoving his snout into his chest like some overeager referee breaking up a fight.

"You've *got* to be kidding me," Callum muttered, though a reluctant grin tugged at the corners of his mouth.

Amy was doubled over now, her laughter a melodic, contagious thing as she nudged Maslow toward the edge of the bed. "Looks like someone needs to go out."

"Someone else needs attention, too," Callum grumbled, glaring half-heartedly at the dog, who now sat proudly at the foot of the bed, head cocked as if to say, *get moving, buddy.*

Amy tossed a pillow at him, still laughing as she slid out from under the covers. "Patience is a virtue."

"Not when you're involved," he shot back.

Maslow barked once, his tail thumping against Callum's leg. Callum sighed, raking a hand through his hair.

"Fine," he muttered, throwing off the blankets and swinging his legs over the side of the bed. "But you owe me, furball."

Maslow barked again, entirely unbothered.

I'll make us some coffee. She kissed him as he trotted to the bathroom for his robe.

"I've added another project to the list. I need to build a fence here too. See you in a bit."

△△△

Amy sat cross-legged on Callum's worn leather sofa, her fingers tracing the curve of the coffee mug. The house was quiet except for the soft hum of the television, tuned to the news—a low buzz in the background as she waited for Callum to return from his walk with Maslow.

Her phone buzzed on the coffee table, but she ignored it. Sleep still tugged at the edges of her thoughts, and she took another sip of coffee, letting the caffeine chase away the fog. The anchor's voice on the television grew louder, her tone shifting to something sharper, more serious.

"And now, an exclusive sit-down with bestselling author and therapist Doctor Mark Rodriguez, whose memoir is climbing the charts. But it's not just his professional success making headlines. His recent divorce and the tragic discovery of Josephine Vega have sparked widespread speculation."

Amy froze, the mug halfway to her lips. She set it down carefully, her pulse quickening as the screen shifted to a live shot of Mark sitting across from the host on *Good Morning America*. He looked polished, his posture relaxed.

The host smiled warmly. "Mark, thank you for joining us this morning. Your docuseries, *In the Shadows of Our Minds*, has touched viewers deeply. But many are curious about the personal struggles you've faced recently, particularly the tremendous losses, and the tragedy surrounding Josephine Vega, which was teased for your upcoming episode. What can you tell us about that?"

Mark tilted his head slightly, the practiced warmth in his expression set. "First of all, thank you for having me. This has been an incredibly challenging time for me personally. Josephine was someone I had a long history with, and her death has been a profound loss. I want to take a moment to acknowledge her family and the grief they must be feeling. My heart goes out to them."

Amy's stomach flipped as she leaned forward, glued to the screen.

The host pressed gently, "Some have speculated about the nature of your relationship with Josephine. What do you say to those rumors?"

Mark's smile faded, replaced by a somber expression. "Josephine was someone I respected deeply, and I think anyone who worked with her would agree she had an incredible spirit." He paused, briefly before meeting the hosts again. "As for the rumors... I think it's human nature to search for meaning in tragedy, to connect dots that aren't necessarily connected. But my focus has always been on telling the truth in my work, and I hope that truth speaks for itself."

The host nodded, her tone softening. "And your divorce? How has that impacted your journey as a writer? A therapist?"

Mark exhaled a carefully timed breath, his gaze steady. "Divorce is never easy, and it's been a painful process. But I think it's also been an opportunity for growth. I just ask for privacy regarding that matter, so that we can move through this difficult time."

Amy's throat was dry, her heart pounding. She barely heard the rest of the interview, the words fading into a blur of polished answers and carefully curated vulnerability.

The front door creaked open, Maslow's nails clicking against the floor as he padded into the room, tail wagging. Callum followed, his jacket slung over one arm and his face flushed from the cold.

"Coffee smells good," he set the leash on the counter. His gaze found Amy, curled up on the couch, her knees tucked to her chest. For a moment, his lips curved into a smile, but the television caught his eye, and his expression froze.

Mark's face filled the screen. "Josephine's death is a tragedy, but I hope it reminds us all how vital it is to address mental health openly and with compassion."

Callum went still, his jaw tightening as he gripped the edge of the counter.

Amy muted the TV, but the damage was done. The silence between them was heavier than any words could be.

"Callum," she said carefully, setting her coffee mug on the table. "Are you okay? You look like you've seen a ghost."

His shoulders rose and fell as he dragged in a breath, his head bowing slightly. "It's nothing. Just…turn it off." His phone started to ring, and he swiped to ignore it.

"Why are you acting like this? What's wrong?"

His throat bobbed, and when he finally lifted his head to meet her gaze, his expression gutted her. Guilt. Pain. Desperation.

"Amy," he started, "I've been meaning to tell you something, but I didn't know how."

Her stomach dropped. "What is it?"

Callum hesitated, rubbing a hand over his face. "Fuck, I don't even know how to process this." His voice cracked, his entire body trembling. "That's… she's my ex–wife."

For a moment, Amy didn't react. The words didn't make sense, didn't compute. But then, like a tidal wave, the truth hit her. Her heart clenched, her chest tightening until it felt impossible to breathe.

"Your ex–wife?" she repeated, "You knew her? You…" Her words cut off, her mind racing.

"Yes," Callum admitted, "I didn't know she was involved with Mark at first. When I saw them together at the mill…"

Amy stood abruptly, the room tilting as she processed his confession. "You've known this whole time?" Each word she spoke was sharp and laced with betrayal. "And you didn't tell me?"

"I didn't know how to!" Callum shot back. "How do you think that would have looked? Hey Amy, I really love you, you're the best thing that's ever happened to me, but your husband is fucking my ex-wife."

Amy's laugh was bitter and hollow, tears brimming. "So, instead, you let me believe you were my safe place. That I could trust you. And all the while, you were hiding this?"

"I wasn't hiding it," he pressed, closing the gap between them. "I was trying to protect you."

"Protect me?" she snapped, stepping back. "From what? The truth? From the fact that the man I love, the man was starting to trust, is connected to her? The woman who's dead?"

Callum winced, his hand curling into a fist at his side. "Amy, I had nothing to do with her death. I swear to you."

"How do I know that?" she demanded. "How do I know you didn't leak the affair? Or that you didn't–didn't push her to do what she did?"

His face crumpled, his anguish raw and unfiltered. "You don't," he admitted, "And I hate that I've put you in a position to doubt me. But I need you to believe me, Amy. I didn't hurt her. I didn't hurt anyone. I was just trying to keep you safe from Mark."

Tears spilled down her cheeks as she shook her head. "I can't do this. I can't trust you. Not after this."

"Amy, please," Callum pleaded, "I love you. I've loved you since the moment you walked into my life, and every decision I've made has been because of that. I didn't tell you about Josephine because I was afraid you'd see me differently. That you'd shut me out before I had the chance to show you what you mean to me."

She froze, his confession slicing through her like a blade. She saw the pain, felt the sincerity, but it wasn't enough to mend the fracture in her trust.

"I don't know if I believe you," she said finally. "I don't know if I believe any of this anymore."

Callum took a step closer, his hands outstretched as if to touch her, but she recoiled. The rejection hit him like a physical blow, and he dropped his arms, his shoulders sagging.

"I'm sorry," he whispered. "I've fucked this up. But I'll do whatever it takes to fix it. Please, Amy. Don't shut me out."

Her tears fell freely now, her chest heaving with the weight of it all. "I need to go."

"Amy–"

She cut him off with a look, her eyes glassy. Without another word, she took to the stairs and grabbed her bag, and then leashed Maslow and headed to the door.

As the door clicked shut behind her, Callum sank onto the couch, his head in his hands. The silence of the room was deafening, the weight of her absence crushing him in a way he hadn't anticipated. *And Josephine.*

THIRTY TWO

The café patio was quiet, the clinking of silverware and the low hum of conversation from inside barely filling the space. Sunlight reflected off the wide windows, catching on the edge of Amy's untouched plate. A spinach salad sat in front of her, the bright greens bruising under her restless prodding with a fork.

Across the table, Charlotte took a sip of her iced tea, her gaze steady on Amy, who hadn't said much since they sat down. Theodore was cradled in a wrap against Charlotte's chest, and the anxiety that seeped from Amy was palpable.

"You're quiet," Charlotte set her glass over the damp ring on the table. "What's going on?"

Amy let out a hollow laugh, flicking her gaze toward the restaurant speakers. "Just thinking about the lyrics of the song that's playing. *Guilty as Sin.* Taylor gets me, damn it…"

Charlotte smirked. "I mean, the woman knows what she's talking about."

Amy looked up, her ebony eyes tired and puffy from crying. She hadn't even tried to mask it today, her hair pulled into a loose knot and her sweater hanging off one shoulder. The weight of everything she had been holding in felt like it might crush her right there in that chair.

"I don't even know where to start," she murmured.

Charlotte tilted her head, placing her arms on the table as she leaned forward. "Just start. Whatever it is, I'm here."

Amy inhaled shakily, the words catching in her throat. She

stabbed at a cherry tomato, the fork sliding off its slick surface before she let the utensil clatter against her plate. "It's Mark," she finally said. "And Callum. And, God, everything."

Charlotte leaned forward slightly, her elbows on the table. "Okay. What about them?"

Amy set the fork down and clasped her hands together tightly. "Mark's affair. I told myself I'd moved past it. That I forgave him because… because that's what I was supposed to do, right?" She exhaled sharply, shaking her head. "But I didn't."

Charlotte's brows furrowed. "I mean… that's understandable, Amy, he hurt you. But, this has all come out of left field."

Amy flinched, the words hitting her in a way they shouldn't have. "Out of left field, is that what this is?" she shook her head in disbelief, lowering her voice. "He fucked another woman for months. Lied to my face. Made me believe we were trying for a baby while he was screwing Josephine."

Charlotte exhaled, pushing a loose curl behind her ear. "I know. And I'm not excusing him. But you were distant, Amy. Detached. Mark called me a few times. He was worried about you. He'd said you'd been shutting him out. And the divorce, its shattered him."

Amy's body tensed. "He what?"

"He told me he'd been trying, that he didn't know how to help you, that he wants to, despite everything, despite the divorce." Charlotte continued carefully. "That maybe you need more support than just talking to me."

Amy laughed sharply, shaking her head. "Of course he did." She leaned back, crossing her arms. "And what, now you think I'm losing it too?"

Charlotte's expression softened, her fingers curling around her glass. "No, Amy, that's not what I'm saying. I just… I don't know. Maybe talking to someone would help? A therapist who isn't connected to all of this?"

Amy clenched her jaw, looking away. "You mean someone Mark *hasn't* already convinced I'm insane?"

Charlotte sighed. "That's not fair."

"Isn't it?" Amy snapped, pushing back from the table abruptly. The scrape of the chair against the pavement made Charlotte flinch. Amy needed air, space, *something*. She started walking toward the open field next to the restaurant.

Charlotte rose, careful to not wake the baby as she caught up to her, linking their arms before Amy could fully pull away. "Amy, come on, I am on your side."

Amy let out a slow, shaky breath. "Yeah? Then why does it feel like you believe him more than me?"

Charlotte's voice was quiet, hesitant. "I know he made a huge mistake, but maybe he's just trying to fix things in his own way. Maybe he's just scared of losing you. People fuck up, maybe you rushed into the divorce."

Amy let out a bitter laugh, her chest tightening. "He's not scared of losing me, he's scared of losing control of me."

Charlotte hesitated, biting the inside of her cheek. "Enough about him, im sorry I brought it up, really." She cleared her throat. "You mentioned Callum, what was that about?"

Amy grunted, dragging a hand through her hair. Her pulse pounded in her ears. " I went to his house last night, and we had sex." Charlotte gasped, but Amy put up her hand. "Let me get this out. It was amazing, and I think I am in love with him, and…" the tears started to fall.

"This morning, I saw Mark on TV, talking about Josephine like…like he wasn't part of the reason she's gone." Her breath shuddered. "He's lying, Char. He's manipulating everyone. He's making *me* question what's real and what's not."

Charlotte's expression wavered, uncertainty flickering across her features. "Do you know anything about their relationship? Mark and Josephine's?"

Amy's laugh was brittle as she shook her head. "No. Only that they were involved, obviously."

Charlotte hesitated. "Lincoln told me after the news broke... He knew Josephine. She and Mark were together as teenagers. She got pregnant, had an abortion. Mark struggled, and Lincoln helped him through it."

Amy stiffened.

"Well, if that isn't the nail in the fucking coffin."

"Why?" Charlotte asked, squeezing her hand.

"For one, because I knew about Josephine, but didn't know her name. Mark told me about that relationship, he just never gave specifics." Amy started to tear up. "After all this time, he chose her over me." she slumped into a bench adjacent to the river.

Amy started to cry. "What's worse, is that Josephine is Callum's ex too, and I can't trust him, not after he lied about this, he lied about his connection to her. What if he had something to do with her disappearance? What if it was Mark?"

"That's...a lot..." Charlotte hesitated before continuing. "Mark told Lincoln you two had a lot more going on in your relationship than people realize. What did he mean?"

Amy pulled her hand away, not out of anger, but out of sheer exhaustion. "I don't know." Her focus shifted to Charlotte who was positioning Theodore to nurse.

"It's too much, and you–you looking so together, so whole, I can't stand it." I see you, I see– him– and all I feel is how much I've failed."

Charlotte's face fell, and Amy immediately regretted the words. But she couldn't stop now, not after finally letting the dam break.

Charlotte reached for her. "Amy... I'm sorry."

Amy swallowed hard, her eyes burning.

"I don't know how to help you," Charlotte admitted. "But I *want* to. Just… tell me what you need."

Amy let out a slow, shaky breath, her walls cracking just slightly. "I don't know," she whispered. "I don't know what I need."

Charlotte reached for her hand, squeezing it. "I know you don't want this, me, right now." She gestured to Theordore. "I get it. But I am here. I always will be."

Amy looked away, swiping a hand under her eyes. "You don't have to fix me, Char."

Charlotte's tone softened. "I know. But that doesn't mean I won't try to be better at… being here."

Amy exhaled shakily, the words settling deep in her chest.

After a moment, Charlotte forced a small smile. "Look, let's just go home. No more serious talk. You go pour a *huge* glass of wine into that ridiculous goblet I got you, and I'll pretend not to judge." She winked.

A shaky laugh escaped Amy despite herself. "I should probably go for a run first."

Charlotte looped an arm through hers. "Okay, but *after* that, check in."

Amy let herself lean into the embrace, but the doubt still lingered.

THIRTY THREE

After heading home to grab Maslow, Amy had run three miles in an attempt to clear her head, but her thoughts and emotions felt just as tangled as before. She tightened her grip on the steering wheel. The road ahead blurred as streetlights streaked across her windshield, matching the rhythm of her uneven breath. Maslow sat panting in the passenger seat, his head resting on the window, occasionally glancing at her.

The drive home felt endless. Each mile churned up memories she had buried, but they clawed their way to the surface, tearing at the fragile seams she'd stitched together to keep herself from falling apart. Her hands trembled as she turned up the radio, trying to drown out the pounding in her chest, *A Little Bit Happy* by Talk was streaming through the car, only making her anxiety worse. Every song seemed to mock her, dragging her back to moments she'd tried so hard to forget.

Josephine's face filled her mind. She imagined her, brilliant, beautiful, desperate. A woman who had reached for help and instead found Mark. What had she been like? Strong, maybe. Or at least she had been before Mark got his claws into her.

Amy's throat tightened. "It's my fault," she whispered. Maslow shifted in his seat, his ears perking up.

"If I hadn't done what I did..." tears blurred her vision.

She thought of Mark's affair, how easily he had stepped into someone else's arms, his body language in those photos, so unlike the man who used to hold her at night.

I pushed him to her. I made him leave.

But it wasn't just Mark. Callum's name crept into her mind, uninvited. She thought about how effortlessly he'd become her lifeline, how his kindness felt like a balm she didn't deserve. And now Josephine hung between them like a ghost.

What did you do to her, Callum? What part of her story didn't you tell me?

Her foot pressed harder on the gas as her thoughts spiraled.

I let Mark do this to her. I gave him the excuse he needed to find someone else, to ruin her. It's my fault she's gone. She let out a shattered breath.

Her chest heaved as the guilt consumed her. Tears spilled freely down her cheeks, and she wiped them away with shaking hands, her knuckles white against the steering wheel.

Maslow barked softly, pulling her back to reality for a fleeting moment. She glanced at him, his warm brown eyes watching her carefully, almost knowingly.

"I didn't mean to," she choked out. "I didn't mean for *any* of this to happen."

But the damage was done.

Her thoughts twisted, dragging her back to the hospital room, the sterile smell of antiseptic, the dim hum of fluorescent lights. She remembered the nurse's expression as she handed him to her. *"I'm so sorry, Amy, can I call someone for you?"*

Her hands clenched the wheel as the memory overwhelmed her. She could still feel the emptiness, the unbearable silence where a heartbeat should have been.

The garage came into view, and a fresh wave of dread washed over her. The house loomed in the darkness, no longer a refuge but a prison. Her hands shook as she turned off the car and stepped out, Maslow following close behind.

The house, once warm, now felt cold, empty. The shadows cast by the low light made the corners of the room appear unnervingly deep. She walked through the garage and into the kitchen, where she placed her keys and phone on the counter. As she rounded the island, the smell of whiskey hit her before she saw him.

Mark emerged from the shadows, his figure slouched, the glass in his hand catching the faint moonlight filtering through the window. His smile was lopsided, amplifying the scar on his jaw. "Amy," he uttered, leaning against the doorframe of the living room. "We need to talk." Her blood ran cold.

"What *the hell* are you doing here?" She clutched her chest.

He raised his glass mockingly. "Celebrating, I suppose. Or mourning. Hard to tell these days." His cold stare set every nerve on fire. "I thought we could share a moment. You and me."

"I want you out of my house," she snapped, trying to keep her distance as she backed toward the kitchen.

Mark's breath thick with the smell of whiskey. "Out of *our* house?" he mocked, an eerie chuckle escaping him. She glanced at Maslow, whose ears were perked, his low growl vibrating in the tense silence.

"Maslow, it's me," Mark called from the other side. His voice was calm, almost soothing, but it sent a shiver down her spine.

"I just want to talk," his tone was warm, almost pleading.

"You shouldn't be here."

"Amy," he began with practiced empathy, "I know things have been difficult between us. I know I haven't been the husband you deserved."

Her stomach churned. He always knew how to twist the knife just right.

"But after everything we've been through, the baby, this media circus, I can't just sit back and watch you go through it alone. You shouldn't have to." He let his tears fall. "Fuck, the fact that I wasn't there for you when he was born." *Step one: empathy. He thought.*

Amy crossed her arms, keeping her distance. "I'm not alone," she said, swallowing the lump in her throat.

Mark's expression tensed for a fraction of a second before he recovered, his smile slipping back into place. "Of course. You have Callum." He said the name with a pointed edge. "Funny how he always seems to show up right when you need him."

Amy stiffened. "Don't do this." Her arms folded protectively, but she didn't move.

Good. Stay put. "I'm not doing anything," Mark raised his hands. "I just think it's interesting, don't you? How quickly he's inserted himself into your life. How much he knows about our marriage." He stepped closer, his gaze narrowing. "You *know* exactly what I'm talking about, don't you?" He closed the gap, his breath hot against her cheek as he brushed his knuckles along her neck. "You're not the only one who has things to hide, Amy. Callum, he's the one who started all this. He's the one who fucked up Josephine's mind. He's the reason she couldn't hold it together. Why she went off the rails."

He took another measured step toward her. *You're scared. Good.*

Amy shook her head, denial already forming on her lips, but Mark pressed on.

"You think I didn't notice the way he looked at you? You think I didn't know what he's capable of?" he sneered.

"Please don't start–"

"Start what?" His lips curled into a smirk. "Telling the truth?" He let the words hang, then took a slow sip of whiskey, savoring the tension. *Let her stew. The silence will do half the work for me.*

"Telling the–" He cut her off.

That Callum isn't who you think he is. That he's been pulling the strings this whole time?"

Amy stiffened, but Mark didn't give her a chance to respond.

"Josephine," he breathed, "She wasn't just his ex-wife, Amy. She was collateral damage."

"What are you talking about?" Amy's balance wavered, her grip on the counter tightening.

Mark tilted his head, watching her carefully. *Hook set. Now reel her in.*

"Josephine came to me in pieces, Amy. She was terrified of him. She told me everything. How he controlled her, how he twisted her mind, how he made her feel like she was the crazy one."

Amy shook her head, the denial already forming on her lips. "You're lying."

Mark smiled, the kind that never reached his eyes. "Am I? Or is that just easier for you to believe? She told me how he isolated her, how he played the victim, how he turned everyone against her until she didn't know what was real anymore. Sound familiar?"

Her breathing quickened, and he saw the faintest flicker of doubt cross her face.

"And then," he continued, his tone hardening, "He leaked the affair. He wanted to destroy me, Amy. To make me look like the villain. Josephine told me he was obsessed with control, with ruining people who didn't bend to him. She said it would never stop."

Mark set his glass down with a sharp clink, his expression darkening. "But let's not pretend this is all about him. Let's talk about *you*, Amy."

Her chest tightened. "Mark, don't–"

"Oh no, we're doing this." His tone dropped. "Do you know what it felt like? To find out from someone else, that my son was gone? That you didn't even bother to tell me?"

Tears welled in her eyes. "I was trying to protect you–"

"Liar." he spat, stepping closer. "You robbed me of the

chance to hold him. To say goodbye. To *grieve*. You took that from me, Amy. You made that decision for both of us, and for what? So, you wouldn't have to see me?"

Mark pressed on. "Do you know what if feels like? Watching you mourn a baby I never even got to hold?"

Her knees buckled, and she gripped the counter for support.

She's slipping. Perfect.

Mark leaned closer, his breath hot against her ear. "You think this is grief? This is guilt. And you should feel guilty, Amy. Because it's *your* fault. You failed him."

Amy's gasp was sharp, a wound opening all over again.

He circled her like a predator, "And now you're letting Callum worm his way into your life, into our son's memory. Do you think he'd be proud of you? Of the mother you've become?"

Her vision blurred as the walls closed in.

"*Stop it*," she whispered, her entire body was tingling, every nerve on fire.

Amy flinched as he slammed his hand against the counter, the sound reverberating through the room. He had her cornered, his looming over hers. Maslow snarled, but Mark ignored him.

"You think anyone will believe you?" Mark hissed. "You'll be just another tragic headline. The woman who lost everything; her baby, her husband, her mind."

Amy backed away, stumbling as her foot caught the barstool. She felt for her phone, her fingers trembling, but Mark grabbed her wrist, pulling her closer.

"Let me go!" she gasped.

Mark tilted his head, feigning confusion. "Stop what? Telling the truth? You want to hear lies, Amy? Fine…" He made sure to pause for effect.

"Callum loves you."

"You're a great mother."

"None of this is your fault." He sneered. "Feel better?"

He grabbed Amy's chin, forcing her to look at him.

"*Listen* to me," he hissed. "You're unraveling, Amy. Everyone sees it. Charlotte, Callum, even your precious dog. They all know you're not okay. And when you break–and you *will* break–they'll leave you. Just like everyone else."

Maslow barked, lunging forward, his teeth snapping inches from Mark's leg. Mark stumbled, releasing her, but he quickly regained his footing, turning on the dog with a snarl of his own.

"Maslow, down!" he shouted, but he didn't flinch. The dog launched himself at Mark, teeth sinking into his ankle, immobilizing him. Mark screamed, trying to shove him off, but Maslow held firm, growling with unrelenting ferocity as he pulled at the tendons of his leg.

"SHIT, get this fucking dog off me!" Blood stained the floor, the scent sharp and metallic. Amy grabbed the leash, pulling Maslow back with all her strength. Her chest heaved as she stumbled into the foyer, Maslow pressing against her side, his low growls vibrating through her. She could still hear Mark in her head, sharp and taunting.

Amy scrambled for the door. Mark straightened, his expression cold and calculating. *Let her run. Let her think she's escaping. It'll make this even better.*

Behind her, Mark stood in the doorway, his face flushed and furious, blood soaking through his pant leg where Maslow had attacked him.

"Go ahead, Amy," he called out, "Run to Charlotte. Run to whoever you want. But remember this: I'll tell them the truth."

He picked up his phone, and dialed 9–11. "This is Doctor Mark Rodriguez." His voice was steady, calm, the picture of professionalism. "I need to report an incident at my home– my ex–wife. She's not well. I'm afraid she's a danger to herself and others."

He glanced down at the blood on his pant leg, at the torn fabric where Maslow's teeth had sunk in. A small smile tugged at the corner of his mouth.

Flawless.

△△△

Amy's lungs were on fire as his words sank in. Her stomach twisted violently. *No, no, no.*

Her steps faltered as her legs trembled, but she forced herself forward, her vision tunneling. Charlotte's porch light was a faint blur in the distance.

"Maslow, come boy, come." She took off, tears streaming, her blood pumping so fast, she thought she'd pass out.

The air outside was biting, the chill slicing through Amy's thin cardigan as she stumbled down the street. Her legs ached, her breath came in jagged gasps, and every step felt like she was wading through quicksand. Maslow stayed at her side, growling softly every time she faltered.

Her thoughts raced. *You'll lose everything. Your job. Your reputation. Your friends.*

Maslow barked sharply as they reached the door, his nails scraping against the wood as Amy pounded on it with trembling fists.

"Charlotte!" she cried, "Please–open the door!"

She pounded again, her knuckles bruising against the heavy wood. The sound of hurried footsteps echoed from inside, and the door swung open. Charlotte stood there, her face pale with alarm.

"Amy?" Charlotte gasped. Her eyes fell to the blood streaking Amy's legs, then up to the frantic look on her face. "Oh my God, what happened?"

Before Amy could answer, her knees buckled. She caught herself on the doorframe, shaking her head. "He–Mark... He was in the house. He..." Her words dissolved into gasps.

Charlotte gasped, grabbing Amy by the arm, she closed the door behind them, locking both bolts.

Maslow stayed glued to Amy's side, growling softly as he watched the door, his fur bristling.

Charlotte guided Amy to the couch, but Amy couldn't sit still. She paced, clutching at her hair, her breath hitching as she tried to find the words. "He was drunk... He wouldn't leave... He said things–awful things. And then–" She clutched her sides, feeling like she might implode.

Charlotte grabbed her shoulders gently. "Breathe, Amy. You're safe now."

Amy's eyes snapped to hers, wide and unfocused. "Safe?" she repeated bitterly. "He's still out there. He's not going to stop, Charlotte."

"What did he do?" Charlotte asked, "Did he hurt you?"

Amy hesitated, her hands shaking as she brushed the hair from her face. "He– no, he–but Maslow–" She gestured to the dog. "He attacked him. Gave me time to get away."

Charlotte's hand flew to her mouth. "Oh my God."

Amy looked around the room. Where's Lincoln?

"He left for the city, the merger, remember?"

"Right, fuck."

"I'm calling the police. Don't worry, all the doors are locked."

"No!" Amy's reaction was sharp, startling her.

"Amy," Charlotte uttered softly, "you have to. He can't get away with this."

Her breath came fast, panic setting in again. "What if they don't believe me? He's already painted me as the unstable one, the grieving wife who lost a baby and can't handle it. He'll turn this into something else. He always does."

Charlotte knelt in front of her, gripping her hands tightly. "Amy, listen to me. You can't let him scare you into silence. You have to stand up to him. For yourself."

Charlotte spoke calmly into the phone before hanging up. "Police are on their way. Dispatched was already called to Mark, they will come and speak with us when they're done."

Amy sank into the sofa, burying her face in her hands as the adrenaline began to wane. Maslow nudged her leg with his nose, whining softly as he pressed against her side. She let out a shaky breath, her fingers curling into his fur.

THIRTY FOUR

The room was heavy with tension, every sound amplified by the stillness that hung between the two women. Amy sat on the edge of the couch, her arms wrapped tightly around her knees. Maslow lay at her feet, his body rigid, his eyes flicking toward the bassinet each time Theodore let out a soft cry.

Charlotte stood near the reclining chair, Genevieve clinging to her neck and crying into her sweater. "Shh, sweet girl," Charlotte murmured. "It's okay. Mommy's here."

Genevieve's small hands fisted in Charlotte's sleeve, her cries growing louder. Charlotte sighed, adjusting her daughter's weight on her hip. She looked over at Amy, her expression lined with exhaustion.

"Can you hold him for a bit?" Charlotte's voice broke the silence.

Amy blinked at her, surprised. "Theo?"

"Just for a little while. I need to put her down, she's overtired and losing it."

Amy nodded quickly, standing as Charlotte moved to the bassinet. "Thank you," she murmured as Charlotte carefully lifted Theodore and handed him over.

Charlotte smiled. "I'll be right back, if you need anything, just holler."

Amy didn't respond, already sinking back onto the couch with Theodore cradled in her arms.

Charlotte disappeared up the stairs, Genevieve's cries

growing muffled as she carried her daughter away.

Amy cradled Charlotte's newborn in her arms, her fingers trembling as she rocked him gently. The weight of him settled against her chest, a warmth she hadn't felt in what seemed like forever. His tiny fists rested by his cheeks, and his dark lashes fanned across his soft, pink skin. She couldn't stop staring at him, at the perfect curve of his nose, the faint smattering of dark hair on his head, the rhythmic rise and fall of his little chest.

Her thumb traced the back of his hand, marveling at the softness of his skin. His fingers twitched slightly in response, curling and uncurling as if he were trying to grasp onto something unseen. She watched him, mesmerized by every delicate movement.

His smallness consumed her, the fragile vulnerability of him pulling her in deeper with every passing second. She counted the creases in his tiny knuckles, memorized the faint whorl of his hairline, the way his lips parted in sleep. He smelled faintly of baby lotion and milk, and the scent brought a lump to her throat that she couldn't swallow down.

Amy felt an ache spreading through her ribs. For a moment, the world narrowed to just the two of them.

Her hand drifted to his chest, her palm resting there as she felt the steady thrum of his heartbeat beneath her touch. It was so steady, so pure, and it shattered something deep inside her.

"Hi, little one," she whispered. Tears welled, spilling silently down her cheeks as she gazed at him. "You're so perfect. You have no idea how perfect you are." Her tears dripped onto his blanket, but she didn't notice. She didn't notice anything beyond the tiny miracle in her arms. Time seemed to stretch endlessly, each second etching itself into her memory with painful clarity.

She thought about Callum, and before she could talk herself out of it, Amy hit the call button.

Her fingers gripped the phone tightly, her knuckles white as it rang. When he answered, his voice was warm, steady.

"Ames?"

The words caught in Amy's throat. She squeezed her eyes shut, forcing them out. "Callum... I don't know what to do."

His tone shifted immediately, concern sharpening. "What's wrong? Where are you?"

"I'm at Charlotte's," she inhaled. "Mark... he's trying to ruin me. He called the police, Callum. He's twisting everything."

She heard Callum exhale, the faint scrape of movement on the other end of the line. "Okay. Take a breath, Ames. Start from the beginning."

Her thoughts were spiraling. "He was in the house. When I got home, he was there, waiting for me. He said things, awful things about you." Her words started spilling out faster. "He said you ruined Josephine, that it's your fault she's dead. He said you leaked the affair–"

"Amy," Callum interrupted, his voice firmer now, though she could hear the tension beneath it. "Listen to me–"

"Did you?" she cut him off, her grip tightening on the phone. "Did you leak it?"

His silence felt like a slap.

Amy stood abruptly, pacing the room as Theodore stirred in her arms. She swayed him instinctively, her movements jerky and uneven. "Callum, tell me the truth. Did you do it?"

His tone softened. "Ames, this isn't the time for this. Let me come to you, and we'll talk about everything in person. I promise."

"No!" she exhaled. "I need to know now, Callum. Did you leak it? Did you hurt her?"

He sighed. "Amy, let's talk in person–"

She interrupted him. "Mark said you destroyed her. That you played with her mind, controlled her, made her think she was crazy. Is that what you do? Is that what you're doing to me?"

"Amy, stop. You know that's not true. You know me."

Her breath came in shallow bursts, her vision blurring as her panic mounted. "I don't know anything anymore. I don't know what to believe. Mark said—"

"Mark is manipulating you," Callum said sternly, cutting her off. "You know that, Amy. This is what he does. Don't let him pull you under."

"But what if he's right?" she whispered, her tears spilled freely now, dropping onto Theodore's blanket. "What if he's right, and I've been wrong about everything?"

Callum's tone had a desperate edge. "Amy, listen to me. I'm coming to you. Stay where you are. Don't do this over the phone. Please."

She shook her head, her grip on the baby tightening as her knees buckled. "I can't... I can't do this."

"Yes, you can, you're stronger than this, Ames. I'll be there soon. Just hold on."

The line was quiet for a moment, her ragged breathing the only sound.

"Callum..." Amy couldn't find the words.

"Stay with me," he said softly. "I'm on my way."

But she couldn't. She ended the call, her hand shaking as she dropped the phone onto the couch. Her legs gave out, and she sank into the chair, her tears soaking into the fabric of Theodore's blanket.

She didn't hear the sound of footsteps or the soft creak of the floorboards behind her. She didn't feel Charlotte's presence until her voice broke the spell.

"Amy?"

Amy startled, blinking rapidly as she turned her head. Charlotte stood a few feet away, her expression soft but lined with concern.

"Oh," Amy breathed, glancing back down at the baby as though trying to steady herself. "I didn't... I didn't hear you."

Charlotte was studying Amy as a deep crease formed between her brows. "You sure you're okay?"

Amy's laugh was brittle, her grip tightening on Theodore. "No," she admitted. "I'm not okay. I don't think I've been okay for a long time." The weight of him, so warm, so steady, sent a fresh ache splintering through her chest. "I lost him, it's my fault because of what I did to Mark."

Charlotte sat across from her, brow furrowed, watching carefully. "Amy, what do you mean you lost the baby because of what you did to Mark?"

Amy let out an exacerbated sigh. "I forced it, Charlotte. I forced *him*." Her throat tightened as the words slipped out, jagged and raw.

Charlotte shook her head slightly, confused. "What are you talking about?"

Amy was staring past her, her gaze unfocused. "That night... the night you and Lincoln came over for dinner," she whispered, "Mark was drunk. Completely out of it. And I knew I was ovulating. I knew it was my last shot before the next round of treatments."

Charlotte was stunned.

Amy's grip tightened around the baby. "He didn't want to, Char. He *told* me he didn't want to. But I–" she swallowed hard, "I didn't care. I wanted the baby more than I cared about how I got it."

Charlotte sat frozen, her mouth slightly open, but no words came.

Amy let out a bitter laugh, her eyes glassy. "And the worst part? It *worked*. I got what I wanted. I got pregnant. And I told myself it was meant to be, that it would fix everything. That if we had a baby, he'd *love me* again."

Charlott's expression was full of worry. "Amy..."

"But I couldn't even keep him," Amy rasped. "Because of *me*. Because of what I did."

Charlotte shook her head, her brows creasing. "That's not– Amy, that's *not* why you lost him."

Amy's gaze snapped to her, her jaw clenched so tight it ached. "Isn't it?" she challenged. "Because that's exactly what it feels like. Like I took something I didn't deserve, and the universe ripped it away from me." Her breathing came faster, more uneven. "Every pregnancy announcement, every baby shower, every single fucking reminder that everyone else gets to have their happy ending except me, it kills me, Charlotte. And I hate myself for it. I hate myself for resenting you, for resenting your baby, because I love you."

Charlotte flinched, pain flickering across her face.

Amy shut her eyes like she could physically stop herself from spiraling further. "Last year, I got pregnant, and it all changed, and I didn't tell you because I was scared I would jynx it. Then I found out it wasn't even a real pregnancy." Her voice cracked. "Do you know what it's like to be *so* fucking desperate for a baby, and then the doctors tell you that all that hope was just…just a cluster of cells pretending to be a baby?"

Charlotte covered her mouth, her eyes wet.

Amy shook her head, biting back a sob. "Mark was devastated. He *wanted* that baby. And I failed him."

Charlotte felt unsteady. "Amy… that wasn't your fault, either, are you hearing yourself?"

Amy exhaled a shaky breath, laughing bitterly. "Everything is my fault, Charlotte. If I hadn't shut Mark out, he wouldn't have cheated. If I hadn't been so obsessed with getting pregnant, I wouldn't have…" her words faltered, "I wouldn't have taken something from him he didn't want to give."

Charlotte reached for her hand, gripping it tightly. A long silence stretched between them, heavy and suffocating. Charlotte didn't have an answer. "Look at how good you are with Theo, Amy, it will happen, I promise."

Amy's grip on Theodore loosened slightly, her hands trembling. "I should've let him go," she whispered. "I should've just let him go."

Charlotte blinked rapidly, wiping at her cheek before exhaling shakily. "Amy… you *didn't* deserve this. No matter how much you think you do."

Amy didn't respond. Because deep down, she wasn't sure she believed that anymore.

Theodore squirmed in Amy's arms, his tiny fingers twitching as a faint coo left his lips. The sound sent a fresh wave of emotion crashing over her.

Mark's words replayed in her mind like a cruel echo, each one cutting deeper than the last.

"You think this is grief? This is guilt. And you should feel guilty, Amy. Because it's your fault he's gone."

Her chest tightened, the air around her feeling suddenly too thin. She stared at Theodore, at the soft rise and fall of his chest, the warmth of his small body pressed against hers. He smelled faintly of baby lotion, that delicate, powdery scent wrapping around her like a noose.

Mark's voice whispered again, louder this time. "You let the stress get to you. You let your body fail him."

Her breathing quickened, and she adjusted Theodore in her arms, as if holding him closer might keep her from falling apart. But it didn't help. The memory clawed its way to the surface; the cold, sterile hospital room.

The nurse's reaction; "I'm so sorry, Amy."

The weight of her son, lifeless in her arms. His skin, cool to the touch.

Tears blurred her vision, and she blinked rapidly, trying to focus on Theodore's tiny face.

"You robbed me of the chance to hold him. To say goodbye."

Amy clenched her teeth, trying to push the memory away, but it was relentless, suffocating her. The way Mark's face had twisted in anger, cutting through her like a blade.

"You made that decision for both of us, and for what? So, you wouldn't have to see me break?"

Her hands trembled as she looked at Theodore, her tears falling onto the blanket. His warmth was unbearable now, a reminder of everything she'd lost.

What if Mark was right? What if it was her fault?

Her stomach churned, and she bit back a sob, but it escaped anyway, a broken, ragged sound. She cradled Theodore closer, her fingers clutching the blanket as if it might anchor her.

"You're so small," she whispered, "So perfect."

Her gaze darted to the delicate curve of his nose, the faint smattering of hair on his head. She couldn't stop comparing him to the son she'd lost, couldn't stop imagining what her baby would have looked like if he'd lived. The thought was too much, a tidal wave of guilt and longing that threatened to drown her.

Mark's narrative came again, relentless. *"You think he'd be proud of you? Of the mother you've become?"*

Her breath came in shallow gasps, and she pressed her forehead against Theodore's, her tears mingling with his soft whimpers. She was unraveling, and she knew it, but she couldn't stop. The guilt, the shame, the overwhelming ache of it all, it was too much.

"I'm sorry," she choked out again, "I'm so sorry."

A knock at the front door jolted her from the depths of her spiraling thoughts.

Not the cops. Not yet.

Callum's voice echoed through the door.

"Amy?" he stepped inside.

Her head snapped up, her breath catching in her throat. Her grip on Theodore tightened, and for a fleeting moment, she thought about running.

Callum stepped inside, his eyes immediately finding hers. His expression was tense, his jaw tight, but his tone was gentle.

"Amy, I'm here. What can I do for you?"

She couldn't answer. Couldn't form words around the panic in her throat.

Callum took a cautious step closer, his gaze flicking between her and the baby in her arms.

"I'm here. Whatever Mark said to you, whatever he did, it's not real. He's not here. You know that, right?"

Amy shook her head, "No, but he... he said things to mess with my head. He always knows how to do that."

Callum's face darkened. "I know he does. But Amy, you *know* who he is. You know what he's doing."

She couldn't look at him. Couldn't meet his eyes when her mind was screaming at her that *maybe, just maybe, Mark was right*.

Charlotte moved closer, her hands held out, cautious. "Amy, sweetheart, why don't you let me take Theo for a bit?" Her demeanor was gentle, careful, but Amy recoiled, her grip tightening.

"No," she snapped. "He's fine. He's...he's fine."

Charlotte hesitated, glancing at Callum, who held his hands up, palms open. "Okay," he said carefully. "But Amy, you're shaking. Just let's talk, alright?"

Another knock at the door.

Amy flinched.

Charlotte turned toward it, but Amy's entire body locked up. "No," she whispered. "Don't open it."

Charlotte froze, confusion flashing across her face. "Amy, it's probably–"

"No," Amy cut her off, her breathing shallow. "It's them. It's the cops."

Amy let out a wild, breathless laugh. "Because Mark *called them* on me."

Charlotte's brow furrowed. "Amy, we called them, remember?"

"Yes, but he called them first! He's holding all the power, Charlotte." She snapped.

Silence filled the room, stretching tight and suffocating.

Charlotte exchanged a quick look with Callum before slowly making her way to the door. She opened it carefully, just enough to reveal the two uniformed officers standing on the porch.

Amy's stomach dropped.

One of them, a broad–shouldered man with sharp eyes, took a step forward. "Ms. Rodriguez?"

Amy didn't answer, she couldn't.

The second officer, a woman with a firm but kind expression, spoke next. "Your ex–husband called us tonight. He's concerned about your well-being. Said there was an incident at your home."

Amy let out a strangled sound, somewhere between a laugh and a sob. "*He* set this up," she whispered.

Theodore stirred in her arms, beginning to fuss.

The first officer glanced down at the baby, then back at her. "Are you alright, ma'am? We are just here to get your side of the story, to help."

Amy shook her head, her breath coming faster now, panic surging hot and suffocating in her chest. "I'm fine. I don't–"

The second officer's voice was softer now, but laced with something that made Amy's skin crawl. "Are you sure? Would you be comfortable putting the baby down so we can talk?"

Amy's stomach twisted violently.

Charlotte's eyes darted between them, panic spilling across her face. "Please," she whispered, stepping forward, her hands trembling. "Amy, just–just give him back."

Callum stepped forward immediately, placing himself in front of her. "She's overwhelmed. Let's not escalate this."

Amy barely heard them. The room tilted, the edges of her vision blurring.

They think I'm crazy.

Mark did this.

He won.

She gripped Theodore tighter, a small, terrified sound escaping her throat. The officers shifted, their posture stiffening.

"Amy." Callum's voice cut through the noise, anchoring her. "Look at me."

She didn't.

He took a tentative step forward. "I understand this–you love that baby. I see it. And he needs you to be okay."

Her sobs grew louder, her body shaking. "I'm not okay! I'm broken! I ruin everything!"

Callum took a cautious step closer, his tone softening. "You're not broken, Amy. You're hurting. There's a difference."

She shook her head, tears slipping down her cheeks.

The baby let out a soft whimper, and her attention snapped back to him. Tears streamed down her face as she kissed the top of his head. "I'm sorry," she whispered.

Callum inched closer; his hands still raised. "Amy, give him to me. Let me help you."

"He's *mine*, Callum, don't you see it? He looks just like me."

"Ames, you will have a baby, I promise you, but Theodore has a mama, and he needs his mama." He shuttered. "Look at him

Amy, he's a beautiful baby, and he loves you. You can love him, but not like this."

Callum reached out, his hands open. "Trust me."

She fought it. Fought the unraveling. But the moment her fingers loosened, Callum gently pried the baby from her arms.

A hollow, broken sound tore from her throat.

Callum turned immediately, pressing Theodore into Charlotte's waiting arms. She let out a sob the moment he was against her chest, cradling him like she thought he'd disappear again.

That's when Amy lost it.

A scream tore from her as she lunged forward. "NO! Give him back! *Give him back!*"

The officers moved instantly.

One gripped Amy's arms before she could reach Charlotte, holding her back as she thrashed, her sobs turning ragged, desperate. "He's mine! He's *mine!*"

"Ma'am, it's okay, we need to stay calm," the officer commanded, his grip firm but not rough.

Amy jerked wildly, her body fighting, her mind spiraling. "You don't understand! He's *mine!*"

Charlotte turned away, curling over Theodore protectively, her body wracked with sobs.

Callum reached for Amy, but the second officer stepped between them. "Sir, we need space," he warned.

Callum's jaw clenched, but he nodded, as Amy crumbled in the officer's grip, her body shaking violently.

Her legs gave out.

The officer helped lower her to the floor as sobs wracked her frame.

Amy barely felt it.

T.D. BOGART

The weight of everything crushed her.
And outside, Mark was waiting in his car.

THIRTY FIVE

The sterile white walls felt suffocating. The air in the hospital room was too still, too clean, stripped of anything warm, anything real. Amy sat curled on the edge of the bed, knees tucked to her chest, fingers clenched in the rough hospital blanket like it was the only thing anchoring her to the ground She had been placed on an involuntary hold, and when deemed safe to return home, she decided that it was better to stay, and they had moved her to a regular room. She missed Maslow, but she couldn't face anyone, not now, not when he was out there. She was weightless, drifting, lost somewhere between exhaustion and the crushing weight of everything she had done.

Charlotte's horrified face. The sound of Theodore's soft wails as he was taken from her arms. The sharp bite of cold air when the police arrived, the way their hands hovered too close, too ready.

She squeezed her eyes shut, pressing her forehead against her knees, but the images wouldn't stop.

The door creaked, and she tensed.

She didn't look up, but she *knew*. She *felt* him, even before he spoke.

Callum.

His presence filled the room like a force, like something too big for these four walls, pressing in, making it harder to breathe. He didn't move at first, just stood there, his breath measured but uneven. A quiet war raged in him, she could feel it in the way the air shifted, in the way his hands, his strong, steady hands, trembled at his sides. She could smell that sweet musky scent, and she wanted to bury herself against his chest.

She stole a glance at him through the hair that covered her eyes.

He looked wrecked.

His hair was disheveled, his eyes shadowed with sleepless nights and something even deeper, something fractured beyond repair. His fists were clenched, the muscles in his forearms tight, like he was physically restraining himself from reaching for her.

The silence stretched, thick and suffocating, until finally, Callum exhaled sharply and stepped forward. "I'm sorry."

Two words. So simple, so devastating.

Amy barely breathed, her grip on the blanket tightening.

"For everything," he continued, "For not telling you the truth sooner. For not being what you needed me to be."

She swallowed hard, her throat dry and aching. "I don't even know what the truth is anymore," she whispered.

Callum let out a slow, unsteady breath. He moved then, lowering himself into a crouch beside the bed, so close she could feel his warmth, could smell the lingering traces of cologne and rain on his jacket.

"The truth is, I love you," there was nothing but absolute certainty in his words. "And I know I fucked up. I know I should've told you everything. I know I should have fought for you harder. But I need you to know, I *need* you to understand, that none of this was a game for me."

Amy's eyes were burning. She couldn't do this. Not now.

Not with him this close, not with the heat of him wrapping around her, making her want to sink into him, to let him fix all the broken pieces even though she knew, *knew*, that wasn't possible.

"Callum, please…" Her fingers twisted tighter around the blanket, holding onto it instead of him.

His body tensed. She felt it. The ripple of restraint.

"Ames." He barely breathed the name, his voice edged with something so desperate, so broken, that she physically felt herself break.

He reached out, his fingers brushing the blanket between them, not touching her, but that sliver of contact sent a violent tremor through her.

"Amy," he tried again, softer this time. "Look at me."

She shook her head, squeezing her eyes shut. If she looked at him, she would cave. She would lose.

"I can't do this, Callum," she whispered.

The words sliced through the air, sharper than anything else that had been said between them.

She felt him shudder.

The breath he took was slow, controlled, but it *shook*.

"If that's what you need, but Ames, I'm here. I will always be here. I'll wait as long as it takes to–"

"It *is*," she interrupted, forcing the words out even as her chest caved around them. "Just… *leave*."

He stilled.

For a long, painful moment, he didn't move.

Amy forced herself to breathe, to pretend this wasn't killing her.

Callum clenched his jaw so tight it looked painful. His hands curled into fists, his body rigid, as if every fiber of him was screaming to *not* walk away. To fight. To push. To stay.

But then, finally, he exhaled, and she felt it before she even heard it. The surrender. The devastation.

Slowly, so slowly it hurt, he reached for her. Not to pull her in, not to demand she stay, but just enough to press the lightest, softest kiss to her forehead.

His lips lingered, like he was memorizing the feel of her.

"I'm sorry," his breath was hot against her skin.

And then he pulled away.

The second he stepped back, she felt the loss like it was physical.

She kept her eyes down as he turned, her entire body trembling with the force of keeping herself still, of *not* breaking, of *not* calling him back.

The door clicked shut behind him.

And Amy shattered.

A sob ripped from her throat, ugly and raw, her entire body curling in on itself. Her fingers clawed at the blanket, her shoulders shaking, but no amount of squeezing, no amount of clenching, could keep her from falling apart.

She was alone.

Again.

Always.

Her phone sat on the nightstand, a silent, glowing presence.

Amy's breathing was erratic as she reached for it, her vision blurred with tears.

Her notifications were endless. Dozens of unread messages. But one name stood out.

Charlotte.

Her stomach twisted painfully.

Her fingers hovered over the keyboard, hesitating.

What the hell could she even say?

She exhaled shakily and typed:

I know 'I'm sorry' isn't enough. I know I can't take back what I did, and I don't expect you to forgive me. But I need you to know that I hate myself for hurting you. For hurting Theo. For everything

I said.

Her thumb hovered over the send button.

No. Not enough.

She swallowed hard and kept going.

You are my best friend, and I don't know if I deserve your friendship anymore. But I miss you. I am so, so sorry.

Her hand was shaking when she pressed send.

The moment the message disappeared, she set the phone down and curled onto her side, wrapping her arms around herself.

And for the first time that week, she let herself cry, before she let herself sleep.

THIRTY SIX

The high-rise office was a gleaming testament to success, all glass walls and minimalist design, offering a panoramic view of the New York City skyline. Mark stood by the window, hands tucked into his pockets, his tailored suit an impeccable shield against the chaos brewing outside.

The recording studio was dimly lit, the microphone glowing red as Mark settled into his chair. He adjusted his headphones, the soft hum of white noise filling the silence. This was his arena, his platform. The one place he controlled the narrative entirely.

"Today's episode is personal," he began, "It's about pain. Loss. And the mistakes we make when we're trying to hold it all together."

He paused, letting the weight of his words settle.

"Infertility," he continued, his tone softening. "It's a word that carries so much weight, so much heartbreak. My wife, Amy, and I faced that struggle for years. It tested our marriage, our faith in each other, and in ourselves. We were drowning, and in that darkness, I made choices I deeply regret." His eyes locked on Nancy's, as she wiped a tear from her face, clutching her clipboard tightly.

Mark exhaled audibly; the sound amplified by the mic. "Josephine... she was the first woman I had ever loved, and when she came back into my life, she set it on fire. Our connection was not a mistake, but not being able to prevent what happened, it's something I'll carry with me for the rest of my life." He took a sip of water.

"Relationships are created and destroyed by outside circumstances that test your will, your beliefs, and your connections. One could argue that my wife and I were broken for years, that the belief of a baby outweighed the fraying edges of what we had, and that circumstance tethered us in a way that, at the time, felt organic. What I learned about these relationships, and these women, was that I was searching for something real, for a connection that felt like I was completing aspects of what was missing in myself, and this is what you should listen to. That inner voice that tells you when something is not quite what your soul needs."

He continued, "Josephine's struggles with mental health were something I couldn't save her from. Her death is a tragedy I'll never fully recover from. The complexity of our past, and what ties us together is something I go in depth with in my book." Internally, his thoughts were colder. *Josephine was a liability, weak and easily broken. But now, she's the perfect scapegoat.*

He leaned closer to the mic, his tone resolute. "I'm sharing this because I believe in accountability. In owning your mistakes and learning from them. My hope is that by being honest, I can help others avoid the same pitfalls."

Mark ended the recording with a sigh, his hand hovering over the stop button. A faint smile played on his lips. *The world loves a flawed hero. And I've given them exactly what they want.*

Mark took off his headphones, and finished up the segment with the producer.

Once back in his office, he sat in his leather chair, the glittering skyline of New York City stretching behind him. The office was a curated display of his success, framed magazine covers, photos from book signings, and awards showcasing his meteoric rise.

On his desk sat the first print of his memoir, *Redemption*, already a bestseller. A Netflix poster for his upcoming special leaned against the wall, its tagline bold: *One Man's Journey to*

Redemption.

He picked up the crumpled restraining order from his desk, smoothing it out as he read the words again. Amy's name, her signature, stared back at him like a challenge.

"She'll come around," he muttered to himself.

His assistant entered, carrying a stack of papers. "Doctor Rodriguez, I've called your driver, he will be here in thirty minutes to get you to the set. The producers are ready, and have made changes that you requested for today's show."

Mark stood, adjusting his tie as he glanced at his reflection in the glass. The lines of his suit were perfect, his smile rehearsed to perfection.

Her voice quivered as she adjusted her blazer. "I just wanted to say that your episode today– it was really heartbreaking, moving. Your honesty, your pain– it, um, it was just raw, relatable."

"Thank you. How did you connect with it, you're only married, no kids?" He took a measured step toward her, his hands finding his tie as he pulled at the knot.

"I identified more with your relationship than I did the rest of the segment." Her brown yes darted to the floor.

"Nancy, close the blinds."

She swallowed hard as she reached for the button, and the outside desks and everything in the lobby disappeared from view.

"Tell me, what about relationships?" He reached for her clipboard as her breathing intensified. He'd hired her for her education, competency a was necessity, but he also hired her because she reminded him of Amy and Josie, both in looks and frailty. She had answered every question in a way that made it almost too easy to see right through her.

"I'm promoting you. You won't be my assistant anymore, but your office will be the one next door. His eyes gestured toward the adjoining door. And that door will always be unlocked, unless you're in here with me." He loosened his tie. "What do you say?" He watched her draw her bottom lip into her mouth as she absentmindedly sucked on it.

"Do that again." The warmth that flushed her cheeks and he was instantly hard. He brushed a strand of hair from her face as his knuckles swiped the length of her neck. She was nervous to look him in the eyes, he could feel her trembling beneath his touch as he stepped back and sat in the chair, tilting his hips forward as his back sank into the confines of the leather seat, motioning for her to come closer.

Mark, you're my– I mean we shouldn't."

"Shouldn't what? Say it." His tone was husky. She hesitated at first before sinking into the chair across from him.

"I don't want to mess this up, I really love working for you."

Mark shook his head. "I said, come here." He exhaled as she rose from her seat and walked toward him. He ran his hands up the back of her legs, inching them past her pencil skirt, as his forearms hiked it up. He hooked his fingers on her underwear, and pulled her down slowly so that she was straddling his lap, the tension between them undeniable.

"Good." His lips found hers as he pulled at her shirt, revealing the lacy fabric that cupped her breast. "I hired you because you're smarter than nearly every person in this office, and–" he sucked on the pad of her ear before brushing his lips on her cheek.

"Because working with you was not enough. I want all of you, I want to start over, and I want it to be with you." He felt a tear fall from her cheek as she kissed him back, her body relaxing into his. *That's right, Nance, you're mine.*

"I'm scared. This is a lot to–"

"I've seen how he treats you, how distant and cold he is. You deserve so much more."

She nodded.

"Just say yes, Nancy. Say yes, and all of this is yours." He took her left hand in his, and slipped her fourth finger in his mouth, his teeth gripping the wedding band that was on that finger. His expression shifted as she gulped, and he slowly sucked on her finger before pulling the ring into his mouth.

"Have dinner with me after my show?" He asked, as she leaned into him.

"You have ten minutes to get to the car. I can ride with you, if you'd like, Doctor Rodriguez, stay with you through the show, and…"

Mark's expression darkened. "Say that again, and I'll bend you over the desk right now."

The words hung in the air, thick with promise and danger. She swallowed hard, nodding as her mouth found his.

△△△

Later, on the brightly lit set, the audience's applause rose like music to his ears. He stepped onto the brightly lit set, the applause swelling as he greeted his audience. His smile widened as he addressed them.

"Good morning, America," he began, his tone infused with practiced charm. "Today, we're talking about turning pain into purpose. Because no matter how far we fall, we can always rise again."

The audience erupted in applause, the sound washing over him like a drug. Mark Rodriguez was scathed, yes, but still standing. Still winning.

And in his world, that was all that mattered.

THIRTY SEVEN

THREE WEEKS LATER...

The hum of the tattoo gun vibrated through the air as Amy sat in the chair, her upper spine bared to the artist. Her skin, pale against the black leather, looked almost translucent under the fluorescent lights. She shifted slightly, a faint tremor in her hand as she spoke. "Oleanders," she murmured. "They're fragile and beautiful but poisonous if you don't handle them right. I think that's why I love them."

"They remind me of myself, I guess." The artist tattooed her baby's birthdate in a small script within the stem.

The artist glanced at her, his eyes narrowing slightly as he traced delicate lines across her spine. "Strong choice," he said simply, the needle buzzing again as he filled in the outline.

"Why the name James?" he asked, referring to the tattoo he could see on the back of her neck.

"It was my dad's name, and also my son's." He called me Ames, felt fitting."

"That's beautiful." He replied, as he wiped the residual ink off her skin.

The tattoo began to take shape; small, intricate, with fine, wispy strokes. The oleanders unfurled like a delicate vine, their leaves barely there, etched in pale, almost ghostly lines, the petals like soft whispers against the skin. Each flower was a blur of pale ink, as if caught in a gentle breeze, its edges feathering out just enough to suggest fragility without losing definition. It wasn't a loud statement; it was more of a quiet rebellion, a reminder of something beautiful, but not to be underestimated.

Amy watched the artist work, her fingers lightly tracing the padding of the table, as though she could feel the soft flutter of the petals beneath her fingertips, their fragility mirrored in the way she held herself.

△△△

When she got home, she swung open the door to an excited Maslow, who was sitting patiently with his leash in his mouth. Her mother was many things, but she had taken good care of him, and his weight showed it.

The bathroom smelled faintly of lavender soap, the floral scent almost mocking against the backdrop of Amy's swirling dread. She sat on the closed toilet lid, elbows on her knees, her fingers tightly interwoven as if bracing for impact. The pregnancy test perched on the edge of the sink, a fragile object holding the power to shape her future. The air was heavy, suffocating, her heartbeat a relentless drum in her ears.

Unprotected sex. It had been one time, but wasn't that all it took?

Her mind flitted back to the nights she had let herself unravel. Mark's touch, consuming and calculated, still clung to her skin like a brand she couldn't scrub off. He'd known how to pull her in, how to dangle the past between them like a lifeline she couldn't resist. She had trusted him again, despite the lies, the manipulation, the dizzying high of his promises.

Callum…

She felt like she couldn't breathe at the thought of him. The memory of him was a different kind of ache. His hands had been steady, his lips soft, his words quiet as they dissolved into each other. It had felt inevitable, like gravity pulling her to him no matter how hard she resisted. It had been raw, unfiltered, and transformative. He had changed her, for the better, he had given her a reason to love herself. It hadn't felt like a mistake, it felt like the universe had given her a gift.

He had stripped her of her defenses, left her bare, and somehow, that had made her feel more whole than she had in years.

But now? Now, everything felt like a mistake.

Amy rubbed at her temples, exhaustion seeping into her bones. Her gaze dropped to her phone; the screen still lit with Charlotte's contact. The name stared back at her, a bitter reminder of how much she had lost. Calling her felt impossible, a cruel fantasy. Amy had burned that bridge, and the ashes were scattered too far to rebuild.

She backed out of Charlotte's contact, her thumb trembling as she swiped to her calendar. The notification for her therapy appointment blinked at her, a reminder of how far she still had to go.

Maslow nudged her leg, his cold nose breaking through her spiraling thoughts. She looked down to find his chestnut eyes gazing up at her, unblinking and filled with quiet loyalty.

"Just you and me, boy," she murmured, bending to kiss his soft muzzle. Maslow huffed, his paw nudging her hand.

For all the chaos she had endured, Maslow had been her anchor. Through every sleepless night and endless wave of doubt, he had been there, steadfast and unwavering.

"You're the best thing that's ever happened to me," she whispered.

The minutes dragged by, each one sharpening the tension coiled in her chest. The timer on her phone buzzed, jolting her upright. Amy hesitated, her hands trembling as she reached for the test.

She stared at the result.

Negative.

Relief and disappointment crashed over her in equal measure, leaving her breathless. Her legs wobbled as she stood, bracing herself against the sink.

The relief was immediate, no ties to Callum, no accidental tether to a life she had finally begun to shed. But the disappointment cut just as deep. Somewhere in the haze of her fear, she had imagined the possibility. A child. A future with *him*. Something more than this endless spiral of survival.

Her reflection in the mirror was almost unrecognizable. The shadowed eyes, the taut expression, this wasn't the woman she wanted to be.

Amy took a deep breath, steadied herself. *Enough.*

She moved into the living room, Maslow trailing behind her, and opened her laptop. The screen's glow lit the room as she navigated to her saved tabs. A modest house in Burlington, Vermont filled the screen, the kind of home where she could start over. A yard for Maslow, a space for peace.

The cursor blinked in the search bar as she typed in something new: *IVF donor sperm clinics near me.*

The idea had been circling in her mind for weeks. She didn't need Mark. She didn't need Callum. She didn't need anyone. For the first time in years, she felt a spark of hope, a fragile but determined belief that she could do this on her own.

Her phone buzzed on the table, pulling her out of her thoughts.

A photo message.

She hesitated, then opened it. The image was of a golden retriever puppy, tiny and wide-eyed, curled in Callum's lap.

Bloom, the text read.

Her throat ran dry. She wanted to block his number, to erase him from her life. But even now, the pull of him was undeniable. Her fingers hovered over the screen before typing a reply.

She's beautiful.

Three dots appeared, indicating his response, but she locked her phone and pushed it away, her jaw tightening as she turned back to her laptop.

This was her life now, and for once, she was the one writing the next chapter.

THIRTY EIGHT

Benson Boone's Beautiful Life echoed through the garage as Callum hummed along. The sandpaper caught the edge of the bassinet, snagging against uneven wood. The memory of Amy, of that night, gripped him tighter than any thought ever could. The way she felt, soft and trembling beneath him, vulnerable, but so alive. Her body in his arms, the way she surrendered. He had never wanted something so badly in his life, not even control.

He closed his eyes, feeling the pull of it. Her lips against his, unsure at first but giving in to him. The way she felt when she opened up to him, body and soul, in a way no one ever had. He could still taste her, the way she unraveled in the quiet moments between them.

She had been broken, yes. But she was also everything. More than he'd ever thought he deserved.

He remembered how she trembled when his mouth found her, her body so raw and exposed, and how he held her as she broke down. There was nothing more vulnerable than that, nothing more intimate. The way she fell apart in his arms, the way her tears soaked into his shirt, and yet, he didn't pull away. He had held her. He had been the one to catch her.

He had given her peace. *He* had been there when the world outside had threatened to swallow her whole.

And still, even now, he wasn't ready to let her go.

The bassinet teetered, unsteady on its legs, but Callum's focus was elsewhere. Sandpaper in hand, he smoothed the wood with slow, deliberate strokes, the rhythmic scrape grounding him. He hadn't really slept since the news about Josephine.

The phone buzzed against the workbench. He let it ring twice before glancing at the screen. *Mrs. Vega,* Josephine's mom.

He exhaled, setting the sandpaper down. He couldn't ignore her, even if the thought of what her loss meant ripped him in two.

"Hi Susan," he answered.

"Callum," her voice cracked. "I just... I thought you should know. Her celebration of life is Saturday. Please come. I know its been a while, but I really wanted the frenzy to die down, its been such an emotional time." She paused. "I have a box of things for you."

A sweat broke out on his brow. "Okay, I'll be there."

There was a pause, the faint sound of her catching her breath. "She didn't deserve this, she was... struggling, I know. But it wasn't supposed to end like this."

Callum swallowed hard. He'd always known Josephine's mind was a fragile thing, caught between her compassion for others and her inability to give herself the same grace.

"She talked about you sometimes, you know," Susan continued. "Even after everything. She'd say how you saved her, back when she couldn't see a way out."

A flicker of memory surfaced: Josephine's tear–streaked face after Callum had pulled her out of that apartment, away from the man who'd left bruises on her arms.

"She never forgot that, Callum," She added softly.

He pressed his fingers against his temples. "I didn't save her."

"You did more than you think," Mrs. Vega replied. "She just... she got lost somewhere along the way."

The line went quiet for a moment.

"Are you okay?" she asked.

Callum hesitated, his grip tightening on the phone. "I will be."

They said their goodbyes, and the call ended. But her words lingered, and his thoughts drifted to Josephine, to that day.

It started with the voicemail.

Josephine had been in the shower, the sound of running water masking the faint vibration of her phone on the nightstand. Callum hadn't meant to snoop, he never would've, if the screen hadn't lit up at the exact moment he glanced over.

The caller ID read "OBGYN"

He ignored it at first, brushing it off as unimportant. But then her voicemail notification pinged, and without thinking, he pressed play.

"Hi, Josephine. This is Emily from Doctor Emerie's office. We just wanted to follow up and see how you're feeling after the procedure. If you have any questions or concerns about your recovery, don't hesitate to give us a call. Take care."

The world seemed to tilt as the words sank in. Procedure. Recovery. His mind raced, piecing together fragments of conversations, her sudden mood swings, and the night she'd cried in his arms, whispering apologies he hadn't understood.

The sound of the shower shutting off jolted him from his thoughts. Callum stood frozen as Josephine emerged, towel wrapped around her, steam curling around her like smoke. Her eyes landed on him, then on her phone in his hand.

"What's wrong?" she asked.

He held the phone out to her. "You tell me."

Her face drained of color as she took it, her trembling fingers navigating to the voicemail. As it played, her expression crumpled, her shoulders sagging under the weight of the words.

"I was going to tell you." her voice cracked.

"When?" His voice was low. "When were you going to tell me that you–" He couldn't even finish the sentence, the word abortion catching in his throat like barbed wire.

She wrapped the towel tighter around herself, her arms folded across her chest like a shield. "I didn't know how. I didn't think you'd understand."

"Try me," he'd said, his jaw tightening.

Josephine shook her head, tears spilling over. "I couldn't, Callum. You don't know what it's like. I had to do this for me, for my sanity. I couldn't bring a baby into this world, not with everything that's happened."

"But you didn't even give me a choice," he seethed. "You made the decision for both of us."

She looked away, silent.

"You lied to me," the realization hitting him like a punch to the gut, "you lied and now it feels like you've been lying about other things, why does it sound like you have so much more to say, but you won't?"

"I didn't know how else to–" She buried her face in her hands, sobbing. "I'm sorry, Callum. I can't do this."

But her apology didn't cut through the ache in his chest, the sense of betrayal that clawed at him. He stared at her, the woman he thought he knew, and for the first time, he felt like she was a stranger.

Callum stared at the bassinet, its unfinished edges mocking him. He'd tried to build something stable, something whole, but nothing in his life stayed steady. Not Josephine. Not Amy.

His phone lit up again. This time, it wasn't a call but a notification:

Start your morning off with Doctor Rodriguez, weekdays at 8:00am on ABC.

A rage simmered when his thoughts shifted to Mark. It wasn't only because she hadn't come back to him. He hadn't been able to fix any of it. His obsession with controlling everything had torn his life apart. He had lost Josephine for it, and now, Amy was slipping through his fingers too. He wished he could kill Mark, watch him die a slow, agonizing death as he stood over him, the life seeping out of him as he pleaded for mercy.

Callum blinked, the vision dissipating. His hand trembled as he set the phone down, his breath uneven.

He turned back to the bassinet, running his fingers over the sanded edge. Amy deserved better than the mess Mark had left behind. She deserved better than him, too, but Callum couldn't let her go. Not now. Not after everything.

Josephine's mother's words echoed in his mind. *"You saved her once."*

But he hadn't. He'd failed Josephine, just as Mark had. And now she was gone.

Callum's chest rose and fell, his breath shallow as the vision played out in his mind. It wasn't just a thought; it was a plan. Clean. Untraceable. Justice.

The soft sound of Bloom's nails clicking against the floor snapped him out of his trance. He looked down at the puppy. She sat at his feet, her golden coat catching the dim light of the workshop. Her head tilted just enough to break the tension coiled in his chest.

"You don't get it," Callum crouched to stroke her head. His fingers trembled against her fur. "Someone has to stop him."

Bloom nuzzled his hand, her warmth cutting through the chill that had settled over him.

He straightened, letting out a slow, measured breath. The bassinet loomed in front of him.

"This is for her."

For Amy.

But as he picked up the sandpaper again, he stared at his work. *What the fuck am I even doing?*

Mark wasn't going to stop. Not until someone made him.

Callum's hand stilled, his gaze fixed on the bassinet's smooth edges. His love for Amy was real.

So was his rage.

And sometimes, love demands sacrifice.

Sometimes, love demands justice.

THE END

...Or is it?

Dissemblance was always intended as a duet. The second novel is in progress, and I hope to publish it by the end of 2025. We'll be diving into some dark waters, uncovering even more along the way. Get ready...

AUTHOR'S NOTE

This book was written in memory of our daughter, Evelyn, who was born still.

I set out to write something that explored the depths of the human psyche, testing the limits of relationships and the hold they have over us. While Amy's journey, her decisions, diagnosis, and marriage, is not mine, her years of infertility, pregnancy, and stillbirth reflect the pain my husband and I have experienced. After three years of trying to conceive and seven miscarriages, we learned I was pregnant with Evelyn. After a severe hemorrhage at eight weeks, I learned alone, that something was wrong with her. I refused to believe it.

Through a brutal pregnancy filled with despair and disbelief, I carried our terminal daughter to 21 weeks and nearly died giving birth due to a rare pregnancy complication. I chose to write this story fictionally because the reality of it was too much for me to face. The biggest difference is that I had the most supportive husband. Why write the story this way? Because a month after Evelyn was born, my husband was deployed. The Navy is his mistress.

I became fixated on getting pregnant again, desperately trying to replace the pain with something positive. I pushed for a frozen intrauterine cycle, even though my husband was reluctant. He agreed, wanting to support me even in his absence. I got pregnant that cycle, only to lose the baby at nine weeks.

The devastation was suffocating. I had failed. I could not give my husband the child we so desperately wanted. Meanwhile, my neighbor, who had been due at the same time as I had been, delivered a healthy baby girl. I watched her son while she was in labor, and the first thing she did when I brought him to her room was place her baby in my arms. A few months later, my niece was born. I was pushed to the edge mentally and emotionally. I resented everyone. No one spoke of Evelyn. Everyone downplayed her stillbirth because "at least she was not full term."

Amy's character takes this pain and transforms it into her own life. Infertility is not pretty. It is devastating. Adding miscarriage and stillbirth to the mix is enough to break you. Every story I write holds a piece of that truth and pain. In those moments of immense pain, there is also an even greater strength.

To my husband, thank you. Thank you for seeing me, for supporting me, for picking me up when I thought I could not keep going, and for being my everything. Thank you to the medical teams who helped us bring our twin boys and daughter into this world via IVF. I would do it all again, every painful step, every loss, to hear them call me mama, to kiss them, and to be their mom.

ABOUT THE AUTHOR

T.D. Bogart is currently based wherever the Navy sends her family, and she embraces each new adventure with gratitude. Her debut novel, A Ripple Through Time was the start of many compelling narratives. Dissemblance is a clear deviation from ARTT, but shows her range as a writer; get ready.

Connect with me by googling Author T.D. Bogart or looking for her on the following platforms:

Website

Goodreads

Instagram

Amazon

ACKNOWLEDGEMENT

Thank you to my husband, you are unapologetically yourself, and there's no one more incredible. You patiently help me shape my writing, even when I ramble, even when I obsess over the same ideas. You're not just an amazing editor, but an even better friend. I love you immensely.

To my babies, you mean the world to me! This story only intensified my love for you. Through everything, we got the three most amazing children. I will always be so proud of you, I will always love you endlessly. <3

Thank you (and apologies) to my mother in law Sally, my cousins Annie, Bianca, and Chiara. You have incredibly busy lives and still take the time to give me pointers, edits, and cheer me on more than anyone else. I'm so thankful for you! <3

Jenny, you don't even read the types of books I write, and yet, you micro–analyze them and make them the best they can be.

Shoutout to Agatha, you have become such a great friend. Thank you for you and for being such an amazing support.

An immense thank you to my beta and ARC readers, especially to Laura, and Laura, Brittany, and Agatha for allowing me to bounce ideas off of you, and for your input.

To all my lovelies on Bookstagram, thank you for loving what I write, thank you for being supportive, and for welcoming me into this amazing community. Cheers to many more stories. Get ready for even more emotional devastation.

OTHER BOOKS BY T. D. BOGART

A Ripple Through Time (a historical romance)

When Ryan Harper inherits an old painting and a set of journals from his grandfather Derrick, he and his girlfriend Natalie, an art restorer, expect nothing more than a quiet project. Instead, they are drawn into a love story set against the backdrop of World War II, pulling them into the heart of the 1940s.

As they uncover Derrick's past, Natalie faces a personal crisis. Her twin sister, Dina, suddenly falls ill, putting their close bond in jeopardy. With the weight of her sister's condition pressing down on her, Natalie's work on the painting transforms into a quest for meaning and connection when everything around her feels uncertain.

Secrets buried in Derrick's journals threaten to change everything Ryan thought he understood about his grandfather and his own identity. As the mysteries of Derrick's life intersect with the fragility of their present, Ryan and Natalie must navigate unexpected challenges while grappling with revelations that will forever alter their lives.

Made in United States
Troutdale, OR
03/16/2025